FLIGHT FROM EGYPT

Also by Michael Vetter

Run Before the Rain—An Antediluvian Adventure
One World Tower—A Babylonian Adventure

FLIGHT FROM EGYPT

ADVENTURES ALONG THE NILE

Michael Vetter

FLIGHT FROM EGYPT
Adventures Along the Nile

iUniverse books may be ordered through booksellers or by contacting:

iUniverse
1663 Liberty Drive
Bloomington, IN 47403
www.iuniverse.com
1-800-Authors (1-800-288-4677)

ISBN: 978-1-4917-6325-4 (sc)
ISBN: 978-1-4917-6326-1 (e)

Print information available on the last page.

iUniverse rev. date: 03/31/2015

To my father
Don Vetter—*Pan Am Pioneer*

Then the LORD said to Moses,
"Now you shall see what I will do to Pharaoh. For with a strong hand
he will let them go, and with a strong hand
he will drive them out of his land."
And God spoke to Moses and said to him: "I am the LORD.
"I appeared to Abraham, to Isaac, and to Jacob, as God Almighty,
but by My name LORD I was not known to them.
"I have also established My covenant with them, to give them the land
of Canaan, the land of their pilgrimage, in which they were strangers.
"And I have also heard the groaning of the children of Israel whom the
Egyptians keep in bondage, and I have remembered My covenant.
"Therefore say to the children of Israel:
'I am the LORD; I will bring you out from
under the burdens of the Egyptians,
I will rescue you from their bondage, and I will redeem you
with an outstretched arm and with great judgments.
'I will take you as My people, and I will be your God.
Then you shall know that I am the LORD your God who brings you out
from under the burdens of the Egyptians.
'And I will bring you into the land which I swore to give to
Abraham, Isaac, and Jacob; and I will give it to you as a heritage:
I am the LORD.'"

Exodus 6:1-8 (NKJV)

ACKNOWLEDGEMENTS

The cover of *Flight From Egypt* is the imaginative creation of Brian Weaver, who has captured the sense of adventure and awe surrounding the fictional lives of Malik, Nathan, Sarina, and their families in Egypt during the time of the Exodus. Thank you for a cover picture that is worth thousands of words! My appreciation also to Johanna Higgins for the professional photograph of the author on the back cover.

Thanks to my team of reviewers: Nadine Lahan, who edited the manuscript twice and made it better each time; Ray Toomey, whose understanding of the Scriptures caught details that made a difference in the story; Jennifer Mitchell, who still found time to review the manuscript with a busy travel and family schedule; Don Dyer, whose keen eye found scores of errors that previous reviewers didn't catch and who educated me about a key meteorological phenomenon; Steve Routhier, who somehow read the manuscript while recovering from a painful surgery and found many typos to prove that he read the entire book. I am indebted to all of you for your corrections, suggestions, and most of all for your friendship. Any misinterpretations of Scripture or literary mistakes are unintentional and entirely my own.

My wife, Mary, deserves an award for her patience with my long absences writing in libraries, the mission office, and (probably too often) in a local coffee shop. This book would not have been possible without your patience and understanding.

It bears repeating that this is a book of fiction that loosely depicts what might have happened in the background of one of the most miraculous and epic events of the Bible. Our information in the Bible about what happened before and during the Israelite's flight from Egypt is an awesome record of the mighty power of God. My imaginative story speculates about how those biblical events might have influenced ordinary people in Egypt. Plausible advanced technologies such as a heliographic network, electric power and lights, and charged capacitors add to the sense of wonder and adventure.

PREFACE

This is a work of fiction based primarily on Biblical events in Egypt taken from the book of Exodus, chapters 5-15. Apart from the principal people named in that section of the Bible, all other characters are entirely fictional.

God's faithfulness is a continuous narrative through the Old and New Testaments. I have used some of the broad, dramatic events of Israel's history, and particularly its miraculous flight from Egypt, to emphasize God's faithfulness in keeping all of His promises.

In what is known as the Abrahamic Covenant (Genesis 12:1-3; 13:14-17; 15:1-21; 17:1-8; 22:15-18), God promised Abraham and his descendants, through the line of Isaac and Jacob, that they would number more than the stars in the sky and become a great nation; inherit the physical land of Canaan which would be their possession forever; and be a people through whom all the nations of the earth would be blessed.

The literal, miraculous plagues that Almighty God brought upon Egypt were unprecedented in scope and terrifying in their severity. There is no indication from Scripture that common Egyptians or Israelite slaves knew, at first, why the plagues took place. The national helio network that informed the nation of God's supernatural works is imaginary, but serves the purpose of the story to magnify God's name throughout the nation. By the time the Angel of Death passed through Egypt at midnight and killed the firstborn (Exodus 11:5; 12:12-13, 23, 29; 13:15), every person knew that the God of the Hebrews was responsible.

The Passover night remembrance (Exodus 12:1-28) holds a unique significance for the Jewish people that has endured unchanged for over three thousand years. To this day, people around the world gather to reflect on God's faithfulness to His promise. They remember the day when His people were freed from slavery and began their journey to a land flowing with milk and honey. Since their flight from Egypt, God's people have seen both blessings and tragedies but have never forgotten God's promise to Abraham. The picture of Christ in the Passover is a blessing and comfort to Christians today (I Corinthians 5:7).

The parting of the Red Sea and the destruction of Pharaoh's army (Exodus 14:16-31) may be the most-referenced miracle in the Bible. Bible writers often mention the parting of the Red Sea and the annihilation of the Egyptian army when they recall the power of God in history. This demonstration of God's mighty hand was so terrifying that when the Canaanites and other nations heard it, they lost all hope of resisting the army of Israel because they knew that the *LORD* of Hosts was with His people.

PROLOGUE

Nile River at Thebes

Pharaoh Thutmose III—*Men-kheper-ra*, The Lasting Manifestation of *Ra*—and his entourage of attendants, lingered at the edge of the Nile River for the monarch's morning bath. Some servants still chattered among themselves about what had happened in the palace the day before. Moses and Aaron, Hebrew brothers, had approached Pharaoh in the name of the *LORD* God of Israel with a demand that the ruler allow the slaves to worship their God in the wilderness. Pharaoh refused them and claimed to know nothing of their *LORD*. When God turned Aaron's rod into a serpent to demonstrate His power, the court's sorcerers duplicated the feat with their occult enchantments. Even when Aaron's serpent swallowed those of the court magicians, Pharaoh remained unimpressed by their God.

A day after that first confrontation in the palace, bath attendants were the first to notice the miracle that mocked the holy river worshipped by Egyptians as the lifeblood of the Upper and Lower Lands. The instant corruption of *Anuket*, Mother Nile, was an affront to Egypt's gods and Pharaoh's authority. Was the *LORD* of the Hebrews more powerful than Pharaoh and the gods of Egypt?

This demonstration of God's might should have been convincing because it turned the full length of the Nile River from water to blood at the same instant. However, Pharaoh's heart was harder than the black granite of Aswan; his advisors demonstrated that they too could turn water red. Unpersuaded by what he considered nothing more than a Hebrew trick, the proud ruler laughed at the two shabbily dressed

Israelites who dared to demand that he set Egypt's slaves free to serve their God in the wilderness.

Luxor West Bank, Lotus House

Iset meditated in her peaceful water garden surrounded by blue cornflowers, daisies, irises, and the fragrance of blossoming almond trees. A scream from the kitchen at the other end of the sprawling house interrupted her morning quiet time. She was annoyed that a servant would dare make noise during her time of quiet meditation. The Egyptian noblewoman gracefully rose from her smooth, sculpted limestone bench, adjusted the light blue wrap around her shoulders and walked with stiff dignity to give the silly kitchen girl a tongue-lashing. Suddenly, a second scream added to the hysterical racket. The lady's pace increased as she walked past the livestock pens and granary to the back of the house. The screeching from the detached cookery was incessant and insistent.

By the time she reached the source of the noise she had a string of scalding words ready, but the sight of dark red blood on the floor brought her to a sudden stop in the doorway. Two Israelite slaves (a young girl and an older woman, both with blood on their hands, clothing and feet) were the source of the commotion. Blood was everywhere! Iset took one step into the room and felt the liquid stick to the soles of her thin sandals. Not one to panic easily, she still nearly gagged when the coppery metallic smell reached her nostrils. The floor around the women was awash with the thick substance which had already begun to coagulate; its warm, thick texture touched her feet and she cringed. She took a pitcher from the hands of the younger, hysterical slave. It was filled with blood. She set it on the counter and slapped the girl as hard as she could. "Stop!" she shouted. The girl's eyes bulged at the sharp sting and her mouth clamped shut. At least the level of screaming was now cut in half. She grabbed the girl's shoulder, pushed her into a chair, and turned toward the second wailing slave. Having seen the violence her mistress was capable of, the older woman fled from the room, still screeching.

"What happened?" Iset asked the girl who sat frozen in the chair as if in a trance. The well-dressed lady closed her eyes when she felt the blood squish between her toes. "Where did all this blood come from? Tell me right now!"

"The water, Ma'am, it was the water!" the maid sobbed.

"What do you mean, 'It was the water'?"

The young girl tried to explain between gasps for breath: "I was... cleaning the dishes from breakfast... when I saw dark water in the sink. I threw that water out, scooped a large bowl of new water from the cistern, and dumped some of it into the sink to wash away the mess; but...but it was blood too. That's when I dropped the bowl on the floor. Then I took a water pitcher to wash it away and it had blood in it too. I'm so sorry, Ma'am. Then the other maid came in with a bucket of water from the river to wash clothes and she screamed when she saw the mess on the floor and she dropped her bucket too. Oh, Ma'am, please don't punish me. I'll clean it all up, I promise."

"Yes, you will clean it *all*! I want this kitchen washed immediately and then we'll see about your punishment." The mistress of the house looked around at the smelly, sticky film that had splashed onto almost every surface in the kitchen. "This place looks like a butcher's shop." The lady removed her bloodied sandals and dropped them in the sink. "Clean these too. I'll wash my feet in the garden and return to my morning meditation—if that's possible now." Without thinking, she wiped her bloodied hands on her blue linen shawl.

Iset composed herself and walked back to her garden leaving crimson footprints on the pink granite tile walkway that encircled the home's main living quarters. She would rinse the blood from her feet in the pond's fresh water. Water that pumped from the Nile nourished her precious golden carp. Several paces away from the pond she noticed that a pulsing red flow rippled the pond's shimmering surface. The fountain in the center of the pond gurgled and pulsed like a severed artery. She fought the urge to scream and then understood how the kitchen maids must have felt. Her precious golden carp floated on the surface of what had once been the twenty-foot ornamental centerpiece of her serene floral garden. She felt sick to her stomach. A sticky substance spattered the blue lotus blossoms that gave her home its name and dried to a dark brown in the sunlight. The cultured, composed mistress of Lotus House collapsed in sobs on her meditation bench. Her ears vaguely detected other cries, screams and shouts coming from the nearby stables and fields. Still sobbing, she looked with a vacant stare at her bare, bloodied feet.

Waset (Thebes)

c. 1445 B.C.

So the LORD said to Moses:
"See, I have made you as God to Pharaoh, and Aaron your brother
shall be your prophet. You shall speak all that I command you.
And Aaron your brother shall tell Pharaoh
to send the children of Israel out of his land.
And I will harden Pharaoh's heart,
and multiply My signs and My wonders in the land of Egypt.
But Pharaoh will not heed you, so that I may lay My hand on Egypt
and bring My armies and My people,
the children of Israel, out of the land of Egypt by great judgments.
And the Egyptians shall know that I am the LORD,
when I stretch out My hand on Egypt
and bring out the children of Israel from among them."

Exodus 7:1-5 (NKJV)

CHAPTER 1

Luxor West Bank, Lotus House

Royal Master Architect Hatep's chariot skidded to a stop in a cloud of dust in front of the stable of his family's Luxor estate. He jumped to the ground and threw the reins to his horse slave. "Water the horse immediately but keep him harnessed in the shade," he commanded over his shoulder and continued walking toward the house.

"Can't do that, Master. No water," the horse slave replied in a voice devoid of emotion.

"What do you mean by talking back to me?" Hatep swung around. The Israelite slave, whose name he could never remember, looked at him without flinching. "Get more water if we're out and don't run out again."

"I beg your pardon, Sir." His horse slave knew his master would not like the news. "There's no water to be had."

Thinking that the slave was refusing his command, he grabbed the horse whip and lifted it with a threatening glare. "Then put the horse in the shade and go find some water!" he shouted. He threw the whip to the ground in disgust. He'd deal with the slave's insolence later.

Almost fifty years old, Hatep was the owner of a rich family estate on the best farmland of Luxor's West Bank. He was at the peak of his career overseeing a thousand tomb builders. The Royal Master Architect expected instant obedience from his slaves. As a landowner and privileged government official, he had a reputation among other landowners for his fairness. It was no secret that he was strict and impatient with his slaves. Thin lips, a small nose and a sloping forehead made him typical of his Egyptian countrymen in appearance. He wore a loose, knee-length tunic of fine white linen with short, open sleeves and a headdress of similar, expensive material which noted his high position in Egyptian society. The wide dark-blue hem of his tunic and sleeves proclaimed him a royal appointee.

Hatep had overheard rumors about the problem with the water in the Artisan Village so he'd decided to return home early to see how far the problem had progressed. The workers' homes and nobles' estates he'd passed on the Valley Road were in obvious turmoil. His home, however, was quiet, which was a good sign.

"Father!"

Hatep put aside his simmering anger with the horse slave when his son, Malik, and his friend, Nathan, ran around the corner of the stables.

Both Malik and Nathan were seventeen years old but world's apart in appearance and status within society. Like his father, Malik descended from a line of educated Egyptian artisans and professional bureaucrats; thin and tall with the lanky awkward movements of a teenager; his copper-colored skin indicated a distant Nubian relation but with the facial features of the proud Egyptian nobility. Nathan was a Hebrew slave whose stocky, muscular build was typical of the people who supplied the nation with labor to fuel its economy. He had short-cropped hair and the sun bronzed his face. Identically dressed in rough tunics, they were as close as brothers.

"We were at Imhotep's aerodrome and came here as soon as we could when we heard." Malik bent over with his hands on his knees to catch his breath. "Have you seen the river? It's unbelievable! The whole valley's in an uproar. What do you think it is? When will it go away?" His excited words gushed out in a torrent.

Nathan shared his enthusiasm. "Sir, all the water has turned to blood! Nothing like this has ever happened in Egypt before! What do you think it is?"

Malik's father raised both his hands. "Both of you slow down! Now, what's all this talk about blood?"

They stepped into the shade of a tree next to the stable where Hatep saw for himself that blood contaminated the animal troughs and buckets. The secondary cistern for the livestock was dark and the smell betrayed that it too was contaminated. The horse slave was apparently correct and couldn't locate any fresh water on the family estate. The horses would have to go thirsty for now.

"Listen, this is what I want you to do," Hatep said, addressing his son and ignoring his horse slave who all the while stood only a few feet away. "Tell the horse slave to harness another horse to my chariot then drive up to your Uncle Beset's house in the hills and see if he has any fresh water. Their spring is miles away from the river so it should be unpolluted. Also, have what's-his-name load an empty cask into the chariot so you can return with enough fresh water for tonight. That should last us until we can cart in more tomorrow; by then I'm sure the river will be cleared up. Take Nathan with you."

"*Reuben*, Dad."

"What's that?" Hatep asked.

"The horse slave's name is Reuben."

"I can never remember Hebrew names—they're too hard to pronounce. Anyway, tell him to harness the chariot and come back here as soon as you can. It's past noon and we'll need water for lunch and afternoon washing." With a dismissive wave of his hand Hatep left the stable to check on his wife.

Malik's face registered surprise. His father had never let him take the chariot out by himself before. Reuben led the newly harnessed vehicle from behind the stable and proceeded to put a damper on the young Egyptian's excitement about driving it himself. Addressing his master's son, he was insistent: "I suppose your father thinks you can drive a chariot by yourself, but I'll give you some advice as an experienced horseman. Do not, I repeat, *do not* drive this mare fast. She's a reliable old horse—not one of your father's stallions. Make sure that the cask is well-secured before you drive with it full. The road back from your uncle's house is downhill and you'll be close to the maximum weight with the two of you and the cask full of water, so be careful. If you bring this horse and chariot back undamaged he might let you take it out again. Do I make myself clear, young master?" His gruff tone and no-nonsense instructions to his master's son were unmistakable. In spite of being an Israelite horse slave, when it came to his master's horses and chariots, Reuben set the rules. He hoped his master would back him up.

"I promise, Reuben." Malik hopped aboard the chariot platform, Reuben handed him the reins, and Nathan joined him. They left the yard at a slow walk. Within an hour they were in the foothills leading to the Great Place Valley—formally known as the Great Place Valley of the

Kings, or simply the Great Place—where small ornate tombs carved into the gleaming cream-colored limestone lined the road. They passed the broken-down tomb of Ramses IV high in the cliffs, the polished black obelisk of a long-forgotten king shining in the sun next to the road, and the abandoned tomb courtyard of Amenophis near the plateau where Imhotep built his aerodrome.

Hatep walked through his estate's pure white Tura limestone entrance into the lush garden where he assumed his wife was either finishing her morning meditation or tending her flower garden.

He paused momentarily at the family altar to touch the obsidian statue of the Egyptian god *Anubis* that greeted everyone who entered Lotus House. As he continued by, he brushed his fingers over the grim face of the black jackal-headed figure trimmed in gold. Hatep did this without thinking each time he entered his house; a gesture of habit more than religious devotion.

From a few steps away he saw Iset meditating in the shade of the almond trees on her favorite garden bench. Her back was to him so he called out to announce his presence. "Dear, I'm home. I left work early." When she didn't turn around, he touched her shoulder. It was only then that he saw her bloody feet and the crimson stains on her shawl where she had wiped her hands. He let out a gasp.

"Are you hurt? Why is there blood on your feet?"

She looked up without seeing him.

"Listen to me. Are you injured? Did you cut yourself?"

A vacant stare was her only answer.

The pond of blood and fish putrefying in the heat escaped Hatep's immediate notice. Something was very wrong with his beloved wife and his heart raced.

He lifted Iset's limp body in both arms and carried her with care through the ornate entrance hall into the home's central courtyard that served as their living room, past a small decorative loggia and into their cool master bedroom. Something had traumatized his wife and he had no idea what it was. He gently set her on the bed and shouted for her servant to clean the blood from her immediately. When no servant responded to his shouts, something that had never happened before, he reached for an alabaster water pitcher next to their bed, dipped his hand in it, and wiped his wife's face.

More blood! The sight of his bloody handprint on his wife's pale face stunned him and he flung the pitcher against the wall in a frustrated, reflexive response. He heard footsteps behind him and spun around.

"Master, what is it?" Rachel, his wife's Hebrew handmaid, stood in the doorway with her hand to her mouth. She looked at the dark red blood dripping down the wall and the blood on her mistress' face.

"Find some water and clean her up. Now!" he demanded. He felt helpless that he had bloodied his wife's face and didn't know what to do about it. Hatep stepped aside to let the slave woman pass.

"I brought some water from my home," she replied nervously. The normally self-assured handmaid was comfortable dealing with her mistress but almost never spoke directly with the temperamental man of the house. She was terrified of his angry outbursts and breathed a sigh of relief when he wiped his hand on the bedclothes and left the room.

Rachel dipped a cloth in the pot of well water from her home. She carefully wiped the dried blood from her mistress' face and gave her a sip from a cup. After washing her mistress' face, hands and feet, she undressed her and settled her under a bed sheet of fine linen. She then adjusted the roof vent to direct a gentle breeze from the river down onto the bed. When Rachel saw Iset's eyes close and heard her shallow breathing, she knew that she was asleep. The slave gathered the soiled clothing and bedding under one arm, held her water pot and cup in the other hand, and left the room.

After she deposited the soiled clothing and bedding in the laundry, she found Hatep on the garden bench staring at the bubbling fountain and pool that reeked of blood and decaying fish. Overcoming her fear, she silently offered him a cup of water. He accepted it without a word and downed it in a single gulp.

Rachel went to the back of the villa to organize the kitchen help and the house slaves. She knew she'd have to browbeat them into carrying fresh water all the way from the slave village to Lotus House. They would clean the kitchen as best they could, prepare some semblance of a noon meal, and dispose of the blood from other household containers.

She lit a fire in the clay stove to warm leftover pheasant and vegetables; day-old bread and fruit would have to do for now. Finally, she would watch for Sarina, Hatep and Iset's daughter, who would probably come home early from scribal school. The young lady's instructor would send his students home early today. Rachel would meet her at the front door to calm her fears because she knew that the sight of blood would drive the young woman into hysteria.

Luxor West Bank, Uncle Beset's Estate

To the two visitors' disappointment, the fresh water spring at the estate was like a hemorrhaging wound. What was once the sweetest water in the area had turned into a sickening crimson wound in the hillside. Beset's horse slave hailed them when Malik turned the chariot around.

"Sir, if you know any Hebrews with a well, you might see if they have any fresh water. I can't explain it, but I've heard that the Hebrews have fresh water and Egyptians don't." The slave shrugged when asked what that meant.

"How's that possible?" Malik asked Nathan as he guided the horse downhill.

"I don't know, but I do know how to find out. We have a shallow well at our house that my father and brothers dug. I know my mother filled buckets from it this morning before we left for Imhotep's aerodrome. Let's see what it looks like." Nathan sounded skeptical but they headed toward the slave village at the base of the hills anyway.

To their surprise, they found fresh water in the well. They watered the thirsty horse, filled the heavy wooden cask, and secured it firmly to the chariot's frame as Reuben instructed. They didn't speak during the ten-minute drive back to Lotus House. The family would be glad to have fresh water even though they couldn't explain how that was possible.

Nile River at Thebes

"This isn't red water!" shouted a grizzled fisherman at a temple priest who had come to the docks to see the river for himself. "This is *blood* and not red water!"

"How do you know?" the priest argued. He had never fished for a living nor spent more than a few hours in a boat on a family holiday. His upbringing did not allow for what his eyes saw. "It looks to me like something spilled in the river. I'm sure it will clear up by tomorrow."

"Can't you smell it?" another fisherman chided. "I've cut up enough fish in my life and that feels and smells like blood. Look at all the dead fish floating as far as you can see."

"I still say it's only a temporary discoloration. *Anuket* will cleanse herself by tomorrow and all will be well once again." The priest was growing more confident after his visual assessment.

"Why don't we toss this smart fellow into 'Mother Nile'," another fisherman suggested. "Then he can tell us if she's made of colored water or something else?"

"I have a better idea," said a fourth fisherman who stepped behind the priest. He lifted a bucket and dumped its contents on the priest's head. His expensive robes were drenched with blood. "Go ahead, wash it off at the community well. Let's see if it washes off like red water." The fishermen laughed at the priest as he ran away.

The usual noontime boat traffic on the Nile, opposite the Karnak Temple complex and the palace of Waset, had become nonexistent. Nobody knew what to make of the sickening change that had transformed their source of drink, food, and transportation into a river of blood a half-mile wide. According to an official announcement from the Great House palace that afternoon, algae had multiplied rapidly in the river; it would wash away naturally with the river's flow during the night. Everything would be back to normal the next day. The Egyptian fishermen and workers didn't believe this story for a moment because it didn't explain why blood contaminated every well, cistern, animal trough and drinking jar.

CHAPTER 2

Luxor West Bank, Lotus House

Seven days after the plague of blood that paralyzed the nation, the pollution finally dissipated and Mother Nile flowed with fresh water once again. Egyptian wells gradually cleared and life returned to normal. Carp, perch, catfish and even tarpon migrated back from the headwaters of Kush and the First Cataract. People's memories were short. The official explanation of an algae bloom satisfied them for now. The priests assured everyone that the gods would supply their needs as they always had. However, the family in Lotus House still debated questions about the incident each night over dinner in the cool of the evening.

"Why should algae from the river suddenly contaminate the water in Uncle Beset's well up in the hills? And what about the cistern water that the workers drew a week before and put into pots? And why were the slaves' wells not affected?" Malik refused to drop the matter even when his father urged him to trust the government officials and forget about the incident.

"I'm sure that the Great One's priests and magicians know what they're talking about. Nobody understands *Anuket* and her moods better than they." Hatep found it best to defer to the priests' supernatural expertise when it came to things that he did not understand.

"That's the problem," his son insisted. "When they don't know something, they invent explanations. From rumors that I've heard, a stranger confronted Pharaoh and the priests at the river that day and predicted that the river would turn to blood. Within minutes, it happened. How do you explain that?"

"I can't," his father admitted, and resumed gnawing on a grilled lamb shank. This meat and the savory lentil and onion dish before him held his attention. He wanted to finish his meal in peace and retreat to the quiet rooftop where he could think.

Iset redirected the conversation before her husband became agitated and got indigestion. She was unaware of the further discomfort that her attempt would cause him. "Well, the thing that amazed me about all this is how readily the slaves shared their clean well water with us. It was very generous of them. They carried water all the way from their wells so we could eat and bathe. Our horse slave even carted water all the way here for our animals."

"They were only doing their duties. They're just slaves," muttered Hatep. He knew where this conversation was going. In his mind, his wife didn't understand that Hebrew slaves were like the horses in his stable or the cows that gave them good milk; they were bred to do hard work so the nation's economy could grow and prosper. It was just the natural order of things. Some, like his favorite stallion, were more valuable than others. The good slaves—the educated, dependable ones like Asher, the chief steward of Lotus House and Rachel's husband—deserved the same affection he felt for his best hunting dogs, maybe a little more. They knew no other life and he assumed that they were happy to work for a stern but benevolent master like him. In his mind, Hebrew slaves were not people like Egyptians.

"I know, dear, but Rachel took care of us when we didn't have water in the house and Asher made sure the barrel always had water for cooking and washing in addition to his other duties. Is it so difficult for you to be grateful for their kindness?"

Malik grew uneasy when his mother became so emotional about their slaves. He remembered many dinners disrupted by arguments on the subject. "I wonder what Sarina thinks about the 'blood episode,'" Malik said in his sister's direction. Any topic of conversation was better than listening to his parents arguing over how to treat their Hebrew household and field slaves.

Malik's sister would be nineteen years old in a few months. Her full lips and high, bronzed cheek bones glowed with youthful beauty. She wore her long black hair in a dozen thin braids that reached to her waist and each braid was weighted with a golden tip to keep it straight. She carried her petite frame with an independent, confident air much like her mother. Since she was almost nineteen, her childhood dinnertime sulking and drama had been replaced with thoughtful silence. A year of educational discipline at the Mittani Scribal School had made her more mature, considerate, and serious.

"Me? Oh, I found it *very* interesting," she said as she chewed a tender piece of grilled lamb. Her dark eyes glanced at her parents. "Especially regarding those two brothers, Moses and Aaron."

"Who are Moses and Aaron? The name Moses sounds Egyptian and Aaron sounds Hebrew. How could they be brothers?" Hatep's quick notice of racial distinctions was typical of an Egyptian nobleman.

Malik was surprised that his sister held a specific view on this. She usually sat quietly through their mealtime arguments and rarely spoke. Her family waited for her to continue.

"I heard that they turned the river to blood when Pharaoh refused their demand." The teen was pleased that she knew something her parents and bossy brother didn't know. She chewed slower to draw out the suspense.

"Tell us what you know," her father finally said. He stopped chewing and held his lamb in midair. She hesitated a few times to feign reluctance to say more. "It's all right," he said, "You can tell us."

"Well..." she began. "The two Hebrew strangers interrupted the Great One's bath that morning with a demand that he immediately free the Israelite slaves to worship their God in the desert."

"No!" her father exclaimed. He threw the half-eaten bone onto his plate. "That's outrageous!"

"The Great One then said that not only would he not allow the slaves to leave to worship, but he would double their workload of bricks to make sure that they had no time for such foolishness. That's when it happened."

"That's when what happened, dear?" Iset asked.

"Moses, or actually his brother Aaron, waved a shepherd's rod over the river and turned Mother Nile to blood. Supposedly, the court magicians did a similar trick with water in a jar, so they said that what Aaron did with the rod wasn't a real miracle. Now, though, nobody can deny that what Moses and Aaron did was supernatural. The entire river turned to blood from Aswan at the First Cataract all the way down to the Lower Land. I don't believe for a minute the official story about red algae contamination."

The ensuing silence made Hatep shift in his chair uneasily. His daughter's superior tone bothered the head of the household more than the wild story she had concocted. "Young lady, I don't know where you came up with this ridiculous fairy tale, or where your superior attitude has come from lately, but you're through with dinner. Go to your room!" His sharp outburst signaled that the meal was over.

"I'm sorry I upset you, Father. I thought you wanted to hear what I thought." She left the table and walked with assurance to her room. It was better that her father couldn't see her self-satisfied smile. She was right and she knew it.

"I heard another rumor that it was Hebrew slaves who sabotaged their masters' wells. Vendors in the bazaar claim that slaves threw some sort of powder into the river at the same time." Malik wanted to continue the family discussion after his sister's revelation.

"I don't feel well," Hatep abruptly announced. He pushed away from his unfinished dinner and refilled his cup of wine. "I'm going to the roof *alone* to catch the evening breeze." He plodded up the stairs where he could mull over the dinnertime conflict in peace. His wife's views of slavery conflicted with his own, his daughter's outrageous opinions were something new, and Malik's conspiracy theories defied definition— these all disturbed him. Not only did he feel that his household's order and tranquility—the Egyptian word was *ma'at*—was disturbed when they argued like this, but he also sensed that Egypt's centuries-old civil order was slipping away. Nothing could be more stable and reliable than Mother Nile! She always had been, and always would be, the same, or so the wise men said. Weren't the powerful gods in charge of preserving Egypt's *ma'at*?

Luxor West Bank, Slave Village

Dinnertime conversation in the simple home of Asher and Rachel was different from that of many other slaves. In many respects, though they lived in poor conditions no different from most other Hebrew slaves, they considered themselves blessed. Their dwelling consisted of rough mud brick walls and a roof of thatched papyrus reeds that was identical to all the others in the closely packed hamlet where the Hebrew field and household slaves lived out their existence toiling for Egyptians on lush estates along Luxor's West Bank. A patchwork of small vegetable gardens surrounded the hovels that housed several hundred families. From its outward appearance, theirs was a nondescript shack; inside it was a tranquil home whose dinnertime serenity would have amazed Master Hatep.

Dinner had to wait for Rachel's return from her evening duties at Lotus House. She made sure that her mistress had clean clothing for the next day, she reminded the last kitchen helpers to be quiet, the proper food was in storage jars ready for breakfast, and she extinguished all but a few oil lamps in the house before she left for the night. Master Hatep was still brooding on the roof after the family's dinner argument. She had overheard them many times before. She looked forward to having a quiet dinner with her family.

When Rachel and Asher gathered around their small table with Nathan and old Ben-Judah, they gave thanks to God for the generous food from their master's house. Iset made sure that the household slaves received all the excess from the lavish meals the Egyptian family enjoyed each night. Of course, Hatep gave little thought to where food came from or where it went. He was a wealthy government employee with a fine villa, many slaves, abundant crops and herds of livestock. His wife managed their home as a model of efficiency and her slaves were well-behaved.

Conversation around dinner in the home of Asher and Rachel soon turned to speculation about the plague that had been the topic each night since the Nile turned to blood. They had exhausted most of the speculation overheard in the bazaar.

"I heard something at Lotus House tonight," Rachel said to her husband. "Sarina told her parents about two Hebrew brothers, Moses and Aaron, who confronted Pharaoh that morning. She said they *demanded* that he allow the children of Israel to journey into the desert to worship the *LORD*. When Pharaoh refused and increased the slave's brick levy, the one named Aaron used a shepherd's rod to turn the river into blood. What do you think of that?"

"I think the master's daughter is imagining things," her husband replied calmly as he dug into the leftover lamb scraps from his master's kitchen.

"She's still only a kid," Nathan added, although she was two years older than him. "Just because she'll graduate soon from the Mittani Scribal School she thinks she knows everything. Malik says she spends all her free time on the roof dreaming up tall tales like that one."

"Maybe that dream isn't so far from reality," Ben-Judah commented. "This reminds me of something." The family waited to hear what the kindly old man had to say. Whenever he thought carefully before saying something it was always worth hearing.

Ben-Judah was a Hebrew, blind from a lifetime working in the sun; decades in the granite and limestone quarries had crippled his black, shriveled body. Rachel came across him one day in the street of Luxor's West Bank bazaar living on handouts. Once in a while, she gave him a crescent loaf of bread when she bought provisions for her mistress; sometimes she gave him a jar of barley beer or water sweetened with honey. She stopped short one day when he blessed her and called her a "daughter of Abraham." He spoke to her of the blessings of Abraham, Isaac, and Jacob and it brought back memories of how her grandfather had told stories handed down from ancient Israelites about their forefathers. The day that Asher agreed to allow the old invalid to live with them began a time of great blessing for their family. Not only did they see increased material favors from their master and his wife, but they experienced a greater love for the God of Abraham whose promises brought them renewed hope.

"My old friends and I have heard these same rumors too. Oh, I know, you think we're just old men reminiscing about times gone by and sitting around waiting to die…"

"I don't think that," Nathan interrupted before he could continue. "You've taught us things about the history of our people that we didn't know before. Your title of '*Rabbi*' in the village is well-deserved and everyone looks to you as a teacher of God."

"It's kind of you to say that, Nathan." The blind cripple reached for the lentil pot from which Hatep had eaten only an hour before. Rachel spooned a large helping onto his plate. "As I was saying, this demand that Pharaoh allow the slaves to worship the *LORD* in the desert could be the beginning of something exciting. God promised Abraham, and later Isaac and Jacob also, that His people would number more than the stars in the heavens and dwell together in the Promised Land of Canaan one day. Yet here we are, slaves in Egypt more than four hundred years later and far from our beloved homeland. Something dramatic needs to happen to move us from slavery in this oppressive land to our rightful home in Canaan, the land of milk and honey. If this man Moses and his brother are really redeemers sent from God, then their role in our future will become more clear in due time. Turning the Nile into blood might be only a first step to change Pharaoh's mind. For now, however, the palace is in confusion and Pharaoh is in denial. When the right time comes, and I pray that it will arrive in my lifetime, the King of Upper and Lower Egypt will realize that he and his gods are no match for the *LORD* God of Israel!"

CHAPTER 3

Great Place Plateau, Temple of Shu Aerodrome

Three weeks after the bloody episode with the Nile and Egypt's contaminated drinking water the matter was a dim memory. The average person accepted the propaganda that algae had turned the water red and killed all the fish. Mother Nile was back to normal and fish once again swam in the warm water, although not as plentifully as before. Drinking water still had a slight coppery tinge but people adjusted to its taste. Months earlier, before the annual *akhet* Inundation season when the Nile overflowed its banks and travel was disrupted, Hatep had begun training Malik and Nathan in the skills they would need for their livelihoods in architecture and design. Soon they would turn eighteen years of age. Egyptians became adults at age nineteen. He realized that they needed much more knowledge and wisdom before they could assume responsible vocations in society.

The Royal Master Architect of the Great Place Valley tombs hoped that his son and favored slave would grow together in their own unique ways to serve Thutmose III and future Pharaohs of The Two Lands. Hatep and Nathan's father trained together in the scribal arts of writing and mathematics as young boys. He wanted Malik and Nathan to follow in his professional footsteps and those of the chief steward of Lotus House respectively when their time came. For now, they had to learn serious responsibilities instead of wasting their time chasing foolish ideas, exotic scientific inventions and daring adventures.

After he dropped off the two at the aerodrome, he expected them to spend the morning with Royal Master Inventor Imhotep on the plateau between Karnak's West Bank on the river and the Great Place Valley of the Kings. The wise old sage was Hatep's chief surveyor. The two young men would fly into the cool pre-dawn air above the Great Place Valley with Imhotep for a lesson in surveying and perspective temple layout.

The *Horus Eye* was a magnificent flying machine aptly named for the falcon-god that Egyptians believed was all-seeing and all-knowing. Imhotep dreamed from early childhood of being able to fly while he watched the falcons, hawks, eagles, and ospreys circle effortlessly over the fertile Nile in search of prey. Their lazy flight made the inventor wonder why he couldn't fly like them. He devised a gossamer, silk tube filled with hot air which floated into the air, though it did not have wings like a bird. Years of experimentation, some funded by Malik's father, resulted in a floating machine that gave surveyors, architects, and artisans from the Kings' Great Place and nearby Queens' Beautiful Place a way to look down on their magnificent tombs, courtyards, and paved causeways in much the same way they imagined that the gods saw them. Being able to picture their carved resting places in the Theban hills from high in the air pleased the tombs' wealthy benefactors beyond words. Contributions to improve and maintain the flying machine were now plentiful.

Imhotep built a launching pad in the large courtyard of the aptly named Temple of Shu, whose name literally meant "he who rises up," on the high plateau overlooking the west bank of the Nile and opposite the temples of Luxor. *Shu*, the mythical god of air, wind and space joined with the all-seeing god *Horus* to watch over the earth below.

The airborne ship consisted of a bulbous, fine silk bag with a hole at its base through which hot air was introduced from an intense charcoal fire suspended on a metal and stone hearth between the bottom of the casing and a woven passenger basket that hung below. On a cool morning, when heated air filled the silken housing, the machine easily lifted upward with two or three passengers and extra fuel. A long, thin umbilical cord of braided linen restrained it from soaring high into the sky. The craft's inventor was certain that all the occupants would perish if it were allowed to float toward the sun. When the outside air warmed later in the day, the ground crew cranked a winch and brought the deflating silk bag back to the aerodrome before it touched the ground. A light, four-pronged mesh structure of papyrus reeds, constructed to fold like the petals of a lotus blossom, gently restrained the silken object until its top was tied down. When fully docked, the limp cloth was held suspended by the rigid papyrus mesh ready to be inflated and launched again.

Although they had been in the *Horus Eye* many times, Malik and Nathan never tired of the exhilaration of flight. Today's mission was a lesson in aerial tomb surveying so as soon as they reached their planned altitude, Imhotep began a lecture on the design of Queen Hatshepsut's burial site spread out below them. The tomb, temple, and courtyard building complex was situated at the base of creamy limestone cliffs and extended deep into the side of the hill. It was an example of the designer's use of colonnades, ramps, and ornamental courtyards that drew the viewer's attention to the double doors through which the body of the land's only female pharaoh had been carried to rest less than a century earlier. To the Egyptians, this extravagant mortuary and its brightly painted interior murals further ensured her body's transition into the afterlife. Today, Hatshepsut's tomb was the subject of an academic architectural study. With less than an hour left before their fuel was depleted, when the craft would inevitably return to the ground, Nathan pointed to something along the top of the ridge that he'd noticed a few minutes earlier.

"Master Imhotep, I see many men over there." He pointed toward the west beyond the top of the hill behind Hatshepsut's tomb. Imhotep and Malik saw more than a hundred horsemen in a depression behind the hilltop that only they could see from their high vantage point. A line of more men on horses and camels strung out into the distance. On the far horizon a cloud of dust hinted at more behind them.

"Who are they?" asked Malik.

"I cannot be certain, but I am guessing from their numbers and mode of dress that they are warriors from the Western Desert—probably Nubians. Their clothing and battle armor are distinctive. They surely see us by now and are wondering what this floating illusion is with the all-seeing eye of Horus emblazoned on its side. We must return to the aerodrome immediately and sound the alarm." The inventor instructed Nathan to deflate the balloon by pulling on lines that hung from above. He waved to the ground crew to reel them down.

While they descended, Nathan offered an idea: "Could we use the *Horus Eye* to coordinate a counter-offense? If the invaders wait until tomorrow morning to attack, this would make a perfect command platform from which to direct Pharaoh's troops. Could we do that?"

"I'm sure that's possible, but you are forgetting that while you and I understand the usefulness of this device as an observation perch, the military is very resistant to anything new. I doubt that they would receive such a suggestion from a slave. Nonetheless, I believe you should try."

"When we land, I'll tell my father what we saw and explain your idea. He'll send a messenger to Pharaoh's court where I'm sure the vizier and others will see the sense in it and send the military to respond." Malik's innocent enthusiasm betrayed his ignorance of Egyptian politics or military strategy. It could take weeks or months for the Great House to make a decision, if they bothered to listen to him at all.

When they reached the ground, the two ran to Hatep's official rooms in the Great Place workers' complex to tell him what they had seen and explain Nathan's idea for helping the army. Hatep listened to their description of the Nubian riders, their positions behind the cliffs and the probable gathering of more troops from the direction of the Kharga Oasis in the Western Desert. The fact that Imhotep identified them as Nubians gave the two boys added credibility.

"Without this information our army would never know that an attack is imminent until it was too late." Hatep paced back and forth muttering to himself. "If I send a courier to the Great House palace it's anyone's guess what would happen to the warning. Some scribe might file it away in an archive or toss it into the fire. I have an idea! Vizier Nakhte is a man of action. I met him when he issued my appointment to the Royal Academy and I know he'd give my message consideration if I sent it personally addressed to him. I also met the deputy to General Bakara at a palace reception some months ago. If I also send the message addressed to him at the army garrison in Karnak, he might take the initiative and do something about it. That's it! I'll dictate the details and send them off this minute." Hatep called for his personal scribe to draft the communication.

"Father, how you can notify them in time? It'll take hours for a messenger to reach them, even if he takes a fast chariot. He'll then have to ferry across the river and make his way through the city. It might be nightfall before the palace receives the message and the Nubians could attack early tomorrow morning."

"No, there's another way. They'll find out about the Nubian attack within the hour." The Royal Master Architect gave the two a knowing smile. "It's time to show you the Royal Signaling Network."

Great Place Valley, Heliographic Tower

A sturdy wooden tower rose fifty feet above the Kings' Great Place with an unobstructed view of the gleaming white limestone Temples of Karnak across the river and the city of Thebes and the Great House palace to the southeast of the temples. Nathan wondered why he'd never noticed the tower before. The still air and the indirect afternoon sun reflecting down the cliffs at their backs made the tower feel like an oven in spite of a patch of shade from a white linen awning. What was this place?

Two scribes, one Egyptian and one Hebrew, sat at small tables on either side of a gleaming copper instrument on an eight-foot pedestal bolted to the center of the tower platform. Malik handed the Egyptian the message prepared by Hatep's scribe and commented on the heat. "How can you work up here in this heat? I'm ready to faint."

"Sometimes there's a breeze. I'm Hakamun, by the way, and this is Elias." The Egyptian, in his mid-twenties and burnished by the sun, glanced over the papyrus while Malik and Nathan stared at the copper machine in the center of the tower. "It's hard to believe, but you do get used to the heat up here. Elias and I have endured much worse. The station in Goshen, with its humidity—now that was insufferable." His Hebrew assistant chuckled. Hakamun handed the message to Elias who scribbled some *sekh shat* demotic script in the margin, sat on a shelf built into the pedestal four feet above the floor and grasped a lever in his right hand while holding the papyrus in his left. A polished, round disk three feet in diameter was attached to a pole on top of the pedestal.

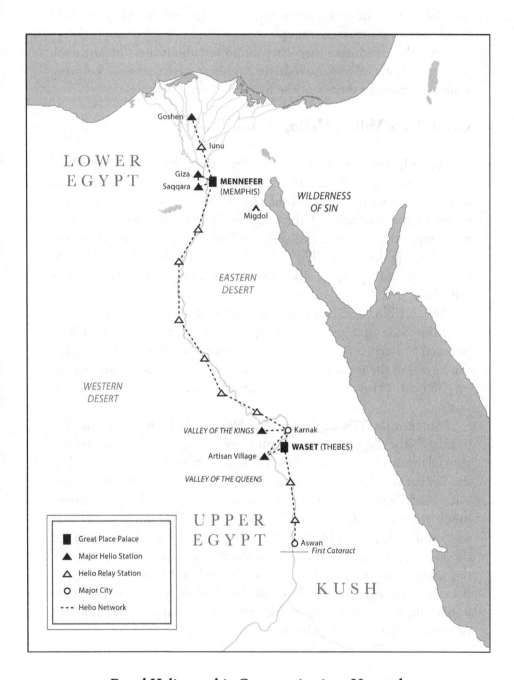

Royal Heliographic Communications Network

"Now it gets really hot," Hakamun warned as he rolled the large linen awning back so the sun shone directly on the curved polished mirror. The Egyptian pivoted the entire mechanism around until a pointer at the base of the pedestal aligned with Pharaoh's royal cartouche symbol on the floor pointing the small copper mirror at the palace. He then adjusted the large mirror until the dazzling reflection of the sun focused a beam of light from its center to a smaller polished disk on the side of the pedestal opposite the mechanism's operator. This caused the concentrated beam to point directly at the palace to the southeast. Elias looked toward Thebes while flicking the lever up and down.

"He's making contact with his counterpart at the Great House palace helio station," Hakamun said casually. "If you look over there, you'll see the reply indicating that they're ready to receive a message."

Nathan and Malik squinted looking across the sloping river valley and noticed a pinpoint of bright light blinking off and on. Then the Israelite at the machine's controls shifted the lever up and down in a practiced, rhythmic sequence while he read from the papyrus in his hand. In two minutes he looked up and watched for a response from the Great House. A short series of flashes on the horizon seemed to satisfy him. He stepped down from his perch on the pedestal and stretched his legs.

"We're not done," Hakamun announced. He rotated the pedestal until a second marker on the floor pointed due east while Elias worked the stiffness from his legs and wrist. When the large mirror was adjusted, the operator repeated the process of making contact with the military garrison in Karnak, and sent the same message and verified its receipt. He laughed when he was finished and stepped down.

Hakamun took the papyrus message from his assistant. "Now we're done. You can put the shade back," he said to Nathan who eagerly pulled the linen awning over them to reduce the temperature by a few degrees.

"Did you see what Tobias said?" Elias asked his boss with a chuckle. This was the first time the Israelite had spoken.

"Yea, '*Nice breeze here by the river. Going swimming this afternoon.*' I hate those guys!"

The two visitors were stunned speechless by what they'd just witnessed. Warning of an impending Nubian attack was instantly flashed through the air in minutes to the palace and the Karnak military garrison across a distance of almost twenty miles. Then the scribes at either end of the solar link joked about going swimming as if they were talking to each other. All of this using sunlight and shiny copper disks!

"That's unbelievable! Who are you guys and what is this thing?" Malik blurted.

"Ah, so your father didn't explain. Sorry. His message was marked MOST URGENT so we had to send it right away. Why don't I let Elias give you a tour of our humble helio station while I take this scroll back to your father and let him know that his message went through to both recipients without a problem. Elias, keep an eye out for more traffic while I'm gone." The scribe disappeared down the ladder with a wave and cheerful smile.

"Since you asked who we are, I'll begin with that. Hakamun and I have had years of schooling in pictographs as well as hieratic script and *sekh shat* shorthand. Have either of you had any scribal schooling?"

"We learned some basic hieroglyphs and hieratic writing at the Mittani Scribal School where my sister goes, but I can't say that we were very good," Malik volunteered.

"We've had enough math so that my friend here could apprentice to be an architect and I could manage his estate when he inherits it," Nathan added. "It sounds like you two have had to learn much more."

"Everyone who works in the system needs two more years of training beyond scribal school to become certified heliographers. We have to learn the helio code well enough to mentally convert the code and write it in *sekh shat* shorthand as fast as it's sent. Even after scribal schooling, it takes years of practice to be able to chat back and forth like you saw us do a little while ago." Their host talked to them while he glanced back and forth at the two stations across the river.

"How is it that a slave came to work here?" Malik was intrigued by this well-educated Hebrew who was the same age as his Egyptian supervisor and was treated as his equal.

"Hakamun is a good boss and friend. We've been through a lot together and he sees to it that I'm paid a living wage, for a slave anyway, in return for my services to the network. I grew up on a farm in Goshen where I was an accountant for a rich rice trader. During years of drought my master sold me to the regional administration as a bookkeeper. It sure beat working in the rice fields! When the helio network was formed, I taught myself code and they hired me on the spot. Hakamun and I have been a team ever since."

"So how many operators are there?"

"Hundreds—from Aswan to Goshen. This is just one station in the local Theban subnet of the nationwide Royal Signaling Network, or the 'helio net' as we call it, that sends information around Thebes and across the river. Besides the three stations you heard about today, there's another in the Artisans' Village in the Beautiful Place Valley of the Queens that can't be seen from here because hills block the line of sight. Any messages from us to them have to be relayed through either the palace or Karnak garrison stations."

Elias reached for a roll of papyrus and a pen while he watched the horizon. The scribe jotted notes without looking at the paper. Then he set the sheet down. "That was an administrative accounting message. I think the royal master scribe likes to make sure we're still here! Now, where was I?"

"You said that there are stations from Aswan to Goshen. I'm astonished that I've never heard of the network before. Why's that?" Malik was growing more curious about this amazing ability to communicate at the speed of light over great distances.

"You wouldn't have had a need to know about it. Since your father sent you here with a sensitive message for transmission, he evidently felt that you needed to know about us. I trust that you won't reveal our capabilities without official approval. Master Architect Hatep is one of the major users of the Theban local network. Information about tomb building materials, payments, construction schedules, personnel assignments, and tomb design changes are all sent through us. He communicates almost daily with royal scribes.

"Hey, I better finish up with my lecture because there might be some responses to your father's warning message in the next hour or so. They'll be marked MOST URGENT." Elias led them to the shiny copper pedestal and mechanism.

"This is the brainchild of Inventor Imhotep, as you might have guessed. He understands the power of the sun and figured a way to turn the sun's rays off and on in a mathematically coded sequence to convey a message. Without going into detail, this thing captures direct sunlight—it won't work on a hazy or cloudy day or at night for obvious reasons—and focuses the intense light into a directional beam. We aim the device at our target station and use this lever to snap the beam off and on. The target station receives the coded pulses sent through the air and skilled operators interpret the code as fast as we can send it. In some sense, it's pretty simple."

"Right. Simple for you." Nathan said. "We need to go now, but can we come see you and Hakamun again sometime?"

"Sure. Whenever the sun's shining, we're here. Unless we decide to take the day off and go swimming, that is," he laughed.

"Thanks for the great tour and explanation. We'll be back," Malik added.

The two descended the ladder and ran to Hatep's office to find out how they could help prepare for the Nubian attack.

CHAPTER 4

Waset, Great House Palace—Vizier Nakhte's Reception Room

A palace runner delivered the MOST URGENT alert message to Vizier Nakhte's personal scribe within minutes of its receipt. Scribe Gobe instructed the runner to wait while he made a copy of its contents. When he finished, he folded the copy of a single papyrus sheet into a tight square package and sealed it with beeswax.

"Deliver this confidential message to Royal Master Scribe Bakenmut *only*. Not to his scribes or anyone else. You will mention this to no one." He handed it to a barefoot palace runner who bowed and ran out of the office and down the corridor. The sound of his bare feet slapping the polished marble floor followed him into the distance.

Scribe Gobe was also a palace informant and a greedy opportunist. His shrunken, almost rat-like appearance and halting speech should have betrayed him, but the vizier was unaware of his disloyalty. As the vizier's personal scribe, he was sought out by high-level palace officials and priests for tidbits of information that they could use to their advantage. The shifty scribe was glad to oblige—for a price. His most generous patron was Royal Master Scribe Bakenmut.

He read the message a second time before he brought it into the vizier's cool, spacious office. His superior sat at a large desk carved from exotic dark wood by craftsmen in some distant land. This and other valuable spoils of the realm's foreign conquests filled the room.

While he stood waiting for his master to acknowledge his presence, Gobe looked around him. As the vizier's personal scribe, he worked amid opulent furnishings and treasured artifacts all day. He spoke with the highest government officials and emissaries on matters of national importance. Yet, the scribe returned home to his wife and three children in their small apartment each night and complained about his meager pay and lack of recognition. His illicit earnings made him the wealthiest personal scribe in the palace, but his love for bribes was overpowered by fear that his treachery would be exposed and he might lose his ill-gotten riches or even his life. In a strange contradiction of logic and emotion, he lived a double existence: risking his life each day as a traitor but living in near-poverty for fear of being discovered.

When Nakhte looked up from the official document before him, his eyes landed on the small roll in his scribe's hand.

"What's that?" he asked. "I hope you're bothering me with something truly important."

"It's from the helio network. It was marked MOST URGENT." He handed the message to the second most powerful man in the nation after Pharaoh. He took one step away from his master's desk to await instructions.

The vizier's large, corpulent form filled the wide chair that strained to support his weight. Even when he worked in his private office, his formal, ceremonial dress and bright red, feathered miter distinguished him as the second most powerful man in Egypt. Dark kohl makeup rimmed his eyes and fine gold powder made his pale face glow in the sunlight. He dressed as if he could become the next Pharaoh at any moment.

The content of the message was of such interest to Vizier Nakhte that he read it to himself three times, but showed no expression on his face. He set the roll on his desk and looked at the man standing before him. His unblinking eyes bore into the scribe standing at attention before him.

"You read this?"

"Yes, master." The scribe was unconcerned for now because he was authorized to screen all messages sent to the vizier's office. He prepared himself mentally because he knew that the vizier's next question would require him to lie convincingly.

"This message is very sensitive. Has anyone else read it?"

"Besides the helio operators and myself, no sir." Scribe Gobe's calculated deception flowed from his lips without hesitation. He dreaded any further questioning if his master sensed the smallest trace of a lie. If there were no more questions, then he would be safe from suspicion—at least for now. He held his breath.

"Very well. Summon the Royal Master Scribe, but don't tell him the subject. This matter is highly confidential."

Resisting the urge to exhale in a sudden rush, the scribe spun about and departed in a slow, unhurried walk to task another palace courier who should be waiting for his order in the hallway. A rivulet of sweat ran down his back and stained his starched linen tunic.

When Royal Master Scribe Bakenmut and his two assistants arrived at the vizier's reception area a few moments later, Gobe met the man's gaze with practiced indifference and informed him that Vizier Nakhte wished to meet with him alone. The two self-important aides scowled at Gobe but left when their superior gave a nod in their direction.

Scribe Gobe was a petty charlatan compared to Pharaoh's Royal Master Scribe. Bakenmut practiced lies and corruption on a national scale, using his trusted position to his maximum personal advantage. He supervised the trusted staff of couriers, messengers, scribes, copiers, time keepers, heliographers, and royal archivists in the Great House palace. He read everyone's mail and ran dozens of blackmail schemes. More importantly, as Pharaoh's personal scribe, he oversaw the transcription of every official royal utterance, saying, edict, and command onto plaster-covered wooden tablets for preservation in the royal archives. Egyptian history was quietly rewritten whenever it suited his plans. At the stroke of his pen, on royal stationary and with Pharaoh's seal, he siphoned gold from the palace vaults into his personal storehouses. His lust for gold was bounded only by the limitless treasures of Egypt.

Bakenmut's eyes bore into Gobe until the scribe was forced to look away in submission. The royal official then entered the vizier's office.

"It was kind of you to come," Nakhte said. He motioned his visitor to a nearby gilded couch.

"You said it was urgent but gave no subject for this meeting," the royal scribe said, feigning mild irritation. "What is this about?" He hated casual, polite conversation and wanted his boss to get to the point.

"This," the vizier said handing him the scroll. He pretended to read the message slowly and ponder its contents, though he already knew what it said.

"So? This appears to be only a small raiding party that poses little threat to the Great House palace or to the Temples of Karnak. I see no reason for great concern." He handed the paper back with feigned indifference and watched the vizier's reaction.

"Is that what you think, Bakenmut? It could also be the precursor to a full-scale invasion. Since we don't know how many Nubian fighters are actually involved, we should prepare for the worst."

"What does General Bakara say? The message indicates that he was sent a copy as well. Have you heard from him?"

"Nothing as yet. I don't think the old man will be too keen to mount an energetic response. He was a good soldier in his prime, with many campaign victories to his credit, but he should have retired to his vineyard years ago. If I get any response from him at all, it will be by courier later tonight. I don't expect anything to happen before tomorrow."

"Precisely my thought," Bakenmut said with newfound conviction. He then pretended to have received a flash of insight. "Wait. I have an idea that might be helpful. Suppose we don't wait to hear from the general. You could send him an order authorizing two parallel actions. First, a small force could be sent to the Great Place Valley to protect the tombs and Artisans' Village. They could fend off the Nubians if they are small in number, or the soldiers could retreat after an initial probe and allow the valley to be taken. They could then return to us with better information on the enemy's strength and disposition. Second, an infantry division, maybe a thousand or more ground troops, could wait on the West Bank of the Nile opposite Karnak in case the attackers' intended target is the temples and palace. They could set up defensive positions there and reinforce them, if needed, using the remainder of the infantry corps back in the Karnak garrison to keep the invaders from crossing the river."

Vizier Nakhte was surprised. "I didn't realize that you had such a grasp of military strategy. That does sound like a reasonable position to take, considering that we don't know much about this attacking force. You are a service to the Great One and his Great House. I will send those orders to General Bakara immediately."

"Would you like me to prepare the order?" the royal scribe suggested. "With your approval and signature, of course."

"Yes! Give the wording for the order to Gobe and he'll put it into the right format for transmission. There is still sufficient sunlight so it should be in Bakara's hands soon. Send a copy to Royal Architect Hatep at the Great Place Valley also, so he knows to expect troops later tonight.

I trust you to word the orders as we discussed without my review since I must leave to meet my afternoon temple obligations." Vizier Nakhte adjusted the tall, bright red miter on his head that complemented his colorful robes and elegant makeup. He wanted to be easily recognized in the crowd of worshippers. The more royal he looked the more he supplanted Pharaoh in the minds of those who saw him in public.

The broad smile on Bakenmut's face lifted Gobe's spirits when he came out of the vizier's office to hurriedly dictate military orders to the vizier's scribe.

"When you finish sending this to the general, be sure to make a copy for my files. Will there be any problem sending me military updates or copies of future messages on this subject?"

"Of course not, sir." Gobe understood his drift.

"You are a faithful servant of the Great One. Your reward for service will be remembered."

Gobe swelled with pride as he watched his benefactor depart. He could hardly wait to tell his wife about the honor and prospect for reward. He prepared to take the military orders upstairs to the helio operator.

Karnak, Military Garrison—Amun Corps Headquarters

The original alert message from the Great Place Valley wove its way through several junior duty officers at the army headquarters. Since the general was secluded at his riverside villa, a courier went in search of the corps deputy, Commander Herihor, to decide if the general should be bothered. While the commander was debriefing his chariot regiment at the garrison stables after a mock training battle, the vizier and master scribe had already decided on a course of military action. Not knowing this, the commander washed, changed into a fresh tunic, and went to the general's office at the garrison headquarters to read the first message from the Great Place Valley.

Herihor was a professional Egyptian officer who bore the marks of a battle-hardened warrior that made him look older than his thirty-two years. He was of medium height, lean muscular build, and quick with a sword and bow. Short, sun-bleached hair above intelligent, piercing gray eyes missed no detail when it came to military tactics and leading soldiers into battle. The few, visible white scars on his face took nothing away from his rugged, dark features that some women found attractive.

Unseen, but a constant source of pain, was a deep gash across his back from an ax that had penetrated his leather armor during the second Egyptian-Canaanite war in Megiddo. He had teetered between life and death for weeks. After surviving loss of blood and then infection, the wound still caused him stiffness that slowed him in hand-to-hand combat but didn't hinder him from firing arrows while braced in a racing chariot. Even when not in uniform he was unmistakably a military man. He distinguished himself early in his short career by victories with minimal troop casualties while exacting a deadly toll from his adversaries. He believed in relentlessly training his men to hone their skills and adapt to new weapons and tactics. To say that his men loved him would be only a slight exaggeration. They respected his fairness, trusted his combat instincts under pressure, and admired his leadership.

On a path lined with palms, regimental ensigns soared over pylons on each side of the solid brick and limestone building that housed the military bureaucracy needed to support the Egyptian Amun Corps of ten thousand troops stationed at Karnak. An identical unit, the Ra Corps, was deployed beyond the First Cataract to deter Nubian and Kushite attacks from the south. Commander Herihor was young, talented, and ambitious. He expected to lead the Amun Corps or another of Pharaoh's five national corps one day.

General Bakara was reported to be convalescing at his villa from an unspecified illness. Speculation among the troops was that he was worn out from a multitude of combat injuries, years of field rations and fetid water, and the overall stress of senior command. His medical advisors recommended that he move to the mountains to escape the heat and the myriad of insect-borne diseases that festered in the swamps, bogs, and irrigation ditches near the Nile. He refused to move and clung to command of the Amun Corps, much to the consternation of his subordinates. Herihor was the *de facto* corps commander but wished that the general would quietly depart, one way or the other, so he could officially assume command of the corps. First however, this matter needed to be dealt with.

The contents of the message warning of a Nubian attack from the western mountains surprised Commander Herihor. There had been no warning from his lookouts, spies along the river, or informers within Nubia itself. It was apparent from this report that a surprise force had assembled deep in the Western Desert, probably at the Kharga Oasis, and traveled undetected to the mountains behind the Great Place Valley of the Kings. The experienced commander studied the message and wondered how two young civilians in a flying bag of hot air could have spotted the invaders gathering beyond the hills when nobody else had reported the enemy's presence.

His gut instinct told him what needed to be done in this situation, but it would take an earthquake to pry General Bakara from his comfortable villa. Commander Herihor intentionally worded a brief communiqué to his general that exaggerated the immediate danger to the Temples of Karnak and Thebes to pry the reluctant general away from his posh retreat. At least it would bring the old man to the Karnak headquarters to approve orders that would move part of the corps across the river during the night. In spite of his understandable ambition, the deputy was wise enough to not overstep his authority by ordering a thousand troops to move now, especially when his superior was only a few miles away.

By the time General Bakara reclined his heavy frame on a upholstered couch in his headquarters office, he was exhausted from the brief chariot ride and the short walk down the hallway. He held the papyrus that a courier handed him as soon as he entered the room. The old soldier's sharp mind absorbed the alert message and quickly grasped its implications. The thought still tired him when he considered deploying even part of his corps across the river to repel an invasion. Hundreds of armed battles, skirmishes and attacks defined his long, distinguished career. This might be his last engagement with the enemy. If he survived, he would beg the Great One to let him live out his few remaining years in peace.

"Commander, issue orders to activate five regiments of the Amun Corps immediately. They will deploy across the river tonight, seek out this Nubian rabble and send them back into the desert with their tails between their legs. And fetch me a drink!" The general was warming to this new mission.

"Wine or barley beer, sir?" his deputy asked, knowing the old man's need for relief from his many aches and pains.

"Neither! Water, honey and whatever juice the steward has in his pantry. Assemble the appropriate regimental staff in twenty minutes. We have work to do!"

Pleased to see that his general still had some fire in him, Commander Herihor was ready to summon the other commanders when another runner burst into the room out of breath.

"With respect, sir," the young soldier puffed. "This just came in for the general from the Great House." The young messenger handed a scroll to the general.

"Humph!" General Bakara grunted when he read the lengthy communication. He shook his head and handed the papyrus to Herihor. "Politicians…" he muttered.

When the staff assembled to implement the latest instructions from Vizier Nakhte, they prepared more detailed orders for each regiment. Commander Herihor suggested, and the general approved, a contact patrol composed of the elite Leopard Charioteers regiment and a few hundred special infantry to engage the invaders at dawn in the Great Place Valley and slow them from reaching the larger mass of troops to be assembled on Karnak's West Bank across from the garrison later in the day. The regiment and their commander would have freedom to execute their delaying mission and gather intelligence before retreating. General Bakara would hold the remaining regiments on Karnak's West Bank and the balance of the Amun Corps would be on standby at the Karnak barracks in case the enemy threatened to cross the river.

Great Place Valley, Artisans' Village

The Leopard Charioteers and the special infantry soldiers were ferried across the Nile by early evening and moved into the Great Place foothills under the cover of darkness. It was impossible to hide a hundred chariots and two hundred marching soldiers, but Herihor had practiced this maneuver in darkness before. Horses walked at a pace that matched that of the soldiers and cloth-wrapped rims muffled the sound of wheels on the rocky road. When they reached the Great Place Village, they were greeted by the inhabitants with appreciation.

Herihor sought out Master Architect Hatep as the senior government representative. They met inside the architect's office around a dim lamp.

"Commander, I was advised of your arrival and place my staff of designers, stone carvers, and artisans at your service. The village elders have gathered all the food they have for your soldiers and water for your horses. Let me know what more we can do."

Herihor liked what he saw in the architect's confident demeanor. He was a civilian but not some panicky appointee or solicitous bureaucrat. "The food and water are most welcome, Architect. My quartermaster will distribute provisions when the men and horses are settled. They'll rest for a few hours then prepare for our deployment before dawn." The soldier looked around the room.

"Who spotted the invaders from that flying thing?" He didn't know what to call the silk hot-air balloon.

"Nathan, come here." Hatep beckoned the Hebrew slave forward into the light. "He and my son, Malik, spotted them and helped prepare the report for your office."

"You mean all this started because a Hebrew slave and an Egyptian teenager claim to have seen something? I hope this isn't some sort of prank. The entire Amun Corps was deployed and placed on alert based on what they supposedly saw." The commander was wound as tense as an iron spring and chafed at the thought that all of this was a waste of time. He issued a terse order to Hatep: "I want everyone out of this room except for you and these two." When the room had been cleared he demanded, "Tell me *exactly* what happened."

For the next thirty minutes Malik and Nathan explained their morning flight in the *Horus Eye* and the men and horses they saw in the hills and desert behind the Great Place Valley. Herihor asked pointed questions about what the Nubians looked like, what they did with their horses, if they were setting up a camp, and other details that held significance to a soldier. He wanted to know everything about the *Horus Eye*, especially its performance limitations. When they were finished, the commander smiled for the first time and his gray eyes sparkled.

"Can the *Horus Eye* fly at night?"

"It's never done so before, to my knowledge," Hatep responded. "I'd have to check with Master Imhotep, who invented it. What do you have in mind?"

"I know Imhotep," Commander Herihor continued smiling. He explained a daring plan that involved a flight into the dark pre-dawn sky and a troop deployment that would culminate in glorious victory or annihilation of the Leopard Charioteers.

CHAPTER 5

Western Mountains, Great Place Valley

The first probe of Nubian mercenaries encamped behind the western mountains waited for dawn to illuminate their quick sweep down into Great Place Valley of the Kings. The Artisans' Village presented a minor obstacle on their way through the valley to the plateau and then down into the fertile farms and estates. Thousands in the main force of the Nubian hoard would surely follow the first wave to secure the rich farmland and begin a cross-river assault on the Temples of Karnak, the city of Waset, and the Great House palace.

Using intelligence agents inside the Egyptian army, the Nubian operation depended on surprise for little or no resistance until they reached the Nile. Commanders anticipated a feeble response from the aged general and his ill-equipped corps. According to their intelligence agents, the senile commander would only manage a weak, uncoordinated response and the rich temples and palace would be plundered with little resistance. Egyptian troops who were not slaughtered or enslaved would retreat into the Red Lands desert to the east.

Great Place Plateau, Temple of Shu Aerodrome

Commander Herihor gathered a small number of aides around him in the dark while the *Horus Eye* was fueled for its daring ascent into the starlit sky. As creator of the wondrous flying machine, Imhotep was eager to see how the silk balloon performed at night. He offered his full services to fend off the attack. Herihor asked Architect Hatep to lead the flight and send reports down the airship's tether to waiting couriers. Although Malik and Nathan felt that they could perform the assignment themselves, they raised no objection. Malik's father would conduct the visual surveillance while Malik and Nathan shared the duties of writing messages and trimming the altitude of the *Horus Eye*. Scribe-couriers on the ground were designated to retrieve the messages and deliver them immediately to Commander Herihor or their designated recipient.

Hatep's orders were specific: Estimate the number and types of troops by identifying them as chariots, mounted cavalry, foot soldiers, or support troops; describe their locations at first light and update their positions as the battle progressed; and send immediate information if any Egyptian troops appeared to need reinforcement. Herihor would tailor his counterattack to the enemy's dynamic order of battle.

"May I make a suggestion?" Nathan asked.

Herihor bristled at being addressed directly by a Hebrew slave who had not been spoken to first. Seeing Hatep nod in recognition, he waited to hear from the insolent slave.

"Information we send to the ground could also be relayed from the heliographic tower to the Karnak garrison as the battle progresses. Even better, if you sent the Egyptian heliographer to General Bakara's field camp on Karnak's West Bank, he could also receive messages sent to the garrison in Karnak because he would be in the line of sight between the tower and the garrison. That way, they could send reinforcements up here sooner, if they were requested." Nathan felt that his suggestion was a logical and reasonable one. He never thought that, coming from a young slave, his comment placed the commander and his master in an awkward or embarrassing position.

Herihor seethed at having a young, impertinent slave offer him military advice. He turned aside to speak with Hatep. "I don't know what infuriates me more, the fact that your slave spoke to me in that manner and that he knows about the secret signaling system, or that he has made such a specific suggestion about military tactics. I'll defer to you, but if it were up to me, I'd have him whipped."

"With all respect, Commander, I take full responsibility for his forwardness. He and my son have been raised and educated together. Sometimes he forgets that he is a Hebrew slave, and not yet an adult at that; he speaks his mind as if he were an Egyptian. I apologize and will reprimand him later. I take full responsibility regarding his knowledge of the signaling system since I instructed him and my son to alert Vizier Nakhte and General Bakara through the helio net about the Nubian attack. If I may say so, I believe that his suggestion indeed has merit. His name will not be mentioned in any reports, however, thus saving the need for any further mention of the matter." Hatep's diplomatic explanation was enough to calm the commander for the moment.

"Very well," Herihor said and swallowed his pride. He turned to his regimental scribe and told him to prepare orders deploying heliographer Hakamun to the general's field camp on the West Bank to read messages between the Great Place helio tower and the Karnak garrison. With that, the commander left to prepare his troops for battle.

The three aerial observers climbed into the confining basket that hung below the hot-air craft and brought supplies that they would need: sheets of papyrus, a wooden ink palette, black ink in a jar with a stopper, small reed pens for *sekh shat* script, string to secure the papyrus messages and small stones to weigh them for their slide down the tether. Their flight would last two to three hours before the heat of the day forced them to descend.

Imhotep handed Hatep a cylindrical tube. "This is a refracting glass to help you see at a distance," he said. "Be very careful with it since it is the only one I have. It has pieces of curved glass at each end. You adjust it by moving the tubes inside each other, like this." The inventor showed Hatep how to focus the magnified image but he could not demonstrate its use further since it was still dark. "Use it as soon as there is enough light. Again, be very careful with it." He stepped back and his impish assistant jumped from his shoulder to the woven basket of the balloon and up into the stringed net above it. Tik-tik was a small, exotic primate from the distant land of Bharata-varsa. The dark monkey, a rhesus macaque, was no larger than a cat. His expressive face mimicked expressions which consisted mostly of full-toothed smiles and screeching laughter. He was a constant source of fun for workers at Imhotep's aerodrome. The agile animal climbed up the outside of the reed docking frame, unhooked loops that restrained the billowing silk bag from collapsing when resting in its cradle, and quickly returned to his master's shoulder. When the air-filled invention was light enough to lift off the ground, the four restraining arms were cranked back by the launch crew and the *Horus Eye* rose into the dark sky while its thin tether was reeled out. Within seconds, all that Imhotep and the aerodrome workers saw from the ground was the flame of the heating hearth that illuminated silhouettes of the three passengers. Minutes later, the pinpoint of light was suspended a thousand feet above the black plateau.

Great Place Valley, Artisans' Village

The remaining inhabitants of the Artisans' Village were frantic with anticipation. Soldiers, horses, and fighting chariots were ready for battle while civilians barricaded their homes against attack. Troops and charioteers had practiced mobilizing in the dark and Commander Herihor was pleased with what he saw.

He drew his hand-picked platoon commanders around him and explained one last time his plan for defense of the Great Place Valley and the West Bank, and ultimately the Temples of Karnak, the city of Waset, and the Great Place palace.

"Our forces are divided equally into two half-regiments of chariots with archers and soldiers waiting to hear from the observers in the sky as soon as there is enough light to see the enemy formation. There are two major avenues that lead from the mountains to the Great Place Valley: the North Canyon and the South Canyon. I have already dispatched regimental sappers, diggers and trenchers trained to work under enemy fire, and all available civilian stoneworkers and quarrymen from the village, to take positions in the heights above the two canyons. They will prepare a surprise for the attackers. If we hear nothing more from the observers, we will move troops and charioteers in pre-arranged numbers to where the two canyons merge into the Great Place Valley, set our ambushes, and execute the attack. Remember, our charioteers must attack their horse-mounted forces while our foot soldiers must engage only their unmounted troops. This is critical! Our orders are to delay the Nubians and slow their descent until the rest of the corps under General Bakara can engage them on the West Bank plain. However, I intend to defeat them *in* the Great Place Valley! That is our challenge as Leopards! You each have your orders, so now is the time to raise any final questions or objections." Herihor looked around at his leaders and was pleased to see confident warriors whom he had tirelessly exercised during the past year. His platoon leaders gave him their full allegiance, saluted and were dismissed to their units.

The Leopard Charioteers were the best-trained archers and fighters in the Egyptian corps. Despite their small number they did not hesitate to take on a force four or five times their size. The modern, double-horse chariots that derived from a proven Hittite design were the most lethal modern weapons of any army on earth. The driver was armed for hand-to-hand, close-in combat while he wove his horses through enemy formations at high speed. The archer beside the driver carried thirty to forty barbed arrows which he fired with precision using the latest composite bow made of wood, metal, and bone. He could put a single arrow through the heart of a key leader or officer at a distance. If either of the chariot crew were wounded or killed, each could perform the duties of the other with equal skill and lethality.

Ground troops were toughened for intense combat. They had been trained to fight for hours in the blazing sun without food or water. Commander Herihor insisted that his special regiment have the latest weapons in addition to the usual leather helmet, body armor, and shield. His regimental armorer had invented a new form of *khopesh* or sickle sword which his troops would use for the first time in combat that morning. The bronze and iron sword measured two feet long; this latest hybrid weapon had a hook for pulling down an enemy's shield or grabbing his leather armor and then plunging the point up into his throat in one swift motion. Alternatively, the sharp, curved blade made a slashing weapon that severed limbs when swung in either direction. Convinced that an overwhelming offense obviated the need for a cumbersome shield, attack soldiers gripped a *khopesh* in their dominant hand and a mace, ax, or spear in their other. Armed thusly, teams of ten infantry met the enemy head-on, mowing down a phalanx of enemy foot soldiers and leaving piles of bodies behind.

High Above The Great Place, *Horus Eye*

Dim, slow-moving figures dotted the mountainside paths in the gray light of dawn. Within minutes, individual soldiers and horses came into focus out of the darkness against the pale limestone and white alabaster cliffs. The calm in the dangling basket of the *Horus Eye* was broken when the three aerial observers prepared their first report.

"This must be brief, but accurate, so the commander knows how to deploy his men," Hatep said. He dictated his observations to Malik and Nathan worked the controls to maintain their altitude. They could trade places later as the mission progressed.

Using Imhotep's vision device, Hatep counted those enemy he could see, realizing that there might be more Nubians hidden from sight behind rocks and outcroppings or in the shadows of the early dawn. "I count about fifty horsemen in the North Canyon with at least three hundred troops marching behind them." He shifted to the South Canyon and counted two hundred horses with only fifty troops. He gave the numbers to Malik who jotted them in *sekh shat* shorthand. The numbers puzzled Hatep at first until he realized that, of course, the two canyons did not offer equally wide or clear pathways into the Great Place Valley. It made sense that the Nubian commanders would send their horsemen down the wider canyon and their foot soldiers through the more constricted entrance. Herihor probably anticipated that too. "Send it now," he instructed Malik. Within seconds, the wrapped package slid down the tether into the hands of the courier waiting below.

The three observers gazed out at the unfolding spectacle of Nubian mercenaries on horseback and on foot below them. The fighters soon stood out clearly in the early dawn light. Their faces, necks and torsos were heavily tattooed to give them almost a demonic appearance, which was their purpose. Their opponents were supposed to flee in terror when they saw a line of screaming, bizarrely painted attackers running at them. Veteran combatants tattooed their sword arms to show how many they had killed, giving their opponents a further sense of dread. Libyan horsemen wore loose, flowing black robes and turbans that marked them as merciless hand-to-hand fighters. Their long swords, held in sashes while they slowly threaded their way down the canyons, flashed in the first rays of sunlight to strike the mountain.

Great Place Valley, North and South Canyons

In response to the first message from the *Horus Eye* revealing the actual disposition of enemy troops and horsemen, Commander Herihor divided his forces in proportion for maximum effectiveness. He led his major force of Leopard Charioteers to the South Canyon where archers could take on the fast-moving Libyans on horseback. The main force of his ground troops headed for the North Canyon with a smaller contingent of supporting chariots.

The enemy slowly descended into both canyons where Herihor's military sappers and village quarrymen finished their surprise. During the night, they used paths high above the canyon floors to position boulders and rocks in strategic locations to crash onto the line of troops at the right moment. In the pre-dawn hours they set a number of smaller rock falls intended to force the attackers into smaller groups. The leading party of invaders—a fraction of the overall attacking force—would rush out of the canyon and into the jaws of a waiting Egyptian regiment. A large part of the enemy force would be trapped behind them in the canyon. They might try to climb over the smaller obstructions blocking their path, but they would be slowed and by the time they reached the valley they would face the Egyptian onslaught that had decimated the first wave.

High Above The Great Place, *Horus Eye*

The view from one thousand feet above the skirmishes between Egyptian chariot regiments and Nubian and Libyan invaders was unique in ancient warfare. The three observers were so mesmerized by what they saw developing before them that they almost forgot to issue their reports. The combat unfolded before their eyes exactly as Commander Herihor had envisioned: rising plumes of dust in the canyons signaled that rockslides were dividing the invaders; clashes broke out at the mouth of each canyon as horsemen and foot soldiers emerged into waiting Egyptian ambushes with no time to form themselves into an effective unit; lines of Egyptians cut into the Nubians like a scythe harvesting wheat; and the Leopard Charioteers met riders on stampeding horses with a rain of arrows where each dart felled a rider. Unable to mount an effective penetration of the Egyptian formations, the invaders either scattered into the valley where they were picked off one by one, or they tried to retreat back to the mountains from which they had come only to find their way blocked.

After pummeling the line of the invading forces with small rockslides, the sappers and quarrymen in each canyon climbed higher to their final positions on the cliff where they would unleash a rock slide to block the canyons entirely. Quarrymen from the Great Place Valley were familiar with the irregular seams and fissures in the mountain's natural rock formations. Normally, they looked for smooth cliffs and mountain sides with minimal faults, cracks, or dislocations into which they could carve beautiful tombs for kings, queens, viziers, and noblemen. Following Herihor's orders, they found places above the canyon with dangerous, unstable fault lines. Like a diamond cutter who knows exactly where to strike a stone to produce a desired facet, the quarrymen chose crevices whose precise dislocation would release thousands of tons of rock into the canyon.

Three hours after dawn, the mountain entrances into both canyons had been completely blocked by landslides that sounded like distant thunder to the observers in the *Horus Eye* platform. The silk air craft was becoming more difficult to keep aloft as the sun rose higher in the sky. Nathan sent down their last message announcing victory in the valley and complete blockage of the two canyons. The surviving force of Nubian and Libyan troops in the western mountains had no choice but to retreat back into the desert in light of the defeat of their advance force and the insurmountable obstructions between them and the Great Place Valley and Thebes.

When the *Horus Eye* settled into its docking cradle, Hatep returned to his village office to see what could be done to return the village to normal. Malik and Nathan ran to the helio tower to find out how the system had worked.

Great Place Valley, Heliographic Tower

Malik and Nathan recognized Commander Herihor's chariot and horses held by its driver standing at the bottom of the ladder of the tower.

"Is the Commander well?" Malik asked the dust-covered soldier who returned their question with a grin.

"Alive and victorious!" He pointed up the ladder.

When the young men reached the tower platform, they found the commander dictating a message to Elias who was writing as fast as he could. The charioteer was splattered with dust-encrusted blood up to his waist and was bleeding from a minor flesh wound in his arm. When he finished his summary of the battle he gave a sigh of relief and noticed Malik and Nathan waiting for him.

"Congratulations, Sir!" Malik said. "We saw the whole thing, of course, and it was a brilliant strategy that resulted in your victory. I hope we were of service."

"You were more than that—much more. Thanks to you, we anticipated their troop formations perfectly and overpowered them as soon as they emerged from the canyons. We lost some men, but far fewer than I was expecting. Your reports were invaluable."

Herihor shifted his tired gaze to Nathan. The anger and hostility of their first encounter was gone. "And you, young man..." He paused to see if the Hebrew slave noticed any difference in his tone. "I owe you thanks for your suggestion." He extended his hand to the slave who had been the object of his contempt only hours before. Nathan shook his hand and looked directly into the soldier's eyes.

"I must check on my troops and have this wound cleaned before returning to the garrison in Karnak, possibly tonight. I want to speak with both of you again sometime—just the three of us." He disappeared down the ladder.

"This has been some day!" said Elias.

"Certainly a historic day when a single regiment fights off an attack by Nubians and sends thousands of enemy troops back into the Western Desert," Nathan agreed.

"I mean for you and all us blinkers," Elias replied, using his slang for heliograph operators. "You reported on a battle in real time from the air and then I sent flashes in minutes over the helio net to the Great House and to General Bakara at his West Bank encampment. Do you realize that we revolutionized Egyptian warfare today? No wonder Commander Herihor wants to see you two later. You're heroes!"

"I don't know about that..." Nathan stammered.

"Tell us what happened. What did you send over the network?" Malik was curious.

Elias handed Malik a scrap of papyrus. "This is the short message I sent when he first arrived here. I'll send his more detailed report in a minute."

To General Bakara:
Attackers annihilated by brave Leopard Charioteers and
loyal troops. Returning to garrison with few casualties.
Full report to follow.
Commander Herihor

"That says it all," Nathan beamed when he read it. "Well, congratulations to you too, Elias. I'm glad you were here to run the signaling operation. I have an idea for a portable heliograph too. I think Commander Herihor might listen to me now."

CHAPTER 6

Luxor West Bank, Lotus House

The regiment of jubilant charioteers and foot soldiers departed the Artisans' Village to the cheers of residents whose homes and lives had been spared thanks to their victory over the Nubian and Libyan forces. It took all day for Commander Herihor's men to reach the Nile at an easy marching pace. They were watered and fed along the way by appreciative estate owners whose lavish homes and crops had been saved from enemy plunder. Egypt's finest warriors were justifiably proud of their victory and of their brilliant commander.

Hatep drove his chariot onto his estate and parked it at the stables where he and the two young men dismounted. They had slept only a few hours the night before.

Reuben greeted his master with a broad smile as he took the horses' reins. "Congratulations, Master. You're a national hero!"

"Really? Who says?" Hatep asked with surprise.

"Why, Miss Sarina is telling everyone. Pharaoh will reward you and Master Malik in a big ceremony at the Great House palace tomorrow at noon."

"Well, I'm pleased about that, but right now I need to wash off this grime and put on clean clothes!" Hatep walked through the gates into Lotus House without giving a second's thought to the Anubis idol facing the entrance. He called out for his wife.

Malik and Nathan were more interested in eating. They raced to see who would make it to the kitchen first. Last night, all food in the Artist's

Village had been consumed by the troops and they were famished. A bath and clean clothes could wait.

Hatep met his daughter in the courtyard. "What have you been telling people about me being a hero? And what's this about a reward from the Great One tomorrow? And where's your mother?"

Before she could answer him, a trumpet blast from the front of the house announced the arrival of an important messenger. "Go see who it is, Sarina. I'm filthy with yesterday's dirt and unfit to receive company."

When Sarina saw that it was a royal courier, she ran to get her father. He walked back to the entrance where he took the gilt-edged, snow-white papyrus from the uniformed attendant. Malik and Nathan came too when they heard the trumpet and walked around the chariot admiring the finely crafted machine—only the best for Pharaoh and his court. The delivery messenger stood at attention while Hatep read the letter's contents.

"It's an invitation for Malik and me to go to the Great House tomorrow at noon for an audience with the Great One." He glanced at the courier standing at attention. "Yes, I heard that this would be coming. An audience with the Great One cannot be refused. Please inform Vizier Nakhte that my son and I will be there with our family, of course. Yes, this is splendid." He admired the crisp, expensive invitation with the embossed gold cartouche of Thutmose III and handed it to Malik.

With a wrinkled brow, the letter carrier seemed puzzled. "Excuse me, Sir. You *knew* this invitation would be coming? Vizier Nakhte was only notified about the ceremony this morning and the invitation was handed to me two hours ago. I rushed here from the palace as fast as I could." He wondered how the recipient could have known about it before he arrived.

"My daughter told me," Hatep answered, oblivious to the implications of what he said. Sarina heard the exchange from the entrance gate and retreated back into the house.

The royal messenger saluted the national hero and urged his horses on for the return trip to the palace. He still couldn't figure out how the man's daughter knew in advance what he had only learned a few hours earlier.

"We need to talk to Sarina," Nathan whispered to Malik as they walked behind Hatep back into the house. "Your sister is up to something fishy and I'm dying to know what it is."

The two hungry teens each helped themselves to food from the kitchen before they found Sarina on the rooftop terrace under the shade of a white linen canopy that waved in a soft breeze and blocked most of the direct sunlight. She stared across the river so intently that she didn't hear them walk up behind her.

"So what are you up to?" Malik said in a loud voice intended to startle his sister.

Sarina jumped and let out a yelp. "Don't do that, you pest! I hate it when you come up behind me and surprise me like that."

"What are you doing up here—daydreaming?" Nathan asked.

"I didn't sleep well last night so I thought I'd rest up here."

"In the heat of the day? You should be in your mom's garden where it's cooler."

"I like it up here. Is there anything wrong with that?"

"I suppose not," her brother said. "Anyway, we want to know who your source is."

Sarina glanced across the river for a second and then looked directly at her brother. "I have no idea what you mean."

"Come on, yes you do. You told Reuben this morning about the vizier's invitation to the Great Place at noon tomorrow. That was before the courier arrived with the invitation. How did you know that?"

"I'd rather not say," she wavered.

"'I'd rather not say...'" Malik mimicked. On a sudden hunch, he asked her directly: "Are you reading someone's messages?"

His sister's eyes widened before she gave a sideways glance across the river again. Sarina's lower lip trembled. "Will I get into trouble? Please don't tell Father."

"What is she talking about" Nathan asked his friend.

"I think my sister is a lot smarter than I gave her credit for." He turned his friend by the shoulder and pointed across the river to the tallest tower of the palace. "She's been reading the palace's helio signals!" He then turned his friend around and pointed to the plateau behind them. "And Elias's signals too."

"I was bored, that's all," she blurted. "I was bored with school so I sat up here thinking of something to pass the time." She looked ready to burst into tears.

Nathan finally figured out what was going on. He looked back and forth between the palace and the plateau. "Lotus House is in a direct line between the two towers! This is the perfect spot for intercepting palace messages!"

By now the two were hopping with excitement. "How did you figure out the code? How long have you been reading messages? This is great!" Questions poured from both of them as they considered the implications of this discovery.

"You have to promise me that you won't get me in trouble for doing this," Sarina insisted. "I'll tell you everything. But this has to be our secret."

"I don't think I can promise you that," her brother said. The seriousness of his sister peering into the royal network carrying military and palace communications was beginning to sink in. "You probably won't get into trouble for doing this. If anything, the authorities might be glad when they learn that their messages can be read so easily. It scares me though that someone with wicked intentions could listen in on official, sensitive messages. No, we need to tell someone. I just don't know who."

"Well, don't tell Mom or Dad. They already think I'm wasting my time doing nothing now that I've almost finished school. Mom wants me to get married and Dad throws up his hands and mutters about all the money he spent on school. I know I could be as good a 'blinker' as Elias, Hakamun or any other operator in the network."

Malik and Nathan were shocked that Salina spoke of the communications specialists as if she knew them personally.

"So start at the beginning and tell us how you cracked the helio code," her brother insisted. He and Nathan pulled up chairs and leaned forward.

CHAPTER 7

Waset, Great House Palace

The procession through the city of Thebes to the Great House in Waset the next day was a majestic pageant honoring the heroes of what became known around Thebes as the Battle in the Valley of the Kings. Soldiers proudly called it the Two Canyons Massacre. The recipients of Pharaoh's appreciation walked at a ceremonial pace through the streets trailed by colorfully dressed princes, nobility, high officials, and priests who hoped for a momentary glance of recognition from the Great One that would give them something to brag about to their families and friends. Since Commander Herihor was the main hero of the battle, the Leopard Charioteers and the half-regiments from the Great Place Valley victory followed at a measured march in their finest uniforms. Crowds lining the streets threw flowers ahead of the heroes and cheered when the Leopards rode by in their spotless chariots. Young boys ran out from the crowds along the road, draped garlands over the chariots' metal railings and scurried back when the war horses snorted and stamped their feet on the pavement.

Commander Herihor savored the moment. Two days earlier, he had fought Nubians and mounted Libyans not knowing if a stray arrow or thrust of a spear would cut his life short. Today was like living in a dream. Overnight, the regimental armorer had made him new breeches of soft leather, a light-weight chest protector, and a helmet decorated with polished metal buttons, clasps, and a tall orange plume. The ceremonial outfit, totally unsuitable for combat use with its thin leather and flashy accessories, made him look all the part of a military hero. The distinctive orange Leopard Charioteers' plume in his helmet waved in the breeze from fans waved by slaves that walked on each side of him. Herihor could not restrain a smile of satisfaction knowing that the Great One would speak his name in a few minutes. Pharaoh's reward for this brave career soldier who had devoted his life for The Two Lands, was well-deserved after such a spectacular victory.

Master Architect Hatep considered himself only a simple, though successfully wealthy, tomb designer and builder who hardly felt deserving of recognition for spending a few hours flying above the Great Place Plateau in a hot air gas bag. He and his son had enjoyed their time in the air and could not believe that the Great One wanted to reward them for such a minor part in the military victory. Hatep never sought personal fame or glory like the military or political leaders. His wealth and status in Egyptian society were the result of family inheritance coupled with education, skill and hard work; seeking fame and daring adventure were the farthest things from his mind. Of course, he would gladly accept whatever accolade Pharaoh wished to bestow upon him.

The procession leading through the city and onto the lush Great House palace grounds was an added opportunity for Iset to show off her finest clothing and jewelry as she walked beside her husband to see Pharaoh up-close for the first time. Before dawn, Rachel and a servant girl carefully wove beads, gold threads, and shining jewels into Iset's black hair in an intricate design that befitted her place as the wife of one to be honored by the Pharaoh himself. When she was dressed in a pure white, full-length linen gown trimmed in azure, they carefully adjusted her finest gold and turquois headpiece so that it accentuated her height and her long, slim neck. An artist from Thebes had painted dark blue *kohl* around her gray eyes to enhance their almond shape. Gold *meket* armlets fit snugly on her upper arms and *masektu* bracelets of the same precious metal inlayed with lapis lazuli and carnelian jangled on her wrists and ankles. Around her neck, a broad collar of intricate gold, etched glass, and turquois stones complemented her ensemble which was finished with a lotus broach, a special gift from her husband when they moved into Lotus House.

In contrast to his stunningly attired wife, Hatep wore his best linen tunic and a simple headpiece on his shaved head. It would be inappropriate to wear his best jewelry, colorful robes, and eye-cosmetics to receive a gift from Pharaoh. He only expected a modest gift commensurate with his minor contribution to the victory.

Hatep and his family walked behind Commander Herihor along the broad road leading to the Great House palace. Cheers of acclaim from the crowds of *rekhet* commoners grew louder. Trumpet blasts echoed into the street from inside the palace courtyard. Pendants atop the massive pylons waved in the lazy breeze. Hatep could hardly believe his eyes when he saw his name and that of his son painted on a large banner draped across the massive palace wall. His wife noticed it at the same time and squeezed his arm.

Once inside the courtyard, they saw that the walled space was filled with an orderly array of musicians around Pharaoh's dais flanked by more princes, administration officials and priests. Thousands of onlookers gathered in the expansive area to catch a glimpse of the Immortal Lord of The Two Lands. The processional line stopped at the foot of a long carpet that led up a shallow ramp to Pharaoh's empty throne flanked by royal officials. Herihor's regiment assembled themselves in a neat formation behind their commander. Malik grinned at Nathan who stood next to him holding a sunshade over his friend.

"Looks like a big deal, doesn't it?" he said out of the corner of his mouth.

"Sure does. You don't deserve it, you know," his friend joked.

Iset gave her son a nudge to behave and he pretended to be serious just in time for the trumpets to announce Pharaoh's entrance. Everyone bowed to the ground as curtains behind the royal dais parted and he walked to his throne. He looked out at his subjects bowed in submission before him and smiled. When the vizier, royal master scribe, and royal priest were in their positions by his side the trumpets gave the signal that the assembled throng could lift their eyes and look at the Great One in all his splendor. They gazed upon the King of Upper and Lower Egypt. The most powerful man in the world was bedecked in a shimmering floor-length tunic with vertical lines of dark and white gold woven into its fabric to accentuate his height. His radiant headdress made him appear even taller.

The music stopped and Pharaoh beckoned Herihor, Hatep, and Malik to approach him. The three walked solemnly up the ramp lined by boys and girls who threw fragrant petals in their path. When they reached Pharaoh they bowed once again until commanded to rise. Upon doing so, Hatep was awed by his king standing an arm's length away. His heart raced to be so close to the man worshipped by the nation as the incarnate earthly form of the god *Ra*. When he noted deep creases that cosmetics could not hide, bloodshot eyes, neck muscles that struggled against the weight of his sumptuous crown, and the slight tremor of his hands, he realized that his Pharaoh was a mortal human being just like him and not a god. That did not diminish the grandeur of the moment, but it was something that struck the architect as ironic when surrounded by the unimaginable wealth and power of a world empire.

Pharaoh spoke to Herihor first. "Commander Herihor, we are indebted to you for your imagination and bravery in the Great Place Valley of the Kings. We are told that, because of you, the Great Place tombs were untouched and the foreign invaders were annihilated or sent back into the desert. Our mother's tomb is sacred to the nation and remains unviolated. We give you this as a symbol of your heroism."

The monarch reached to his side and took a gold pectoral *wesekh* from the hands of a servant and fastened it around Herihor's neck. He adjusted the necklace made of hundreds of intricately carved golden bees in a mesh that extended across the commander's neck and chest from shoulder to shoulder. The honey bee, source of energy and vitality for a man's body and yet possessing a deadly sting, was a symbol cherished by the military. Before he could admire its workmanship, he sensed that Pharaoh was not finished.

"We have been told by your superior that you are the finest soldier in Thebes. Your victory over the Nubians confirms his assessment and thus we are giving you command of the Amun Corps, *General* Herihor. You will not disappoint us."

"I will not disappoint you, Great One." Promotion to replace General Bakara had not entered his mind. The broad pectoral necklace was more than enough, he thought, and now this too!

Turning to Hatep, Pharaoh was handed another golden *wesekh* whose weight required both of the monarch's hands and assistance from a servant to fasten around the architect's neck. Weighing more than ten *debens* and clasped with a sturdy chain, the collar was a single, thick arc of polished gold engraved with row upon row of intricate palm leaves and pomegranates. The heavy weight around his neck was cumbersome and exhilarating at the same time. This piece of jewelry exceeded the value of his entire estate!

"For you, Royal Master Architect Hatep, this trinket is a token gift for your part in saving the Great Place Valley from its attackers and preserving the tombs of our ancestors. Furthermore, your work as Royal Master Architect has not gone unnoticed. In recognition of your fine work, you will henceforth be known as *Amkhu* Hatep. You and your descendants are granted a perpetual tomb in the Great Place Valley of the Kings to usher you into the hereafter."

Pharaoh smiled for the first time when he turned to Malik. He saw that the teenager before him was nervous but unafraid in his presence. This reward gave him more pleasure than the others because it reminded the aging monarch of his own youth. When he raised both of his arms above his head there was movement in the crowd at the far end of the courtyard. People quickly scattered to allow a chariot pulled by a single horse to trot forward and stop at the foot of the ramp. The iridescent coat of the narrow-faced, muscular horse glistened blue-black in the noonday sun. The driver clenched the reins in both fists to keep the high-spirited animal from bolting.

"You may turn and look behind you, Malik son of *Amkhu* Hatep," Pharaoh said.

When he turned and saw the glistening horse and sleek chariot he didn't understand.

"When we were your age," Pharaoh intoned with the royal plural, "all the gold in The Two Lands meant little to us. A fast horse, a light chariot, and the wind in our face on the Royal Road to the City of the Horizon were our greatest joy. For your part in the victory, this is your gift."

"I am your servant, Great One." Malik bowed and his voice trembled.

The ceremony had lasted less than fifteen minutes, but to the honorees it seemed like hours; later they would recall every word and gesture. Pharaoh lifted his arms in acclamation and thousands of voices exploded in a deafening roar. The three heroes walked backwards down the ramp with their heads bowed until they reached the base of the incline where they turned to be engulfed by happy well-wishers.

Without hesitation, Malik took the reins of his new chariot from the attendant and motioned to Nathan to join him. "My friend, you deserve this as much as me. Here, you drive."

"Seriously? You trust me to drive this beauty?"

"Sure. Just don't wreck it on the first turn!"

The crowd opened ahead of the snorting horse with flashing black eyes and mouth foaming at the bit. Malik shouted over his shoulder that they'd meet his parents back at the house later. The two friends headed toward the main highway out of the city to see if they could outrace the wind.

CHAPTER 8

Luxor West Bank, Lotus House

Malik and Nathan pulled up to the Lotus House entrance at dusk where they were met by Reuben and a young helper who grabbed the bridle of the snorting stallion. The chief groom appraised Pharaoh's gift with pride.

"Master Malik, this is the most beautiful animal I have ever seen! This is a much better gift than gold, is it not?"

"That is exactly what the Great One said to me. Has my sister been spilling secrets to you again?"

"You have me there. She enjoys sharing little secrets with me so I can appear intelligent," he boasted with a grin. "Does your horse have a name?"

"Nathan said he should be named *Sapphire* because he shines dark blue in the sunlight."

"Then I shall carve that name above his stall first thing tomorrow morning!"

"Whose chariot is that?" Malik pointed to an unfamiliar one-horse vehicle propped against the stable.

"The new general is here. He arrived only a few minutes ago. His horse is cooling down in the stable."

"General Herihor is here? I wonder what that could be about?"

"Why don't you ask him? He's standing just inside the front door talking with your father."

As they approached the home's entrance they overheard Hatep and Herihor speaking on the other side of the icon entrance. The two men made no attempt to lower their voices.

"Then you agree with me that *Anubis* is without power or influence? That worshipping him or the other mythical deities is a waste of time?" the general was heard to ask.

"I'm not saying that," Hatep insisted. "What I am saying is that I have *doubts* about any god that never says or does anything. To me, a god must at least prove himself to be superior to a man. A carved image or some priest's dream lacks credibility, that's all."

"That I agree with, but be careful, Hatep. Don't let our Pharaoh or his advisors hear you say such things. He wants us to believe that he is a god himself. After seeing him up close today, I'm convinced that he is a man just like us—only much richer!" The two men laughed.

Malik thought it best to make his presence known before the conversation went any further. "May I add our family's welcome to Lotus House, *General* Herihor," he said with emphasis on their visitor's new rank. "I thought you would be celebrating with your men tonight."

"Malik, what a pleasure to extend my congratulations to you also. Your father tells me that you have been enjoying Pharaoh's gift. You must give me a ride in it someday." He looked at Nathan standing nearby and extended his hand with a genuine smile. "I heard that Nathan has been driving it too."

"General, I'm honored to shake your hand once again." The Hebrew slave was still puzzled by Herihor's complete change in attitude toward him since they first met two nights ago. "If you will excuse me, Sir, I must attend to my chores." Nathan left to see if his father or mother needed help.

Out of courtesy, Iset had invited the general to Lotus House to join their celebratory feast and was pleasantly surprised when he accepted. Like Malik had done, she assumed that he would rather spend time with his troops in a night of drunken revelry. Instead, he readily welcomed her invitation and joined them after refreshing himself and changing clothes at his barracks residence. He was dressed in a simple white tunic with a beaded turquois belt and comfortable sandals. He left his golden *wesekh* behind for the evening and appeared glad to relax after such a momentous day.

Iset had the cooks prepare a sumptuous banquet to impress their distinguished visitor. The amount of food was many times more than needed for the five diners. It was tastefully displayed on a long table surrounded by floral decorations and fresh fruit: roasted gazelle, fowl, and fish sizzled straight from the grill, bread was baked into a half-dozen artful shapes, fruits and vegetable dishes lined the low table. The fact that they were reclined instead of sitting in chairs at the family's dinner table meant that they would be eating for hours.

Their guest's exciting military career was the principal topic of conversation through course after course of delicacies. Herihor had been raised by a prominent Egyptian couple who found him abandoned by the river as a baby. This was during a time of internal upheaval in the kingdom when Pharaoh schemed to eliminate all the Hebrews from the land. His parents educated him as their own son and when he expressed interest in joining Pharaoh's army, his adoptive father found a sponsor to enroll him in the officer ranks. He was both successful as a warrior and as a leader of men. Expeditions against the Hittites and Canaanites and an incursion into Kush distinguished him as an exceptional commander. His Leopard Charioteers set the standard against which all other Egyptian chariot regiments were compared. Now he was Commanding General of the Amun Corps and at the peak of his career.

Iset turned the conversation to his childhood. "Please excuse me if this is an indelicate question. Is it possible, general, that you could be of Hebrew blood?"

"Dear, maybe our guest does not wish to discuss that," her husband admonished her in a gentle tone.

"No, I don't mind. The simple answer is that I don't know. As far as I am concerned, I'm as Egyptian as they come. My parents raised me as an Egyptian and I've taken the military oath to serve the Great One with my life."

Hatep lowered his voice. "But maybe you think that the Great One is not so great after all. That he is not a god?"

"Now *I* am uncomfortable with this conversation," Hatep's wife said as she stood to leave the table. "Sarina, come with me to arrange for after-dinner drinks. The men may wish to go up to the roof to catch the night air."

"Do I have to, Mother? This conversation is getting more interesting!"

"Yes, come. When we return in a few minutes, the talk will have changed to a more suitable topic." Iset and her daughter walked down the hallway to the kitchen while Hatep, Herihor, and Malik went up the steps to the roof.

Before Iset rejoined them with liquid refreshments, Hatep cautioned his guest. "I apologize for my wife if she made you uncomfortable with such an indelicate question. You are our honored and distinguished guest tonight so I do not wish to give offense with what I am about to say. In the past few days it seems that there has developed a friendship between you and our family which I truly welcome. Let us keep our talk about the gods and our Pharaoh in private. I would hate to see your honorable military reputation tarnished or turned into an accusation of disloyalty by imprudent questions." He watched for Herihor's reaction.

"I accept your apology as a friend. I too have great respect for you and your family. I give you my promise that if we speak of these things in the future it will be between us only."

When Iset and Sarina came up the steps to the roof they were glad to hear the general describing more of his regiment's campaign above the third cataract in the jungles of Kush and Punt. They listened to his stories of exotic people, animals, and foods. The vivid storytelling continued well into the night.

During a lull in the conversation, Hatep politely suggested that it was getting late and their guest may wish to return to his garrison.

The general cleared his throat. "Would it be possible to speak with Malik and Nathan alone first? I would like to hear their ideas about the helio network and military tactics. I don't mind the hour if it is no trouble to you."

"Iset, Sarina, and I will say goodnight, then. You're welcome to stay up here talking and spend the night in our guest room, if you wish," Hatep said. "The room is prepared with fresh linens and water. If you need anything, you can ring for a servant."

'I'll take you up on the guest room, thank you. Could you have your groom put my horse away for the night? And have Nathan come up here too?"

"Of course." Hatep thought his last request to summon the young slave unusual. "Good night then. It's been an honor to have you as our guest tonight and I wish you a restful sleep." The couple descended the stairs to their bedrooms. Iset motioned for Sarina to follow them.

Sarina brushed past her brother and whispered, "I'll be back. I have something to tell the general."

Malik suspected that he knew what it was, but figured he'd wait for his sister to explain it herself.

When Sarina snuck back to the rooftop ten minutes later, Nathan was already there. He, Malik, and the general were seated around a low table. The night air had finally cooled to a refreshing temperature. Sarina's return sparked Herihor's immediate interest.

"And to what do we owe your charming return, Miss?" he asked with mock formality.

"My sister has something to tell you about the helio network that may have an effect on what you wish to discuss with us, I think." The general's eyebrows went up when he heard this. Malik continued, "A year ago, when she said she wanted to attend the Mittani Scribal School, our father and mother tried to discourage her, but she was persistent. The school instructors doubted that a girl could learn the intricate language of glyphs…"

"It shouldn't matter that I'm a girl!" Sarina's eyes blazed at her brother.

"You are *not* a girl. You are a young lady," Herihor said in a soothing tone. "Please let Malik continue."

"In less than a year she had mastered the curriculum and finished at the top of her class. She could have obtained employment as a palace scribe if she were old enough and if our parents would let her. With that as background, I'll let her tell you what she's discovered about the royal helio network."

"I'm impressed already," their guest said as he turned toward Sarina. "Please tell me what you've found."

"I was on this rooftop a few weeks ago when I noticed a flashing light coming from the Great House palace across the river and thought that it might be some sort of signal. Within a week I figured out which sequence of flashes represented symbols in a hieratic alphabet. I've been reading signals between the palace and my father's architect offices in the Great Place Valley ever since. I thought you should know how easy it was for me to do this. Some of the messages from the palace were sensitive but I swear that I've not told anyone about them." Sarina's main worry was that she would get in trouble for breaking the helio signaling code. To her it was only a game or a puzzle.

"This does change some things," the general observed. He looked across the Nile at the lights shining in palace windows. "I've been telling General Bakara for almost a year now that military messages should be encrypted, but he never listened to me. He said that nobody could figure out what the flashes of light meant. He was obviously wrong."

"Does that mean I'm in trouble?" Sarina asked.

"No. It means that Egypt's leaders have been foolish to think that a simple code—converting writing symbols into a sequence of light flashes—could never be broken. Now that I'm in charge of the Amun Corps, I can do something about it. Thank you for letting me know." Sarina's oval face was outlined in the lamp light. Her bangs nearly obscured her eyes. Her intelligent analysis had earned the respect of the nation's top military hero, but it was her beauty and innocence that captured his heart that night. "If I need advice on how to encipher our military messages, would you be willing to help me? I'll get your parent's permission, of course."

"Do you need their permission?" she pleaded. "I'm afraid they'll think that my puzzle solving was frivolous or 'unladylike'."

"I'll tell your father that it's a matter of national security for you to do occasional scribal work for the Amun Corps which you can do here at Lotus House. While I don't expect any of this to be dangerous, some very powerful people might be upset when I tell them that an unnamed young woman was reading their mail. Don't mention your work outside of your family and I'll get your father's approval."

"Oh, that sounds wonderful!" Sarina clapped her hands.

"Now, your first assignment is to leave before your mother finds you up here talking after midnight." Herihor secretly wished that Sarina would stay.

"Good night, General." She slowly descended the stairs and resisted the urge to turn for one last glimpse of the ruggedly handsome soldier.

It was late and Herihor thought it best to leave the two young men with some things to ponder before he retired for a few hours of sleep. They would speak more about the helio network and a portable device at some other time.

"I'll meet with the Karnak garrison heliographers and my military scribes tomorrow about ways to make the signals more secure. I must also notify the Great House palace that their signals are vulnerable—without revealing how I know, of course. Meanwhile, I want you to give me your thoughts about how a *portable* helio machine could be used during military maneuvers. Also, I will speak to Inventor Imhotep about building me a prototype portable unit which I will pay for from corps funds. If I had a small device that could be set up in a few minutes on a hilltop, regiments could contact each other and send messages to headquarters during engagements. My question is: could we duplicate the tactics used in the Great Place Valley on a smaller scale between regiments?" He sensed his two new friends' excitement.

"We'd love to help!" Malik exclaimed. His friend nodded in agreement.

"Then sleep on it and we'll talk about this again. I'll be gone before dawn to return to my garrison," the general said as he shook their hands before he went downstairs to the guest room, "so I bid you good night and good bye."

"Wow!" Nathan could hardly contain himself after their guest left. "Did you see the look on his face when Sarina told him she'd been reading secret messages from the palace? I wouldn't be surprised if the general paid a visit to the royal master scribe first thing in the morning. As soon as they change their coding scheme your sister will be bored again with nothing to do."

"Don't be so sure. Sarina is smarter than both of us put together. General Herihor said he wanted to keep all of this under wraps and I can see why. If word ever got out that Sarina had such easy access to palace secrets from this rooftop, it could put everyone in our house in danger."

CHAPTER 9

Great Place Valley, Artisans' Village

The excitement of the foiled Nubian attack and Pharaoh's awards had diminished two weeks later when Malik and Nathan immersed themselves in their ongoing apprenticeship in the offices of Royal Master Architect Hatep. After they explained General Herihor's use of a portable signaling instrument to Imhotep and gave him suggestions for a design, they ran out of things to engage their hyperactive minds. They were assigned to the draftsman, Thethi, to learn drawing techniques for new tombs carved into the hillsides of the Great Place Valley. They saw the necessity of painstakingly tracing old drawings for the elaborate underground necropolis, but spending hours bent over tables inking fine lines on large sheets of papyrus was boring, tedious work.

"I can't stand this anymore," complained Malik. "All we're doing is copying drawings made by someone else. Where's the fun in that?"

"Your father said that drafting is a skill you'll need to master before you can be an architect and follow in his footsteps," Nathan reminded him.

"I know, but let's take a break while Thethi is away. It won't hurt to be away from these torturous tables for a few minutes. He is a mysterious one, though, isn't he? He receives sketches from Deputy Architect Imani, gives us minimal instructions to copy them, and then leaves for hours at a time. Where does he go?"

"I assume he goes to the tombs under construction to check that the stone cutters and artisans are following the drawings. Who knows? Who cares?"

"Well, I never see him drawing anything himself. How do we know for sure that he knows anything about drawing?"

"How can you say that?"

"Let's look through his desk to see if there are any drawing rolls with his name on them," Malik said with a grin.

"Not a good idea," Nathan said as Malik pulled scrolls from the cubbyholes above Thethi's drawing table. After opening dozens of oversized sheets, none containing Thethi's name, Malik concluded that their drafting teacher was not who he claimed to be.

"So," Nathan chided, "he's not a real draftsman. Big deal! Now put those back."

"What's this?" Something odd in Malik's voice drew Nathan back to his side.

He spread an old papyrus sheet before them and weighted its corners with smooth rocks kept on the desk for that purpose. This drawing was older than those Malik first pulled from Thethi's desk. The faded ink showed aboveground and underground details of the magnificent tomb of Queen Hatshepsut, Pharaoh's step-mother who had been dead for over fifty years. Two things captured their attention: the original draftsman was named 'Imani,' maybe Deputy Architect Imani's father, and a recent addition had been freshly inked onto the dried paper.

With only rudimentary knowledge of architectural drawing and notation, Malik and Nathan struggled to figure out what the superimposed lines meant. They both arrived at the same conclusion.

"This looks like a new tunnel," Nathan whispered as if he expected someone to be eavesdropping on them.

"Queen Hatshepsut's tomb was finished and sealed by Pharaoh long ago. Why would any additional underground work be done?" Malik asked.

His friend sounded even more certain now. "This is a new tunnel leading into the underground burial chamber from an entrance on the other side of a hill. That notation is the hieroglyph for a well. Someone recently added another entrance into the tomb that doesn't appear on the original drawing. Why would they do that? Maybe it was a design that was never built."

"There's only one way to find out," Malik announced. "Let's go see if there's a well on the other side of the tomb's front entrance."

"That, my friend, sounds like something that will land us both into serious trouble. I want no part of it."

Malik rolled up the papyrus sheet and put it back in a slot over Thethi's drawing table.

"It'll take us all of twenty minutes to see if there's a well where that drawing shows it. We'll be back here in no time." Shaking his head in disbelief, Nathan reluctantly followed his curious friend out the door toward the tomb of Queen Hatshepsut.

Walking along a worn path in the Great Place Valley toward the famous queen's tomb, the two friends drew no special attention from the stone cutters and artisans shaping other tombs in the cliffs. The roar from copper foundries casting new tools, the screech of stone wheels sharpening chisels, the rhythmic sound of hammers chipping soft rock, and the chants of hundreds of artisans at once all gave this part of the valley a loud musical rhythm that hardly sounded like the final resting place of the dead. When they came over a shallow rise they saw the beautiful ramps and colonnades leading to the tomb entrance of Queen Hatshepsut gleaming in the sunlight. The architectural wonder dominated the Valley. They paused a moment to admire the monument's artful balance of design that was a tribute to Egypt's greatest Pharaoh-Queen. No sooner had they left the noise of new construction behind them, than they heard voices ahead. Starting to feel guilty about being away from their desks, they hid behind a large pedestal that marked a long row of steps leading up to the magnificent tomb.

Deputy Architect Imani and Draftsman Thethi were sharing an animated conversation as they strolled along the worn path. The two couldn't hear exactly what was said, but it was punctuated with laughter as they apparently shared a joke. They disappeared over the rise a minute later.

"Now we're in trouble," Nathan said. "Thethi will report our absence to your father and we'll be in hot water."

"I can tell that those two are up to something! Now I *must* see if that well is there," Malik insisted. He was more interested in seeing if there was a secret tunnel into the tomb than getting into trouble with his father. He figured that he could always explain their need to take a break as long as nobody questioned where they went.

Walking past the queen's tomb and over the hill as the drawing depicted, they saw a well in the middle of a dusty clearing surrounded by scrub bushes. Two men suddenly stepped from behind bushes on the opposite side of the clearing from where the boys hurried behind a low, stunted tree. Nathan grabbed Malik's arm and pulled him to the ground. The men hadn't seen them.

From their large physiques, leather armor and sharpened swords, they looked like soldiers. What convinced Malik and Nathan that they were probably not from the Egyptian army were their matching jackal headdresses that covered their heads and faces. The black jackal represented *Anapa*, the ancient god of mummification and the dead, before modern priests made *Osiris* the god of the dead. A jackal's head was symbolic of the agony of physical death and all its horrors. The unmistakable pointed ears, narrow jaw and snout, thin lips formed into a grim half-smile, and gleaming black eyes on the body of a human warrior would scare away anyone who approached the well.

When the guards walked back into the bushes, the two young men retreated over the hill to the safety of the tomb of Queen Hatshepsut. It took them a few minutes to calm their nerves.

"I think that answers your question," Nathan said definitively. "Are you satisfied now?"

"No. I want to go back and see what's inside that well."

"Are you crazy! Not only do you want to get us in trouble, but you want to get us killed by those jackal-headed sentries."

"Don't you see? Imani and Thethi are part of this. The tomb of Queen Hatshepsut has been sealed forever. If someone is using a secret tunnel to steal treasure from her burial chamber then we need to tell my father so he can tell Pharaoh."

"All that is quite a leap of fantasy from an old drawing and two thugs in scary jackal masks guarding a well. How does that equate to tomb robbery?"

"That's why we need to go back tonight and explore that well."

When Thethi returned to his office and found Malik and Nathan missing he was mildly annoyed. He considered his job teaching them drafting nothing more than babysitting the royal architect's son and his slave. He had more important things on his mind. He stood at his desk and absentmindedly reached up for the Hatshepsut drawing to refresh his memory about the complex interior chambers. When his hand touched an empty compartment, his eyes darted up and his heart skipped a beat. He saw the scroll one cubbyhole lower than where he had left it. The top of his drawing table was littered with flakes of old, dried papyrus. Someone had very recently unrolled the drawing! It took only a fraction of a second to conclude who the likely culprits were. Thethi tucked the scroll under his arm and hurried upstairs to inform Imani.

CHAPTER 10

Great Place Valley, Artisans' Village

"What will we do if Thethi is in the drafting room? What will we tell him when he asks where we were?" Nathan asked Malik. "I know he and Imani didn't see us near the tomb, but if he asks where we were I don't want to lie to him."

"That won't be necessary," Malik replied. "I'll tell him we went for a walk and if he asks where we went, I'll tell him it's none of his business. If he presses me further on our whereabouts, I'll report him to my father. He won't bother us then."

"I hope so. This whole thing is creepy. Do you really think the two of them are tomb robbers?"

"We have to find out for sure. You're right that we can't go accusing them without evidence. We'll look inside that well tonight and if there's a tunnel back into the queen's burial chamber like the drawing showed, then we'll tell my father and he can notify the authorities."

"Look!" Nathan pointed at Thethi's desk.

"What?"

"The drawing scroll of Queen Hatshepsut's tomb is gone! He must have come back here and taken it with him."

"Do you think he knows that we opened it and saw the tunnel drawing?"

"Who else could it be? How could he miss that layer of dried papyrus flakes on his desktop?" Nathan pointed out.

"Let's go see my father," Malik insisted.

Within minutes, the two youngsters reached Hatep's office. Nathan stepped back and allowed Malik to enter the room first. Hatep was placing some drawings into a carrying bag in preparation for returning to Lotus House.

"Father, are you leaving?" Malik asked casually from the doorway.

"Oh! It's you, Malik. Yes, I'm taking work home to finish before your mother and I go out to dinner with friends this evening. We'll be home late. Will you and Nathan be coming home soon too?"

"No. I think we'll take a ride around Queen Hatshepsut's tomb to see what it looks like around sunset. We'll probably be late too."

"Well, Malik, be careful driving the chariot home in the dark. There is a new moon tonight so go slow." Hatep gave an absentminded wave on his way out. "Have fun!"

When Hatep stepped into his waiting chariot and drove off, Malik turned to Nathan. "Apparently neither Imani nor Thethi spoke to him or he would have mentioned something. So let's go into the village, get something quick to eat, and then hide Sapphire and the chariot closer to the well."

Great Place Valley, Queen Hatshepsut's Tomb

By the time the sun set, they had put on darker long sleeve tunics to make themselves nearly invisible and to ward off the evening chill. Nathan and Malik walked Sapphire from his stall in the village to the edge of Hatshepsut's elaborate colonnades and left him harnessed to the chariot in the shadows near some grass to keep him quiet. They climbed up the wall leading to the Middle Court of Hatshepsut's tomb and walked across the open expanse leaving the causeway ramp to their left. They were still a few hundred yards from the well and approaching it through the low acacia underbrush.

"Why did we pick the darkest night of the month to do this?" Nathan whispered.

"What? And risk those guards seeing us walking up to the well? This is the *perfect* night to do this." Malik relished the danger and excitement.

They moved from bush to bush listening for any sounds that would reveal the presence of the guards that they knew must be nearby. The glow of a campfire illuminated where the guards probably warmed themselves between their rounds. From the edge of the clearing they saw three guards seated on the ground around the fire. Their jackal headdresses rested next to them but these men still looked menacing.

Malik crawled closer to learn if there was another guard somewhere. They didn't have to wait long.

"Shouldn't one of us get back to the well," the younger of the three men asked.

"We still have time," another said. "They don't usually show up until a couple hours after sunset. We'll hear them coming anyway. That big digger stomps along the trail and snorts like an elephant." The other two laughed.

Malik backed away from the edge of the clearing and took a roundabout path to the well. Nathan was close on his heels.

"This is the best time to go. If we hurry, we can be down the well before anyone comes."

"Then how do we get out without being noticed?"

"When the time comes I'll think of something. We need to go *now!*"

When they reached the well they saw that it was much larger than it appeared from a distance. The sides of the circular well were made of creamy limestone blocks about a foot thick and four feet high. The opening was eight feet across, which was larger than any well used by a home or estate. Starlight revealed short steps inside the well that descended in a spiral around its edge. The two sleuths climbed over the side onto the steps.

Malik led the way down the pitch-dark shaft that disappeared into the earth. They leaned against the wall away from the center to keep from falling into the abyss. After no more than twenty steps their feet reached moist sand. They felt the outline of a large opening at the foot of the steps, almost as wide as the diameter of the well. A dim light in the distance outlined the opening once their eyes adapted to the darkness.

"Somebody's down there," Nathan said.

"I don't think so. There's no sound and the light isn't moving. Let's keep going."

As they walked closer, they saw lights in the ceiling. The passageway was higher and wider than any access tunnel they'd seen in other tombs. The walls were rough-cut stone and not the smooth, polished surface found in pyramids. From this, Malik concluded that it was dug quickly and yet was large enough to accommodate the removal of the tomb's larger contents. They continued following the down-sloping floor which they assumed would take them to the burial chamber of Queen Hatshepsut.

They stopped under the first light and stared at the glowing object in the ceiling. They had never seen anything like it before. Shaped like an onion, the glass bulb about the size of a fist cast a dim orange-yellow light in all directions. Malik reached up then quickly pulled his hand back when it touched the hot glass.

"What is it?" Nathan asked.

"No idea," Malik replied, blowing on his fingers to cool them off.

They craned their necks up to examine the thin flickering thread that glowed like gold inside the bulb. Nathan was fascinated by the silent, flame-less torch. "There are two strands of something attached along the ceiling that lead from this one to another of those things further down the tunnel."

They walked faster and traced the two strands to a line of more bright globes evenly spaced in the tunnel ceiling. It didn't take long for them to reach where the passageway met a small room that did not appear to be the main burial chamber. They found stacks of wooden boxes and large pieces of ornate, royal furniture—chests, beds, wash stands, chairs, tables.

Still intrigued by the ceiling lights, Nathan followed the twin strands to a squat, black storage chest or cabinet on the far side of the room that measured four feet on each side and three feet tall. Other strands emerged from the box and went in other directions. On closer inspection, he realized that the strands were tightly wrapped in papyrus and sealed with black tar.

"What's that smell," Malik asked when they stood before the large, squat object. He felt its sides and realized that they were warm, but not too hot to touch like the glass bulbs.

"Pungent. Like some sort of chemical. Maybe like the acid used for tanning hides," Nathan speculated. "Whatever it is, it's making those globes give off light and heat. Wouldn't surprise me if Imhotep had something to do with this."

"Do you think he's a tomb robber?"

"That would be unlike him, but the crooks behind this wouldn't hesitate to use any invention of his."

"Well, forget that for now. We need to find the main burial chamber and then get out of here." Malik led the way down another lit corridor.

When they emerged into a large, brightly-decorated room it was clear that this was the final resting place of Queen Hatshepsut. Her enormous gold sarcophagus filled the far end of the chamber and its smooth, ornate surface gleamed under the overhead lights. Much of the large vault, whose colorfully decorated ceiling was reinforced by two fluted, decorative columns, was otherwise empty except for pieces of a broken chariot, a ceremonial reed boat that wouldn't fit through the tunnel, baskets of decayed fruit and grain, and open boxes in the center of the room waiting to be sealed.

"I've seen enough," Nathan announced. "Robbers have pretty much cleaned out the tomb of the queen's riches. They could come along any minute now." He didn't wait for Malik and walked alone back to the smaller room that held boxes packed with treasure waiting to be removed. No sooner had he reached the room than a man's deep laugh came from the well tunnel. Nathan beckoned to Malik to come and hide. It was too late for him to move when Nathan noticed that he'd picked a hiding place next to the warm box that gave the ceiling globes their light. He hoped that the approaching men didn't have anything to do with the lights or the box.

When the two robbers stepped into the lighted room they didn't even look around. They headed straight for the queen's burial vault. Both were dressed in the loose, dusty clothes of stone cutters.

"Let's get these boxes closed up and stacked so they're ready for tomorrow night. The gold sarcophagus will go out when all the other treasures have been loaded. I'll be glad to be done with this place so I can collect my pay," the larger of the two said in a booming voice that echoed in the small room. He must be the loud, clumsy one that the guards joked about. The burly stone cutter looked like he could singlehandedly lift the boxes of treasure. The other man was smaller and limped behind him with a jerky gait.

As soon as they disappeared around the corner, the two terrified intruders ran down the tunnel to the well entrance. The carved path from the burial place of Queen Hatshepsut led, they hoped, to an unguarded well and safety. While he ran uphill, Nathan thought about what Malik said earlier when he asked how they'd get past the guards at the well. He wondered if his friend had come up with a plan yet because they needed one in the next few minutes.

They emerged from the tunnel without a sound onto the moist sand of the well bottom and looked up. Stars dotted the small, dark circle above their heads. Nathan grabbed Malik's arm before he began to climb the narrow steps to the surface.

"Now would be a good time to tell me how we get out of here without being captured," Nathan whispered.

Malik replied in a casual drawl. "We're going to climb out of the well and pretend that we're the two robbers leaving early. Let me be the big lug and I'll speak if a guard challenges us. You keep quiet and tag along. Walk with a funny limp like the little guy. It's dark enough that they won't know it's us."

Nathan shook his head in disbelief but followed his friend up the stairs anyway since he didn't have a better idea. The two paused on the top landing and peeked over the edge of the well. Two guards talked at the far edge of the clearing.

Malik gathered his thoughts to utter the right sounds when they came out of the well.

He climbed over the lip of the well and fell onto the ground with a loud thud. "Ooof!" he shouted. He grumbled loudly as he got up and stomped off up the path and out of the clearing.

"Mukka, be careful. I felt the earth quake." The guards laughed.

The two continued to walk away with Malik stomping his feet and Nathan limping along behind him.

"Will you be back later?" one of the guards called after the departing figures.

"No!" Malik grunted in his deepest, gruffest voice. They kept walking. When they were over the crest of the hill they broke into a run to get to Sapphire and the chariot tied near the temple.

Nathan hurried Sapphire away for home at a quick trot. Malik urged him to slow when he remembered his father's caution about driving too fast in the dark.

"What will happen when the real robbers come out of the well?" Nathan asked.

Malik thought while the horse steadily walked on the road to his West Bank home. "I'm sure the guards will report it to Imani. It won't take much for whoever's behind this to figure out that someone else knows about the tomb robbery scheme. There's a fortune at stake here. They won't play nice if they think that the plan could be exposed."

"We need to tell your father about this," Nathan said.

"Maybe."

"What do you mean 'maybe'?"

"I mean that we don't have any solid evidence of a robbery. If we accuse Imani and Thethi, they'll simply deny it. It's only our word against theirs."

"We can show your father the well and the tunnel into Queen Hatshepsut's tomb. That should settle it, right?"

"Maybe. We need to catch them taking the treasure out of the well tomorrow night."

CHAPTER 11

Great Place Valley, Queen Hatshepsut's Tomb

The next night, Malik and Nathan left Sapphire in a narrow alley between Hatshepsut's tomb and the Chapel of Hathor which was still under construction. The first sliver of a new moon was low in the sky. They approached as close as they dared to see if the treasure was being taken away that night, like the two robbers had planned. The muffled sounds of men and animals guided them straight to the well.

The robbers took advantage of the darkness to gather ten ox carts and several dozen armed men around the well. Not a word was spoken. The lowing and snorting of restless oxen, the creaking of carts and harnesses, and the shuffling of nervous guards and drivers filled the clearing with muted tension. Soon, a line of men emerged from the well laboring under heavy boxes which they handed off to other workers who filled a waiting cart. The process was repeated for the next two hours until all the treasure boxes had been loaded onto the carts. The guards and drivers watched in amazement as the riggers, drenched in sweat from pulling on the ropes, pulled the lid of Hatshepsut's golden sarcophagus from the well using a sturdy tripod set over the well opening. The value of this much gold was beyond their imagination. It took twenty men to carry it to an oversized waiting wagon pulled by eight oxen where the gold object was covered with a tarp. When the operation was repeated with the base of the sarcophagus, the convoy of carts left the clearing in single file; armed guards walked beside them on a path that twisted through the acacia underbrush. A few workers stayed behind at the well to clean up all traces of the carts and oxen.

"We need to follow them," Malik said as they ran back to their chariot.

"Why? I've seen enough." Nathan protested.

"Not me. They're moving all that treasure someplace. I suspect that they'll ferry it across the river tonight and then it'll disappear into the city. If we tell my father exactly where they've taken the treasure, he can alert the Medjay police and they can arrest the robbers red-handed."

"We're getting ourselves deeper and deeper into this and I don't like it. What if they capture us? What makes you think we wouldn't disappear without a trace?"

"We can pretend to be a couple of kids out for a night of fun who just happened to cross paths with them."

"You forget that if word gets back to Imani and Thethi about us they'll realize that we know about their operation. By the way, I really wish you'd stop referring to us as 'kids'."

"Fine, so we're 'teenagers.' Does that make you feel better? We need to follow them now and at least see where they go. I promise we'll stay at a safe distance so we don't get caught."

Still uncomfortable with his friend's casual assurance, Nathan took Sapphire's reins and drove through the dark toward the West Bank waterfront where the ox carts were already being loaded onto barges.

Nile River at Thebes

It was almost midnight when they reached the West Bank shore and saw the heavily laden cart with the gold sarcophagus being driven up a ramp and onto a flat barge to ferry it across the Nile. Once again, they tied Sapphire up where he could munch on some grass on the high river bank until they returned later that night. To Nathan's bewilderment, Malik "borrowed" a small punt to row them across in the dark. He promised they would return it to its mooring before dawn. Nathan didn't like what his friend was doing, but he went along with it anyway.

The last barge carrying treasure was tied up to a wharf on the Theban waterfront that was busy with commercial activity even this late at night. They watched as the barges were unloaded and the ox-drawn carts disappeared into the slow-moving traffic of other vehicles, pack animals, and river cargo.

"We have to follow that last cart or we'll lose their trail," Malik insisted. He tied the borrowed punt to a piling and waded ashore with Nathan close behind him. Nobody took note of two young men emerging from the river soaked from the waist down. They hurried to keep the cart in view before it disappeared into the dark, winding streets.

Fortunately, the cart moved slowly enough for them to keep up with it and the accompanying guards were too preoccupied making sure that nobody touched the treasure boxes to notice them as they followed at a distance through Theban back streets. Walking together a couple of dozen paces behind the last cart, Nathan chanced a quick whisper to Malik: "When we see where they unload the cart we'll leave, right?"

"Maybe," Malik replied with his usual grin.

"Not again! Why do I always find myself tagging along so you can get both of us in trouble?"

"Because you enjoy it," Malik whispered as he jabbed his friend. "Besides, don't think of it as 'trouble' but rather as an 'adventure'."

Minutes later, the cart stopped at a building with large double doors. A guard immediately opened the doors to reveal the dimly lit interior of a warehouse. Pedestrian traffic from the waterfront had thinned on the back street so that Malik and Nathan were forced to slip into a shadowed alleyway to watch unobserved. Men swarmed from the building and emptied the cart in less than a minute. The doors were slammed shut and the cart drove off into the night. The street was suddenly quiet.

"Where are we?" Nathan asked.

"Somewhere near the bazaar," Malik observed. "This is probably a warehouse for merchants who use the bazaar. I don't see a name or address on the building, so this must be the back entrance. Let's go around and see what it looks like from the front. Maybe there'll be a name there."

"And then we'll go home, right?"

"Maybe."

A narrow alley separated the warehouse from an adjacent building which offered them a shortcut. The alley was narrow and they had to climb over some discarded boxes and step on shards of broken pottery and garbage to get through. They couldn't help making some noise when they stumbled into a pile of trash in the dark. One pile of wooden boxes was directly under an open window. Malik couldn't resist climbing onto the boxes to sneak a peek inside. Nathan groaned at his friend's disregard for caution. He helped Malik balance on the top box to peer over the windowsill. As expected, the large room was filled with articles of all sizes for the bazaar. The crates taken from the tomb were piled almost to the ceiling on a far wall and what he assumed was Hatshepsut's sarcophagus and cover, were draped with rugs. Someone stood under a lamp counting out copper pieces and giving a fistful to each of the guards and workers. Malik couldn't make out their faces.

He was about to ask Nathan to steady his feet so he could get a better view when he felt an iron grip on both of his arms. At the same moment a wet cloth was pressed against his nose and mouth. The cold liquid stung his eyes. Everything went black before he could utter a sound.

Waset, Great House Palace

"All the treasure has been delivered according to your instructions, Master. Some of the 'merchandise' will be distributed to the usual middlemen for sale to private collectors and the public. The gold will be melted down at the usual foundry." The trusted courier made his report before dawn and waited for some indication that his master was pleased by the outcome of the latest business venture. Instead, the face of the powerful man who went by the code name "Black Falcon" to all but an intimate circle of insiders, hardly registered any expression. His conscience and emotions were desensitized to the feelings of either guilt or pleasure from another robbery.

"Did they cover their tracks? Are you sure nobody can trace the operation or the artifacts back to me?"

"Yes, Master. The well was filled in and the ground swept clean of any evidence or tracks. The cart and barge transporters have been well-compensated, as have the riggers and handlers. They know that if anything is revealed, they will pay with their lives. The warehouse is secure and a small incident has been remedied."

"A small incident?" The Black Falcon showed the first trace of emotion since the courier gave his report.

"We caught two teenagers looking through a window. They saw the workers being paid off but the guards made sure they won't be telling anyone what they saw."

"Very well, that will be all."

The messenger closed the door quietly behind him.

The Black Falcon leaned back in his chair. His mind worked through each intricate step of his latest operation and the people aware of its choreographed steps. The secret, systematic emptying of Great Place Valley royal tombs by secret tunnels was untraceable back to him. By tunneling into the burial chambers from a distance, their decorative exterior façade remained undisturbed and Pharaoh had no idea that the treasures of his ancestors were either melted into ingots, sold in the bazaar, or shipped to foreign lands. The Black Falcon's secret satisfaction was that Pharaoh was making one of his closest advisors rich without even realizing it. His growing wealth might one day equal that of the Great One himself. Then he would buy an entire army and replace that ancient relic of a pharaoh.

He should have been more concerned about the incident of the two teenagers but the thought never crossed his mind again.

CHAPTER 12

Temples of Karnak, *Per-Nefer* House of Mummification

Nathan regained consciousness in the dark. His head pounded with pain and his tongue and throat felt like he'd eaten desert sand. When he finally rolled his tongue over his lips he tasted something sweet. The smell made him retch uncontrollably. He tried to wipe the vomit from his chin and realized that his hands were tied behind his back. He fought to clear the throbbing pain in his head while he took inventory of the rest of his body. He remembered steadying Malik's feet on some boxes in an alley behind a warehouse when someone grabbed him from behind and put a wet cloth over his face. Now he was either blind or blindfolded but glad that he could breathe. He tried to call out but only a weak croak emerged from his dry throat. The bottom of his tunic was still damp from when he and Malik waded ashore the night before and now he had vomited on his tunic.

Malik! Where was he? Nathan contorted his body and bumped into what he assumed was his friend tied next to him. It felt like he was lying on a hard slab of cold granite. If the two put their backs to each other maybe they could untie each other's hands. He moved again and groped behind him in the dark. He felt a hand and pulled it to see if it was tied with the same cord as his own. The icy hand slipped from his grip. He felt further and sensed that whoever was next to him was slathered with oil. Rolling over again brought his face against that of a corpse. The smell of embalmed flesh caused him to retch again between attempts to scream.

"Malik! Malik!" He finally managed to yell between gasps for air. "Malik!"

His cries were enough to rouse his friend who lay on another granite mummification table nearby. Like Nathan, the drug that knocked them out caused him to vomit uncontrollably as soon as he awoke. He tried to speak. His first coherent words revealed that he was as terrified as Nathan.

"Where are we? What happened to us?"

"Try to calm down. How do you feel? Are you injured?"

"I don't think so. My head feels like it's about to explode, but nothing's broken. I think I'm going to be sick…" He threw up again and Nathan heard the last contents of his stomach spill onto the floor. When Malik screamed in surprise Nathan knew he'd discovered a dead body next to him too.

"Listen to me, Malik! We're both on tables which means I'll have to somehow get down from here to untie your hands. I'm going to sit up, if I can, and slide off this table."

"I don't know how you're going to get to me. There's a dead body between us."

"My hands and feet are tied too, but if I can get off the table, onto the floor, and stand up, I can hop over to you. Hang on."

"I'm not going anywhere. What a mess I've gotten us into!" Malik lamented. He thought he was going to be sick again.

"Well, I'm glad you finally admit it. This is not my idea of an adventure—it's more like a *nightmare*."

When Nathan fell off the table onto the floor, his head hit the pavement with a loud crack. He lay in a heap between the granite tables.

"Are you all right?" Malik asked. Silence gave him his answer. He remained on the mummification table for almost an hour trying to not think of the dead body next to him before he heard Nathan groan.

"Nathan! Wake up!"

"Oooh… now my head *really* hurts. How long was I out?"

"I don't know. A long time, I think. Can you stand up?"

Nathan slowly rolled onto his stomach, bent himself at the waist with his forehead pressed into the slippery floor until he was kneeling, and tried to stand up. He was weak from whatever liquid had been used to knock him and Malik out during the night and was still dizzy from his fall off the table. When he eventually stood, he hopped and wobbled until he felt the side of Malik's table and used it to steady himself. The cords binding his feet seemed looser now. He took short steps around the table until he felt a warm, moving body.

"Finally," Malik exclaimed.

"Roll over so I can reach your hands and untie them."

"That means I need to face the dead body…"

"There's no other way, my friend."

Malik slowly rolled and tried not to touch the cold corpse.

Within a minute, Nathan had untied Malik's hands who in turn removed his blindfold, untied his feet and climbed down from the table.

"Wow! You won't believe where we are," Malik said.

"Just untie me and spare me the details. I know where we are and the sooner we get out of here the better."

They stood in the center of the *Per-Nefer* House of Mummification, also known as the House of Death, in the Karnak Temples complex. The room held almost twenty black granite tables, most of which held naked bodies in various stages of ritualistic embalming and mummification. Scented oils, gum-resins, natron salts, and creams did little to mask the sour odor of decomposing human flesh. Nathan had heard enough about the ritualistic mummification process to know that the canopic jars on shelves lining the room contained preserved organs. Sharp, curved metal hooks and forked probes lined up on small tables between the slabs gave him the shivers when he visualized how they were used to extract brains.

"What are you doing here?" a voice behind them boomed.

They nearly jumped out of their skins, which would have otherwise sounded funny had they not been in the House of Death.

"I said, 'What are you doing here?' This is a sacred place forbidden to anyone but priests of *Anibus*." The pale, wizened man who stood before them wore a linen tunic covered by a blood-spattered apron. He held a sharp, hooked metal rod in his hand in case the intruders had designs on attacking him.

"We…that is, someone tied us up and left us here during the night." Nathan spoke up because, for once, Malik seemed at a loss for words.

"It was some sort of sweet-smelling liquid that knocked us out. We woke up on those tables with our hands and feet tied. Believe me, we don't want to be here."

"Come here, let me see that residue on your mouth." The diminutive man reached out with his free hand while he kept the sharp rod handy just in case.

"Stay away from me!" Nathan reacted, but he was too slow and his confronter was surprisingly quick and strong. The man grabbed Nathan's shirt and pulled him closer.

"Yes, I believe you," he sniffed. "I am familiar with that formula. I have used it in the past on my patients."

"You do this to living people?" Malik recoiled in horror.

"No! Of course not. I am a priest of *Anibus* but also a physician. You were both drugged. Do you have painful headaches?"

"Yes!" the two answered together.

"And judging from your dilated eyes," he gestured to Nathan, "you have also recently struck your head on something hard."

"Yes to all the above," Nathan agreed. "Can we get out of here now and return to our homes on the West Bank?"

"Of course," the priest of *Anibus* replied as he led them to a door that opened into dazzling sunlight that nearly blinded them. "If you are ever interested in learning the fine art of embalming and mummification, please come back. I would be glad to have two more apprentices." He chuckled as the two intruders ran down the street to the riverfront.

Luxor West Bank, Lotus House

By the time Malik and Nathan pulled into the driveway of Lotus House later that morning they were almost too tired to stand upright. Reuben came out of the barn, took the reins from Nathan's hand, scowled at them and shook his head. "You two should be ashamed of yourselves."

"It's not what you think, Reuben," Malik said in a weak voice. "And don't speak so loudly. I have a headache."

"Like I said, you should be ashamed. You spend the night in the city consuming strong drink and then you drag yourselves in here and tell me it's not what I think. That's vomit on your clothes and you both stink. I can see that you two are still drunk. The master will have a fit when he finds out."

"Reuben," Nathan said more forcefully while the groom unhitched the chariot. "We have *not* been drinking. Something happened that we don't want to talk about right now. We need sleep and then we'll talk about it."

"I can't wait to hear that story," he said with sarcasm. He spun on his heel and led the horse into the barn.

Hoping they would reach Malik's bedroom without running into his mother, they instead met Sarina standing in their way.

"Well, well, well...look who decided to drag themselves home after a night in town!" his sister smiled cheerfully.

"Oh, not you too..." Malik moaned. "Must everyone shout when they speak?"

"Some fine influence you've had on my brother," she scolded Nathan.

"*My* influence on him?" he replied. "I'll have you know it was *his* fault for bringing me into all of this against my better judgment." He followed Malik into the bedroom and fell onto a pile of blankets on the floor. He was asleep within seconds.

"What's his problem?" Sarina asked her brother, but he was already snoring on his bed and never heard her.

"Fine company you two are! I want a full report from you when you wake up. Then I'll tell you about something new and interesting I've discovered on the helio net." She covered Nathan with a sheet, closed her brother's bedroom door, and skipped down the hallway and up the stairs to her observation perch on the roof.

CHAPTER 13

Luxor West Bank, Lotus House

Malik and Nathan slept for twenty-four hours. After eating all the food they could find, they realized that Lotus House was deserted except for Sarina who was in her usual spot on the roof under a shade awning. She had sheets of papyrus spread before her and several pots of ink and writing sticks at the ready. When she heard her brother and Nathan ascending the stairs, she greeted them with a smile.

"I wondered when I'd see you two drag yourselves out of bed. Did you find your breakfast in the kitchen? I asked the servants to leave it out for you."

"Yes, thank you. That's the first place we went." Malik said. He figured his sister had something to do with the cold lamb, dried fish, and grape juice they found on the counter.

"Where are Mom and Dad?" he asked.

"Dad's gone to work and Mom went shopping…of course."

"Were they upset about us being away overnight?"

"Not that I could tell. They're so wrapped up in their own lives that I wonder if they'd miss us if we disappeared for a week." Malik and Sarina were thoughtful and serious young people beginning to make their way in the world; lately their parents seemed to have grown distant and indifferent to what went on around them.

"I know what you mean. Well, maybe it's best that we don't have to explain what happened to us in Thebes." Malik knew that his sister wanted all the details, so he and Nathan recounted how they found the drawing in Thethi's desk, discovered the strangely lit tunnel into Queen

Hatshepsut's burial vault, followed the trail of stolen treasure into the city, and then woke up in the House of Mummification in Karnak. Sarina could hardly contain her excitement.

"I wish I'd been with you!" she blurted. "You were in the *Per-Nefer* embalming room itself—how exciting! Did you look inside any canopic jars?"

"You're very strange," her brother remarked in disgust.

"I would call our time there more like *terrifying*," Nathan observed. Malik's sister had no idea what it was like to wake up in the dark next to a cold decomposing body. That was an experience he never wanted to repeat. He quickly changed the subject.

"I vaguely remember you saying something about a discovery on the helio net. Did I dream that or have you come across something new."

"The morning you came home I was up here at first light to read messages. There were some short, routine notices sent from the palace to the valley offices. Helio operators mixed in tidbits of gossip with the official messages. After the usual back and forth between operators, there was an urgent message from the palace to somebody named Deputy Architect Imani."

"We know him!" Malik exclaimed. "He's mixed up in all this somehow."

"I was stumped by the message because it was the first *encrypted* helio signal I'd ever seen. I was caught unaware without pen and ink since I can now read the signals visually without writing anything down. Elias, the operator on duty at the Great Place Valley, was caught by surprise too and had them slowly repeat the message so he could write it down accurately. I got it all on the second transmission. The encrypted script makes no sense, of course, but I'll figure it out later," she said. "I love a good puzzle!"

"If anybody can crack that mystery, you can." Nathan observed without sarcasm. "Do you think there's any significance to the timing of that signal from the palace?" he asked Malik.

"There could be… Maybe it was meant to tell Imani and Thethi that the treasure was delivered to the warehouse."

"Or it could be warning them about us," Nathan said. Having their names connected with the stolen treasure was frightening. Given the enormous value of the gold and artifacts at stake, their knowledge posed an obvious threat to the thieves' operation. "We'll have to go back to the drafting room and eventually face Thethi. We'll run into Imani sometime, too. What will we say to them?"

"Nothing unless they confront us directly. If they do, then we'll have to tell my father everything."

"I think we should tell him everything before that happens."

"Maybe."

"There you go again. You don't listen to me, do you?" Malik's exasperated friend lamented. He and Malik argued about that for the rest of the morning.

Later that evening, in a quiet corner of the home's center courtyard and away from the rest of the family, they told Malik's father everything that had happened. After telling him about the tunnel to Queen Hatshepsut's tomb, the treasure shipment to a warehouse in Thebes, and their experience in the embalming room in Karnak, the royal architect was astonished by their story.

"What you've told me is almost unbelievable. Of course, first thing in the morning I'll check the well for that tunnel which you claim you saw before I question Imani and Thethi. It's too bad that you don't remember the name of the warehouse or I would check that too. There aren't many verifiable details to go with your story."

"You mean you think we made this up?" Malik wondered.

"I don't know what to believe. Maybe your imaginations carried you away and you saw something that looked like gold being carried by a cart to Thebes. There was only a sliver of moon that night, remember?" Hatep was struggling to make sense of the wild tale.

"On top of that, I'm very disappointed in both of you. I was told by the horse groom that you came home drunk that morning. That's partly my fault for not keeping a closer eye on you. I expected more of you but you have obviously proven me wrong. No more nights out, understand? I'll speak to Asher about this too."

"We weren't drunk…" Malik injected.

"I mean it." Hatep's word was final.

"Yes sir." Both Malik and Nathan agreed. They left to sulk in Malik's bedroom.

"See?" Malik said when they reached the other side of the house. "You talked me into telling him what happened and not only doesn't he believe us, but he thinks we were drunk and now we can't leave the house at night."

"You must admit that our story sounds far-fetched. That is, if you didn't see what we saw."

The next two days passed uneventfully. Malik and Nathan spent their days in the Great Place Valley architect offices where they did their drafting apprenticeship. They watched Thethi for any indication that he knew of their discovery. He seemed irritated about something but grudgingly commended his two charges on their neat annotation of a drawing for a nobleman's tomb. Something was on his mind but it didn't seem to involve them. Even when Deputy Architect Imani delivered more drawings at the end of the day he hardly gave them a second glance. When they drove Sapphire home at the end of the day they hoped Hatep would have something to say about the tunnel.

After a late dinner, Malik brought the subject up again with his father. Nathan was at home because his father had also imposed a curfew when he heard of Hatep's restriction. They'd have to do further investigating during the daytime.

"Nothing," Hatep told his son. "I went to the well you described and, as I suspected, found nothing."

"But we went down more than twenty feet to the tunnel!"

"It's an abandoned well. It was filled with dirt and rocks and hasn't been used for years. I looked all around the area and saw no evidence of ox carts, guards, or camp fires. Whatever you think you saw, it wasn't a tunnel in that well. Now, let's drop the matter. I have work to do before tomorrow." Malik knew when it was pointless to press the matter further.

"What about the warehouse?" he asked his father.

"If you can give me a name or an address for the place, I'll look into it. Otherwise, it isn't worth my time. I think you should forget the whole thing."

It was clear that his father was finished. "Yes sir. I'll try to remember where it was."

Malik lay in bed that night trying to remember the location of the warehouse. Something bothered him that he couldn't quite place. It might come to him in the morning.

As soon as he opened his eyes the next morning he visualized something that his mind had sifted and dredged up from his memory during the night. He concentrated to make sure it stayed with him and didn't slip back into his subconscious. He smiled because he knew exactly how he and Nathan could find the warehouse. Then a second thought came out of nowhere. He had to talk with Nathan right away.

As they drove together to the Great Place Valley that morning, Malik explained the two things that had popped into his mind when he woke up. They would ask Thethi for the afternoon off. He probably wouldn't object, and then they could go to Thebes to investigate. They'd find where the carts were unloaded, write down the address, and then decide what to do.

"Whatever we do, we shouldn't give the information to my father until we know for sure that he's not involved himself."

"That's the most absurd thing you've ever come up with," Nathan exclaimed over the sound of Sapphire's hooves on the road up to the Great Place Village.

"That would explain why he said the well was abandoned and doesn't want to talk about it anymore."

"Your father tied up with tomb robbers? You think he lied about the well? Now *that's* unbelievable!"

"I know. I find it hard to believe too. But what if he is involved in some way?"

"Look, I agree that we should first locate the warehouse in Thebes. I'm warning you though, we have to do it without drawing attention to ourselves. If someone sees us poking around again, that would bring them down on us hard. I do not want to be the stiff on the granite slab this time!"

Nile River at Thebes, Main Bazaar

As expected, it was easy enough to get the afternoon off. Nathan drove Malik's chariot to the West Bank docks where they left Sapphire at a stable and jumped on the next ferry crossing the river to the city. As Malik visualized the last time they were there, he found the pier where the carts drove off the barges and took the treasure through the city's back streets. He instinctively walked through the winding streets and came to the back entrance of the warehouse. The usual afternoon crowds in the streets and in the shops allowed the two to watch the warehouse from a distance without being noticed. They bought snacks from a street vendor and casually strolled around the block while they ate.

"Golden Scarab Imports. Doesn't tell us much, does it?"

"The word *Gold* in its name says something," Nathan observed.

Malik and Nathan studied the front of the large mud brick building while they hid behind a display in a clothing store across the street. The warehouse was some kind of storage and distribution center for merchandise. People left the building carrying fruits and vegetables as well as furniture, bolts of cloth, and bags of items. With all the activity going in and out, it would be easy for stolen goods to move unnoticed in broad daylight.

Without warning, Nathan grabbed Malik's arm and pulled him deeper into the fabric store from where they'd been watching the warehouse. Malik's mother walked across the front of the store, paused to look at some cloth on display and then turned down the street to avoid an over-zealous salesman.

"That was close!" Nathan exclaimed.

"We're not doing anything wrong, but she thinks we're working. We need to be more careful."

Nathan peered up and down the street and didn't see Malik's mother. He and Malik started crossing the street and were almost run over by a horse-drawn vehicle. They stepped back just in time to look up at Reuben pulling vigorously on the reins of the family wagon.

"You two!" His anger at almost hitting two pedestrians who walked in front of him was tempered by his surprise at seeing Nathan and Malik where he least expected them.

Unable to avoid speaking with him, Malik explained that they were investigating something and begged him to not tell his mother that they were in the city. Reuben promised that he would not volunteer the information but explained that he had to catch up with the mistress of the house. Her recent purchases were in the back of the wagon and he had to take her home before it got dark. He left in a cloud of dust.

"That was close again!" This time, Malik was still shaken by almost being run over by Reuben and his own family's wagon. "We need to get across the river and back to the house before anyone figures out where we've been."

Nathan was worried about what would happen if it turned out that Hatep was involved in the tomb robberies. "Even if your father investigated the owner of Golden Scarab Imports, the treasure is probably long gone anyway."

"I want to tell my father about the warehouse anyway. Don't you want to see how he reacts?"

"Yes and no. I still can't fathom why he would be involved with gold robbery."

"Tonight we'll find out."

Luxor West Bank, Lotus House

Hatep had no reaction when they told him about their trip to town and Golden Scarab Imports. The name elicited no reaction other than a promise that he would inquire about who owned the warehouse and the types of business they conducted. He speculated that the 'Imports' in their name meant that they had commerce outside of The Two Lands, probably with Nubia and Put and Kush to the south and maybe as far east as Canaan. He then mentioned casually that Malik's mother had been shopping in the city that afternoon and wondered if they had seen her in the bazaar.

"Nathan caught a glimpse of her, but she didn't see us," Malik said. He hoped he wouldn't have to explain to his mother why they'd been there.

"Well, she spent a small fortune on a table and some emerald jewelry. The horse slave cleaned the table and put it in the sitting room earlier this evening and I suppose I'll like it even less when I get the bill." He left Malik and Nathan and walked into the living area where the new table held a bowl of fresh flowers and Iset admired it in the glow of lamp lights placed around the room.

"What do you think, Hatep? Isn't it the most beautiful table you've ever seen? The man who sold it to me said it was fit for a queen. I assure you, it was worth every gold piece I spent on it." Iset looked for her husband's approval.

"Yes, it is lovely." Hatep admired the large round table and matching chairs for six. The gold trim around the edge of its polished surface highlighted the intricate river scene carved in its top. It was modeled after the design of a royal offering table. The royal architect's expert eye could tell that it was indeed some of the finest workmanship he'd seen in Upper Egypt. After examining the table's four sturdy legs shaped like the powerful limbs of a lion, he admitted to himself that his wife had purchased an item that enhanced their home's decor. He would compliment her on the quality of her purchase, but refrain from saying that it was a bargain lest she buy more furniture than they could afford. He hoped that the jewelry was of equally high quality.

"My dear, you have such good taste. This adds to the tasteful decoration of the room."

"Thank you. The man who sold it to me said his shop recently acquired it and that I was fortunate to have it delivered so quickly. He also received a shipment of jewelry which absolutely captivated me. I'll wear it at dinner tonight so you can see how it goes with a dress I also bought."

Malik and Nathan walked into the room and let out a gasp together. They stood paralyzed before the new addition to the room. It was one of the tables they'd seen offloaded into the warehouse! The item's size and design were unmistakable. Even the chairs were identical to those they'd seen.

"Oh, you boys like it too?" Malik's mother asked with a smile.

"Yes, Mother. It's very…nice." Malik's face was pale with shock. "Father, we need to speak with you again."

They told him about seeing the same table and chairs offloaded two nights ago at the Golden Scarab Imports warehouse. Their description was detailed enough to gain Hatep's full attention. He promised to send his chief steward, Nathan's father, to investigate the warehouse the next morning and find the vendor who sold Iset the table, chairs, and emerald jewelry. He further urged Nathan to tell his father everything he had seen and to omit nothing, no matter how insignificant. He would instruct Asher to take two men with him in case there was trouble.

Before Nathan left to speak with his father, he and Malik stood in the dark outside the front door of Lotus House.

"It looks like things are starting to move along again," Malik said. He was pleased that his father was finally taking them seriously and doing something to find the robbers.

"Yes," Nathan said with caution. "Only now *my* father is getting involved too. Whoever is behind the robbery won't be too happy when vendors are questioned about where the furniture and jewelry came from. I will need to make sure my father realizes the danger involved."

"Don't worry about it. Everything should get straightened out tomorrow."

"Maybe," Nathan said, mimicking his friend.

CHAPTER 14

The Two Lands of Egypt

Asher's investigation into the source of the furniture and jewelry stolen from the tomb of Queen Hatshepsut never happened the next day because three divine plagues, each in rapid succession and unprecedented in scope and magnitude, inflicted harsh torment along the Nile from the Upper Cataract to Memphis. Most Hebrew slaves were still unaware that the plagues affecting the land of Egypt were from the hand of God and the direct result of Pharaoh's stubbornness.

Shortly after sunrise, billions of frogs emerged like a tidal wave from the river and hopped across the landscape. God had been keeping the tiny green reptiles in the Nile until it was time for Aaron's command. When they jumped onto dry land, they covered the ground and slithered into every Egyptian home, garden, bedroom, water jar, shed, and barn. The frog-goddess *Heket* could not stop them. Even Pharaoh's palace was not safe from the slimy creatures that slithered into sealed hallways and inner chambers. Frogs had multiplied before in large numbers during the *akhet* Inundation but never in such overwhelming numbers and never so suddenly. One minute there were none and then they were crawling over each other to the depth of a person's ankles.

Lotus House was not spared either. No sooner had the servants swept the tiny reptiles from the inner court and rooms, than more poured through windows and doors and squirmed through any crack. Nothing could keep them out. Iset screamed in fright each time one of the tiny green intruders became tangled in her hair. She spit them from her mouth and cried even louder. The servants struggled to clear the hoards from the house, but to no avail. After a sleepless night of removing the pests by the hundreds of thousands, the frogs began dying as suddenly as they appeared. The house slaves shoveled them into the yard in heaps where the dead bodies soon turned into a moist green carpet.

When the bodies of dead frogs had finally been swept from Lotus House, the servants thought that the ordeal was over. Almighty God then caused gnats to swarm out of the dust and infest the people and livestock with lice. There was not much that the servants could do to help their Egyptian masters assuage the constant biting and itching that afflicted them all. Into the night, the parasitic infestation persisted amid cries of pain from man and beast. Bathing with cool water did little to relieve the suffering. Egyptian and Israelite servant alike endured another night without sleep.

As with the frogs, the gnats died in the morning as quickly as they appeared. By this time, in Lotus House, as in thousands of other homes in The Two Lands, Egyptians called out to their gods for help but received no response. They cursed *Anuket*, Mother of the Nile, for bringing such suffering upon them. Then the One True God of the Hebrews brought another plague designed to soften Pharaoh's heart.

Clouds of winged insects sprung from the moist soil near the river, like sprouts of new reed grass. The dark army of flying bugs rose in the warm morning air, partially obscured the sun, and headed for the open-air homes. Inhabitants of The Two Lands were tormented by the attacking, biting insects almost to insanity. Carved, golden flies that had once been worshipped as gods were cursed and cast out of Egyptian homes. The loud buzzing continued all day and into the night. They were so thick that no one could eat or drink without insects flying into their mouth and up their nose. Even nets of fine woven linen could not keep them out.

Unnoticed until much later, Goshen in Lower Egypt was strangely devoid of the frogs, lice, and flies that enveloped the rest of the country. The majority of Hebrew slaves in Egypt labored in the rich, productive farms of the Nile delta and its vast mud pits used to fashion bricks. They were spared the overwhelming infestations because the Self-existent One the Hebrews called *I AM* was using the supernatural plagues to teach Pharaoh and the Egyptians about Himself. The *LORD* of Abraham, Isaac, and Jacob was mightier than any of Egypt's so-called gods. Everyone in The Two Lands would eventually appreciate the full strength of God's mighty hand as He prepared to redeem His chosen people.

Waset, Great House Palace—Royal Gardens

"My concern," said Vizier Nakhte in a low voice as he and Royal Priest Metjen of *Amun-Ra* walked in the palace gardens one week after the last plague, "is what will happen to the country if these plagues continue. The pain and suffering of the people, to say nothing of lost revenue from stalled commerce, has been a serious blow to the balance of harmony—*ma'at*—in The Two Lands. Reports from up and down the river are that the swarming infestations reached into all of the *nomes* or provinces except Goshen."

"But we've had infestations during the *akhet* flooding season before," the royal priest, objected. "We've always recovered with abundant, multiple harvests by the next *akhet*. Why are you so concerned this time?"

"You know very well why. That Hebrew Moses and his brother seem able to predict the plagues that erupt within minutes of their demands. The pattern began with the river turning to blood and then in the most recent invasion of frogs and insects. Even your own priests admit that the lice and flies were the result of their God's power. They couldn't duplicate those miracles and gave up trying."

"What are you suggesting?" Metjen was uncomfortable with the direction of their conversation.

"I am not *suggesting* anything...yet. The events of the past weeks have the potential of upsetting the stability of the entire country. I'm worried about more than the discomfort of our countrymen and the temporary loss of commerce. What if our people find out that this man Moses is asking—no, demanding—that all Hebrews be allowed to journey three days into the wilderness to sacrifice to their God? What if they find out that it is the Great One's stubbornness that is bringing the plagues upon them. Egyptians could turn on their leader if they thought it were his fault that all this has happened. If the Hebrews rally behind this miracle worker we could have a revolt on our hands. What would we do then?"

"We'd call out the army and stop any uprising in quick order. How could a bunch of slaves stand up against the mightiest army in the world?"

"Don't be absurd. We can't fight off a swarm of insects, let alone repel a million slaves. If they organized themselves into a united force, even six of our military corps could not withstand them."

The royal priest stood close to the vizier when they stopped in the shade of a juniper tree. "So is *ma'at* completely lost? Has the Great One already destroyed our country?"

He and his friend exchanged a long stare in silence. The vizier chose his words carefully. "What I am saying is that you must advise our Great One to carefully consider the power behind this upstart Hebrew and his brother. As our leader's spiritual conscience, you must guide him toward decisions that increase *ma'at*—order, harmony, stability, calm—and not diminish it, which will destroy the nation if the present course continues unchecked."

"And you, my friend. What will you do?" the priest asked with equal caution.

"I will continue to monitor the attitude of the people. Many Hebrews and their descendants have been assimilated into Egyptian families for centuries and are not treated as subjugated inferiors. A Hebrew revolt or internal civil war could cripple us. I pray that the Great One will consider this when he is next confronted by Moses' demand."

Bakenmut, the Royal Master Scribe, watched from the shadows of his balcony overlooking the royal garden as the two men parted ways and returned to the cool hallways of the palace. His twisted, cunning mind could guess what they were planning and he would turn it to his benefit.

CHAPTER 15

Luxor West Bank, Lotus House

By the time life at Lotus House had returned to normal and Hatep remembered his promise to investigate the source of the royal table, the chance of identifying the tomb robbers, if there were such people, was gone. Hatep's son and Nathan cleaned the scroll storage rooms in the architect's Great Place offices after the plague of frogs left a green, sticky coating on the papyrus drawings. He sent Asher into the city to contact the vendors his wife identified but he returned empty handed. Either the vendors had moved to another city or they claimed to not know the person from whom Iset had purchased the objects. His chief steward was more interested in bringing his master's estate back to top efficiency and productivity, so he reported his findings and suggested that no more time be wasted chasing suspicions of tomb robbers. Hatep agreed.

"Great! Now what do we do?" Malik asked when he and Nathan were told the results of Asher's investigation.

"I'm not surprised that he found nothing. My guess is that the robbers always planned to sell the goods or ship them out of the city as quickly as possible to avoid being traced. Either that, or they use trusted vendors who won't divulge where they got the valuables. It looks like we've run out of clues."

"I don't want a face-to-face confrontation with Imani and Thethi. They surely must have figured out by now that we know about their scheme. Why haven't they said anything to us?"

"Why should they? Nobody's believed us so far. I'm sure they've covered their tracks and have good explanations for everything we saw. They'd deny everything. Let's just drop it."

"You know me better than that." Malik broke into a mischievous smile.

They heard Sarina's excited voice calling them from the roof. The two ran upstairs. It must be something she found on the helio net. She now spent every daylight hour on the roof reading the palace's mail.

"I did it!" she exclaimed when she saw her brother and his friend. "I did it!"

"Did what?" Nathan asked.

"I broke the encryption! I unscrambled that message that the palace sent to the Great Place Valley." Sarina jumped up and down with excitement.

"So what does it say?" Malik asked.

"Don't you want to know how I did it?" She sounded disappointed.

"I knew you'd figure it out eventually. What does it say?"

His sister's feelings were hurt that her brother *assumed* she would break the cipher. He was so focused on results that he sounded unimpressed with her hard work and intelligence.

"Tell me how you did it," Nathan injected. "I want to know."

"Finally some respect from one of the men in my life." She pointed to scraps of papyrus sheets scattered on a table. Some were still stained green from the frogs the week before but she didn't seem to mind. "It's a simple substitution written in the hieratic alphabet, of course."

"Of course," Malik said dryly.

"Let her talk," Nathan urged. "You know how smart she is."

Sarina beamed at the compliment and continued. "Anyway, I spent days trying different substitution combinations and concluded that I could try random sequences for years without hitting on the right one. So I looked at the symbols that occurred most frequently and guessed what they might be. Some short words started to pop out that revealed a couple more symbols that might fit next to them. This morning they all came together and now I know the substitution sequence. It turns out that the hieratic alphabet was shifted by three symbols. When they send another message I'll be able to figure it out right away. Even if they shift by a different number, now that I know what to look for. Neat, huh?"

"You're terrific, Sarina. Your time wasn't wasted on this. The message sent to Imani from the palace must be important." Nathan steered Sarina toward the content of the message because Malik was about to explode with curiosity

"It doesn't seem to be all that important. It's just a list of furniture and things. I don't know what can be so important about that." Having solved the intricate puzzle, she was disappointed that the deciphered text was an administrative list to her father's assistant.

"Can I see it?" Malik asked with barely controlled restraint.

The two young men held the papyrus between them and they skimmed down the list. Their eyes bulged when they came across the description of a table and six chairs. Then the name at the bottom of the message grabbed their attention. They looked at each other and then at Sarina.

"Why would a list like this be sent using a complex cipher?" She found the content of the list as puzzling as the cipher. "I've seen lists of things on the network before and they're all boring. Some were sent to the Deputy Architect or to the Royal Master Architect or one of the construction superintendents. They all have to do with tomb design, building materials and supplies, or payments to workers. I assume that this is a list of valuables being shipped for placement into someone's new tomb. It doesn't say whose tomb they're for, so Imani probably knows. Whoever will be buried in a Great Place tomb must be very wealthy. I wonder though—so much expensive clothing, women's jewelry, stone and wooden artwork, even carved furniture."

"What do you make of the name at the bottom of the list?" Nathan asked her.

"Now that's more of a mystery," Sarina admitted. "Why would it be signed with that name? It was addressed to Imani so he must know who the 'Black Falcon' is. I've never seen that name used in any other messages. Still, it must be someone important in the Great House palace."

It suddenly clicked in Sarina's mind that Malik and Nathan were showing an unusual interest in the message. "Wait a minute!. Tell me what you know. Who's this 'Black Falcon' and what's going on? I won't stop pestering you until you tell me."

Malik knew his sister well; it would be useless to feign ignorance now so they had to tell her. They sat down in the shade of the awning and he and Nathan pointed out that the description of the round table and six chairs on the list matched the items her mother purchased in Thebes two days after the robbery. Sarina then recognized an emerald necklace with a carving of *Osiris* on a large green gem that matched exactly what her mother bought. The list must be an inventory of items stolen from the tomb of Queen Hatshepsut!

When Nathan insisted that they had to show the list to Hatep, both Malik and Sarina objected. Sarina knew her father would be angry at her for reading a secret message from the palace and Malik figured he would further reprimand him and Nathan because they insisted on sticking to their story. When they reluctantly agreed to tell him, it was only after Nathan promised that he would continue the pursuit if Hatep grounded his two children, although he'd probably be grounded too.

Their meeting with Hatep that evening began well. The master of the house summoned Asher to listen to their explanation of the secret message sent from the "Black Falcon" in the Great House to Deputy Architect Imani in the Great Place Valley. Asher confirmed that the table and jewelry purchased by his mistress matched those on the list. He had to admit that it was not a coincidence. The fact that Sarina had broken the enciphered palace code was a sticking point with Hatep which he could not overlook.

"Your curiosity has landed you in bigger trouble now, young lady," her father scolded. "Not only have you been reading royal messages for your own amusement, but now you have read something that, for whatever reason, was intended to be a palace secret. I want you to stop this nonsense immediately!" Under her father's increasing fury Sarina was close to tears.

"I was only doing what I thought General Herihor wanted me to do," she sniffled. "He… he gave me permission to watch the helio traffic and make suggestions to him on how the network and the sending device could be used by his troops." Sarina's lower lip quivered. "I thought you said I could do that."

"Well, I suppose I did," Hatep sputtered, "but I didn't know you'd sneak into such private messages that could be from the Great One himself."

"Do you really think the 'Black Falcon' could be Pharaoh?" Malik blurted. "Would he secretly steal the treasure from his own step-mother's tomb?"

"Of course not! All I'm saying is that this has gone beyond snooping on helio signals from our rooftop. Now someone powerful in the Great House is involved and that means there could be trouble for our family that puts us in danger. I don't want this to go any further!" Hatep was insistent and Asher agreed with his master.

"One way to protect the family would be to tell General Herihor about the matter and ask him to make further inquiries at the Great House without using your names," Nathan suggested.

"I don't want to bother him with this," Hatep said. "Besides, I don't know him that well."

"But we do, don't you remember?" Malik offered. "Nathan and I spoke with him late that evening, after the awards, and he said we could come to him if we had any questions about the helio network or suggestions about improving it. Obviously, Sarina's cracking the cipher shows that even enciphered messages are not as secure as the palace thinks. If the general uses the same cipher for military secrets, the Nubians or Canaanites could be reading palace secrets just as easily. That would be reason enough to go to the Karnak garrison and show the evidence to him, don't you think?"

"Could we please go, father? I think General Herihor's scribes should know about the cipher before something terrible happens. Please?" Sarina sensed her father wavering.

"I don't want my eighteen-year-old daughter visiting an army garrison," he insisted. "Who knows how a young lady would be treated there?"

"I'm almost nineteen," she reminded her father.

"I hardly think General Herihor would allow anything to happen to my sister," Malik said. "He's a national hero and a fine man. He spoke highly of her when he was here."

"Besides," Sarina said to persuade her father further, "I have an idea for a *new* cipher that would take ages to crack. I'd have to explain it to his scribes personally, of course. Malik and Nathan couldn't begin to understand it enough to explain it to him." She hoped her brother would support her and not react to her veiled insult.

"I think Sarina needs to go with us," Malik agreed, to her relief. "Nathan and I will accompany her."

Hatep let out a resigned sigh when he realized that his children were right. "You have my permission, but this isn't about your wild story of a tunnel and grave robbers and being tied up in the mortuary. This is about a valuable table and jewelry that appeared in a coded message. Let the general decide where to go with it. If he says the matter should be dropped, then will you promise me to not investigate further?"

"Yes," Sarina said immediately with a smile.

"Yes sir," the two young men agreed.

"I'll send a messenger to General Herihor tomorrow with a letter asking him if he would meet with you about what you discussed when he was here. I'll tell you what he says." Hatep got up and walked to his bedroom shaking his head and muttering to himself.

Sarina left without a word to prepare her notes for the meeting she knew would take place as soon as they received the general's response. Malik and Nathan were excited about finally making some progress in their investigation. Their enthusiasm clouded any thoughts of harm that could come to their families from the Black Falcon if their discovery came to his attention.

CHAPTER 16

Karnak, Military Garrison – Amun Corps Headquarters

As expected, General Herihor readily agreed to meet with the three young people since the message intimated that they had something important to relate. On the chariot ride from Lotus House to the Karnak garrison they agreed to begin by showing him the message that Sarina had deciphered and to let him deduce the significance of the contents. They would let him speculate as to why a list of expensive articles deserved a cipher and who the Black Falcon was. Malik and Nathan hoped that the general would be open to their explaining the connection between the expensive articles in the message, the tunnel into Hatshepsut's tomb, and the warehouse in Thebes. Would he be willing to help them discover the identity of the Black Falcon? Would he believe any of their story?

The double gate into the garrison was a twenty-foot tall structure of acacia wood two feet thick between black granite pylons three times the height of the doors. The pair of uniformed guards at the entrance expected them and the gates swung open when they were still a hundred yards away. A captain dressed in the familiar spotted skin and plumed helmet of the Leopard Charioteers waved them through the gate and saluted Malik as he passed. Sarina balanced herself on the chariot's webbed floor and gripped the railing. She was dazzled by their formal welcome. When they reached the largest building of the garrison they stopped in awe under a painted image of *Amun* that covered the façade of the fortress-like structure. The bearded, ram-horned deity, namesake of Herihor's powerful corps, held the thin *was* scepter of dominion and cast a lifeless stare into the distance. The imposing building with its gigantic mural, thousands of troops camped around the compound, and Charioteers maneuvering in practice formations on the parade ground represented the concentrated power and military might of Egypt.

A groom took Sapphire's reins from Nathan and another soldier escorted the three to Herihor's offices inside the fortified headquarters building. The cool hallways were refreshing after the hot, dusty ride from the ferry dock to the garrison. The visitors craned their necks at the painted walls and ceilings depicting scenes of battle and conquest. By the time they arrived at Herihor's office they were overwhelmed.

"My friends, how nice to see you!" The general's greeting was warm and genuine. After having worked on administrative matters all morning he welcomed their visit. When he visited Lotus House after the palace awards ceremony he had found his conversation with the three refreshing.

After pleasantries and inquiries about Malik's and Sarina's parents, Herihor offered them facilities to wash off the dust of their trip and for Sarina to freshen up. When they returned to his office, he was eager to find out what news they had regarding the helio system. Sarina's announcement that she had intercepted an enciphered message from the palace and unscrambled the letters caused his face to darken with concern. He listened to her describe how she unraveled the hieratic substitution sequence. When she finished, the general was visibly disturbed.

"First, I must compliment you on your brilliant analysis." General Herihor was torn between respect for Sarina's sharp intellect and concern that one of the nation's greatest secrets had been so easily compromised by an eighteen-year-old woman. He thought of the many military orders and battle plans that had been sent using that cipher which the scribes assured him was unbreakable. "Who else has read the contents of the secret message?"

When they told the general that it was limited to Hatep's household, he was somewhat relieved. He paced the room while the three watched with increasing concern. What would Vizier Nakhte do, Herihor thought, if he found out that the general was not only aware of Sarina's helio monitoring activities but actually encouraged them? What if Pharaoh became involved? It could become a national scandal.

"I came up with another cipher that will be much harder to break," Sarina suggested to lessen the tension in the room. "It's as easy to use as the other cipher but mine would take much longer to break, if it could be broken at all."

General Herihor stopped pacing and returned to sit on a chair opposite Sarina. "You are amazing!" he said with unabashed admiration. Malik rolled his eyes. "Would you show your new cipher to my Corps Master Scribe? Would you do that for my corps and for Pharaoh?"

"I would do that for *you*," she replied with a dreamy smile.

Malik and Nathan could barely contain their laughter.

Their host was caught off-guard by her implied devotion. The battle-hardened soldier inside him wondered how a young woman like her could be so captivating. He snapped out of his private reverie and hoped that nobody noticed, but Sarina sensed the reaction in his eyes.

He summoned his Corps Adjutant, who in turn called Ahmes, the Amun Corps Master Scribe, who entered the room a few minutes later. General Herihor introduced Sarina to the puzzled man in the scribal uniform who wondered why he was being asked to speak to a civilian, and a young woman at that. When he heard the order from his commander to listen to what she had to say about a new cipher, he readily obeyed although he didn't believe that she could know anything about ciphers. He'd been encrypting and decrypting military messages his entire career. What could she tell him that he didn't already know?

When Sarina gathered her notes to show Ahmes, she handed General Herihor the scroll with her deciphered text. "You never asked me what sensitive palace secrets we learned from the message. My brother and Nathan will tell you the details." She gave the general a parting smile over her shoulder as she left the room with the confused and still-skeptical scribe.

After Herihor read the list of household and personal items in the text of the message he was no less enlightened. "What's all this about? I don't understand why a list like this should be protected by our cipher which is supposed to be used only for our most sensitive secrets. What's so secret about this?"

Malik and Nathan took turns explaining their story, beginning with their discovery of the tunnel into Queen Hatshepsut's burial vault and ending with the royal table and jewelry purchased by Malik's mother that appeared on the list. When they finished with their deduction that the Black Falcon must be someone high in the Great House palace, Herihor was even more troubled than he had been before by their discoveries.

"I agree with most of your conclusions," he said. "The compromise of the cipher is certainly something that endangers the security of the nation. However, knowledge of potentially plundered royal items on this list and specifically their connection to the palace and someone called the Black Falcon places you and your family in great danger. Your father was right to not want you or Lotus House identified."

"We think Deputy Architect Imani also knows, or at least suspects, our involvement from the tunnel scroll we saw in the drafting room. If he works for the Black Falcon and makes the connection between us and the two caught in the alley next to the warehouse, that's a further link to put us in danger," Nathan pointed out.

"Can you help us?" Malik pleaded. "We're in way over our heads. Now I am sorry I ever opened that tunnel scroll or went down into that well."

"Time will tell if you did the right thing. Any theft from Queen Hatshepsut's tomb would certainly be a shameful national tragedy. She was the first and only woman Pharaoh of The Two Lands since we became a united nation a millennium ago and by all accounts she was a good ruler until Thutmose III became old enough to assume the throne. She deserves to be honored and not disgraced in her final resting place. Someone in the palace apparently doesn't care about that."

General Herihor expected that by now his master scribe would be enthralled with Sarina's new cipher and was be scribbling notes furiously.

"I have some an urgent matter to take care of, so I suggest that in the meantime my aide give you a tour of the garrison. Then, I would like the two of you and your sister to join me for lunch before you return to Lotus House."

He saw the two escorted away for their tour and sat at his desk to write a letter outlining his meeting with them. Within a few hours, one of his loyal officers would deliver the letter by hand to a person who the general had known from childhood; a person whom he could trust like a brother. His letter urged his friend to find and expose the Black Falcon, whoever he turned out to be.

It was no wonder that the nation's *ma'at* was disintegrating. It wasn't only because the God of Moses was putting the false gods of Egypt to shame. It was because people like the Black Falcon thought they could pillage and rob the land for themselves and disregard the thousand-year old traditions of his nation. He could not allow that to happen.

The four gathered for lunch in the lush inner courtyard of the fortress in the cool shade of a stand of sycamore trees. Herihor was a generous host. The Amun Corps quartermaster prepared a main course of roast duck stuffed with walnuts, perch grilled in sesame oil with savory herbs, and a spicy pork dish flavored with peppers and garlic. Somehow the general knew of Sarina's liking for coconut. For dessert, he presented her with a box of candy made from the seed of a rare type of coconut palm mixed with honey. Laughter and conversation over the sumptuous lunch allowed them to set aside the seriousness of their morning meeting. Sarina assured the general that his Corps Master Scribe understood the new cipher. He had agreed to send her some examples to prove that he used it correctly. As Herihor expected, the normally dour Scribe Ahmes was enchanted by the young woman who had brightened his day, and elevated the scribe's esteem within his unit. Later, Scribe Ahmes would be honored for "inventing" the new cipher while Sarina's identity and role remained secret. She didn't mind as long as she had a reason to visit the general again.

The three said farewell under the *Amun-Ra* mural when Sapphire and Malik's chariot were brought around by a uniformed groom. Sarina held the box of coconut candy and a bouquet of blue cornflowers as tokens of appreciation from their host.

"You will be contacted at Lotus House by a man named Hezbak. He's a trusted friend who will investigate the matter we discussed. Tell him *everything*—leave nothing out." He shook hands with Malik and Nathan and when he turned to say good-bye to Sarina he nearly bumped into her.

"I'm...I'm sorry, Sarina." He stammered. It was the first time he had spoken her name out loud. That realization caused them both to pause and stare into each other's eyes.

"That's all right," she replied automatically. She didn't realize that she was blushing..

"Will...will I see you again?" The usually self-confident soldier stammered once again.

"I hope so," she answered. With a warm smile and slight wave, she ran around the chariot and climbed aboard with Nathan and her brother.

As the three drove off between the pylons, Herihor spoke sternly without turning so his aide wouldn't see him smiling. "I'll have your hide if any of that gets around to the men. That's a promise!"

"Yes sir!" His personal assistant grinned knowing that his commander was only half-serious.

Medjay Police Headquarters, Robbery Squad

Early every morning, Second Auditor Hezbak trudged to the Robbery Squad room in the basement of Theban Medjay Police Headquarters to thumb through another pile of paper slips reporting stolen objects—a cooking pot that disappeared from a kitchen, an old mule that probably chewed through his rope and walked away, a copper coin that the victim may never have had, or a hammer borrowed by a neighbor without permission—his days were occupied chasing down vague reports of supposed thefts. His police credential, or badge, was a cheap, thin copper piece that identified him as a second-level auditor on the Robbery Squad. A superior officer he never met dropped trivial assignments that nobody else wanted into his basket. Showing his official badge and asking questions was enough to satisfy an unsuspecting public that the Theban Medjay cared about their lost articles when in fact he was a nobody wasting his time on a forgotten squad of nobodies.

When he opened the personal letter from General Herihor the night before asking him to look into a robbery of great national significance, it was as if a death sentence had been lifted from his shoulders. Finally, he could breathe again. The fact that his friend sent the request to his home and not through official channels to the Medjay brought a smile to his face for the first time in almost a year.

The Chief Medjay's idea of punishment was proving effective. A year ago, whenever Hezbak flashed his intricately engraved, gold Chief Inspector credential, witnesses, victims, and other policemen took notice. When he began a murder investigation—back then he only took on the most difficult cases—he always captured the offender, brought him before the Royal Magistrate, and personally witnessed his execution. Among hardened criminals in the Theban underworld he had a reputation for making them confess using methods that terrified and confounded them. The suspects who lurked in the winding alleys and crooked bazaars could stand police beatings, torture, and depravation but Hezbak's mental trickery and overwhelming evidence of guilt elicited confessions without him lifting a hand. Activities and identities of criminal elements were transparent to him because of his extensive network of informants. He'd seen every murderous, corrupt scheme that human minds could invent. He was admired or feared by everyone. That was, until he confronted a wealthy merchant a year ago with indisputable evidence of murdering a competitor that brought him before the Royal Magistrate for prosecution. Within an hour, the Chief Medjay came down on Hezbak like a block of granite. His gold identification badge was confiscated and, without a word of explanation, he was assigned to the hated Robbery Squad to chase stolen donkeys. Finally, thanks to his friend General Herihor, he had something of consequence to investigate.

Luxor West Bank, Lotus House

The Second Auditor handed the reins of his tired horse to the Hebrew slave who met him at the front of Lotus House. An official Medjay chariot was "unavailable" to him so his arrival at the estate riding bareback on a worn horse meant that he was a lower-class official, no more respectable than an Egyptian farmer or cattleman. The slave demanded that he state his business before going further. Even when Hezbak handed him his thin Medjay identification card, the skeptical servant handed it back with a condescending shake of his head.

"We've had no robberies in this house," Reuben said firmly. "What do you really want?"

"That is of no concern to you, slave. I wish to speak with Master Malik. Is he here?"

"Master Malik? Why? Is he in trouble with the Medjay?"

Hezbak had dealt with cheeky Hebrew slaves before. It was time to put this one in his place. His face reddened with anger and he stepped closer to the burly horse slave. "Take me to Malik *now*," he growled. He had not lost his intimidating touch.

Reuben held his tongue and motioned for the Second Auditor to follow him to the front gate. Conscious that he was still responsible for guarding the household entrance, the slave told the visitor to wait just inside the gate while he went to see if Malik was available. When he found him, he freely gave his low opinion of the man who had ridden on a tired nag and who claimed to be a Medjay official. He was surprised when he heard that his master's son was expecting him.

Malik greeted Second Auditor Hezbak at the front gate and understood why his groom did not care for him. His first impression was of a man who had slept in his tunic—which was probably the case. He was filthy from his long ride on horseback, but nonetheless, General Herihor seemed to have enough confidence in the man's ability to solve crimes. Malik asked a young servant girl to bring refreshments to the courtyard where he introduced Hezbak to his sister and Nathan.

"May I ask why a Hebrew slave is included in this conversation?" Hezbak remained standing and stared intently at Nathan.

"Let me make something clear from the start." Malik didn't like the man's arrogant tone, even if he was the general's friend. Most Egyptians were bigots when it came to dealing with Hebrews and Hezbak seemed to be no exception. "Nathan is my personal steward and one day he'll be head over all the affairs at Lotus House and this estate. You will address him as you would me. Will that be a problem for you?"

The investigator sat on the couch and lifted his chin. His reply took long enough to make Nathan feel uncomfortable. He replied simply: "No. That will not be a problem."

Hezbak shifted his gaze to Sarina who sat opposite him on a couch with her bare feet tucked under her. "And your sister…she is somehow involved in this mystery?" She responded to the man's condescending tone with a sweet smile.

"This very much involves her. You will learn that this is a mystery unlike any that you have ever investigated." Malik definitely didn't like their visitor's attitude and didn't understand why his sister smiled at him.

"Well, with all respect, I doubt that." Hezbak removed one scroll of blank papyrus, two quill pens, and a jar of ink and meticulously arranged them on the table before him. He took his time sharpening the quills and opening the ink jar. His tired look around the room indicated that he was ready to begin.

Malik had had enough of Hezbak's pretentious manner and was about to call Reuben to throw the man from the premises. Before he could call for the horse slave, their visitor continued.

"General Herihor said only that you would give me all the details of a supposed mystery of great importance. I am doing this as a favor to him. Assume that I know nothing and start at the beginning. I will take notes as you speak. Please begin and I will ask questions as you go along."

"You might need more paper," Nathan observed with a wry smile. Sarina suppressed a giggle which momentarily unsettled their visitor. He struggled to maintain control of the interview.

"Proceed," their visitor instructed.

Malik calmed down and began by telling him about the discovery of the tunnel drawing at the Great Place Valley. Then, Nathan filled in details while Hezbak wrote in a neat, compact *hieratic* script. After thirty minutes he stopped taking notes because he had filled both sides of his single sheet of papyrus and the point of one of his quills was bent. Sarina brought him a handful of blank sheets and more pens without being asked.

When Sarina explained her reading of the intercepted helio messages from the palace and her ability to decrypt the secret code, Hezbak's eyes widened, he stopped writing, and held his hand up to stop her.

"How old are you?"

"I'm almost nineteen," she replied curtly. "What does that have to do with this?"

"Oh, nothing...." He had been following the sequence of events about the tomb robbery until Sarina began telling him about unscrambling enciphered heliographic signals from the palace. He reached for a pitcher of grape juice, poured himself a cup of the sweet, diluted liquid and drank it slowly. He struggled to regain his composure.

"Please continue," he murmured.

By the time they had explained the connection between the stolen treasures and the list of objects in the coded message from the Black Falcon, Hezbak's hand was cramped and his head ached. He had filled ten pages of papyrus—covering both sides—by the time the sun set across the river.

When Malik finished, Sarina added to his throbbing headache: "What exactly is a *Second Auditor*? We were under the impression that the general knew someone who could discover the identity of the Black Falcon and bring him to justice. All you've done is take notes. You never asked us a single question about the case. What kind of Medjay are you, anyway?"

"Miss—and I address you with the utmost admiration and respect—your brother was correct. This is a mystery unlike any in my experience. I apologize for my initial arrogance and confess that my first intention was to listen, assure you of a swift solution, return to the city, and forget the matter. I see now that I was mistaken."

The man before them was exhausted from listening and writing notes in his careful handwriting. Still, he evidenced a reserve of inner strength and determination that his punishment on the Robbery Squad had not dampened. He told them of his long career solving crimes of violence and murder to justify that he indeed knew something about solving mysteries, while he glossed over his most recent demeaning work. The three young people felt a combination of pity and disappointment until he explained that his demotion was due to charging a prominent merchant with murder. He had been publically humiliated and demoted from his once-powerful position in the Medjay force. He reluctantly admitted that he had neither official authority to investigate their mystery nor any resources to draw upon for expenses.

"Well, I think my father can pay for some of your expenses, if that is what you mean. We're ready to help you investigate too in any way we can." Malik offered.

"I may have some minor expenses and I appreciate your offer to help. However, I work best alone. Besides, some of my methods are… unconventional. It would also be best for your safety if you remained anonymous."

"I do have one request, however." Their visitor turned to Sarina. "Can you draw?"

"Of course!" she responded enthusiastically.

"I would like you to draw pictures of the table, chairs and jewelry that your mother purchased. Each article should be on a separate sheet. Make them as accurate as possible."

"It will take me several days. Should I send them to you at your office?"

"No!" he nearly shouted. "That is, they might get lost in the clutter at my office. I have a suggestion, however. The slave who met me at the front door, do you trust him?"

"Reuben? Yes, completely," Malik said without hesitation "He's been with our household his entire life. Why?"

"Send him to Medjay Headquarters with the drawings sealed in a package as soon as you can. He must wait for me outside the building entrance in the early morning and hand the package to me only. As you have already suspected, this involves someone so powerful that he will have informants everywhere watching for any threats to his safety. If this Black Falcon suspects that you are seeking to uncover his identity he will not hesitate to harm you and your family. He might not suspect or know who you are...yet. Trust me, I know how criminal minds work; their twisted reasoning is the same whether they are filthy murderers in the city underclass or perfumed, corrupt officials in the palace. I promise that I will eventually find him. Of that you may be sure."

When he stood and bid his hosts farewell, his face showed a cold determination. It softened when he shook Sarina's hand at the front entrance to the home. "It has been a most unexpected pleasure to meet a young woman of your skill and accomplishment. I will do my utmost to protect you and your family." He gave a low bow and left to retrieve his horse.

Reuben was startled when the departing Medjay climbed onto his horse, gave him a cheerful wave and said, "I'll see you again in a few days."

CHAPTER 17

Luxor West Bank, Lotus House

The fifth plague from Almighty God on The Two Lands sent a more ominous message than those before. The infestations of frogs, lice, and flies, like the Nile turning to blood, were similar: they were universal, except for the flies that did not invade Goshen; they caused temporary inconvenience or suffering but not death; their material or commercial damage was not long-lasting. The consequences of Pharaoh's continued stubbornness, however, would be economically severe in the next plague.

Moses told Pharaoh that all Egyptian livestock would die. His God would spare the Israelites' animals as a demonstration of His specific wrath against Pharaoh. After Moses left, a quickly convened council of advisors suggested that the effects might be avoided if Egyptian landowners temporarily "gave" their livestock to the Israelites before the plague arrived. A reverse scheme could take the animals back when the sickness departed. If this didn't work, then they would confiscate the Hebrews' remaining livestock. Either way, the royal advisors concluded that the plague could easily be avoided.

A short message from the palace went out over the helio network to all government agencies warning of a coming disease that would inflict only Egyptian domestic animals. The announcement said nothing about the source of the calamity. By order of Pharaoh, officials were to sign over all royal herds to their Hebrew slaves for safekeeping. The order was dutifully transmitted and would reach the far northern helio station in Goshen and the southern station in Aswan just before sunset. Most recipients would be confused by the order and issue a flood of questions back to the palace that would queue up at the helio stations until sunrise the next morning.

Sarina intercepted the order from Pharaoh that went out to the Great Place Valley station and wondered what to do with it. Her brother and Nathan had no immediate suggestions.

"The message doesn't say it in so many words, but if this is another of Moses' plagues," said Nathan, "Pharaoh's dodge won't alter anything. God is all-knowing and all-powerful. He'll turn Pharaoh's plan around on him."

"You're right, it doesn't say it's a plague from your god," Malik said. "Just in case, though, I hereby give you Sapphire for your own. You keep him for me until this passes."

"Malik, I don't think this will work. I love Sapphire as much as you do, but he's Pharaoh's gift to you and not me. I'm afraid that he'll die no matter what we do."

Malik would not be deterred. "There's nothing to be lost if you take him. If your god is as all-knowing and all-powerful as you claim, then my horse will die either way. So, he's yours to keep. I mean it."

"Should I take him home or leave him in your stables?" Nathan asked.

"Take him home and keep him in the slave village. Tell Reuben this is done with my permission."

"What about the rest of Father's herds?" Sarina asked. "He's at work and won't be back until dark."

"When he receives that helio message I'm sure he'll come home as quickly as he can. Let's wait and see. If he isn't back by an hour before sunset then we'll have to think of something."

"Then, I'm off to see Reuben." Nathan reached to shake Malik's hand. "Thanks for the horse!" he grinned.

Two hours later, Hatep arrived in a cloud of dust with Asher at the reins of his chariot. His steward handed the horses off to Reuben. Malik and Sarina waited for their father at the front door.

"You saw the message?" he asked them.

"Yes. We've been waiting to see what you wanted to do about giving the livestock to the Hebrew slaves." Malik replied.

"I picked up Asher on the way and we've discussed this briefly. He says he's sure that this is a plague from his god and that it cannot be circumvented as the palace ordered."

"That's what Nathan said too, but we figured that whether it worked or not, I should give Sapphire to him."

"We're thinking along the same lines then," Hatep agreed. "And Asher has an idea to distribute my livestock among all my slaves. I'll let him explain."

Asher picked up where his master left off. "If the God of Abraham desires to punish the Egyptians, then nothing we do can prevent that. If, however, His desire is to also bless us, the Hebrews, then He can do that too. I will draft a contract between the master and his slaves that gives them his herds of horses, cows, bulls, donkeys, camels, and sheep. My understanding is that he is willing to sign the contract and see what happens." Asher was still unsure if his master fully understood what he was doing or even if he intended to follow through with his idea.

"I agree," Hatep stated after thinking more about what he would do. "It's a risk I'm willing to take. Go inside now and prepare the contract and I'll sign it." Asher left to draft the agreement.

Malik's father was tired from the ride, but the thought of losing all his herds left him weak with worry. He settled onto a bench in the courtyard and stared at the garden fountain. Its soft gurgling in the dwindling sunlight was soothing.

"I'll get you a drink," Sarina offered and headed toward the kitchen.

"Father, you're doing the right thing," Malik said sitting next to him.

"I hope so." His father said without taking his eyes from the fountain. The family had weathered the other plagues from the Hebrews' god and survived with no lasting effects. This time, the risk of great financial loss weighed on him.

Over dinner, Hatep was quiet and didn't want to bother Iset with the impact that the loss of their herds might have on the value of their estate or their future lifestyle. He'd tell her about the coming plague when they retired later that night and try to sooth her fears. She'd have many questions that he couldn't answer. On top of that he wondered why the ancient gods of The Two Lands were so powerless to stop this god the Hebrews called *I AM*. He stopped before the statue of *Anubis* on his way to bed. It stared back at him with dead, black eyes.

The Two Lands of Egypt

The next day the Egyptian people suffered losses unlike anything they'd ever experienced. There were seasons in the past when Mother Nile refused to renew her precious water and drought ruined entire crops and decimated herds; modern-day priests of *Amun-Ra*, like the ancient priests of *Ra*, lifted their prayers to the goddess *Tefnut* and the rains always returned. In other years, when the Nile overflowed to wipe out homes and fields and they could not plant for an entire season, the people went hungry. Again, the priests prayed to their gods and the next year all returned to normal. Even the recent infestations of frogs, lice, and flies did not totally ruin their crops or kill their animals. Through times of disaster and depravation, the Egyptian people remained resilient and hardworking. They flourished for centuries in a hydraulic civilization that submitted to their deities who ruled the water, land, and sky. Now everything was changing in ways they had never experienced. Their priests and their gods could not stand against the powerful God of the Hebrews.

Unaware of the warning that had gone out to a small number of government officials the day before, the slaves tending their master's flocks were confounded when a mysterious disease caused animals in the fields to drop by the thousands. Ignorant of the cause, they reported the losses and many fell victims to retribution for allowing the animals in their care to die. Local magistrates and estate masters accused the slaves of poisoning their animals. Their wrath only increased when they confiscated an ox or lamb owned by a slave and it died as soon as it came into their possession. God's purpose was to show the Egyptians that they could not escape His might. They did not fully realize this purpose yet. It would take more plagues of increasing severity before the people of The Two Lands understood that the God of the Hebrews was more powerful than Pharaoh, his armies, and all their so-called gods.

It took days for reports of nationwide damage to trickle back to Pharaoh's palace from the seventeen *nomes*, or provinces. With each report that flashed through the helionet came questions directed to Pharaoh: 'Why did this happen? How could the earthly cow-goddess *Heset* not prevent this national disaster? How can the cult of *Mut* function in the Temples of Karnak if there are no animals to sacrifice?'

When the vizier and the master scribe brought reports of the losses to Pharaoh he tore the message sheets into pieces and raged against the gods. This was all Moses' fault! Pharaoh ordered the Egyptian Army on alert in preparation for a revolt by Israelite slaves; he demanded that any resistance be brutally suppressed. He actually hoped for a slave insurrection for the perverse pleasure of exacting a bloody retribution. If he couldn't fight against their god, then he would fight against them.

What Pharaoh did not grasp, nor could he from his comfortable palace surrounded by nodding courtiers, was that some Egyptians actually had a peculiar affection for their Israelite house slaves. When plagues fell upon an Egyptian family, some of their unharmed slaves cleaned them, gave them food, or replaced an animal here and there. Seeds of kindness such as these were planted throughout The Two Lands.

Luxor West Bank, Lotus House

The century-long close relationship between Hatep's ancestors and their family slaves was brought out by the events that followed the latest plague. In other Egyptian households, animals died regardless of the complicated, fraudulent paper-schemes that masters forced on their slaves. None of the animals covered by the contract between Hatep and his slaves died! Could it have been because he made the gifts with a sincere heart and not with deceitful motives? If he reneged on his promise, the animals would probably die as soon as he confiscated them, so he accepted their loss as a matter of personal honor. When many of his cattle, horses, and sheep were *voluntarily* returned by his slaves out of appreciation to their master, they lived. This God of the Hebrews confounded him!

During the night, Hatep lay awake frustrated by the weakness of Egypt's countless deities against the one deity worshipped by lowly slaves. The earthy cow-goddess was powerless because no cows in Egyptian barns or fields survived the plague; likewise, the celestial cow-goddess *Hathor*, who carried the sun disc between her horns, and the bull-god *Mnevis*, could do nothing to protect the herds. Every sacred black bull of *Kemwer* in the Great Temple of *Amun* in Karnak was dead. Nothing could survive before the *LORD* of the Hebrews. Hatep quietly rose from his sleepless bed, walked barefoot through the dark house, seized the obsidian statue of *Anubis* from its niche near the front gate, and smashed the grinning jackal into bits against the outside wall of Lotus House. He returned to his bedroom and slipped under the linen sheet trembling with rage. The next morning he was too upset to speak to his wife and left for work before she got up. On his way out he placed a fresh lotus bud on the altar where the black icon once rested. He felt better now. The chariot drive in the cool morning air cleared his mind by the time he reached his office.

The plagues were taking their emotional toll on Iset too. The mistress of the house spent hours in her garden meditating about the ancient gods who watched over The Two Lands, but she had no peace.

Her husband had tossed and turned in bed most of the night and she knew not to say anything to him when he arose before sunrise. At first light, Iset called a servant for her shawl and breakfasted in the courtyard. She needed someone to talk to about her unsettled spirit and she knew Rachel would listen. The one the Hebrews called the God of Abraham—did He care enough to help her? It was clear from what she had seen so far that He was powerful and all-knowing, but could He calm her heart and give her hope? What did the future hold for her and her family?

"What can you tell me about your God?" Iset asked when Rachel answered her summons a short time later.

"What do you wish to know, my lady?" Rachel replied cautiously. "One can spend a lifetime learning about Him. I can tell that you are upset about something. How may I help you?" That was all the encouragement Iset needed to pour out her fears, uncertainties, and doubts. Her pleasant life on the Luxor West Bank could end at any time. Her handmaid listened patiently. When it seemed that she had finished, the servant hesitated before making a suggestion that her mistress might not like.

"There is a teacher of my people—we call him Rabbi Ben-Judah— who can tell you more about our *LORD*. The flame of God's Word burns in his heart. I am confident that he can answer your questions."

"Then bring him here immediately! I want to hear what he says."

"My lady, he is blind and crippled. You would have to come to our home in the slave village to speak with him. If you do not wish to go there, I understand."

"I will go." Much to Rachel's surprise, her mistress gathered the folds of her long tunic, slipped into her sandals, and headed for the front entrance of Lotus House.

When she ordered Reuben to harness a chariot and drive her to Rachel's home in the slave village, the horse slave was dumbfounded. Rachel shushed him before he could protest. They had to hurry before their mistress changed her mind.

Luxor West Bank, Slave Village

Iset ignored the stares of the village residents when Reuben drove her to the home of Rachel and Asher. Rumors raced from door to door when Rachel led her inside the simple brick dwelling. They had never seen the wealthy mistress of Lotus House in the village, let alone enter the home of a slave!

They found Rabbi Ben-Judah seated on the dirt floor in the dark. For Iset's benefit, Rachel lit an oil lamp and they sat close to the old man so they could hear his weak voice. Unwashed bodies, dusty clothing, and cooking smells in the one-room shack were uncomfortable for their visitor, but she needed answers to burning questions. When Ben-Judah asked how her family had fared through the livestock plague, she appreciated the concern of this thoughtful, kind man. The Hebrew teacher spoke to her before she could ask a single question.

"You have many questions, I can tell. I sense that you are afraid about the turmoil in your land and in your family. Is this correct?"

"I am afraid that all I have ever cherished is falling apart. Our family is being turned upside down and that is tearing at my heart." It was difficult for her to admit her inner anguish to a stranger, let alone an old blind slave, but it was true.

"Perhaps you would allow me to explain why we, although poor Hebrew slaves, are hopeful about the future. Your handmaid Rachel, like other devout daughters of Abraham, has a hope inside her that is grounded in a three-part promise from her God that cannot fail to be fulfilled. It is a promise that He made hundreds of years ago to our forefathers Abraham, Isaac, and Jacob: that we would one day live in our own land and be multiplied in numbers more than the stars in the sky. How can we believe this, you may ask, when we have been slaves in a foreign land for more than four hundred years? It is because *we know for certain* that God, who cannot lie and is always faithful to His Word, is able to perform all that He says."

"How can you be so sure of this? Has your *LORD* ever shown Himself to you?" Iset asked.

"To me? No, not directly. How many times does God have to prove Himself for you to believe Him? The miraculous demonstrations of the past months should be enough to convince you that He is more powerful than all the gods of Egypt. The *LORD* is the self-existent *I AM* of all peoples, not just of the Hebrews. Do you believe that to be true?"

The wealthy woman dressed in Egyptian finery sat in the dust and gloom of her slave's dwelling and pondered the gravity of what he asked. The inner conflict brought tears to her eyes that the teacher could not see, but he heard them in her voice when she answered, "Yes."

With attention to every word, Iset listened to Rabbi Ben-Judah explain the faith of Father Abraham and how she too could be right with God. The fact that Abraham believed what God told him and was declared righteous was an astoundingly simple spiritual principle which God repeated over and over throughout Hebrew history.

"Do you remember that I said God made a three-part promise to Abraham? The first two parts apply to Abraham's descendants, specifically through Jacob, whom He named Israel. So we, the Israelites, will have our own land and countless descendants. It is the third part that involves you."

"How could it involve me?" Iset asked. "I'm not a Hebrew."

"God, in His infinite grace, promised blessings on the peoples of the whole world through Father Abraham and us, his descendants. That means that you, an Egyptian, will be blessed through your relationship to us. You too can have the same peace that we have by trusting in the One True God and His promise to you through Abraham and His people."

"You must help me understand what that has to do with the plagues." Iset glanced to Rachel for support. "The plagues are not a blessing to our people but a curse. Where does this blessing come from?"

"I'll try to explain," Rachel began. "We have clung to God's promise of a land for many centuries because we believe that God always keeps

His promises. To reach our Promised Land we must have a deliverer or redeemer to take us from bondage to the special land reserved for us. You know that place as the land of the Canaanites. Somehow, and this requires a miracle, God will take us from Egypt to Canaan, clear out the inhabitants and other tribes, and settle us and our children where the land flows with milk and honey."

"And the plagues?"

"The plagues coincide with the arrival of a man named Moses, born a Hebrew but raised years ago in the household of Thutmose II. We believe that Moses is that deliverer who will take us out of Egypt to the land God promised to us. The terrible plagues are the result of Pharaoh's refusal to let us go to serve our God. Until he allows all Hebrews to worship in the desert, the plagues will only continue and grow worse."

"Why have I not heard of this before? Why has the Great One or his priests not told us of this?" That the plagues were punishment on all the people of Egypt because of Pharaoh's stubborn refusal explained the almost total collapse of peace and tranquility in the land.

"But you suffered from some of the plagues too." Iset observed

"Yes," replied Ben-Judah, "but they were minor compared to the added burdens inflicted on Hebrew slaves working for Pharaoh in the brick factories of Giza and Karnak, in the granite quarries of Aswan, and on the farms in Goshen's deltas. The brutality meted out against our people has been doubled in recent months. Yet we have hope because this means that our deliverance is drawing closer. I believe that soon we will be leaving Egypt for the Promised Land."

"I must think about this more," Iset said and stood to leave. "This news overwhelms me. I envy your peace of mind and confidence in your God in the face of suffering, but I still don't see how this involves me."

"Before you leave, allow me to give you something to meditate on when you sit in your garden each morning." She wondered at his knowledge of her daily routine. "If you wish to have the peace and confidence that true Hebrews have from God, there is something you can do."

"What is that?"

"If you truly believe in the God of Abraham, then come with us when we depart for the Promised Land. It can be your land too."

The blind rabbi couldn't see Iset's shock at what he said but he sensed her fear. She rushed out the door without another word and climbed into the waiting chariot. Rachel followed her and stood next to Reuben who assumed that the lady of Lotus House wanted to return home. None of the occupants of the chariot spoke during the brief journey. Iset alighted from the vehicle as soon as it stopped and ran through the front gate of her home. A sideways glance at the family altar brought her to a sudden stop. The grim, black jackal was gone—a pink lotus flower lay open in its place.

CHAPTER 18

Luxor West Bank, Lotus House

By the time Malik and Sarina awoke late in the morning, their parents had left for the day. This was nothing new. The plagues in the land disturbed Hatep because the vast wealth of his estate was at risk. Maybe it threatened his architectural work in the Great Place as well, though his children couldn't understand how. Their mother was probably upset for a similar reason: the security and comfort that she and her family enjoyed at Lotus House was threatened by a powerful, invisible force. It was difficult for Malik and his sister, maybe because of their age and upbringing in a wealthy Egyptian household, to appreciate the ingrained national trait of maintaining *ma'at* at all cost. The divine Great One, chosen and guided by the gods, was responsible for the stability, tranquility, and prosperity in The Two Lands. Yet an old Israelite and his brother could counteract Egypt's gods and shake the foundation of the greatest nation on earth.

When Nathan joined the brother and sister at Sarina's usual post on the roof, he found them in a discussion about the messages flowing back and forth over the network.

Nathan jumped into the conversation with Sarina. "Something new?" he asked.

"Not really," Sarina answered as he sat down next to her and looked at the notes in her delicate script spread across the table before them. "Just reports of lost herds across the country. What's unusual is the volume of message traffic on the net. It's been literally nonstop since the plague began. Instead of writing down each message, which was impossible, I've compiled brief notes. For example, every province was devastated at the exact same time and only Egyptian livestock were stricken. Just as Moses predicted, Hebrew animals were not affected. If a slave's animals were later confiscated by their Egyptian masters, those died too."

"Was it only the farm animals?" Malik asked.

"No, it was every type of domesticated animal. In addition to temple herds for sacrifices and palace herds used to feed the royal family and court, Pharaoh's prize horses died immediately. One message said that he *walked* from the palace to the river for his morning bath instead of taking his royal chariot—imagine that!"

"Does that mean the Leopard Charioteers lost their horses too?"

"I'm afraid so. I saw a report from General Herihor that his troops have begun digging a mass grave for hundreds of their war horses. He must be heartbroken. On top of that, his troops have no meat to eat and are living from their grain stores, as is the rest of Karnak and Thebes."

"That's probably sensitive military information," Nathan observed. "The Amun Corps would be hard pressed to defend against another attack by the Nubians without chariots. Did General Herihor say anything about what he's doing about it?"

"Vizier Nakhte authorized funds for the Amun Corps to purchase horses from Canaan and Put as quickly as possible, but it will take time to replenish their stables and then more time to train new war horses. A report from a newly arrived caravan said that animals outside Egypt did not die. That further confirms that it was limited only to our country."

"Is there anything else?" Malik asked his sister. It seemed she had put together a comprehensive picture of the plague's devastation of their country. He could not imagine a worse disaster.

"The economic effects will reverberate for decades. Every province reports heavy losses and asks Pharaoh to help them. So far, he hasn't answered." Sarina set her notes down and gazed across the river at the helio tower in Waset that had not stopped flashing since sunrise. She had not bothered to follow any of the traffic during their conversation. "There are some things that bother me more than the economic loss of livestock and the crippling of the army. There are things going on inside the palace that few people know about." She paused to choose her words carefully.

"Like what?" her brother asked impatiently. "Maybe it's just gossip and not true."

Nathan held his hand up to stop Malik from interrupting. Sarina was visibly shaken and would tell them in her own time.

"None of this is from official messages. The helio operators in the palace chat back and forth with Hakamun and Elias in the Great Place Valley, with operators at the Karnak garrison, and the relay stations above and below Thebes. It seems that this last plague was the fifth in a series; all of them have happened after Moses and his brother Aaron confront Pharaoh to let the Israelites go into the wilderness to worship."

"My people already know that," said Nathan. "Rabbi Ben-Judah says that Moses is our redeemer and will eventually lead us to the Promised Land in Canaan."

"That's exactly what the operators have been talking about," Sarina explained. "The palace blinkers say that higher-ups in the court are worried that Pharaoh would rather see the country destroyed than give in to Moses. The palace runners reported overhearing Vizier Nakhte tell the Royal Priest of *Amun-Ra* that if the gods of Egypt cannot stop the God of the Hebrews then Pharaoh should release all the Hebrew slaves."

"The *LORD* cannot be stopped!" Nathan blurted. He surprised even himself with the outburst. "What I mean is that Pharaoh won't be able to stop Moses; the plagues are bound to continue until my people are let go." He expected his Egyptian friends to defend their deified leader.

"I agree," Malik said.

"Me too," Sarina added.

"So what can we do?" Malik asked his friend. "Things look grim for Egyptians if the plagues continue. I suspect life for Israelite slaves will get worse too. The slaves are already being blamed for everything bad that happens. They always are."

"Oh, I forgot," Sarina added. "Yesterday, the vizier ordered the army on alert to put down a slave revolt which he said could arise at any moment in support of Moses' demands. There's been no evidence of such a rebellion, of course, so it looks like the palace is preparing a scapegoat in case things take a turn for the worst."

"You asked me what I think we can do, so let me tell you my plan." The germ of an idea had been in Nathan's mind for days. "The national helio network could give both Israelites and Egyptians some advance warning of another plague in the future. Better yet, it could be used to tell the truth about their source and why the plagues persist. Only a handful of people outside the royal inner circle know the connection between Moses' demands and Pharaoh's refusals, and the fact that the plagues are from the *LORD*. Almost everyone in Egypt believes the royal propaganda about the plagues. What if an alert or warning message were sent on the helio net as soon as Moses predicts the next plague from God? It could tell them the nature of the plague and the reason for it."

"At least it would be the truth instead of a palace lie," Malik said. "Even if the destruction were unavoidable, it couldn't hurt for people to know that is was Moses the Hebrew, or rather your God, who continues to bring the plagues because of Pharaoh's stubbornness."

Sarina shook her head. "What you're saying is *treason*! Anyone speaking against the Great One like that could be imprisoned or executed."

Nathan thought that the benefits of more information outweighed the risks. "Even the vizier and the royal priest seem to be thinking along those lines. Your point is well-taken, though. Think of it this way: If Egyptians knew the truth, they'd be less likely to turn on the Israelites and blame them for what's happening. They would learn that Pharaoh is the one ultimately responsible for these plagues continuing."

"I agree with Sarina's reluctance but also see what you mean," Malik said. "It would help if both Egyptians and Israelites knew what was said between Moses and Pharaoh so they could decide for themselves and take precautionary action, if that were even possible."

Nathan leaned forward to further outline how everyone in The Two Lands, from Aswan to Goshen, Egyptian and Hebrew, could learn how the God of Abraham was dealing with the world's most powerful leader. They were in agreement that they needed to share the plan with Hakamun and Elias as soon as possible. As the three friends discussed the pros and cons of Nathan's suggestion further, they had no way of knowing that his idea would impact millions of lives.

Great Place Valley, Heliographic Tower

Mild apprehension tempered her excitement when Sarina accompanied her brother and Nathan to the Great Place Valley helio tower to meet with Hakamun and Elias the next morning. Although confident in her scribal and numerical skills, she was shy with strangers and she was still unknown to the two professional heliographers. Sarina knew about them from eavesdropping on their chats with other operators. She hoped that the two would recognize her unique abilities and accept her as a near-equal.

"Welcome, my friends!" smiled Hakamun as the three stepped from the ladder onto the helio platform. He beamed brighter when he saw a woman close to his own age with his two friends.

"This is my sister, Sarina," Malik said as the two exchanged formal bows. Elias waved to them from the machine where he sat transmitting a message.

Hakamun led Sarina on a tour of the station's sparse administrative accommodations where the gleaming copper heliograph dominated the platform. His description of the machine's operation was superficial since he assumed that Malik's sister was here as a mere courtesy to *Amkhu* Hatep. While the tour continued, Elias concentrated on his transmission. Malik and Nathan waited for the operators' reactions when Sarina finally told them what she knew.

"I've wanted to see an actual heliograph for the longest time," she said admiringly. "Seeing Elias operate it in-person explains the different signaling patterns used by the different operators. I always suspected that…"

"What did you say?" Hakamun exclaimed. Elias overheard this and slowed in the middle of his message. He sent a quick sequence to mark a pause before he turned around to listen.

Sarina gave them both an innocent, charming smile. "Look across at the palace tower in the distance and then down to the large estate on the West Bank directly in line with it. That's where my family lives. From my rooftop I can see both towers and read your messages. I've been doing that for months." She had agreed beforehand to make no mention of the enciphered message.

"I don't believe it," Elias blurted. "I mean…sorry, Miss, it's just that only certified operators can do that."

"Well, that isn't the case, is it? I taught myself how to read the codes." Sarina stopped when she saw Hakamun's jaw drop. "I apologize for making your signaling sound trivial. That was not my intention."

"My sister is actually being modest," injected Malik. "She graduated from the Mittani Scribal School at the top of her class. She noticed your helio signals from our rooftop one day and figured out the code by herself. If I know my sister, she can probably sight-read signals as well as either of you."

"My buddy in the palace is getting impatient with my pause," said Elias. He gestured toward the distant tower. "Can you tell me what he's saying?"

Sarina glanced at the spot of light and repeated: "'*Will you hurry up and finish so I can go to lunch?*' That looks like Ventiu's hand, I think."

"How did you know it was Ventiu?" Elias was incredulous.

"First of all, he's new and doesn't blink very fast. Second, and this is what I meant about realizing something after seeing the heliograph; I suspect that Ventiu is naturally left-handed and Imhotep invented the helio machines with right-handed levers. There's a certain hesitation when Ventiu sends complex characters using his right hand." Sarina looked to see if these observations made sense. "And each of you has your own characteristic signature when you transmit. But you probably already knew that."

"I'm more than impressed," Hakamun exclaimed. "I'm overwhelmed! Nobody's ever heard of a girl—sorry, a woman—helio operator. Wow, and to think that you're Malik's sister too."

"Hey, what's that supposed to mean?" Malik bristled.

"I'm just kidding, my friend. There must be some reason why you brought her with you besides to embarrass us," the Egyptian operator said. Sarina blushed.

"Nathan has a proposal for you in light of messages coming out of the palace about the plagues. We think the helio network could be used to save lives if or when there's another plague."

They waited for Elias to finish sending his message, much to the relief of his counterpart at the palace who was impatient with his many pauses, so they could all talk. The five gathered under the awning to go over Nathan's idea. Their discussion went on well past the operator's lunch break but they seemed unconcerned. When they finished, they had agreed to spread word of a coming plague up and down the length of the country using helio signaling.

"So," summarized Hakamun, "I'll personally visit my counterpart in the palace tomorrow and get his agreement to initiate an informal 'plague bulletin' to blinkers at all sites if he learns of another disaster threatened by this man Moses. I don't foresee any problem doing that because we've already talked about how Pharaoh and his court seemed to know about the plagues in advance. I'll stress the need to send short, unofficial bulletins as soon as they have something to report. If operators are prepared ahead of time, a short message could theoretically be relayed to the farthest stations of Egypt in two hours or less."

"That ought to be enough time to warn everyone unless a plague comes without warning. Oh, and one more thing," Nathan reminded the group. "Once a station receives a plague bulletin and relays it to the other stations it must also pass the word to all the Egyptians and Israelites in the towns and villages around the station, although how they do that will be different for every location. We'll depend on the operators' initiative and local contacts to spread this information as quickly and widely as they can. That's all we can do from here."

"When do you think the next plague will hit?" Elias asked.

"My friend, that is in God's sovereign hands," Nathan said. "It could come at any time."

CHAPTER 19

Luxor West Bank, Lotus House

Lotus House was jolted the next day without warning by a plague that hit every other Egyptian household—from sprawling estates to the Great House itself. Moses unfolded a sixth demonstration of God's power to convince the ruler of The Two Lands to let the Hebrews go. Mocking the medicinal ritual of the Egyptian magicians that evoked their god *Thoth* to heal diseases using soot from a furnace, Moses threw handfuls of ashes skyward. Instead of being curative, boils instantly erupted on Pharaoh and everyone in his court; magicians could not even heal themselves. The fine ashes mysteriously spread in the air. Cries of agony rippled through the palace as the disease flared and covered every Egyptian with oozing sores from head to toe. Within minutes, ashes miraculously dispersed over the entire countryside where they contaminated Egyptians and any of their remaining livestock; the Hebrews and their animals were spared the aching misery of God's latest demonstration of His power.

Hatep's family was fortunate to have devoted Hebrew slaves to care for them and their livestock during their illness. This appreciation was replicated in only a few other Egyptian households. At Lotus House it was an opportunity for Rachel to again share her faith in the God of Abraham while she made the family as comfortable as possible. Hatep suffered silently while anger toward the impotent gods of his forefathers churned inside him. Malik and Sarina were touched by the soothing care they received from other household slaves.

After five days, the itching sores dried only to be replaced with painful, open wounds. Traditional ointments helped somewhat, but it was another five days before boils on the soles of their feet were healed enough for them to walk. Slaves brought pillows to Malik and Sarina in the small courtyard where Nathan could speak with them about the latest helio intercepts in private. He pulled a small scroll from his pocket to read from the notes that Elias sent packaged with a stack of official communiques addressed to Hatep.

"When the boils started, the Great Place blinkers sent a short message to all sites explaining how and why they started. I'll skip the details, but Moses used handfuls of soot from a furnace which immediately infected everyone in the palace. Magicians called on *Thoth*, their god of medicine, but they were incapable of healing anyone. Other messages arrived describing how the disease started in other provinces at the same time. Someone observed that this was the first plague that actually hurt people—some even died from infections when they didn't receive proper care."

"And your people were not affected?" Malik asked.

"That's correct. That too was confirmed by many helio stations."

"Well, our family is grateful for all that your mother and father, and the other slaves, have done for us," Sarina said.

"Our people look forward to following Moses one day to the Promised Land. That day will be soon, I'm sure." Nathan's tone turned serious. "You two are like a brother and sister to me. It would break my heart to leave Egypt without you. If only..." In the silence that followed, Malik and Sarina glanced at Thebes in the distance across the river. Malik broke the silence.

"What else did you hear? Did Elias take over at the Great Place Valley station when, I assume, Hakamun got sick?"

"Hakamun was cared for in the Artisans' Village while Elias continued operations. Actually, there's been little official traffic on the net today except for chatter among the Hebrew operators up and down the line. One official matter did come up that caused a bit of a commotion."

"Did it have to do with General Herihor?" Sarina asked.

"Yes, how did you know?"

"Just a guess," she answered as she shifted on her pillows to find a more comfortable position. "I thought of him and how his entire army must be bedridden. He must be very concerned for his men."

"I heard from Elias a few days ago that the vizier asked the general about the readiness status of the Amun Corps. It's not like they couldn't have guessed what it was. Maybe they hoped the army was somehow immune."

"Was the general able to answer? Is he all right?"

"I assume it was painful for him just like everyone else. The Amun Corps is completely out of commission. They've been able to replace only a few horses by now and those became covered with the same boils as the soldiers. It was the palace's order that got everyone's attention."

"What order could the palace possibly give to the army under these circumstances? If they felt anything like I did until a few days ago, they couldn't get out of bed!" Malik observed.

"Pharaoh and his top advisors are paranoid about the plagues tearing the country apart. They ordered the Amun Corps put on battle alert—I know that doesn't make sense—for an imminent slave rebellion. They must be in a panic about not having any military defense against a possible insurrection or a Nubian or Libyan attack."

"Did the general respond to the order?" Sarina asked.

Malik was puzzled by his sister's interest the army general.

"Nothing more from him," Nathan continued. "Informal evidence, coming from Hebrew helio operators of course, suggests that the country has been relatively quiet. There are reports of a few slaves caring for their masters." Nathan wanted to explain why this was happening. "You know, my people don't hate Egyptians."

"You're probably right. I suppose if Hebrew slaves wanted to escape to their promised land," Malik speculated, "this would have been a good time to do it; steal whatever they wanted while their masters were bedridden, head for the Eastern Desert, and be at the Red Sea in a few days."

"Israelite slaves have been subjugated and mistreated in Egypt for centuries. If it was me, I'd hate my oppressors with a passion," Sarina confessed.

"I'll admit that some Hebrew slaves probably do hate Egyptians, but I'll also be the first to admit that it's easy to care for Egyptians when they treat you well, like your family has treated us. Many children of Abraham live for a better hope that rests in the *LORD's* promises for the future and not in daily circumstances. It's not a matter of escaping slavery but of being led by God and His servant, Moses, to worship the *LORD*."

"I've heard recently that Moses once killed an Egyptian taskmaster. If your people follow him, why couldn't they rationalize doing the same?" Malik asked.

"That was forty years ago. I'm sure he now regrets doing that. Something life-changing happened to him in Midian and he's learned to trust the *LORD* of Hosts to do the fighting for him."

"I was wondering..." Sarina said in a voice that could scarcely be heard above the background of the bubbling fountain and waving palms, "I was wondering if your God would allow Egyptians like us to go to the Promised Land too. Is that possible?"

Nathan's heart pounded with excitement when he heard her question. He was quick to answer: "God promised that through Abraham and his Hebrew descendants all nations will be blessed. The God of Abraham, Isaac, and Jacob welcomes all who call upon His name. Yes, Sarina, the Promised Land is a place for Israel's descendants and for all those who trust in *Jehovah*."

City of Thebes, Hezbak's Apartment

The plague of boils kept Second Auditor Hezbak bedridden in his run-down apartment for a week. Like all other Egyptians, when the dry scabs appeared, his recovery was uncomfortable and slow. Hebrew slaves were unaffected by the disease that struck its Egyptian victims with a sudden fever and then covered them in burning, painful pustules. As Malik had observed, it was curious that the slaves did not seize the opportunity to add further affliction on their masters when they easily could have done so.

A one-time informant of Hezbak's was a runaway Hebrew slave who lived in a hovel next to the former inspector's apartment. The slave offered to take care of him and accepted a few coins to buy food when the Egyptian could barely lift his head. Still exhausted from his sickness, he tried to remember the slave's name but drew a blank.

Before the plague struck, Hezbak had interrogated his usual contacts in the alleys of Thebes' aromatic food shacks, rowdy wineries, and dank tenements. He dug for any information about stolen items of expensive furniture or jewelry passing through the bazaars. The picture that emerged after bits of intelligence were pieced together was that a consignment of priceless articles had been split into two shipments:

one sent west by caravan across the Red Lands to Libya and another by
boat downriver to Mitannia. Shippers assumed that their cargos were
destined for royal families who could afford such expensive treasures. A
few items, such as the table and necklace that some recognized from the
drawings, were probably skimmed from the shipments, passed through
multiple hands, and sold by merchants in Thebes who knew nothing
of their origin.

A prosperous coppersmith who was rumored to melt gold on the
side was identified but had not yet been interrogated when Hezbak took
ill. At least he confirmed that the items purchased by Iset were taken
from a larger shipment that was probably already melted down or sent
out of the country.

Now, more than two weeks later and almost recovered from the
boils, Hezbak was ready to resume his investigation. He'd had time to lie
in bed without interruption and think while the scabs healed. He wasn't
self-conscious of the dark red marks on his face and hands because every
Egyptian had them. When he sat up wide-eyed one night, the thought
flashed through his mind of what would happen if his inquiries about
stolen treasure found their way to the Black Falcon. Discrete questions
and a heightened vigilance should have been watchwords from the start.
Only now they were a matter of life and death and he scolded himself
for thinking like a petty-theft policeman and forgetting the tradecraft
of a high-profile homicide investigator. Would the Black Falcon seek
him out if he came too close to discovering the mastermind's identity?
Probably. Better yet, would word of a formal Medjay inquiry force the
Black Falcon to quash the charges or make a mistake? Trickery that
brought an adversary out into the open was more like the tactics he'd
used throughout his police career to capture criminal deviants of the
Theban underworld. He was looking for someone high up in the palace
this time. That meant that they would use subtle and deadly tactics to
silence him before he brought them to light.

Another idea popped into his mind as it raced through different
ways he might die if this investigation came too close to his quarry. He
could ask royal permission to unseal the tomb of Queen Hatshepsut
and examine its contents. Even the suggestion of such a petition would
circulate inside the palace and surely come to the attention of the
Black Falcon. Hezbak would have to bring the Chief Medjay into his
confidence, only partially, of course, and convince him to schedule an

audience with Vizier Nakhte. Yes, petitioning the vizier to unseal the queen's tomb would be like illuminating a dark room with a flaming brand to expose the cockroaches. His job would be to find one cockroach before it escaped or turned on him.

Karnak, Military Garrison—General Herihor's Quarters

Like any professional military leader, General Herihor's concern for his men's welfare was strained to the limit by reports from the barracks that his entire corps was bed-ridden by the plague of boils. Whether off duty in the garrison, conducting unit training in the field, or on leave in the city, all soldiers became feverish at the same time and returned to the Karnak barracks for medical help. By the end of the day, covered with painful boils, every soldier in the Amun Corps was incapacitated. In fact, the corps was less than useless as a defensive force; it was a national security liability.

Nobody appreciated this military vulnerability more than the corps commander who brooded in his darkened private quarters. His windows were shuttered and doors locked. He ordered Khan, his personal aide, to leave him alone.

The plague had no effect on him. After hours of mental turmoil, he reached one inevitable conclusion: he must be Hebrew by birth and not Egyptian. This horrible disease infected every Egyptian in his Amun Corps, yet the Hebrew slaves were untouched. His heritage would be apparent to anyone who saw him. Khan had been stunned to see him healthy and pacing back and forth in his room. Swearing loyalty to his general, Khan left him to himself and wondered what this could mean.

The exchange of corps readiness messages with the palace actually worked to mask his true condition. It seemed best for now to let them assume that his health was no different from every other Egyptian. Speculation about what would happen to him if the palace discovered his Hebrew birth haunted him through the night: immediate discharge from the army, public humiliation, imprisonment, and either exile to the granite quarries or execution for treason. The implications were terrifying.

For now, he'd fulfill the obligations of an Egyptian general even though he'd already begun to think of himself as an Egyptian-Israelite with conflicting doubts and allegiances. What a contradiction this was: a Hebrew general in Pharaoh's army!

CHAPTER 20

City of Thebes, Medjay Headquarters

"You must be out of your mind!" The disagreeable Chief Medjay was perspiring heavily before Hezbak could answer him. Second Auditor Hezbak was mostly healed of the boils and in this meeting with his boss he omitted saying that it was General Herihor who had started him on this investigation; he said that he had received a tip about a royal tomb robbery and confirmed it with reliable informants. He didn't mention that he suspected someone in the palace who called himself the Black Falcon–that would only complicate matters. It would be best if his superior knew as little of the background as possible.

Second Auditor Hezbak, demoted from Chief Inspector in the Homicide Division and assigned to humiliating duty on the Robbery Squad, had nothing to lose by putting the burden on the chief's shoulders to make a decision. "Wouldn't the Great One want to avenge his mother's memory if the thieves could be apprehended and the treasure returned?"

"I could explain it that way, of course," the chief admitted. "Do you really think he'd give his approval to open the tomb?"

"If the tomb was plundered and you caught the thieves, I'm certain that the Great One would make you Minister of Justice!"

The Medjay chief's eyes gleamed with interest. He summoned his scribe and a courier to carry a request to the palace for an immediate audience with the Vizier. He would stress the importance of the meeting without revealing its purpose. Before Hezbak departed, he had one final request of his chief.

"I respectfully ask that I be allowed to accompany you."

"Remember your inferior position! Your presence is no longer necessary. You are no longer a Chief Inspector, but a Second Auditor. Return to your duties in the Robbery Squad and I'll take the investigation from here."

"Again, with respect, I think it would be helpful in case the Vizier has questions. All of this hinges on the credibility of my secret informants. It would be disastrous if your request were denied because you couldn't explain details about the evidence."

"Very well, but don't speak unless spoken to directly. Remember your inferior position!"

Waset, Great House Palace—Vizier Nakhte's Reception Room

Scribe Gobe ushered the two Medjay representatives into the Vizier's official reception chamber and closed the doors for their private meeting. Within minutes, it was apparent to Vizier Nakhte that the Chief Medjay was a buffoon. He fumbled through the rationale for unsealing Queen Hatshepsut's subterranean resting place. The supreme administrator of the kingdom directed his stony gaze at the ill-dressed man standing to the side while the Chief Medjay babbled on without noticing that he was being ignored.

"Who is that man?" the Vizier interrupted. "Why did you not introduce him to me?"

"Him? He is a Second Auditor on the Robbery Squad—a man of no official consequence. He is only here to answer any questions in the unlikely event that I cannot answer them." The chief was perturbed that his practiced monologue was sidetracked.

"Does this man of *no official consequence* have a name?"

The Second Auditor broke his silence: "The name is Hezbak, sir."

Nakhte beckoned him to come forward. He bowed before the vizier who was reclined on an upholstered couch.

"Now, how did all this come about and what questions am I supposed to ask that only you can answer?" He stared at the Chief Medjay while he directed his request to Hezbak.

The demoted inspector used this opening to review the highlights of his investigation but omitted the letter from General Herihor and skipped any mention of Nathan, Malik, and Sarina. He referred only to "confidential informants" and stressed the need to verify the robbery immediately and pursue the caravans to recover the treasure. He watched the vizier's eyes during his account for a reaction, especially noting his pupil dilation for indication of surprise, anxiety, or fear. He saw none of these. The Vizier was a good master of his emotions.

Hezbak mentioned that other royal tombs had been plundered in centuries past; the culprits were apprehended within days because evidence of their break-in through the main tomb entrance was in plain view. In this instance, a tomb was supposedly robbed without leaving outward evidence. Queen Hatshepsut's tomb *had* to be unsealed and inspected.

Anticipating another objection, he stated that Pharaoh might see opening the tomb as sacrilege against the memory of Queen Hatshepsut and a personal insult against himself and his family. To that objection, he noted that there was precedent in Egypt's ancient religious traditions for re-entering the sacred tomb of a dead Pharaoh if the royal priest did so with proper ceremony and solemnity. The real risk was a palace scandal if Queen Hatshepsut's treasures were found intact. Her eternal resting place would have been violated for no reason.

"Your Excellency, if there has been a theft of *national treasures* that rightfully belong to Queen Hatshepsut and our Pharaoh's family, then the Great One would surely want to correct this unspeakable injustice."

"Of course," Vizier Nakhte agreed as he sat up and leaned toward his visitor. "I am no expert on police work, but it sounds like your investigation has been exceptionally thorough and professional. I have just one more question." He turned his attention to the Chief Medjay.

"You said Second Auditor Hezbak is a mere policeman of no official significance and yet he is clearly an intelligent person with much ability and experience. Why is he only a Second Auditor?"

Hezbak suppressed a smile at his superior's discomfort. The vizier was an exceptional judge of character who came to his position of power by shrewd insight and not by birthright. Unlike the Great One who inherited his authority, Nakhte rose to Pharaoh's side in The Two Lands by, among other skills, possessing an uncanny ability to discern truth and deception. Far from infallible, he was correct much of the time and confident that most of what Hezbak told him was true.

"This man is a Second Auditor as punishment for insolence and disobedience. He refused to obey my direct command in an investigation that resulted in great embarrassment for the Medjay force. Besides, he has refused to apologize to me." The Chief's firm jaw accented his personal indignation. The vizier saw his pettiness for what it was.

Redirecting his attention back to Hezbak, he smiled. "What was your position before this demotion?"

"I was a Chief Inspector with gold credentials in the Medjay's Theban Homicide Division for almost thirty years, sir."

"Now I remember you! I've seen you testify before the Royal Prosecutor in a number of trials," Nakhte admitted. "Your meticulous gathering of evidence and faultless logic have sent many guilty murderers into the vicious jaws of *Anubis.*"

The turn of events caused Hezbak to give an inner sigh of relief. This could only mean that the queen's tomb would be unsealed and the horrific desecration finally exposed! His euphoria lasted for a few seconds.

"I refuse your request to open the tomb of Queen Hatshepsut. In a refreshing way, I find you to be a man of integrity, reputation and ability in your area of expertise, Inspector Hezbak. Thus, I will tell you my reasons: the Great One is still weak from the outbreak of boils and too frail to handle the emotional strain of seeing his step-mother's tomb unsealed; it may be weeks before I could bring up this sensitive subject. In light of that, the treasure, if it was indeed stolen, would be in Libya or Mitannia by then anyway and it would take an act of war to retrieve it; I will *not* take our country to war based on the testimony of your informants."

"I... I don't understand what you mean, sir." The confused Chief Medjay spoke in a cracking voice.

"Inspector Hezbak understands, don't you?" the vizier observed.

"I do, sir. You require irrefutable evidence of a theft that you can take to the Great One when he is well enough to receive it. With your permission, I can uncover such evidence." Hezbak was elated that the investigation could continue. After all, his plan did not require that the tomb actually be unsealed. The *threat* of it being unsealed was sufficient to force the Black Falcon to make the next move.

"I'm curious," the Vizier said. "Why have you not mentioned the need to identify the thieves who stole the royal treasure and bring them to justice? That would seem to be your highest priority—more important than recovering the treasure itself. Do you know who they are?"

Hezbak stared into Vizier Nakhte's eyes without blinking. The penetrating look communicated much between the two men. They both understood that the thief would be a highly placed official who was yet to be exposed. It would take guile to flush him out into the open.

The Chief Medjay was bewildered by what was left unsaid. The Vizier turned to the chief who had been ignored for most of their visit.

"Chief Medjay, you will reinstate this man today to his former rank of Chief Inspector with gold credentials. He will report to me, through you, when he has incontrovertible evidence of a royal robbery. Do you understand?"

"Incontrovertible evidence. Yes sir, we will get it."

"*Chief Inspector* Hezbak will be given every Medjay resource he needs—no questions asked. Is that understood? You and he will report back to me when you have the evidence."

"Yes sir. Incontrovertible evidence. Everything he needs. Report back to you." The rattled Chief Medjay's tunic was drenched with nervous perspiration.

"May the gods of The Two Lands be with you, Chief Inspector Hezbak."

Hezbak left the palace with the Chief Medjay wondering quietly if Vizier Nakhte really believed that the gods of Egypt retained any influence in The Two Lands.

City of Thebes, Medjay Headquarters

The next day, Inspector Hezbak sent a three-man digging crew to excavate the well near Queen Hatshepsut's tomb to uncover the tunnel that Malik and Nathan described. While Hezbak waited to hear from the crew, he walked around the city inquiring about the coppersmith rumored to have melted large quantities of gold. By the end of the day he had nothing new to lead him to the man's identity or his location in the city; at least now he learned that there were scores of coppersmiths around Thebes who melted gold on the side. He returned to his former office at Medjay headquarters that was luxurious compared to his dirty corner in the Robbery Squad room. He came across one of the diggers slumped in a hallway chair opposite his office wearing nothing but a tattered loincloth smeared with red clay and dried blood. He was badly beaten and needed medical attention.

"Why weren't this man's wounds attended to?" Hezbak shouted for his assistant. "Call a doctor immediately!"

"Sir, I told them not to call anyone until I reported to you," the digger's voice strained. He supported a bloody arm with his opposite hand and grimaced in pain. One eye was caked with blood.

"We'll get you help right away. In the meantime, tell me what happened."

"The other two diggers are dead. We were jumped by four stone workers while we shoveled out the well just like you instructed us and hauled the dirt and rocks out of the hole in baskets. We'd only gone down about eight feet when the man on the surface was grabbed from behind and his head was bashed in. When the other digger and I climbed out of the well to see what had happened, we were surrounded. They moved in swinging heavy clubs and even though we had tools to defend ourselves, we didn't stand a chance. I don't remember how I got away, but I assume the other digger is dead. We hadn't been there an hour before they showed up. I'm sorry."

"Don't be sorry. This is my fault for not realizing the danger involved. I should have sent you with Medjay protection. Here's Physician Meketre now." Hezbak stepped aside so the doctor could attend to the wounded worker. Now Hezbak's investigation was forced to change direction.

He called for his assistant to have a horse slave bring the inspector's official chariot around to the front entrance of headquarters. No longer did he ride bareback on a worn-out nag; the sleek pursuit chariot and fresh horse made excellent time. When he crossed the river to the Great Place Valley where the well was supposed to be, he found that the stone structure had completely vanished and the clearing, or what should have been the clearing, was nothing but packed dirt covered with scuffed footprints and dried brush. All trace of a well had been obliterated.

Upon Inspector Hezbak's return to headquarters in early evening, the pained look on the face of his assistant waiting for him at the main entrance elicited a groan. He handed the reins of his chariot to a horse slave. His assistant met him halfway down the steps.

"What is it?"

"It's the Chief. He wants to see you. Now!"

"About what?"

"He didn't say. A palace courier delivered a confidential message to him after you left and when he read it he called for you right away. I told him you were out on a case."

"Very well, I suppose I'll find out in a few minutes. First, I'm going to wash up in my office. He can wait for me to clean off the road dust." Hezbak splashed his face, neck and arms from a basin of water in his office, dried them with a towel and put on a fresh tunic and headdress. He might as well look calm and refreshed. Call it police intuition, but he expected this meeting to be unpleasant. Maybe Pharaoh had approved his request to unseal the tomb and this would be the break he needed, but he doubted it.

"Where have you been? You certainly took your time getting here," the chief complained when Hezbak was announced into his office. "You returned twenty minutes ago. I gave instructions for you to come here immediately."

"I thought it best to clean up first. I apologize for the delay." He would keep his whereabouts to himself. No sense in making the chief mad before he found out what this was about.

His superior held up a folded sheet of bleached white papyrus with royal blue and gold trim. "This instruction from the Great House is marked SECRET. You can read it later but it orders you to stop your current investigation. You are to open a new investigation into the plagues and the Hebrew unrest. Begin by finding out how all our countrymen were infected at precisely the same time by this recent infestation, why the Hebrews were immune to the disease, and ask the physicians for an antidote in case the disease returns. There must be some reason why not one Hebrew was stricken and every Egyptian was infected. Also, you will use your network of informants to learn about a rumored Hebrew rebellion, when it will happen, and what the army and Medjay can do to subvert their plans. The palace demands regular updates on your progress."

This reversal of Vizier Nakhte's instructions from two days ago sounded peculiar. "Is the Vizier's seal on the order?" Inspector Hezbak asked, suspecting a forgery or some deception.

"No, but it's on palace stationary and marked SECRET," the chief answered with irritation. "It *must* be from the Vizier."

"What about my reports? Are they to be sent only to the Vizier?" The whole thing smelled suspicious.

"One palace courier, mentioned by name in the order, will be summoned. I assume he will take your report to the Vizier to maintain absolute secrecy. The orders are very clear about that." The officious Chief Medjay saw nothing amiss in the instructions and Hezbak's questions only irritated him further. "Come back in a week and we'll send our report." He shoved the sheet of gleaming royal papyrus at the inspector and dismissed him with a grunt. The interview was over. There was no use arguing with the Chief, so the inspector returned to his office.

The palace order changing everything must be the work of the Black Falcon, he reasoned on the way back to his office. This was not the break in the case that he expected. Inspector Hezbak was almost certain that the Vizier was not the mastermind behind the tomb robberies. No doubt the one he was looking for had access to royal stationary and the palace courier system. It made no sense for the Vizier to give him explicit directions in their face-to-face meeting and then two days later send thugs to cut off his search for the tunnel entrance by attacking his investigators and then reversing his orders. He could have easily instructed him from the beginning to not pursue the robbery. Hezbak concluded that someone, either the Black Falcon or an accomplice, sealed this new order with the Vizier's cartouche. In fact, as he read the exact wording on the fine papyrus, there was no reference to the tomb robbery; simply a mention of his "ongoing investigation" and nothing about his meeting with the Vizier, which led him to believe that the writer did not know all the details of the meeting or of Hezbak's exact assignment.

For the sake of appearances, he would begin a superficial investigation into the plague of boils and the supposed Hebrew rebellion, although he believed the rumor of a slave revolt to be a desperate fabrication. While his team of investigators interviewed Medjay informants about the supposed revolt and the physicians examined evidence of the disease of boils, he would use this city-wide investigation to mask further inquiries into the whereabouts of the elusive coppersmith—his only other lead for now.

CHAPTER 21

City of Thebes, Medjay Headquarters

A week of relentless, exhaustive questioning of slaves, merchants, household servants, Hebrew rabbis, and community leaders uncovered not a bit of evidence that an internal slave revolt was planned. In fact, the Israelites were patiently waiting for their God to humble Pharaoh so that their redeemer, Moses, could lead them to their promised home in Canaan. Hezbak wanted to interrogate Moses but learned that he was hiding somewhere in Goshen. His Egyptian informants also confirmed the absence of any organized, armed rebellion plans that would present a threat to the nation; some of his countrymen even speculated that the cause of the plagues might rest with Pharaoh and not with the Hebrews. He also held this view, but it would be unwise to express such an opinion openly.

Practitioners of the ancient Kemetic medical healing arts had never encountered a disease of boils like the one that swept the country, nor did they know how to cure it. One report by a Royal Physician attributed the outbreak to the displeasure of the war-god *Set*. The antidote, according to a consensus of physicians, magicians, and priests, was a jumble of spells and incantations that they admitted had proven ineffective when they first tried to cure Pharaoh. However, they urged physicians to try every variation of the traditional chants to see if any would work. Hezbak threw the useless report onto a pile of similar "expert" opinions that cluttered his desk. Nobody knew anything about a Hebrew rebellion and the plague of boils was a total mystery. His report back to the palace would be brief, but he had an idea that might open another avenue to expose the Black Falcon. He told his assistant to summon the head of the Medjay's best surveillance team.

The Chief Medjay was distracted by other active investigations. When he received Hezbak's perfunctory report he gave it only a quick reading before signing his name to it. The report said that the inquiries were ongoing, they had accumulated a wealth of testimony and evidence, and would eventually send a full report to the palace. That should buy him another couple of weeks. Hezbak left his chief's office and sent a policeman to the palace to inform the courier named in his orders that a confidential report was ready to be picked up. He would personally hand the sealed report to the palace courier.

The special courier was older than Hezbak expected, with the arrogant attitude of a courtier or high-level confidential scribe. Junior palace runners did precisely what they were told and hurried to complete their tasks—this courier swaggered into Hezbak's office. He knew he had a powerful sponsor and regarded the chief inspector with contempt.

"Deliver this to Vizier Nakhte for me," the inspector said as casually as he could manage.

There was a momentary flicker of the official messenger's eyes before he answered coldly, "I have my orders, Chief Inspector."

"Yes, I'm sure you do. Well, that will be all."

The courier's cocky attitude revealed nothing more before he gave a casual nod and departed from the office. From his window, Hezbak watched the man's sure, determined stride down the Medjay headquarters front steps and into the crowded streets of Thebes. The surveillance team would follow him without being noticed. Now that he had met the courier and sensed his devious attitude, he held little hope that the surveillance team would follow him to the Black Falcon.

What else could possibly go wrong? His adversary obviously knew that he was being pursued and his resources far exceeded those of even a top Medjay inspector. Before he allowed himself to slip into a despondent fog, he turned his attention to the only promising lead he had.

A tip from an informant led another of the inspector's surveillance teams to check out a shop that repaired copper cooking pots. An undercover policeman reported back that he found traces of gold on the shop tools when they broke in during the night before. The coppersmith was being watched from across the street until the team was ordered to bring him in for questioning. He had no idea that he was under surveillance.

Hezbak called his assistant. "Tell the team to pick the coppersmith up for questioning and make sure he's transported safely, but don't bring him here." It was likely that the Medjay headquarters building was being watched. "Take him to that Medjay station just outside the gate of the Temple of *Mut* in Karnak. They have a few holding cells there. Use my name and tell the officer on duty that the man is my prisoner and he is to be held in isolation until I arrive."

"That station is way over in Karnak, sir. Why not hold him here or closer to the city?"

"I don't want to be disturbed by the Chief, if you know what I mean," he said with a wink.

"I understand, sir. They'll take him to Karnak and wait there for you."

When his assistant left, Hezbak considered how he would conduct the questioning without revealing too much of what he already knew. It was unlikely that the tradesman personally knew the identity of the Black Falcon, but he hoped for a contact name or some new piece of information to crack his quarry's impenetrable shield. He would accuse the coppersmith of illegally melting gold, which the Medjay knew for certain that he had done, and hint at wanting a cut of his earnings as a bribe. If the man agreed too readily, then he melted gold articles for a common criminal ring. If he melted gold articles for the Black Falcon and his powerful network of thieves, then he would fear for his life. If he refused to talk, then harsher interrogation methods might be necessary.

Temples of Karnak, *Mut* Precinct

An hour later, Inspector Hezbak arrived at the *Mut* substation. He vaguely recalled having seen the duty officer behind the desk before. The officer greeted him cheerfully when he walked through the small entryway. The building was typical of small Medjay outposts sprinkled throughout Karnak and Waset. This was a visible police presence in the crowded neighborhoods with bazaars and temples where zealous religious demonstrations took place and sometimes erupted into violence. The hot afternoon lull in activity around the station meant that he and his team could question the coppersmith undisturbed.

"Good day, Chief Inspector. We have six cells here and I personally assigned your prisoner to the last cell at the back. Let me know if there is anything more you need. I have other men on duty if you require assistance." The officer in charge, like all Medjay, knew of Inspector Hezbak's reputation for solving capital crimes and prosecuting the worst criminals. If his name was mentioned in the inspector's report as helping solve an important case, he might get a promotion.

"Thank you, officer…"

"Constable, Sir. Constable Sebni."

"Well, Constable Sebni, we appreciate the use of your fine facility. No matter what you hear back there, we do not wish to be disturbed. Understood?"

"Yes sir. I and my men will remain out here." Any thought of assisting the inspector evaporated, but at least he'd given him his name and maybe he would remember it.

Down a hallway the inspector found his men playing a game of *senet* outside a substantial wooden door that led to the cell block.

"How's our prisoner?" he asked as the men rose to their feet.

"Quiet as a mouse, sir."

"Has anyone spoken to him about the case? Does he know why he's been detained?"

"No sir. We picked him up as instructed and brought him here chained between two of us in a chariot. He insisted that he was innocent," one of the guards chuckled, "but these types always say that. We gave him food and water, as you instructed."

"Food and water?"

"Three of us were on the arresting squad and the other fellow brought him food and water per your orders. He said you didn't know when you would get here for the interrogation. He took bread and a jug of water to him and then returned to headquarters about fifteen minutes ago."

"Open the door immediately!" Inspector Hezbak shouted.

The startled guard fumbled for the key and flung the door open, Hezbak raced to the far cell where the coppersmith lay face down on the floor. When the cell gate was finally unlocked, he entered and put his finger to the man's neck. No pulse. The bread was untouched on the cot.

The clay water jug was smashed on the floor next to the prisoner. The inspector knelt and sniffed a small puddle. The remaining liquid that seeped into cracks in the stone floor had a strong fruity odor. The agony of his prisoner's last seconds was unmistakable: the frozen, contorted scream on his face told of instantaneous death.

"Who was the man who brought him this?"

"He joined us at the coppersmith's shop and said you sent him as backup in case the suspect resisted. He wore a Medjay tunic and spoke like one of us. We didn't think it was necessary to see his credentials. He followed us here in a Medjay chariot," the second guard said.

"I never sent backup," Hezbak sighed. The two guards standing outside the cell looked at each other as the grim significance of their oversight sunk in. "It's not your fault men," he assured them. "I underestimated my adversary once again. I'm sure we'll never find the imposter who poisoned the prisoner." He felt lightheaded and leaned against the metal cell gate for support. "Leave everything as it is. You," he said motioning to the first guard with the keys, "lock the cell and the outer door and don't let anyone else in. And you," nodding to the second man, "take my chariot to Medjay headquarters as fast as you can and bring Physician Meketre back here to examine the body. He's a real physician and not one of those Kemetic fakes. I'll wait for your return outside. I need fresh air."

Hezbak walked unsteadily past Constable Sebni and the pale, pained look on the inspector's face concerned the duty officer. Something had unsettled the famous investigator. Hezbak struggled to clear his mind after he slumped on a bench in the shade of a date palm tree and gasped for air. He gripped the sides of the bench to stop a sudden convulsion. The pain in his chest and shoulders was paralyzing. Physician Meketre should be here soon, he thought, but even in the bright sunlight his vision was dimming into a dark blur. Soon he'd find out what the Black Falcon used to kill his prisoner. Until then, he had to stay awake...

City of Thebes, Hezbak's Apartment

"It's a wonder you didn't die." The disembodied voice said when the inspector opened his eyes for the first time in three days. "You still have plenty of fight left in you, Hezbak." The patient removed the cool cloth from his forehead and tried to sit up.

"What was it?" he rasped.

"What was what?" the voice asked.

"What poison did he use? What killed my prisoner?"

"Ah yes, the poison," Medjay Physician Meketre said with professional enthusiasm. "As best I can tell, it was probably from the gland of a puffer fish peculiar to the Phoenicians. From what I've read, it's very rare. There was so much poison in the jar that they added concentrated fruit juice to mask the bitter taste. One sip and your prisoner's heart stopped before he hit the floor. Look at what it did to you and you only sniffed the spilled liquid! You could have died from that one whiff."

"Then thank you for saving my life. I'm glad I sent for you when I did." He realized that he was in his apartment.

"I insist that you take a long rest before you return to duty, and I mean that. You had a heart attack that was induced by the poison and there's no telling how much damage was done." The Medjay doctor put his medicines and instruments in a small bag and turned to his patient.

"Before I leave, I need to know how much of this to put in my official report. A prisoner died in a Medjay outpost jail while under your authority. This is serious enough to catch the Chief's eye. We have a fine history together Hezbak, so I'll word it any way you want."

"I take full responsibility for his death. It's unfortunate because he was my only lead on a special case for the vizier. I don't want any details of the case known within the Medjay."

"The last thing I want is for my report to end up on the vizier's desk. I can be as vague as you wish."

"Just say that the prisoner was being held on suspicion of dealing in stolen artifacts and died of cardiac arrest while in custody. From what you told me, that's accurate. Be sure to say that you found no evidence of Medjay torture or other mistreatment, which is also true. Mention the excellent cooperation of Constable Sebni who bears absolutely no responsibility for the death. He must think that his career is ruined because a prisoner died in his station." Hezbak was tired from speaking and lay back in his bed. "Your report need say nothing about my 'illness' or the poison. Can you do that for me? I'll add a few details verbally when I speak with the Chief later."

The doctor nodded. "Get some rest. I'll check on you in a few days. Oh, by the way, your Hebrew slave has been inquiring about your health and offering to bring you something to eat. I told him you can eat anything that you can keep down. He sounded genuinely concerned." The physician closed the door softly on his way out.

The inspector passed through hazy rounds of sleeping, eating, and staring at the ceiling. After a week, he was well enough to sit on the rooftop in the evening and take short walks. He paid his Hebrew slave to buy and prepare more substantial food as his body recovered.

When Inspector Hezbak finally returned to Medjay headquarters two weeks later, he found that he had not been missed. He summoned the surveillance team leader that he'd assigned to follow the palace courier.

"That fellow was a slippery one. We had a full team on him—even two women—and he must have known he was being followed, though I'd stake my reputation that he didn't spot any of my team."

"I'm sure he didn't see them. Did he go to the palace?" Hezbak asked.

"We lost him before he went near the place. He used every counter-surveillance technique we've ever seen, and a few new ones. I tell you, he either *knew* he was being followed or he assumed so from the beginning and took expert measures. One minute he was in sight of three of my men and the next minute he disappeared into thin air. They searched everyone and everything in the vicinity and I tell you, he became invisible—like he'd never existed. I'm sorry."

"No apology necessary. Your team is the best and I'd use them again. I'll be sure to mention that to the Chief if he asks."

That evening, Hezbak made a pivotal decision: it was only a matter of time before the Black Falcon stopped sparring with him and struck back with deadly vengeance. So far, the criminal in the Great House palace had only managed to block Hezbak's investigation. The criminal mastermind behind the greatest tomb robbery of the century would keep turning up the heat. For his part, Hezbak was not about to give up his pursuit of justice. The gambit back and forth would continue until one of them was dead.

That night, after Hezbak bathed and ate dinner, he had a long talk with the Hebrew slave. After hours of intense inquiries he concluded that the man was genuine in his loyalty. This still puzzled the inspector since Hebrews and Egyptians were supposed to be bitter adversaries, but so be it. The mutual arrangement between them would be that of a master and paid servant. Hevel—he finally learned the tall, quiet man's name—would be compensated to take care of his master. The two would become an undercover investigative team. They would change their appearances and identities to melt silently into obscure Theban life. The search for the Black Falcon would continue.

Medjay Chief Inspector Hezbak would have to disappear to stay alive.

Mennefer (Memphis)

(c. 1446 B.C.)

Now the LORD said to Moses,
"Go in to Pharaoh; for I have hardened his heart and the hearts
of his servants, that I may show these signs of Mine before him,
and that you may tell in the hearing of your son and your son's son
the mighty things I have done in Egypt,
and My signs which I have done among them,
that you may know that I am the LORD."
So Moses and Aaron came in to Pharaoh and said to him,
"Thus says the LORD God of the Hebrews:
'How long will you refuse to humble yourself before Me?
Let My people go, that they may serve Me.

Exodus 10:1-3 (NKJV)

CHAPTER 22

Waset Great House Palace

The Black Falcon approached Pharaoh in the ruler's private courtyard where he lay recovering from the boils that almost killed him. Trusted Israelite nurses had attended to his bodily needs during his illness when Egyptian servants were also felled by the plague. Strangely, the Israelite nurses still did this while fully aware that it was Pharaoh's heart of stone that kept Moses from leading their countrymen out of Egypt. When royal Egyptian attendants became well enough, they resumed his care, but with a sense of dread that their land was descending into chaos.

"May we speak privately, Great One?" the visitor announced as he bowed before the monarch reclined on his royal couch. Pharaoh opened his eyes at the sound of the voice and focused on the supplicant before him.

"Oh, it is you. This had better be important," the tired leader stated with no emotion.

"Excellency, may I dismiss your attendants for a few moments so we may speak in private?"

Pharaoh nodded and his advisor turned with a stern look that sent the nurses, the cup bearer, the boy fanners, and two guards out of earshot.

"What is so important this time? I am weary of this sickness. When I am well, this battle with the god of the Hebrews will surely resume with renewed vigor. My Vizier and Royal Priest have assured me that this is so. Do you believe this too?" In spite of his body's weakness,

Egypt's supreme ruler set his jaw and looked at his visitor with clear, unblinking eyes.

"I do, Great One. In fact, the purpose for my visit is to suggest a way to gain victory over this Moses and his god."

"That is finally good news. I was wondering if all my advisors had turned into cowards."

His visitor was pleased that Pharaoh was open to a suggestion. "This god of the Hebrews is no different than the gods of all the other nations that you and your fathers have conquered. You crushed the kings of the Nine Bows because their gods could only defend their small plots of territory; their power diminished when they dared enter our Two Lands."

"But the Hebrews' god has shown himself to be…persistent."

"Yes, but that is because the *ma'at* of the Upper Land has been disrupted by unrest and treachery. The strength of our gods is sapped by those stiff-necked slaves; almost as if there were a curse on Thebes. If your majesty were to return his throne to the place known to the ancients as *Ankh Tawy*— Mennefer, That Which Binds The Two Lands—you would bind the upper and lower regions together once again and regain *ma'at*. Your presence in the Mennefer Palace would restore the calm and stability of times past. When you and your mother Hatshepsut held court in the palace there the land was at peace within itself, was it not?"

"That is true…" Thutmose III thought back to the palace of Mennefer where he grew up with his step-mother, Pharaoh-Queen Hatshepsut. He was tired of Waset and Karnak. He wanted nothing more than to sleep at night without having to face Moses in the morning or worry about the constant threat of a slave rebellion. On top of that, his attendants shuffled through the somber hallways expecting him to die at any moment. His wife dreamed of their son becoming Pharaoh in her lifetime, so she was in a hurry for her husband to die too. Yes, a move to Mennefer would give him a change of scenery and, maybe, it might even give the gods of Egypt a chance to overcome this *LORD* of the slaves. Deep inside, however, he knew that he'd not seen the last of Moses and his brother.

"Very well, give the order to move the Great House palace from Waset to Mennefer." The leader felt a brief moment of relief. He didn't give much thought to the displacement of five thousand officials, citizens, servants and slaves as a result of this casual decision.

"May I ask also, Excellency, for two additional orders?"

"What are they? Get to the point!" The leader was becoming annoyed by his advisor's intrusion into his quiet time. He was having difficulty keeping his eyelids open.

"The concern about a possible Hebrew rebellion instigated by this man Moses is justified; the high concentration of slaves to the north in the fields of Goshen presents a clear national security threat if they were to move south into the populated cities. As you know, General Djehuty and his Sobek Corps in Saqqara have always been there as a token presence to guard the temples, pyramids, and tombs of Giza and the palace in Memphis. Until now, those cities have never been in real danger. My suggestion is to swap the full-strength Amun Corps in Karnak with General Djehuty's weaker Sobek Corps. That will put experienced, battle-ready troops closer to the northern cities in the event of a slave uprising in Goshen. General Djehuty's corps can reinforce itself in Karnak later. A second Army corps, General Intef's Ammit Corps, can also be stationed to the east of Saqqara on the opposite bank of Mother Nile to defend the Great House palace in Mennefer in case Midian or Canaan attack from the east. A total of twenty thousand troops should make the area secure against even the god of the Hebrews."

"Approved. And the second order...?"

"This was meant to be a surprise Great One, but you should know about it now so you are adequately prepared."

"I don't like the sound of this..."

"No, it is something you will enjoy, Great One. Royal Master Inventor Imhotep, has conjured a special tribute to you in your new pyramid in Giza. You have been following the monument's construction, which is almost completed, but Imhotep has devised what he calls the *Breath of Osiris* which will emanate from the pinnacle of your pyramid into the night sky for all to see. He requires the services of *Amkhu* Hatep, your Royal Master Architect, to finish the pyramid building so his unique invention can be demonstrated. With your permission, I will have Imhotep, Hatep and his workers relocated from the Great Place Valley of the Kings to Giza where they can supervise the completion of your exquisite memorial."

"Is that the same *Amkhu* Hatep I honored after the Great Place Valley battle?"

"The very same, Excellency. I am certain that he will be honored to move to Giza where he can guarantee the successful completion of your everlasting monument."

"Very well, approved. Now leave me." A slight movement of his hand summoned his attendants from their waiting posts. "I don't want another visit from you with bothersome requests. Do whatever else you think is necessary."

Pharaoh did not notice the broad smile that crossed the Black Falcon's face that hid his inner elation about another matter. When Pharaoh moved the court to the Mennefer Palace the Black Falcon would recover the very gold he had stolen from Queen Hatshepsut's tomb and which he sold back to Pharaoh to construct Imhotep's invention. After Imhotep showed off his *Breath of Osiris* contraption to Pharaoh, the Black Falcon would lay his hands on more gold than he could have ever imagined.

Luxor West Bank, Lotus House

Messages from the palace flowed in a steady stream later in the day alerting countless numbers of recipients that the Great One and his entire court would be moving to Mennefer. The transition itself would take months to complete, but military orders directed that the Amun and Sobek Corps begin their exchange mobilizations immediately. A directive addressed to the Great Place Village elicited a cry of surprise from Architect Hatep's daughter when she intercepted the helio signal on the roof of Lotus House.

"My life is ruined!" Sarina screamed. "This can't be happening!"

Servants rushed to see if she was hurt. Even her mother hurried up the steps to find the cause of her daughter's cries.

"What is the matter, dear?"

"Daddy's being ordered to move us and his office to Giza! We have to leave Lotus House and go to that dirty, dumpy house between the crumbling pyramids." She was in tears when she remembered that her mother didn't know about the royal signals.

"What in the world are you talking about?"

"It's probably only a rumor," she recovered, "but it's upsetting just the same. If it's true, we'll have to move." Sarina composed herself and dried her tears.

"I don't know where you heard these rumors," her mother stated. "Your father has enough work in the Great Place Valley to keep us here for as long as he wishes. If it's true, though, we still own the house in Giza where you and Malik grew up. Do you remember Jasmine House, dear?"

"I remember it and I hated it! Stuck miles from the river on a stinking canal between two abandoned pyramids, not a breath of wind, and nothing but Red Land dirt and dust everywhere. How could you stand it there?"

"Your father had the house built there to be close to his work. It wasn't so bad in Giza, but we were all younger then, I suppose. Designing and building pyramids for Pharaohs was your father's lifelong dream—fulfilling his father's ambitions before him. At least I could cross the river to the city of Memphis every few weeks to shop. Besides, whoever told you the rumor about moving back to Giza was probably mistaken. I'm going back to the garden." Iset descended the stairs to her secluded courtyard wondering why her daughter got so worked up over a silly rumor.

Sarina spent the rest of the afternoon monitoring the instructions that flashed back and forth from the palace that further confirmed the order that thousands would move in stages to Giza, Saqqara, and Mennefer. At least General Herihor's Amun Corps and the people she was closest to would be moving too. With Asher and Rachel doing most of the hard work, her mother would immerse herself in the less complicated details of moving the household and servants. Hatep would be occupied full-time with transporting his draftsmen, accountants, overseers and hundreds of artisans and their families to Giza. His estate's land holdings on the Luxor West Bank —with what few livestock remained—would still be maintained by trusted stewards.

Sarina would fill in Malik and Nathan when they returned from their apprenticeship, although Hakamun or Elias might have already tipped them off. The Great Place Village would be abuzz with the news!

A passing signal made mention of Imhotep's special *Breath of Osiris* project in Giza. He was ordered to leave for Giza immediately with a small crew. Sarina made a mental note to ask her father what the *Breath of Osiris* was.

Then, it occurred to her that the Jasmine House in Giza might not offer a view of a heliographic station; certainly nothing as well-positioned as Lotus House. She'd been too young to remember exactly where the old house was located but it seemed to be in the shadows of towering pyramids. What if neither the Giza nor Mennefer helio stations were visible from Jasmine House?

Great Place Valley, Heliographic Tower

As Sarina speculated, Elias sent a runner to fetch Malik and Nathan as soon as the station received notice of the move. Their two friends came running and they spoke hurriedly between messages while Elias and Hakamun alternated reading signals and writing orders as fast as they could. Runners were busy delivering the messages throughout the village.

"Thanks for calling us about the new orders," Malik said.

"I guess it means 'so long' for now, anyway," Hakamun said while his quill flew across a message form.

"I hope you and the rest of the helio operators can keep up the exchange of information we set up," Nathan began. "If the plagues continue after the move, as I'm certain they will, the Great House palace in Mennefer will become the new center of activity."

"I'm afraid you're right. With your father and the entire Artisans' Village sent to Giza, our tower might as well shut down. Maybe we can put in for a transfer to Mennefer or Giza. What do you think, Elias?"

"Sounds good to me. I'd rather be busy while I bake in the sun anyway. Maybe we can visit the pyramids as tourists!" Elias was his usual upbeat self.

"Well, we'd better go see if Father can use our help." Malik and Nathan shook hands with their friends and descended the ladder to the ground.

"We'll look you up when we get to Giza!" Elias shouted.

"And maybe we'll see your sister too," Hakamun added. He and Elias grinned at their friends as they waved in reply.

"Seriously," the Egyptian said to his Hebrew assistant when their two visitors were gone, "do you think we'll ever see them again?"

"Only God knows," Elias said.

River Nile, Between Thebes and Memphis

Mobilization of the Amun Corps was logistical pandemonium in spite of the many times that they had practiced a mass deployment. A week after receiving their orders, General Herihor finally had time to think about Sarina as his barge sailed toward Saqqara's garrison in the second fleet of troops and supplies. He'd learned that she and her family would be living in nearby Giza.

Why did I think of Sarina just now? he wondered. Her image had flashed through his mind only a few times since she and the two young men from Lotus House visited him at the Karnak garrison a month ago. Yes, she was pleasant to look at, engaging to speak with, and smelled of fresh lavender, but what did he like best about her? He pondered that question for the next hour while the serene shoreline drifted past. Their two encounters played over and over again in his mind, especially the last time he saw her.

City of Thebes, Medjay Headquarters

A month after Hezbak's disappearance into anonymity, the Chief Medjay concluded that the inspector had finally asked too many questions of the wrong people and died a violent death in an alley somewhere. One day his corpse would surface in the river. Having lost interest in any further controversy, the Chief sent a quick message, via the designated courier, to inform the palace that the investigation into the tomb robberies and the suspected uprising was suspended until he could assign a new investigator. The smug courier seemed pleased with the news. When the senior Medjay was informed that the entire palace would move to Mennefer and he would remain in Thebes, he breathed a further sigh of relief at the prospect that his workload would diminish. He relished the thought of turning to more leisurely pursuits.

Inspector Hezbak changed his appearance and he and Hevel took menial jobs cooking and cleaning dishes in the large banquet hall of the Great House palace. He watched for the Black Falcon's courier who he would recognize again. Meanwhile, he scoured the city for anyone who might know anything about the murdered coppersmith.

Scores of kitchen workers and servers carefully packed Pharaoh's richly appointed banquet furniture, tableware, gold cutlery, decorations, and supplies for the move to Mennefer. Hezbak moved among them with his eyes and ears open for clues to the identity of his quarry. He was determined to continue his search for the Black Falcon even after the move to the Mennefer Palace.

CHAPTER 23

River Nile, Between Thebes and Memphis

The Nile carried the daily commerce of a hydraulic civilization originating in the heart of a dark continent in the south to the Great Sea in the north more than one thousand miles away. It pulsed like a thick, blue artery with life-sustaining energy. Thin green rims of vegetation on each side of the never-ending course gave The Two Lands its prosperity and power. If the *Horus Eye* were released to fly untethered, its passengers would see black dots scurrying like water bugs back and forth between the lush banks and up and down the constant flow as far as they could see. When the palace mobilized from Waset to Mennefer, it spawned an unending trail of boats, barges, and luxurious floating resorts that slowly but purposefully followed the lazy current northward.

Imhotep departed Thebes on his private watercraft with a small team of engineers and artisans as soon as he received his orders. He was eager to reach his destination to ensure the secrecy and completion of the *Breath of Osiris*. He had more experiments to conduct before its dramatic demonstration to Pharaoh. The *Horus Eye* flying platform would have to be disassembled, packed, and transported to Giza later by barge and then through the Great Memphis Channel to Thutmoses' unfinished pyramid where a new aerodrome would be built for it. The famous inventor was excited by the prospect of seeing a full-scale demonstration of the *Breath of Osiris* at night from his airborne balloon. It would be the largest man-made aerial spectacle ever seen.

In the wake of Imhotep's boat, the Amun Corps filled more than one hundred bulging barges in a steady stream of troops, animals, military machines, carts, wagons and provisions. The long, wide, flat wooden vessels designed to transport slabs of granite and alabaster from quarries upriver, were crude but rugged floating platforms. Herihor commandeered enough of the craft to move his corps as swiftly as possible. Soldiers were crammed below and above decks in conditions that were only marginally better than slaves' quarters. They were thankful, however, that they weren't forced to march five hundred miles along the banks or to tow all the supplies to their new garrison. The general was occupied with keeping his fleet together and maintaining the morale of ten thousand restless soldiers who were used to vigorous daily exercise. When they finally reached the new garrison at Saqqara it would take them a month to return to full battle readiness. In the late evening darkness, while the general reclined on deck, watched the stars, and listened to the sounds of birds, insects, and crocodiles along the shore he wished Sarina were with him. He tried to dismiss the idea that an intelligent, refined, vibrant young lady would find anything attractive in a tough, scarred warrior like him, but the memory of her crept into his mind again and again. He wondered if she ever thought of him.

Sarina was too involved with packing to give the general much thought until the family was under way on the private barge that her father hired. Hatep delved into his personal wealth and claimed his royal position as *Amkhu* to hire a furnished, floating apartment that accommodated his family, their servants and enough comforts for a month-long river voyage.

The passenger vessel was similar in hull design to the big obelisk-carrying barges—a broad beam and a flat bottom kept it stable in the Nile's shallow water—but it was different in its propulsion method and comfortable passenger amenities. Commercial and obelisk barges were propelled by slaves pulling on oars. One, two, or three tiers of oarsmen sped transports downriver with quarry stones for the Giza projects and upriver with grains, produce, and livestock from the rich delta in Goshen. They had to meet tight schedules and turn their owners a profit. Hatep's barge was quietly pushed along by slaves using long poles as they walked barefoot up and down each side of the ship on smooth, worn wooden planks. A single paddler steered from a high perch on the stern where he could guide their way down the middle of the river.

If the ship ran aground, the slaves leapt into the water and pulled the craft forward using long ropes or pushed it back into the middle of the river, while avoiding the crocodiles that lined the banks. Fully furnished apartments on the expansive upper deck gave the passengers privacy during the hot, still days. The barge was anchored to the shore before sunset so that servants could prepare the evening meal; the slaves and crew disembarked to sleep on shore at night and the passengers had the boat to themselves.

Hatep looked forward to a slow-paced respite from his duties as royal architect and more time with his family. Sometimes it was hard to remember that his son was almost an adult and his daughter a young woman who would marry someday. He and Iset may never have a relaxing time like this again with their children.

River Nile, Royal Dockyard at Thebes

Weeks later, after the military, passenger, and supporting commercial vessels had left northward for the new capital, Pharaoh's fleet of gilded barges began their slow departure from the near-empty Theban city. The floating Great House was composed of two dozen luxurious palace ships. Transportation barges stayed ahead of Pharaoh's fleet with servants and provisions to meet every royal need on the six-week journey to his Great House in Mennefer.

Since he had not fully recovered from the plague that struck the nation almost a month earlier, Pharaoh's personal barge drifted slowly during the day and stopped early each evening. When he arrived at the Mennefer Palace he would continue his convalescence and, so his advisors assured him that he would not need to face Moses and Aaron again. The crowned head of Egypt was determined to never yield to the demands of those upstart Hebrews. Release all the slaves in Egypt? Absolutely not!

River Nile, Asyut Helio Tower

Asyut was the capital city of the 13th *nome* district of Middle Egypt and halfway between Thebes and Memphis. Tired of being confined on their drifting home, Malik and Sarina begged their father to stop at Asyut for a few days so they could walk around the city and climb a small mountain to the west for exercise. As soon as their boat was tied to a tree and the gangplank touched the shoreline, Malik, Sarina, and Nathan raced through the small fishing village to reach the looming summit shortly after noon. A heliographic signaling tower stood a short distance back from a cliff's edge with a view for fifty miles in all directions. The familiar tower shape dominated the peak.

"Hello!" Malik called when his head came even with the instrument platform at the top. Sarina and Nathan followed him closely.

"Hello!" replied a voice from the other side of the copper signaling instrument shrouded by a thick tarpaulin. "I'll be there in a minute." A light brown smiling face topped with curly sun-bleached hair popped up from behind the tarp and approached them with an energetic step. "You must be Sarina," he said in welcome while he ignored Malik and Nathan.

"How did you know?" Sarina replied with surprise as she shook his hand.

"Elias said you'd probably stop at one of the towers along your river journey, and we were told to offer you every courtesy. It's a privilege to meet a self-taught blinker. You're famous, didn't you know?"

"Famous? My sister?" Malik was puzzled that this young blinker was so fascinated with Sarina. "I'm Malik, by the way, and this is Nathan. Who are you?"

"Oh, sorry. I'm Levi—the Hebrew blinker."

"So our visit here is not a complete surprise," Nathan stated. "I wasn't sure if we'd be welcomed or if we'd have to go through a long explanation of who we are to get a tour or even to hear news from Thebes and Memphis."

"Well, as far as the station goes," Levi said sweeping his arms around the platform, "If you've seen one outpost, you've seen them all. Helio towers and the instruments are nearly identical. We're a relay station so we only see long haul traffic passing through. We rarely originate traffic ourselves like the Great House palace helio station that sends hundreds of new orders per day.

"However," he motioned his visitors to the writing table under the awning, "we've had a lot of traffic in the past several weeks about this move. It seems everything happening in Thebes, Karnak, or the Great Place Valley has to be relayed to the Mennefer Palace, Saqqara Army garrison, or Giza. This is the first break I and my boss have had all day today."

"Anything new about Moses?" Nathan asked.

Levi hesitated before answering. "There's been some mention of him, yes."

"Well, what about him?"

"I'm not sure I'm at liberty to discuss that. I'd like to, but since I'm only a Hebrew slave operator, I'll defer to my Egyptian supervisor to tell you."

An awkward silence followed. The visitors had read so many sensitive royal communications that they assumed they would be given access to messages here as well. They were about to bid farewell to Levi when his superior came up the ladder behind them.

"I didn't know we had visitors," an Egyptian announced in a gruff voice as he stepped onto the platform. The lead operator was an older man, with small eyes, nose, and mouth punctuating a creased, weather-beaten face. He glared past the three visitors at his assistant.

Levi quickly introduced Supervisor Chufu and explained that he had been speaking with the visitors for only a few minutes. When he mentioned their names, the man's annoyance turned to unveiled animosity.

"Ah, the *famous* Sarina," he said with a forced smile that grew more creases around his mouth.

Sarina wasn't sure how to interpret the man's sarcasm. His underlying hostile tone took her by surprise. She almost responded in kind when her brother stepped in.

"Thank you for the compliment, Sir. However, I wish people would stop calling her 'famous' just because she's a woman and a self-taught blinker. We thought we'd stop by and see if there was any news that our father, Royal Master Architect *Amkhu* Hatep, should learn before we continue on our way to Giza."

Chufu ignored his last statement. "But she is famous! The royal cipher was unbreakable until she cracked it. I understand you wrote the new helio encryption method for the military." His dark eyes were fixed on her as he waited for a reaction.

Sarina was stunned by his statement. How did he know this? Was this common knowledge among the helio operators? What other strangers knew that she had cracked the country's most private cipher?

"Sir...I don't know what to say."

"Nor do I." Malik said stiffly. "That is supposed to be a military secret. Her identity is very sensitive information and, if it were too widely known, could place her in danger. I must report this irregularity to General Herihor who is a close friend of our family and a sponsor of my sister's work."

"I'm sorry if my statement distressed you or broke a military confidence. I thought this was a public achievement worthy of compliment. Please forgive me." His hollow-sounding apology did little to reduce the tension.

"Since you already have access to our nation's most sensitive secrets, I will be glad to share other news with you. What would you like to know?"

"Sir, they asked me..." Levi began but was cut off by a sharp look.

Malik picked up on the strain between the Egyptian and his Hebrew assistant. "We came here to pick up messages for our father. That's all."

"Yes, we have a few administrative orders. Levi, get them from the files. Anything else?" Chufu obviously wanted his visitors to leave.

"Have you heard anything about that man Moses?" Malik tried to make his question sound casual.

"Are you one of his followers?" Chufu's question sounded like an accusation. His face darkened further when he looked at Nathan.

"I just thought you might have heard something. He was the talk of Thebes before we left." Malik hoped that Nathan would keep his mouth shut and let him talk his way out of what had become an unexpected confrontation with the station manager.

"I suppose you'll find this out when you speak to General Herihor in a few weeks. The Amun Corps was ordered to take that Hebrew rebel and his brother into custody. They're hiding somewhere in Goshen but General Herihor will find them and have them executed, I'm told."

Sarina let out a gasp. "The general would never do that!"

"Why not? Moses and Aaron have caused this nation nothing but pain and suffering ever since they came back from Midian. They deserve to die!" Chufu hated Israelites and was itching for an argument.

"We'd better leave," Malik said. He took his sister's arm and steered her toward the ladder. Nathan helped her descend and then he followed.

Malik said over his shoulder, "Send those messages for my father by courier later today. Our ship leaves the fishing village early tomorrow morning. Thank you, Sir." Malik spun around and hurried down to the ground before he exploded.

The three friends discussed their experience as they hiked back down to their waiting barge. Feeling Chufu's eyes on their backs during their descent down the mountain, they refused to look backward.

"Can you believe that bully?" Nathan exclaimed.

"I'm glad you didn't say anything to further provoke him," Malik added. "There's no telling what he might have done to you, even though you're technically my property. He obviously hates Hebrews."

Sarina had learned something of the humiliation and abuse that even well-educated slaves endured. "I feel sorry for Levi. He cowered like an animal when his boss looked at him. Did you notice how cheerful he was when we first met him?"

Nathan felt that an explanation was in order. "Your father's treatment of his slaves is the exception, Sarina. Most Egyptians are cruel and take out their anger and frustration on Hebrew slaves. Slaves can be beaten or even killed by their masters if they so much as object to their treatment. I thank God that I'm part of your family." They continued hiking in silence.

Later that night a helio courier delivered a packet of messages to Royal Architect Hatep and then asked for Malik by name. A servant escorted the courier to where Malik and Sarina were finishing dinner on the deck under the stars.

"Levi! It's you!" Sarina exclaimed when he was announced.

"I'm sorry to bother you at your mealtime. A friend of mine does courier chores for Chufu and I offered to deliver the messages to your father myself so he could have some time off. I wanted to see you again anyway and give you some other news."

"I'll get Nathan. Here, have some sugar dates and fresh pomegranate juice," Malik said as he got to his feet and headed to shore. "Sarina, pour him a drink. He looks thirsty."

"Sit down, Levi." She motioned to where Malik had been sitting. The young slave gave her a bewildered look. "What's the matter?" she asked.

"I've...I've never shared food with an Egyptian before. Is it all right?"

"Yes, it's all right. You're among friends here. Sit down and drink this."

The Hebrew blinker reluctantly sat on a plush cushion and took a long gulp of juice. "This is very sweet. What is it again?"

"It's pomegranate juice. Haven't you ever had it before?"

"Never. It's very good."

"Have you had dinner? If not, I'll ring for some pheasant we have left over."

"I don't know what to say. You're very kind."

Malik returned with Nathan to find Levi stuffing sugar dates into his mouth. The young slave tried to smile with a full mouth when the two sat beside him.

"It's good to see you again, Levi. Take your time eating those dates and tell us what you have whenever you're ready." Nathan noticed that the bright-eyed helio operator was enjoying the sweet treats.

Their visitor self-consciously wiped his face on his sleeve, swallowed the dates and drank more juice. After a satisfying burp, he began.

"My news is from your friends Elias and Hakamun. As they suspected, the helio tower at the Great Place Valley has been decommissioned. They have orders to move to the station in the 18th *nome* district of Lower Egypt, in the Goshen region. It's not what they wanted for an assignment, but they didn't have much choice."

"When will they get there?" Malik asked.

"They left a few days ago so they're about two weeks behind you. They said they'd try to look you up at the Giza station when they pass by Memphis but might not have the time. They like you three and I can see why. I wish I had a boss like Hakamun instead of Chufu. I'm stuck where I am and there's nothing I can do about it."

Nathan tried to cheer up the dejected youngster. "If everything that our holy men say about Moses is true, then the Hebrews will be released from slavery someday soon. Imagine, our people have waited four hundred years for this and it could happen in our lifetime! All I can say is watch the helio messages for news about Moses. One day soon we'll all leave Egypt together for the Promised Land. Won't that be great?"

"Yes! But I'm puzzled. You two are Egyptians," he said gesturing to Malik and Sarina, "and you're all right with that? Releasing all the Hebrew slaves, I mean. I thought you'd be against it."

"If that's what the God of Abraham has planned for his people, then that's what I want," Sarina said.

"Me too," Malik added. "We haven't decided yet, but we might be going with the Israelites. What do you think of that?"

"I don't know... I've never met anyone like you before." Levi got to his feet and looked longingly at the few sugar dates left on the plate as he said, "I must be going back but I'll keep watching the helio net for news."

Sarina, having taken an immediate liking to the shy Hebrew blinker, motioned for him to wait. "I'll have the cook pack you a dinner and include more sugar dates and a jug of juice in the basket."

Malik and Nathan spoke with Levi at the gangplank for a few minutes then bid him farewell after Sarina handed him a heavy bag that their new friend slung over his shoulder. With a wave and a broad smile he walked into the night.

CHAPTER 24

Giza Complex, Jasmine House

The house in Giza was beautiful in its own way. Jasmine House was a stark dwelling of bricks made from the red clay of the Giza Plateau. Unlike the estate on Luxor's West Bank, surrounded by rich fields and a view of the Nile River, this structure squatted amid crumbling, thousand-year old pyramids and featureless rows of above-ground *mastaba* tombs built from identical red bricks. The dry, hot air was often motionless until whirlwinds formed out of nowhere to sweep clouds of fine dust into the air and deposit a red film on everything. One positive feature of the location not far from the Giza Artisans' Village was the deep barge canal that cut through the necropolis complex and connected the towering pyramids to the Nile River two miles away. The canal's Nile River water was an inexhaustible source of irrigation during and after the Inundation. It was also a convenient highway to the city of Memphis and a commercial route that delivered large blocks of stone to the doorsteps of Giza's pyramids.

Iset looked over the home that she and Hatep had occupied when first married and remembered their small children playing on the lush green grass of the large inner courtyard. The tamarisk trees they planted back then now shaded the outer perimeter of the lawn. Thanks to maintenance by the groundskeepers, the house had not fallen into disrepair during their absence. Varieties of jasmine still washed the house with their sweet fragrance which almost compensated for the ever-present dust. Iset would make Jasmine House an oasis of comfort for her family during their stay in Giza, no matter what happened outside its walls.

The building was designed with the same single-story, open floor plan as Lotus House in Luxor but on a larger scale with nearby buildings for animals, cooking, and food storage. Thanks to the nearby canal, Iset's meditation garden of countless varieties of flowers and trees surrounding a fish pond and fountain was well-watered. Like Lotus House, a set of double doors led into the traditional altar entryway. An *Anubis* idol would never greet visitors to Jasmine House.

Within a week after arriving in Giza, the servants settled into their daily schedule of cleaning, food preparation, and grounds maintenance. Iset busied herself overseeing the house while Hatep ensured that Thutmose's pyramid would be completed soon. He also managed to design some new blocks of *mastaba* tombs for wealthy Memphis patrons. Pharaoh's continuing ill health prompted pyramid overseers to hurry completion of the monument before its namesake passed into the netherworld. All indications pointed to the imminent death of their ruler if he had to endure more plagues.

Malik and Nathan obtained Hatep's permission to take Sarina with them on their rounds of the three heliograph stations in the area—the army garrison at Saqqara, Giza, and the Mennefer Palace. They would also meet with Imhotep before returning to their apprenticeship duties. Sarina wanted to see General Herihor as soon as possible to offer him and Corps Master Scribe Ahmes more encryption suggestions. At least that's what she told her brother.

Giza Complex, Unfinished Pyramid of Thutmose III

When they had visited operators in the area's three helio towers, Malik, Sarina, and Nathan were satisfied that news of Moses and any future plague forecasts would be exchanged with other stations in the long network. Unlike their hostile reception from Chufu in Asyut, the Egyptian operators they met in the Memphis area were eager to share information, especially when they met Sarina in person. She was a celebrity in the tight blinker community. To Malik's annoyance, his gifted and beautiful sister overshadowed him and his friend wherever they went. Nathan pointed to the advantages of her notoriety, but Malik chafed when the others spoke of her brilliant work on the signals and ciphers and completely ignored him.

Malik paused with Sarina and Nathan outside the pyramid entrance that gaped like a black mouth. "We should ask Imhotep to find Sarina a place near Jasmine House where she can observe at least two of the three helio stations in the Memphis local network. Even though we have assurances from the Saqqara, Giza, and Mennefer operators to share information about Moses and the plagues with us, we'll need to know immediately if the Black Falcon sends any more secret messages."

Nathan also had more questions for the Master Inventor. "We should also find out when the *Horus Eye* will be ready to fly. I'd like to see the giant Khufu and Khafre pyramids from the air. He could give us a first-class aerial overview of the Giza complex layout."

"And what about the *Breath of Osiris* I've heard about?" Sarina asked.

"Right," Malik said. "If he has time we should be able to get answers to all our questions."

The three checked in with the pyramid supervisor—it was still considered a construction site—who knew them by sight as members of Royal Architect Hatep's household and gave them smokeless torches and directions to the first intersection inside the pyramid where they would meet another custodian to direct them through the maze of corridors to Imhotep. Their gradual descent down a smoothly polished passageway with painted walls and ceilings took them about fifteen minutes. When they reached an intersection of multiple corridors, the custodian collected their torches and directed them to a wider and taller gallery that descended further into the dimly lit depths of the building. There was just enough light from glowing globes on the ceiling to see the floor and the colorfully decorated walls.

"That's the same lighting we saw in Queen Hatshepsut's burial vault," Malik observed.

"Where does the light come from?" Sarina had never seen the bright globes before. "Is there a flame inside those glass balls?"

"Keep going. You can ask Imhotep when we find him."

They found the Master Inventor in a giant, brightly lit chamber on his knees working on a gold cylinder more than twenty feet tall and five feet in diameter in the exact center of the open room. A thin golden tube went from the top of the cylinder to a hole in the ceiling forty feet above his head. Imhotep noticed their arrival and rose to his feet.

"Welcome my friends. I wondered when you would be paying me a visit." His twinkling blue eyes and gleaming white hair reminded them of a jovial grandfather. He was old even by Egyptian standards, but still active in body and mind.

"And this must be Sarina," he smiled.

Malik rolled his eyes and once again braced himself for the words "famous" and "legendary" describing his sister.

Imhotep turned to Malik with a wise suggestion. "I could not help but sense the sibling rivalry. You should be thankful that your sister is a talented blinker enthusiast who could be a great help. If you gave her half a chance, she would prove that to you. Take my advice and you'll not be disappointed."

"I told you," Nathan whispered when the old man turned his back on them to speak to Sarina who studied the rows of hieroglyphic symbols that covered the curved surface of the golden cylinder.

"Please don't touch it," Imhotep cautioned. "It's been disconnected from its energy source but one can never be sure how much energy it retains since I last tested it. It is designed to store a large amount of energy before it is released in an instant."

"Is this the *Breath of Osiris*?" she asked. Malik and Nathan stepped closer to hear Imhotep's answer.

"This is the machine that produces the *Breath of Osiris* which has yet to be demonstrated on a large scale, so I cannot tell you exactly what it will look like until I see it for myself. What you have before you is the machine that produces living breath or *exoflux* that will fly into the air."

He led them to an adjacent room where he pointed to a large, black sarcophagus-like box or chest covered in a black substance. "That is a *flux* box. It is the source of energy for the golden cylinder through those cloth-covered tubes."

"Like the one we saw in Queen Hatshepsut's tomb!" Malik exclaimed.

"What? When were you in her tomb?" They had never seen Imhotep this surprised before. "That tomb has been sealed for over fifty years!"

"You and your big mouth..." Nathan murmured.

"We... we saw a black box like that tied to glowing glass bulbs in a deep tunnel into her tomb. I'm sorry. Forget I said anything about it."

"I built such a system for Deputy Architect Imani some years ago. He said he installed it to light a burial chamber under construction in the Great Place Valley of the Kings. So he used it in Queen Hatshepsut's tomb?"

Nathan explained how they came across the concealed tunnel that led into Queen Hatshepsut's tomb, watched thieves steal her treasure, and traced the stolen objects to Thebes before they disappeared. He omitted any details about the encrypted list, the Black Falcon, and Inspector Hezbak.

"Is that what you came to see me about?" Imhotep asked.

"Not really," Malik said. He desperately wanted to turn the conversation away from the tomb robbery.

Sarina came to his rescue. "We were wondering if you could find a location for me to observe two or three of the Memphis helio stations, preferably somewhere near Jasmine House. General Herihor asked me to work on more helio encryption methods and I will need access to some signals to test my ciphers. Could you do that for us?"

"I can do better than that! After his victory over the Nubian attack in the Great Place Valley, the general asked me to construct a portable heliograph. I've been so busy with this project and the move from Thebes that I haven't had time to finish one. I promise that you will have your own portable signaling machine and experimental station in a short time.

"Is there anything else? I must finish this exoflux generator before my slipping mind forgets why I'm here." He chuckled at his own exaggeration so his visitors did not take him too seriously.

"Will the *Horus Eye* be available for a flight over the pyramids anytime soon?" Nathan asked.

"I'm afraid not. The barge carrying it and its crew broke down on the river and required extensive repairs. Since it is not essential to finishing Thutmose's pyramid I told them to fix the ship and bring the aircraft to Giza when they can. I cannot say when it will arrive or be ready to fly."

"Oh, I'm sorry to hear that. Please let us know when you're ready to test the *Breath of Osiris*. We don't want to miss seeing it."

"According to my theoretical calculations the exoflux released into the sky should be impossible to miss. I'm fairly confident of that," he said with another chuckle.

Imhotep's cryptic comment about the exoflux being impossible to miss was the subject of much speculation during their walk back up the incline of the inner gallery to the main intersection of narrow corridors inside the pyramid. When they stepped into the blinding sunlight of the Giza plateau the three began making plans to visit General Herihor at his new garrison.

CHAPTER 25

Saqqara, Military Garrison—Amun Corps Headquarters

General Herihor had been in Saqqara for only three weeks when Malik, Sarina, and Nathan visited him at mid-morning at the army garrison camp that also housed General Intef's Ammit Corps. The recently arrived Amun Corps was bivouacked in tents that extended across the Saqqara plain. Ready to deploy at a moment's notice, the ten thousand men replenished their supplies, maintained their weapons and vehicles, and tended to the new foreign horses recently purchased to fill out the charioteer regiment. Both corps were on alert in anticipation of a Hebrew slave rebellion.

The three visitors were escorted into the reception area of the general's spacious octagonal tent in the center of the encampment surrounded by the smaller tents of his regimental commanders and division captains. Colorful rugs on the dirt floor, thin cushions around the perimeter of the room, and a low table with food and drinks gave the impression of a quiet family living room.

Their friend greeted them as soon as they came through the curtains at the entrance of the tent. He shook hands with Malik and Nathan without taking his eyes off Sarina. She blushed and her face darkened further when he took her hands in both of his and uttered his sincere thanks that she had safely arrived with her family.

After settling on cushions and being served drinks by the commander's aide, they made idle conversation before turning to the purpose of their visit.

"And are your parents well?" the concerned general asked Sarina, still ignoring Malik and Nathan who waited their turn for their host's attention. Malik wondered if Herihor's attention toward his sister could be any more obvious.

"Yes, they are well. Father is, of course, busy finishing the pyramid for Pharaoh and has taken on a number of contracts for new *mastabas* in the necropolis. Mother is recovering from the long trip and tending to Jasmine House. Everyone is well, thank you." For once Sarina was at a loss for words. "Oh, and they wish you good health and send their best regards also."

When the silence dragged on, Malik gave a slight cough. "Well, now that we know that everyone is healthy and happy, may we please talk about the reason for our visit?"

"Of course." General Herihor tore his eyes from Sarina and turned to Malik. "I assume you're here about the portable heliograph and a new station for Sarina near your home."

"Well…yes."

"Inventor Imhotep delivered the machine last night and said you'd be coming here this morning. He has a site picked out in southern Giza between your home and my station on top of the Zoser pyramid near here where you can see all three stations of the Memphis network. This morning, my quartermaster and his crew leveled the top of the old Menkaure pyramid in Giza for the instrument and cleared a small stone shelter at the base for supply storage. It should be ready when you arrive there."

"I look forward to seeing the site," Sarina said. "But what's going on here at the garrison? It looks like you're preparing for war. Do you really anticipate a Hebrew revolt?"

"Personally, I think an uprising is unlikely. However, I have my official orders."

"When we stopped at the Asyut station four weeks ago we heard that you were told to arrest and execute Moses. Is that true?" Nathan asked.

"Those were my orders, but I… Listen, my friends," he said in a low voice, "what I am about to tell you is for your ears only. I sent an undercover team to Goshen a week ago. They easily found Moses and followed him to daily meetings with representatives of the twelve Israelite tribes. One of the Hebrew slaves accompanying the team listened in on his talks with the elders and assured me that he is not advocating a revolt. In fact, Moses spoke of patience and non-violence until the time when God is ready to lead them to their Promised Land. I have decided to not arrest him unless he makes violent threats against Pharaoh or Egyptian citizens." Herihor looked to his visitors for a reaction.

"I support your decision, of course. Hebrews will be glad to leave slavery and Egypt behind them when the time is right." Nathan's view was not unexpected.

"What do you think of my decision?" the general asked Sarina.

"Nobody doubts your courage in battle to defend our country or attack our enemies. You are a kind man. There is something else troubling you that you haven't told us, but I believe you will do what is right."

Malik was puzzled by his sister's cryptic remark. She often sensed things that eluded him and Nathan. Apparently she had hit upon something because Herihor quickly changed the subject.

"Was there something else you wanted to tell me?" the general asked.

"When we stopped at Asyut the station manager there was a brute and a racist. He said some things that upset us. Among them was a reference to Sarina's breaking the royal encryption code. He made it sound like it was common knowledge among all the blinkers." Malik continued, "He flung this secret information in her face as if he knew it would upset her. What do you know about this?"

"Nothing, but I'll look into it as soon as you leave. In the meantime, I'll assign a special guard to protect her and your home."

"Is that really necessary?" Malik objected.

"Believe me, it is. If this Black Falcon thinks that his plans have been discovered, he'll stop at nothing to silence those who could expose him."

"Speaking of that, have you heard anything from your friend Inspector Hezbak?"

"Nothing. But his methods take time and often involve great secrecy. The last I heard, a month before I left our Karnak garrison, he was on to something and knowing him, he won't give up chasing leads until he solves the case."

"If the Black Falcon is someone high up in the Great House, does that mean he's in Mennefer now?"

"I'm sure of it, and that is all the more reason to provide protection for you and your family."

Malik and Nathan knew who he really wanted protected.

South Giza, Menkaure Heliographic Research Station

The pyramid of Menkaure was built more than a thousand years earlier during the time of Egypt's Old Kingdom. Its original construction called for giant black granite blocks for the pyramid's underlying structure covered with gleaming white alabaster and limestone slabs. A solid gold cap was placed at the apex at its dedication. The miniature gold pyramid on top seemed to float in the sky on a white cloud. The sharp edges of the pyramid's bright triangular sides stood out against Egypt's clear blue sky and shimmered in the desert heat. The tribute to Pharaoh Menkaure glistened above the flat skyline of Giza fifteen dynasties before the reign of Thutmose III.

When the three friends, escorted by two uniformed soldiers, finally came across the Menkaure pyramid in the half-mile space between the much larger and greater monuments to Khufu and Khafre, it was not impressive. Workmen had cannibalized the white alabaster and Tura limestone slabs centuries ago to cover above-ground tombs in which the families of noblemen and public officials were buried. The practice of removing outer materials from pyramids erected four or five generations earlier to build other structures was common among those who regarded their own memorials more worthy than those of long-forgotten ancestors. By this time, even the granite substructure of the two great pyramids had been pillaged to build other pyramids, temples, palaces, and buildings. Of course, the four-sided gold cap atop the Menkaure pyramid was stolen soon after the Pharaoh died and a white limestone replica was put in its place. That too was long gone. The rest of the stripped edifice had been eroded by centuries of desert winds, vandalized by looters in search of hidden entrances, and picked over for a carving or engraving here or there that might have value.

When Malik, Sarina, and Nathan saw it for the first time, Menkaure's pyramid resembled a worn pile of rubble rather than an artistic memorial to a royal Pharaoh. In spite of its weathered surface and severely blunted top, it still stood almost one hundred feet above the surrounding red plateau of Giza in the shadow of its two great neighbors. Thanks to its uneven granite block sides, it was easy enough to climb and the three visitors ascended to its summit ahead of their bodyguards. A man and a boy stepped from the shade of an awning near what they assumed was a portable heliograph covered with a linen sheet.

"You must be Sarina. My name is Akhenat." By this time Malik and Nathan were used to being ignored by helio station personnel. The man who extended his hand to her, evidently the team leader, was a heavy-set, older Egyptian dressed in a military scribe's threadbare tunic that was probably his only set of clothing. Like so many of the blinker teams they had come across, his assistant was a small Israelite slave boy named Uriel who showed a Hebrew youth's single side lock of dark hair that fell over his ear. He bowed from a distance and gave a shy smile, not sure how he should greet them.

After a formal introduction of her brother and Nathan, Sarina pulled the sheet off the portable heliograph near the southern edge of the pyramid's top. An attempt had been made to level the stone surface around its base. The small copper instrument was built according to the solar reflective principles of the larger heliographs. A tripod elevated the machine while an adjustable mirror captured the sun's rays and focused them on a second mirror that aimed the single solar beam outward at a distant target. A control lever attached to the second mirror flashed the beam on and off. When disassembled, two men could carry the entire machine.

Sarina turned to Akhenat. "How well does the helio machine work? Have you sent or received any messages with it yet? Can I see them?" Looking around her, she continued, "And what are the sight lines to the other stations? Do you have a map of the area?"

The Egyptian operator seemed puzzled. "I am sorry, Ma'am. I am only a scribe and not a heliograph operator. We were told that you are the new station manager."

Malik and Nathan shook their heads in disbelief and a long silence followed. Sarina looked around the rectangular expanse of rubble that measured fifty feet on a side. She removed her shawl and handed it to Uriel.

"Well then, I suppose we should get to work."

Taking her brother and Nathan aside, she was determined to make the best of it. "You might as well leave now because I'll be here until sunset. The bodyguards can escort me home later. Don't worry, I'll be fine."

"If anybody can make something out of this junk pile, you can." Nathan tried to encourage her before Malik said something stupid.

"I agree," Malik spoke up as his friend expected he would. "If they need someone to boss people around, you qualify."

"I'll take that as a compliment coming from you." Her distracted tone indicated that her mind was on other things.

"Really, Sarina," Nathan said, "you'll be fine. We can come for you this evening, if you want."

"No, two guards should be enough."

After confirming arrangements with the soldiers to escort Sarina home later, Malik and Nathan climbed down the crumbling side of the pyramid and made their way back to Jasmine House.

Sarina sat with the Egyptian scribe and Israelite boy servant in the shade to explain what a heliograph was. Soon thereafter, she sent Uriel to Corps Master Scribe Ahmes in Saqqara with a requisition note for a supply of papyrus, ink, and pens. She also asked for a map of the Saqqara-Giza-Memphis area and food, water, and bedding for her assistants and the guards so that they could stay at the Menkaure pyramid around the clock, if needed. She resolved to sleep in Jasmine House each night and not on the rock pile where she figured she would be spending all her daylight hours for the foreseeable future.

CHAPTER 26

Giza Complex, Great *Mastaba* Highway

Hatep's horses arrived on a livestock barge from Thebes a week after Sarina started working at the Menkaure research site. Reuben made sure that Sapphire was well-rested from the trip at the stables before he allowed Malik and Nathan to take the sleek chariot out to explore the tombs east of the Great Pyramid of Khufu, the largest structure in Giza. Row upon row of decorated tombs lined broad avenues between Khufu's pyramid and the silent monument of an enormous lion with a man's face where processions of mourners and worshipers trod centuries ago to honor their dead. Funeral crypts, partially underground, fashioned from locally quarried limestone and carved with the names of their occupants, once held coffins and sarcophagi of Pharaoh's extended family, viziers, influential courtiers, and government officials. They lined both sides of the Great *Mastaba* Highway from Jasmine House to Thutmose's unfinished pyramid. The two chariot riders would stop at the pyramid construction site later to visit Imhotep and water Sapphire at the canal.

Nathan worked the familiar reins while Malik closed his eyes and felt the wind blow through his hair. How Sapphire could run! He was content to let Nathan drive as he drank in the sensation of freedom. The abandoned highway between the *mastabas* was perfect for reaching top speed in a chariot. Worn by the feet of thousands of pilgrims and smoothed by centuries of wind and sand, the hard-packed road was devoid of the larger stones and wagon ruts that made racing impossibly dangerous on commercial roads. Speed on the open stretches was exhilarating for horse, driver and passenger.

Malik's eyes snapped open when he felt the chariot jerk violently. Sapphire tossed his head from side to side. Nathan tried in vain to keep him from twisting around. Sudden movements by the horse ran the risk of flipping them over.

"What's gotten into him?" Malik shouted above the sound of the wheels.

"I don't know, but something's spooked him." He tugged on the reins with all his strength but only managed to reduce their speed a fraction. Malik and Nathan hauled on the reins together until the gasping stallion finally drew to a stop. His dark eyes bulged out from his face in obvious terror and his coat twitched in nonstop convulsions.

"I've never seen him act like this before," Nathan observed. "Even when he's smelled a leopard he usually outruns the scent."

"Something's given him a terrible fright." Malik looked at the tombs on either side of the road for someone or something that could have startled the horse. A distant roar made him look behind them.

"I think I know what it is. Look back there."

Nathan turned to see where his friend pointed. The pyramid of Khufu, less than a mile away, was lost in a dark red wall moving toward them. The billowing line of sand stretched across the horizon and high into the sky. A cloud that beautiful ought to be harmless, he thought to himself. The opaque wall was approaching faster than he realized.

"We need to find shelter right away," Nathan yelled as the volume of the rumble increased. "We'll never make it back to Thutmose's pyramid or the Artisans' Village in time. We need someplace to hide *now*!"

"There! Head for that abandoned *mastaba* with no doors. Take the chariot inside and at least we'll be sheltered from the direct blast of the wind." Malik had to shout to be heard above the howl that had not yet reached them with its full force. Nathan turned Sapphire toward a *mastaba* with the name of Prince Ankhaf, the son of a Pharaoh in the Fourth Dynasty, written over its door in eroded hieroglyphics.

Particles of fine dust pushed ahead of the storm's frontal wave forced them to wrap their headdress scarves over their faces. The blue-black horse needed little prompting to run toward the opening of the mastaba a few hundred feet away. By the time they reached it the wind was fierce and each grain of sand stung their skin like a shard of glass.

The chariot skidded to a stop inside the shelter when the horse abruptly stopped in front of a pile of rubble. He stumbled momentarily on loose stones but regained his balance.

Nathan dismounted and checked the horse's legs for any injury. "He looks fine," he shouted. "I'll take him around these rocks and get as far from the doorway as I can."

"Good idea. I'll look for something to block the opening."

Within a minute, Malik joined Nathan at the far back of the large tomb structure.

"Nothing," Malik said. "This place has been stripped. There's nothing here but piles of dirt and rocks. I don't know where all this dirt came from though. It's piled to the ceiling from front to back on either side. It's a good thing that pile of rocks wasn't any closer to the entrance or Sapphire could have been badly injured if we'd crashed."

"Do you think this storm is another plague?" Nathan asked.

"That's unlikely. Sandstorms are common this close to the desert and this one doesn't seem to be any worse than others that I've seen. It's not like the sun was completely blotted out. Now *that* would be a miracle from God. I'm sure that this will be over in a few hours."

"I hope you're right."

They looked around their refuge in the dim red light that penetrated through the dust swirling inside the tomb building. The howl of the storm diminished somewhat due to their distance from the doorway so that they no longer needed to shout. They tied their head scarves tighter to keep out the fine dust. When his eyes adjusted to the darkness, Nathan was the first to notice a large flat stone propped against the far wall.

"What's that?"

"It looks like an old funerary stele memorializing the tomb owner or the exploits of some family warrior." Malik ran his hands over the carved hieroglyphics on its dusty limestone surface and saw that the slab was a fragment from a much larger commemorative stone.

"What does it say?" Nathan asked. He could barely make out the pictographs on the worn surface. The carvings were deep but the edges of the once-crisp inscriptions were chipped and smoothed making them almost illegible.

"I can only make out a few words. This must be written in some ancient Egyptian dialect. The original stele was huge if this is only a piece of it." He ran his hands around the broken edges. He felt a current of air coming from behind the slab.

"Let's see if we can move this."

Nathan helped him tip the flat stone onto its side where it slipped from their grip and hit the floor with a solid thud. Before them, in the dim reddish glow, was a black opening.

"Let's see where this goes," Malik said as he stepped into the pitch darkness.

"Wait, I don't think that's a good idea," Nathan cautioned. "Why do you always want to see where dark tunnels lead? This entrance was covered with a stone slab for a reason. People aren't supposed to go in there," he muttered. When Malik didn't give him a smart reply, he gave up. "Why am I wasting my breath?"

Malik's muffled call from deep inside the tunnel was lost in the wind's noise.

"Fine, now I'm talking to myself. You never listen to me anyway so I might as well go along so I can bail you out. I'll tie Sapphire to a rock and hope he's here when we come back—*If* we come back." Nathan secured the horse and gingerly stepped into the dark hole.

"Wait for me," he called. "Malik?"

South Giza, Menkaure Heliographic Research Station

Sarina had more warning of the sandstorm than Malik and Nathan. By now, she had trained Akhenat and Uriel to keep a constant watch for distant helio flashes. They called to her when they noticed the red cloud on the horizon.

She hadn't thought of what to do if the Menkaure station had to be quickly evacuated but knew that the portable heliograph instrument must be protected from the blowing sand. The gritty blast would scratch the polished mirror and other parts of the mechanism, delicate parts would be thrown out of tolerance by the flying pebbles, and tiny sand particles would find their way between the smooth, lubricated surfaces. It could take weeks to refurbish the instrument if it were damaged.

"Akhenat and Uriel, disassemble the machine like I showed you." She motioned to the guards. "Wrap each part in a piece of awning and carry them to the storage room below. There should be enough room there for us and the heliograph." They immediately began their chores and soon the men made their way down the side of the pyramid.

The wall of sand was almost upon them. The hot air was oppressive—the sun's glare was blinding.

"Uriel, fold up the rest of the awning and carry it down to the store room. If it's too heavy for you to carry then leave it behind and get to shelter. The heavy material will shield us from the direct force of the wind. I'll come behind you with the writing instruments."

"Miss, I should stay with you to make sure you reach the ground safely. The storm will be here in minutes," little Uriel said. His anxious eyes pleaded with her.

"Go! I'll be right behind you."

As Uriel struggled down the rough rocky steps with a piece of the awning, the rising scream of the sandstorm descended on the pyramid. The awkwardly folded awning and growing fear caused Uriel to stumble on the uneven stones but he finally reached the safety of the ground where a guard took the material from him.

By the time Sarina had put the blank papyrus sheets and writing instruments into a food basket, the wall of sand had darkened the sun. She wrapped her scarf around her head leaving a slit for her eyes. If she could just reach the bottom of the crumbling pyramid without falling, she'd be all right. She concentrated on balancing the food basket in the wind and stepping down as fast as she could without tripping over her skirt, wishing now she'd removed her expensive sandals first. When she lost sight of the stone steps in the dense, swirling red mass, she slowed and felt for the edges of the granite blocks with her free hand. How would she know when she reached the bottom? She should turn right to reach safety, but how far away was the storage room?

She stopped when she couldn't see her feet before her and the sand stung her bare hands and ankles. When the wind tried to knock her over she sat down in despair. She was terrified of being buried alive in the powdery sand.

A strong pair of hands grabbed her shoulders and snapped her out of her misery. "We're right over here, Miss" one of her bodyguards said as he helped her bent, shaking form walk twenty feet to the storage room where the awning cover flapped violently. She sat between her assistants while the two soldiers weighed down the corners of the awning with stones. The material didn't keep out the noise of the wind or prevent the fine dust from seeping around the edges, but it excluded most of the biting grains of sand.

"Miss, we will survive this storm. We've seen much worse storms in the middle of the desert with our general. Don't worry."

Little did the soldier realize how much his comment lifted her spirits. Maybe *her general* was thinking of her at this very moment. Uriel huddled next to her and tried not to cry. She put her arm around him. She'd wait out the storm with her eyes pressed shut and ponder what to say to the general when she next saw him.

Giza Complex, Great *Mastaba* Highway—Abandoned Tomb

The rough sides of the down-sloping tunnel seemed eerily familiar. It felt identical in dimensions to the tunnel dug from the well to Queen Hatshepsut's tomb. Nathan took tentative steps forward into the darkness hoping to reach his friend before he got into more trouble. When he heard footsteps ahead he called out and then stumbled into him seconds later.

"Let's go back," Nathan whispered. "This goes nowhere."

"I think I see a light ahead," Malik said.

"Your eyes are playing tricks in this darkness. This tunnel has no end."

"It must, I'm going to see where it leads."

Sure enough, he soon made out Malik's dim silhouette ahead. He stood before a sliver of light coming from the other side of another slab of limestone. There was enough light to see that the stone blocking the tunnel was similar to the stele fragment that covered the entrance behind them. He and Malik pushed the covering aside to reveal a sparse room carved into the rock.

"Look familiar?" Malik asked his friend when they stepped into the room and their eyes adjusted to the light.

"I'll say. That's the same glowing globe in the ceiling that we saw in Queen Hatshepsut's burial chamber. And over there is another of those smelly black flux boxes. Didn't Imhotep say that it made some sort of energy for the lights?"

"Not only that, but he said it was the source of energy for his golden cylinder and the *Breath of Osiris*."

"Not this one, though. That was back in Thutmose's pyramid. This must be another one."

"I don't think so. We're *in* Thutmose's pyramid. The large vault with the golden cylinder should be right through there." He pointed to a decoratively carved wooden door.

Nathan noticed that another set of tubes, wrapped in papyrus, led from the black coffin-like box through a hole in the wall.

Malik walked to the door and listened. "I hear someone talking on the other side. It sounds like Imhotep's voice!"

"We should peek in first and see who he's with. They probably don't know that there's a sandstorm raging outside and may not appreciate two dirty stragglers barging in on them."

"Good idea."

Malik opened the door a crack. He and Nathan locked their sights on the gold cylinder gleaming in the center of the brightly lit vault. Two expensively dressed men examined the cylinder while Imhotep pointed out the inscription around it. Tik-tik sat on his master's shoulder staring at the two men with unblinking eyes.

"The warning on the device is very clear: Anyone in this room when the *Breath of Osiris* is released will die. The crackling sound of energy flowing in from the flux source is unmistakable and grows in intensity until the cylinder is filled to its maximum capacity. In one sudden burst the pent-up flux flows up those tubes to the golden apex of the pyramid and is released into the sky. The *Breath of Osiris* will be seen in the heavens as far as the Great Oasis to the west and the Red Sea to the east."

"Brilliant! Brilliant!" one of the men exclaimed.

"Thank you, Vizier Nakhte," the inventor replied modestly.

"And you, Master Scribe Bakenmut? Are you also impressed?"

"The device is certainly beautiful to look upon," he said in a bored tone, "but does it work? How do we know that the substantial investment in royal gold will produce the glorious display that you predict so eloquently? Maybe it will only give off a tiny spark. How can we be sure?"

"Those are reasonable questions. If you return tomorrow I will give you a demonstration on a smaller scale that should convince you. I built a prototype using the same principal for General Herihor and the Amun Corps to use as a weapon. You will be the first people besides me to see it in operation."

"Then we will be here," Vizier Nakhte pronounced happily. "Now, we must go. We do not wish to be late for our audience with Pharaoh. We will give him a positive report of your progress, won't we Bakenmut?"

"Of course." the master scribe dutifully replied.

When Imhotep left with his guests to escort them to the front entrance, Malik opened the door further and stepped into the vaulted room.

"What are you doing?" Nathan hissed, trying to stop his friend.

"Don't worry, Imhotep's gone and we'll have some time to look around. I want to see if I can find that smaller version of the cylinder he mentioned." He walked around the periphery of the large room lifting the lids of wooden boxes and looking under tarps. He found a miniature version of the gold cylinder the size of his fist inside an ornate chest. One end of the cylinder was attached to a small flux box and thin tubes at the other end led to a golden sword two feet long with a forked tip. The handle of the sword was wrapped in leather. Malik held the weapon over his head. "*Breath of Osiris!*" he exclaimed in mock triumph.

"Be very careful with that, my friend," a loud voice commanded.

Tik-tik shrieked.

Malik nearly dropped the two-pronged weapon.

Imhotep stepped forward, gingerly lifted the golden sword from his hand and returned it to its scabbard. He acknowledged Nathan's presence with a nod. "I am a bit surprised to find you here. Did you come through the *mastaba* tunnel?"

"You know about it?"

"Of course I do. Tik-tik heard them digging and warned me days before they broke through the wall into the flux storage room. They weren't very good diggers and stone carvers, by the way. How they thought they'd get in here without being heard is beyond me. So how did you find it?"

They told him of the sandstorm outside, how they had entered the abandoned Prince Ankhaf tomb for shelter, and just happened to notice the slab that covered the tunnel entrance. They admitted to overhearing his explanation about the cylinder to the vizier and master scribe. Malik was intrigued by his description of the small-scale demonstration.

"I'm sorry for taking the sword out," Malik apologized.

"You are forgiven. I always admire one's curiosity and bravery. I'll be delivering that model to General Herihor in a few days; if you see him after that maybe he'll show you how it works."

"That's very kind of you, sir. Again, I'm sorry I went where I shouldn't have."

A quizzical look came over Imhotep's face. "If there's a sandstorm outside, I wonder how your sister is faring on top of the Menkaure pyramid. I hope she was able to find shelter."

"We need to find her!" Nathan exclaimed. He and Malik ran for the flux storage room and the tunnel exit.

"Wait! Do not touch anything that you find in the tunnel, especially anything hanging from the ceiling. I positioned some surprise traps for my clandestine diggers which you would not want to trigger by accident. Tik-tik knows how to activate them but I will make sure he stays here with me while you go ahead. Be careful." Imhotep waved farewell and his two visitors ran off to see if the sandstorm was over.

They walked in the dark as fast as they could while being mindful of things dangling in the dark.

"So the tunnel is booby trapped. Great! I told you we never should have come in here." Nathan couldn't resist scolding his friend.

Malik grinned in the dark. "Imhotep sounds like you—'Be careful.'"

CHAPTER 27

South Giza, Menkaure Heliographic Research Station

Sarina was reviewing messages from the previous day when Uriel called out for her attention.

"Miss! A message from the Zoser station!"

A small dot on the pyramid of Zoser in Saqqara blinked with the station's familiar header. When she realized that it was a plague alert message relayed from the Mennefer Palace, she grabbed a pen and papyrus to transcribe the warning:

> *ALERT-ALERT – Plague from Jehovah tomorrow morning...thunder, lightning, rain, hail from heaven... crops, livestock, anyone in the fields will be destroyed...seek shelter inside...worst storm in Egypt's history!*

The alert system was working!

Throughout the morning, more messages circulated within the Memphis network about preparations for the plague. News relayed in from distant stations acknowledging receipt. The news was like a virus sweeping across Egypt! By late afternoon an official announcement from the Mennefer Palace stated that the plague warning was a hoax and should be ignored. Sarina read a later comment suggesting that a Hebrew blinker in the palace station had been severely disciplined as an example to other blinkers.

How could people in the palace be so stupid? Didn't Pharaoh realize who he was up against? The gods of Egypt were no match for the God of the Hebrews. The palace could not tolerate the truth.

Sarina read the transcribed message for the hundredth time:

Plague from Jehovah tomorrow morning...

Why did the blinker insert God's unique Hebrew name in the message? He may have paid with his life for such a bold declaration of faith. Pharaoh and those around him were blind to the power of God. They'd rather destroy the country than submit to the God of Abraham!

Sarina shook her head in frustration. Her two assistants and the guards waited for her orders. Sarina's station contingent had great respect for this bright young woman who trusted in the God of the Hebrews more than in the gods of Egypt. If she believed that the plagues were from that God then maybe there was something to what was happening in the land after all.

"We'll be closed tomorrow," she announced in a calm voice. She instructed Akhenat and Uriel to disassemble the heliograph, secure it in the storage room at the base of the pyramid, and return to their homes. The soldiers wrapped up the awning and their tents and carried the basket of writing materials for Sarina.

As she and the two guards walked under the stars through the Giza complex on their way to Jasmine House, one of the soldiers spoke to her: "Miss, may I say something?"

"Of course, what is it?"

"We were told by our regimental officers and religious advisors that the plagues are a trick by the Hebrews. They said that much of the time the Hebrews are not affected and yet Egyptians suffered and died. It appears that our gods still cannot protect us. Our commanders tell us that we must kill the Hebrews first before they attack us. Do you believe that to be so?"

"I believe that the gods of Egypt can never stop the *LORD* of the Hebrews. I also do not believe that the slaves are enemies of Egypt. Since you have spoken freely, I will speak freely to you. Someday soon, Pharaoh will release the Israelites to return to their Promised Land. They will not attack their Egyptian masters but will trust their God to fight their battles for them. Until now, Pharaoh has refused to let them go although the plagues increase in severity. One day, Pharaoh will eventually have to give in to the God of the Hebrews but until then we must suffer because of our ruler's stubbornness." Sarina's treasonous statement against the supreme leader of the land surprised her. Yet what she said was true.

They continued walking toward Jasmine House. "Miss, you sound like our general." She sensed pride in the soldier's voice although she could not see him in the dark. "The rumor is that he confided to his personal guards that this *LORD* of the Hebrews is the One True God above all other gods. I don't know how he knows this, but he says that the divine purpose of the plagues, and the Great One's resistance, is to make God's name known among all the earth. He has also confided that we will never attack the Hebrews unless attacked first."

"I am very pleased to hear that. Thank you for your courage to speak to me about that."

Encouraged by her frankness, he continued: "We also hear that the general thinks of you often. They say he softly speaks your name when he is alone. I beg you not to tell him that I said this."

"What you say pleases me very much." Her face flushed with excitement. "Have I answered your question about the plagues?"

"Yes, Miss. Thank you."

They walked the rest of the way to Jasmine House without another word.

When the guards took their positions at the front gate, Sarina turned to them. "Be sure you take shelter tomorrow morning. I don't want either of you hurt."

"We plan to do that, Miss." Both soldiers saluted her smartly.

The Two Lands of Egypt

In spite of the warning on the helio net, most of the common people in Egypt were still taken by surprise. Wise Hebrews, and forewarned Egyptians who heeded the helio announcement, spent all night harvesting produce from their small garden plots and fields. God's judgment on Egypt was very real and, ready or not, they had to bring in the produce of the vines, bushes, and trees before they were destroyed. Barley and flax were a week or two from harvest while wheat and rye were more than a month from maturity. If the green vegetables and fruits were indoors, they should be safe. Likewise, their animals would not be harmed if secured in stables, sheds, and covered pens. Some brave slaves harvested some of their masters' crops and sheltered their livestock even though they were told to ignore the warning of coming destruction.

Proud Egyptians sided with their Pharaoh. They discounted the warnings as hysteria by a pair of zealous Hebrew brothers. When dawn broke the next day they looked out on their fields of standing grain and their groves of laden fruit trees and laughed at the God of the slaves. By mid-morning, however, the skies darkened and thunder rolled across the narrow, green ribbon of the Nile valley. A violent storm raged all day from Aswan to Memphis, exactly as the warning had predicted. First the winds ahead of the black line of thunderclouds bent the ornamental aspens and eucalyptus until they could bend no further. Elegant sycamores and poplars that lined the roads to old estates snapped like twigs. Lightning illuminated the houses and farms that were exposed to the full force of wind, rain, and hail. The plague grew into a disaster unlike anything seen in Egypt's history.

Thunderstorms this late in the growing season were not uncommon in Egypt. Hail formed when the rising humid air from the Nile valley met freezing air high in the sky which turned water droplets into ice pellets that fell to earth when they reached a critical weight. This storm was different. By God's divine hand, the falling pellets were carried up and down by fierce wind currents until they became the size of a man's fist and finally plunged to the ground at a high velocity. The bullet-like projectiles of rock-hard ice killed any workers, cattle, sheep, and horses not under shelter.

The deadly hail pummeled field crops and fruit trees until they were flattened under a heavy layer of ice. Those who found shelter were terrified by the lightning that accompanied the violent storm. Roiling rain clouds, lightning, and thunder were also familiar phenomenon to the Egyptians but they had never experienced a storm of such frightening scope and intensity. Bolts from heaven in all colors mixed with the hail. The people had seen brilliant flashes of lightning before, but this was very different. Balls of lightning fell from the sky and bounced along the ground where they made the layer of hail glow with a deadly blue light. Any man or beast caught in the open and not struck by hail, was incinerated when the lightning reached them.

That fatal day, the dawn was warm and tropical but by late afternoon puddles of rain were covered with a film of frost. Any undamaged fruit and vegetables were frozen inside shells of ice. The lightning, thunder and hail continued for the rest of the day as man and beast huddled shivering inside homes and covered stalls. When darkness came, it swallowed a shattered, humbled country. Besides the killing hail and lightning that seemed to have a mind of its own, Egyptian history scrolls would record the greatest temperature drop in memory. It did not record the more miraculous fact that the land of Goshen was completely untouched by the plague.

The sky goddess *Nut* and wind god *Shu* offered the nation no protection from the Almighty *LORD*. Pharaoh sent a messenger to tell Moses that he and his people could leave Egypt. Within hours of his order, Pharaoh's defiant spirit caused him to change his mind and cancel his permission as quickly as he had given it.

CHAPTER 28

Mennefer, Great House Palace

A breakfast of farina cereal in warm cow's milk with a dollop of honey was all that the world's most powerful monarch could eat. He had not bathed in the river this morning because it was too cold. He hunched over his bowl wrapped in a heavy, embroidered blanket and wondered why there were no birds singing their carefree melodies in his private garden this morning. Had he bothered to look outside, he would have seen a denuded landscape under his window. The lush fruit trees, flowering shrubs, and ornamental lily ponds were gone. During the night, servants cleared the shattered trees, raked the red dirt, filled in the pond, and rearranged the rocks in a barren courtyard. Pharaoh was willfully unaware of the bleak view from his window. He lamented bygone times when he had breakfasted on a roasted chicken stuffed with onions and garlic, a mound of boiled crocodile eggs, a hot loaf of bread, and a jug of wine. Bland porridge was all his digestive system could tolerate these days. He looked up to see Moses and Aaron standing before him. Bewildered by their sudden and unwanted presence, he scanned the room for his guards. How did those two get into his private room?

Moses repeated the same demand which Pharaoh's advisors had assured him would cease after the palace moved to Mennefer. This time, Moses demanded that *all* Israel—young and old, sons and daughters, flocks and herds—be allowed to depart into the desert to worship the *LORD*. While Moses spoke this new demand, a retinue of advisors, priests and scribes hurried into the room flanked by a half dozen armed guards. Their sovereign raised his hand for them to stop. The Hebrew prophet continued saying something about an infestation of locusts greater than any in the history of Egypt. When Moses finished his proclamation Pharaoh smiled and motioned for the guards to step aside so he and Aaron could leave. The two Hebrews remained before him awaiting a response.

The monarch broke into a broad, toothless grin. "This is most amusing! Locusts are nothing new in Egypt," he laughed. "Our crops have survived these invasions for many centuries. The corn gods *Nepri* and *Nepit* protect Egypt's fields from harm, do they not, Royal Priest?" Pharaoh's tired eyes searched for his top religious advisor somewhere in the group assembled before him.

The priest in charge of the temples of Mennefer gulped and stepped from behind Vizier Nakhte. "Of course, Great One," he replied with timid conviction.

"Then it is so!" Pharaoh spoke up cheerfully as if his words dismissed reality. "Allow this deluded Hebrew and his brother to leave here unharmed. There is nothing he or his god can do to the all-powerful forces of our gods who protect The Two Lands. I, the earthly incarnation of *Ra*, proclaim it to be so!"

The audience of advisors, priests, scribes and guards held their collective breaths in astonishment. They parted ranks and allowed the two Hebrews to leave the room. Moses had Pharaoh's answer.

The royal advisors filed out into the hallway and closed the door behind them. They could think of only two possible explanations for what they had witnessed: either Pharaoh was completely blind to the previous day's destruction—unimaginable even for a sick, elderly monarch—or he was mentally deranged. A third remote and more terrifying possibility was that he knew exactly what he was doing. This meant that he'd rather ruin the nation than give in to a slave's demand.

"You *must* do something, Vizier! Egypt is being destroyed all around us while the old man drools over his bowl of mush and grins like an imbecile." Royal Priest Metjen clenched his teeth in rage.

Nakhte and Royal Master Scribe Bakenmut exchanged quick glances.

"I will speak with the Pharaoh later. He's tired and still not fully recovered from the river voyage." Vizier Nakhte did not want the royal priest's heresy to grow contagious.

"It's more than that," the royal priest continued undeterred. "He must know about the devastation from the hail and lightning. The nation's economy is in tatters, yet he still insists that the gods will protect us. Up to now they've done nothing for us!"

"Now I too am worried, Royal Priest." The vizier's eyes narrowed and his voice turned icy. "When you, the palace spiritual leader, lose faith in the gods, where does that leave the rest of us ordinary men? It would seem that you and your gang of overpaid charlatans are not offering the proper sacrifices, interpreting the daily entrails correctly, or concocting more powerful curses against the god of Moses. Maybe it is you who have a problem and we should find your replacement?"

The priest recoiled at the Vizier's threat. The Royal Priest had only expressed what everyone in the palace must be thinking. Nobody noticed that a messenger slipped away from the entourage and ran down the hallway.

South Giza, Menkaure Heliographic Research Station

Later that day, a forecast of another plague issued from the palace. "Incoming message from Mennefer Palace, Miss." Uriel's sharp eyes were always the first to see new transmissions from the surrounding stations.

"Another alert so soon?" Sarina sighed when she recognized the message preamble. This one was from the palace and came too quickly after the hail and lightning plague. She hoped that the damaged towers and heliograph instruments at other stations were repaired enough so the alert could reach the distant towns and cities. The small network around Memphis was operational but so far today she hadn't seen any traffic from stations further away.

This alert message was framed in a more official style than the hailstorm warning. Either the Hebrew palace operators were more tactful or this one was drafted by an Egyptian supervisor with a better sense of political correctness. Either way, the warning would surely be heeded this time.

> *ALERT-ALERT – Warning to all – repeat all – stations…*
> *large swarm of locusts tomorrow…seal all seed, grain,*
> *and foodstuff in containers…pray to Nepri and Nepit for*
> *deliverance…*

"I suppose the propaganda about praying to Egypt's gods serves some official purpose. Not that anyone will bother praying to the corn gods this time," Sarina remarked.

She did not transmit an acknowledgment of most messages because the Menkaure site was technically only an Army experiment for General Herihor. Any message for her was sent through the Zoser station in Saqqara while she continued to intercept other messages between Giza and Mennefer. She mostly used the portable helio machine to chat with her fellow blinkers. A note from Hakamun and Elias in Goshen found its way to her a few days earlier. They reported that the storm produced only light rain and that the crops in the Nile delta were completely unharmed. One million Hebrew workers in the nation's breadbasket continued to harvest grains; vegetables and fruits prospered in the rich soil.

Late in the afternoon, Sarina gave orders to disassemble the equipment once again and store it and their supplies in preparation for a wave of insects. The station would be closed, of course, and her assistants returned to their homes. She and her bodyguards hurried back to Jasmine House to prepare for the inevitable.

The Two Lands of Egypt

The *LORD* sent a wind from the Red Sea and Arabia all day and night over the Eastern Desert and the Red Hills that carried hundreds of billions of winged invaders. When they descended on Egypt at dawn they feasted on every blade of grass, flower, bud, green stalk, and seed that had survived the hail and lightning.

At first, the sound was mistaken for a gentle rain. Soon, the soft hum became a loud, harsh, metallic buzz. Sunrise turned dark in the eastern sky as clouds of locusts rained down on Egypt. In years past, hoards of locusts originated in faraway Arabia and flew to the fertile Nile valley in search of food. Unlike any insect invasion they had experienced before, the great power of Almighty God extended beyond Egypt. He truly was the God of all the earth!

Soon, voracious insects covered the ground so deeply that not a speck of dirt or vegetation was visible. They feasted on anything that remained after the day of hail and lightning. Stray grains of barley or oats in the field were instantly consumed and then the invaders gnawed at the stalks until even bare nubs disappeared into the dirt. When the locusts found an enclosed grain storehouse they seemed to know how to break into it. They pried at the smallest crack or chink in the walls or doors with their strong legs and chewed away at any wooden obstructions with powerful jaws until they exposed an opening large enough for two, ten, hundreds, then thousands of the swarm to squeeze inside. Every building containing precious grain was soon emptied and the ravenous army moved on in search of more.

They flew into temples, homes of the rich or poor, even the Mennefer Palace in search of the tiniest scraps of food. The Hebrew homes were not exempt from the locusts that didn't care whose food they ate. The night before, wise slaves and some of their discerning masters had taken precautions to preserve raw grain, ground flour, wine, and fermented drinks in tightly sealed containers. They had emptied salt casks, barrels of clothes, stone cisterns—anything made of strong materials with a tight lid or covering. Household servants stood around the secured containers of food and beat insects away all day.

Wave upon wave of winged predators washed over Egypt. When one wave disappeared and before another arrived, a barren landscape of red soil extended to the horizon. The stone pyramids, stark against the dark sky, remained untouched. The lush green vegetation on either side of the Nile—Egypt's life-sustaining storehouse—was wiped away in one day. Without seeds, there would be no crops the next year and without grain the population would starve.

Even Pharaoh was touched by the grim scene from the Mennefer Palace. The songbirds were gone, his garden courtyard was a bare patch of red dirt, the servants were in a panic, and his bedroom was ankle-deep in the corpses of stinking insects.

He sent word that Moses was free to take his people into the wilderness.

Giza Complex, Jasmine House

No sooner had Pharaoh given Moses permission to take the Hebrews into the desert to worship, than the wind blew from the west and the locusts, those still alive and heavy with food for the return trip, flew back to Arabia. By sunset, a humbled country wondered how they would survive. Not only had the God of the Hebrews put the corn gods *Nepri* and *Nepit* to shame, but even the wind god *Shu* was obedient to the One who commanded the wind from Arabia and then turned it back again. Few appreciated that this plague and its reversal were actually God's mercy toward the Hebrews and Egyptians. Nobody died from this plague. He wanted them to acknowledge His power over life and death.

Jasmine House was left standing but not one tree, plant, flower or stalk of grass remained. All that Iset valued in the serenity and peace of her prosperous family home—lily pond, fruit and shade trees, blooming plants and vines, flower arrangements, sumptuous meals and drink—was gone. Hatep held his wife in his arms and felt her slim frame shake in helplessness. They wondered what more could possibly happen to their family.

Hatep was startled when Iset suddenly broke from his embrace and ran from their bedroom. He followed her to the front of the house where she threw open the double doors, ripped away a golden locust amulet she had strung around her neck for protection, and flung it away into the dirt outside the entryway. She cursed every god of Egypt she could name before she collapsed on the ground in tears. Hatep held her sobbing body and heard her cry out to *Jehovah* for deliverance.

Sarina's bodyguards saw and heard everything. They stood by their posts like stone statues on either side of the entrance to Jasmine House and stared wide-eyed into the distance.

Mennefer, Great House Palace

Pharaoh watched the clouds of locusts disappear into the eastern sky. He chuckled to himself and called for a courier.

"Tell Moses that he and his people will be stopped by the army if they attempt to leave the country. He will not get away so easily."

The courier ran through the palace to find the Vizier. Nakhte muttered to himself when the courier relayed the brief verbal order.

Pharaoh is insane!

CHAPTER 29

The Two Lands of Egypt

Each plague that demonstrated God's supernatural power increased in severity. Some came with advance warning; some harmed the Egyptians but not the Israelites; some were only annoying and some brought death and destruction. The next-to-last plague—though no one realized it at the time—was an unmistakable insult to the god at the core of Egypt's religion and culture. It came without warning to the general population and, while not physically painful or destructive, it contradicted what every Egyptian had been taught about the world's order.

They had been told from time immemorial that the sun-god *Ra* sailed his boat across the heavens during the day with his daughter *Sekhmet* and descended into the west in the evening. He was reborn again with new life each morning in the east to bless the earth with his energizing rays; all living things sprang to life and prospered under his warming care. The sun, with its many names: *Sacred Disc, Giver of Life, Circle of Light*, was the most visible and faithful of all Egyptian gods upon whom the other gods depended. People went to bed every night with the full expectation that their supreme deity would greet them in the morning with its life-giving warmth and light. Even when a bygone Pharaoh proclaimed the worship of *Amun-Ra* combining the invisible and visible deities, it was *Ra* that everyone knew dominated their daily life.

Ra was absent the next morning.

People sensed 'daybreak' in different ways. Children's hunger pangs told them it was time for breakfast, yet it was pitch black outside.

Farmers' and their livestock's inner clocks told them it was time to tend to their flocks or eat. Poor and affluent alike, who normally awoke to crowing roosters, heard nothing. Even Pharaoh, who slept only an hour or two at night, lay in bed and wondered why it was so dark and quiet.

As the morning—if you could call it that—drew on, more Egyptians and Israelites arose from their beds to a dawn like none in recorded history. The magicians always announced an eclipse in advance; they never passed up an opportunity to collect more votive temple offerings to *Amun-Ra* when the moon-disc passed before the sun and darkened the land at mid-day. Maybe another storm or swarm of insects had darkened the eastern sky, or perhaps it was smoke from a grass fire.

Not only was it dark to the eyes, but the all-penetrating darkness was *felt*. Walking inside or stepping outside was like wading through liquid darkness. The absence of natural or artificial light was absolute: a lit lamp gave off heat that burned fingers but produced no illumination; a cooking fire was invisible and servants quickly extinguished flames before they burned unnoticed and out of control; family members called to each other and reached out in panic for reassurance. Nobody dared walk outside for fear of being swallowed by the ink-like substance that washed over them. The unseen, oppressive grip of supernatural darkness even made it difficult for Egyptians to breathe.

The significance of the thick darkness confounded temple priests who predicted solar eclipses and attributed them to the power of *Amun-Ra*. The duration of a total solar eclipse was measured in minutes; however, this daytime darkness was absolute and lasted longer than anything they'd ever experienced. Those nobles who were dependent on servants or slaves waited for someone to bring them a lamp or a meal. Midday was indistinguishable from evening and everyone huddled in their homes. They prayed to their powerless gods and implored that this would pass so their lives could return to normal. Egyptians, immersed in total darkness, pondered the significance of this unusual plague.

Giza Complex, Jasmine House

Jasmine House was as upset as any other Egyptian household. Reuben, the faithful horse slave, looked after Hatep's few remaining horses and livestock. He knew the layout of the barn by heart and carefully opened a sealed grain bin to scoop enough feed to keep the animals quiet. All the hay had been eaten by the locusts and they had enough grain in barrels for about a month. When he realized that the darkness would not disappear anytime soon, he covered the nervous horses' eyes with strips of linen. They calmed enough so that he could exercise them in the barn aisle before watering them. He would ration their feed as long as he could.

Behind Jasmine House in the slave village, the humble one-room dwelling of Asher and Rachel was a testimony to God's mercy and faithfulness. Like other Israelite households, theirs was illuminated by lamps and a small cooking fire. Rabbi Ben-Judah spoke in the corner with Nathan and his friend Malik who had joined him earlier for companionship. "*Jehovah* is more powerful than all the gods of Egypt!" the blind teacher taught emphatically. "He is the Light of the world. All the gods of Egypt are nothing before Him." Malik and Nathan hung on his every word.

Rachel carried a bubbling kettle of porridge that she had prepared for her master and his family. She and Asher felt their way along a worn path through the darkness to Jasmine House. She found Iset clinging to Hatep on a couch in their bedroom. Her mistress had been crying but stopped when she heard her handmaiden's voice.

Rachel spoke to her as she placed the bowl of porridge in Iset's hands.

"I'm sorry that this is all I could bring you, Mistress. I'll bring something more later."

"Thank you, my dear. You are so gracious."

"It is only my duty. I wish I could do more."

"The LORD sent you to me. I am so thankful to Him."

Tears welled unseen in her slave's eyes.

"Thank you Asher," Hatep said when he felt his slave guide his hands to a bowl. "You are a true friend."

Before they left, Iset said that they would probably find Sarina in her bedroom.

"We'll be back later with some bread, dried fruit, and drink," Rachel said, although she had no idea whether it was daytime or night.

"How can you bake anything in this terrible darkness?" Hatep asked. "How did you see to make this porridge?"

Asher thought carefully before answering. "I cannot explain it fully, Master, but the thick darkness has not penetrated inside our humble home. We have lamps and a cooking fire." He didn't know how his next statement would be received.

"Master, you would be welcomed to seek shelter in our home."

Iset felt her husband tense. She'd been in the slave's home in the West Bank slave village, but she knew her husband felt differently about associating too closely with slaves. "We'll wait here," he replied. "We appreciate what you've done for us." He was not ready to admit dependence on his Hebrew slaves or their God.

Rachel felt her way to Sarina's room where she found her sitting on a carved settee by the window. She sat in the darkness with the invisible, fresh breeze on her face. Asher left to make sure that the house kitchen fires were fully extinguished. Rachel sat next to Sarina and pressed a bowl of porridge into her hands which she held without eating.

"Are you all right?" Rachel asked. "Aren't you going to eat?"

"I'll eat later. Thank you for bringing this to me. I know you love me like your own daughter. I wish I had your peace about all this."

"I do love you—I have since you were a baby," she said as tears welled for the second time in minutes. "What else have you been thinking about?"

"Like everyone else, about what these plagues mean and what the future holds for me and our nation. Your people will be leaving soon for your Promised Land—I can tell that the plagues will only get worse until Pharaoh finally relents. Mother and Father disagree about this, but I've made up my mind."

"Made up your mind about what?"

"About whether to go with you and the other Hebrews or to stay here in Egypt."

"You've made your own decision?" Rachel was surprised by how much this young woman had grown in the past months. At Lotus House she had wasted her days on silly puzzles and riddles after finishing scribal school, and she could pout like a child if she didn't get her way. Now she ran a helio station on Menkaure's pyramid and military bodyguards obeyed her commands.

"Don't ask me to tell you my decision because I must tell Mother and Father first. You'll know when the time is right."

"Of course, I know your decision will be a wise one." She secretly hoped that Sarina would leave Egypt with them.

"Could you make sure my guards are fed? They're very loyal to me; I expect they'll be at their usual post by the entrance."

"Of course, Miss." The Hebrew slave felt her way out of Sarina's room and called for Asher to take her to the front of the house.

The supernatural darkness continued for days; without distinction between dawn and dusk it seemed much longer. Hunger and boredom compounded with fear and isolation took their toll. Some panicky Egyptians ran outdoors, became disoriented, and lost themselves in the maze of tombs and pyramids in the Giza complex or in the featureless, dusty fields of flattened wheat and barley. Others stumbled into marshes and canals where they drowned or were attacked by crocodiles. Those who stayed in their homes listened to the terrifying howls of blinded men and beasts who stumbled about outside in the darkness.

South Giza, Menkaure Heliographic Research Station

As soon as Sarina saw the first hint of a sunrise, she dressed and hurried out of the house to the Menkaure station. She startled her bodyguards who were dozing at their post. They trotted after her across the barren landscape.

The sun's rays came over the horizon for the first time in three days. Long shadows of the nearby pyramids stretched toward the red western hills. Sarina craved a message from anyone. The sun had to rise higher in the sky before the mirrors could reflect its rays to other stations to the north or south. By the time Akhenat arrived with her breakfast, she detected the first points of light flickering through the shimmering thermal layers low on the horizon.

An hour later, clear signals arrived with news of the locusts and the darkness. Blinkers from distant stations made no attempt to minimize the total destruction of all the food in Egypt. By most accounts, there remained only 30-60 days of food in the nation! After that food was gone, nobody knew what would happen.

One blinker, obviously a Hebrew operator, issued a long, uninterrupted transmission about how four hundred years ago when the Hebrew Vizier Joseph guided the land. Joseph foretold seven years of famine and when Pharaoh made him vizier in charge of the harvest he accumulated vast storehouses of grain in preparation for the days when harvests ceased and nothing would grow in Egypt. *"I wish we had a man like Vizier Joseph today!"* the operator boldly declared in blinker code across the network. He then signed off from his station and said he was leaving to join Moses.

"How true," Sarina admitted to herself. "I wish someone would take charge of this nation, but neither this Egyptian pharaoh nor his vizier seem capable of doing that. If The Two Lands had a Hebrew vizier today, he would take us all in a new direction."

Mennefer, Great House Palace

When Moses informed Pharaoh that a final plague remained, a momentary ripple of relief went through the audience assembled in the royal throne room. However, when they heard what it was, Moses' description of God's judgment only brought hopelessness and despair.

The *LORD* was not yet finished with Egypt and its Pharaoh. One more demonstration of His mighty power would tip the scales of Pharaoh's heart and force him to set the Hebrews free. Not only would each household free its slaves, but their masters would give them gold and riches to take on their journey. By this time, most masters had concluded that their slaves would eventually leave Egypt and not return. Many masters were secretly thankful for their slaves' past kindnesses toward them throughout the plagues. Many secretly acknowledged that the Hebrew's God had humbled the gods of Egypt, including the Pharaoh, the Great One—*Men-kheper-ra*—the Manifestation of *Ra*.

Moses and Aaron left the Mennefer Palace for the last time.

One grain of fine sand followed another through the official hourglass in the center of the palace. A sand counter, only twelve years old, was in charge of the delicate timepiece. He wrote with chalk on a large board the number of hours and days remaining until the Angel of Death visited The Two Lands of Egypt at midnight.

CHAPTER 30

Saqqara, Amun Corps Garrison

"What is this?" Malik asked as he and Nathan pulled up next to three horses harnessed to a silvery chariot unlike any they'd ever seen. The standard two-horse military configuration was replaced by a wider harness that tied three horses to a yoke whose single shaft attached to the undercarriage of a wide chariot body and pivoted on a single peg. Compared to Malik's one-horse speedster, this horse-drawn weapon platform towered over him.

General Herihor greeted them with a proud grin. "Imhotep delivered this yesterday for the Leopard Charioteers to evaluate. It's a revolutionary design that has my men excited. It's just a prototype, of course, but I believe this design is the future of Egyptian chariot warfare. Even the Hittites, who invented the chariot, have nothing like this."

Nathan ran his hand over the seamless, shiny metal that curved around the platform. "This isn't silver. What is it?"

"It's some sort of miracle metal that Imhotep's metallurgists concocted in their foundry. He came across the formula in ancient scrolls written by his ancestors. It's lightweight and yet strong enough for armor." Herihor reached into the chariot and withdrew a two-piece set of body armor.

"Feel how light this is," he said as he tossed the pieces to Malik. "Our heavy leather armor works well enough against most arrows and knives but not against long swords and axes. This metal is lighter and all but the hardest thrusts bounce off."

Malik banged the armor against the chariot wheel producing only a slight scratch on the burnished surface. The lightweight material was also used for the frame of an awkward-looking elevated structure behind the driver's position.

"The three-horse harness allows for a wider chariot platform which gives room for this tall device." Herihor climbed four ladder rungs to the top where he leaned against a solid railing as high as his chest. He was eight feet above the ground.

"Is that for the archer?" Malik asked.

"Two archers, and they don't have to stand exposed in the open. Behind this armored railing they can shoot over the top and duck down whenever arrows come their way. Up here, they can't be reached by ground troops with swords or mounted cavalry with spears. My men ran through mock engagements this morning, and nobody could reach the archers. I've already petitioned Vizier Nakhte to authorize funds for many more. If I had one hundred of these," the general mused out loud, "I wouldn't be afraid to take on the Hittites, Canaanites, Amorites, or whoever stood in our path."

"Is that what this weapon is for?" Nathan asked. "Not for use against Israelites?"

"Never!" General Herihor reacted instantly and emphatically. He jumped down from the archer platform. "No!" His eyes flashed with rage. "I'll *never* use this or any of the Amun Corps against them." His emotions subsided when he realized what he'd just said. "Of course," he continued with more composure, "if I was ordered to repel an Israelite attack, then I would obey the orders of my Pharaoh." His compressed lips formed a thin line.

"Let me show you something else Imhotep made for us." He changed the subject by climbing into the cockpit of the chariot and removing what looked like a short forked sword from a scabbard. The handle of the sword was wrapped in leather and two strands of tubing sheathed in papyrus led from it to a box on the floor.

"We've seen that before!" Nathan said.

"You have? Imhotep said it had never been tested before he delivered it to me."

Malik explained, "He showed it to us but we've never actually seen it work. Can you show us now?"

"I'd rather describe its effect than give you a demonstration. Imhotep called it a *muscle exciter* or *stunner* that incapacitates anyone stabbed by these two sharp prongs." Herihor gestured toward two tiny needles at the tip of the spear spaced about an inch apart. "When these pierce an attacker's clothing, an invisible force runs through his body and sends him into a violent convulsion. He falls to the ground where he is unable to move for several minutes. The pain is intense but of short duration and wears off quickly. Our toughest soldiers were reduced to whimpering children. The drawback is that it only works once before its energy must be renewed."

With the tour of the chariot and its stunning weapon over, General Herihor stepped back to admire the gleaming body of his new chariot.

"This chariot is very nice," Malik said with admiration. "I don't suppose you'd let us take it for a spin, would you?"

"Malik! Please don't!" Nathan was aghast that his friend would ask such a thing. The general would never let them drive this one-of-a-kind war machine. What if they wrecked it?

"I don't see why not." General Herihor said, to Nathan's surprise. "Imhotep designed it for rough combat use and my men put it through every maneuver they could think of this morning. It seems almost indestructible."

"You don't know my friend…" Nathan warned.

"Can we take it on the Great *Mastaba* Highway and see what it'll do there?" Malik's thirst for breakneck speed was insatiable.

"Oh no!" Nathan had visions of them losing control of the horses and destroying the general's new chariot. "Let's just take it for a short ride around the parade ground."

However, the general seemed unfazed by Malik's request. "Yes, you may take it on the highway under two conditions." He motioned for Nathan to join him in the driver's compartment. When he stepped up into the chariot he handed him the reins.

"First, Nathan must drive. Second, my squadron captain will show him how to control the three horses since I assume he has never driven such a configuration before. Will you agree to those conditions?"

Malik nodded in agreement. Nathan gulped and took the reins from the general. For the next half hour he received instructions on the large rig while a crowd of bystanders watched him maneuver around the parade ground. When the chariot pulled up to the general, the captain was smiling.

"General sir, the young man is a natural with horses!" He clapped Nathan on his shoulder and saluted his general. "I'd let him drive my chariots any day."

"Excellent!" Herihor motioned for Malik and Nathan to join him in the shade of a nearby tent. While they drank cups of cool water, the charioteer captain had the horse grooms water the animals and rest them briefly before they left the garrison toward Giza.

Giza Complex, Great *Mastaba* Highway

Nathan was cautioned about running the horses at a full gallop for any extended time. It was senseless to press such valuable animals to their limits in peacetime. Wartime combat was different—chariot and cavalry horses had to give their lives to protect their riders and achieve victory in battle. They would still run faster on the Great *Mastaba* Highway than Sapphire could pull Malik's chariot.

For their first run down the highway, Nathan drove at a fast trot and Malik stood on the archer platform in the fresh wind. Above the dust and flying rocks, he closed his eyes to feel the thrill of racing into the wind.

"We'll do one more run at a full gallop and that will be it," Nathan yelled above the pounding of hoofs on the packed pavement. He turned the chariot around in the middle of the wide thoroughfare and looked ahead at two miles of smooth, straight road. They'd cover that distance in minutes!

While Nathan's mind concentrated on handling the reins and Malik stood on the archer platform with his eyes closed, neither saw three chariots with royal markings pull out of the old Prince Ankhaf tomb and race to intercept them. Although the three-horse war chariot was faster, the others had timed their exit from the abandoned tomb perfectly to intercept them. Nathan felt his steeds pull to the left as his attackers, still unseen to him, came closer. The sound of his horses drowned out those of the chariots closing in on his right.

Movement out of the corner of his eye drew Nathan's attention from the thundering trio in front of him. He turned his head just in time to see a chariot with two men in it nearly next to him. He instinctively jerked the reins away to the left and the pursuer followed directly behind him. The sharp turn snapped Malik out of his dream. The chariot tried again to pull alongside them. Nathan felt his horses tiring after running at full speed for nearly two miles. It was just as well that they slowed because the Great *Mastaba* Highway made a ninety-degree turn onto a narrow stretch of road with rows of tombs nearby on either side.

Each time the chariot tried to pull beside them, Nathan swerved to cut them off and they pulled back. With his horses tiring and the narrow road that weaved among the *mastabas* fast approaching, he no longer held a speed advantage. The war chariot was more ruggedly built than his pursuer's fancy vehicles and this gave him an advantage. If he had to crash into them they'd be the worse for it.

What was Malik thinking when he asked to take the brand new metal chariot out for a spin? If he crashed General Herihor's new chariot he'd never forgive himself, or Malik!

His momentary lapse of attention allowed the other chariot to pull beside them and the passenger, brandishing a curved scimitar connected to a heavily tattooed arm, jumped onto the rear of the platform. Malik kicked him in the head from above and knocked off his ragged turban. Another kick caused him to lose his balance and he wavered precariously before he grabbed the railing with his free hand.

"Nathan! I can't stop him forever. Do something!"

In spite of the close confines of the narrow road, Nathan swerved back and forth in hopes of knocking their attacker off. Instead, Malik lost his balance and nearly tumbled into the road. He hung to the outside of the elevated archer stand. If he let go he might fall onto the driver's platform next to Nathan, or he might bounce off and onto the road.

Suddenly he had an idea. He concentrated on timing his drop to happen when Nathan wasn't swerving. Fortunately, the man with the razor-sharp scimitar was also preoccupied with keeping his balance and staying in the chariot. Malik let go, fell onto the driver's platform floor, and gripped the railing with his left hand. With his right he pulled Imhotep's muscle stunner from its holster and pointed the large fork at the assailant who looked him in the eye and broke into a sickening laugh. His yellow checkerboard teeth, disheveled filthy hair, and rags for clothing were laughable but the tattoos on his arm marked him as a mercenary killer. Malik wondered why they would be chasing him in a royal chariot?

With a loud yell the assailant aimed the point of his scimitar at Malik's face and lunged forward. The length of the stunner in Malik's outstretched hand was a few inches longer than the scimitar in his attacker's hand and the two prongs pierced his thin shirt first. His face contorted in shock and he literally flew backwards off the chariot. His scream was drowned out by the horses' hooves as the second chariot ran over his body. It swerved away and the third chariot took its place. This one carried an archer whose arrow was notched and ready to fire.

"Great!" Malik shouted. He took cover in front of the elevated platform just as an arrow whizzed past his head.

"Don't let this guy get beside us. We're shielded from behind for now."

"I'll try, but these horses are tiring." Nathan struggled to keep them under control.

"If he comes up on either side we can always hide behind the metal railing."

"You can, but I can't hold the horses that way. I'll have to stay here."

Another arrow flew past them and stuck in the heavy wood and leather harness of their nearest horse. Another inch and it would have hit the horse's neck.

"He's aiming at the horses now!"

"I'll keep swerving as long as I can but there's not much more I can do. I think the road widens up ahead and then he'll have plenty of room to pass and cut us off."

While Nathan concentrated on driving the horses, Malik glanced back every ten seconds to see what their pursuer was doing. He saw the archer's bow bend for a shot and quickly pulled his head back behind the metal shield. When nothing flew past or hit the metal screen, he took a quick peek. The archer was gone and the chariot with only a driver remaining swerved down a side road. The last chariot slowed and also turned away.

"They're gone! You can ease up now."

Much to Nathan's relief, he let the reins fall slack and the exhausted horses responded immediately. Nathan slowed them to a walk, their bodies gleamed with sweat, they snorted, and their mouths foamed from working their bits for nearly an hour. Another chariot approached from behind them at a fast walk.

When Nathan caught sight of the orange plume of the Leopard Charioteers on the passenger's helmet he brought his own horses to a stop. "It's General Herihor!" he exclaimed. He leaned his tired frame on the metal railing. His hands ached from working the rains.

Malik dismounted and walked toward the general's chariot as the officer and his driver stepped down. "Thank you for saving us from those assassins, General. Were you following us? If so, I'm very grateful for that."

"Yes and no. We wanted to see how the chariot performed at high speed so we watched you from a distance. When those three chariots came out of nowhere it took us a few minutes to gather our things and join the fray. You both did a fine job repelling that attacker who jumped aboard."

"Malik tested the muscle stunner on a live subject," Nathan announced as he joined the group. "It sure worked!"

"I was impressed," the general's chariot driver said. "You fellows know how to take care of yourselves."

"I'm only sorry he died because of this. I know it was either us or him but it's still upsetting." Neither Malik nor Nathan had seen someone killed before.

It was hard for the seasoned army general or his driver to fully sympathize so they said nothing.

After a minute, General Herihor fetched a wooden device from his chariot. He showed them another product from Imhotep's workshop. It was a bow affixed to a short stock of wood that shot small arrow-like projectiles called bolts. The sharpened bolt was placed in a groove along the stock and notched into the bowstring. Then the archer drew the string back until it was extremely taut where a lever held the string under tension until ready to fire. The device was aimed and fired by simply releasing it with a trigger in the stock. Imhotep said it and the metal chariots would revolutionize warfare.

"Where's the archer?" Malik asked.

"We'll find his body and the one you stunned on our way back to the garrison. They're not going anywhere," the general replied.

"You both know my friend here, of course." General Herihor nodded in the direction of his driver. They realized for the first time that instead of a soldier's tunic he was dressed like a palace servant. The front of his shirt was stained with grease. He was a cook!

"I don't think so," Malik shook his head.

"Good," the man replied. "That means nobody else will recognize me either."

He extended his hand, "Medjay Chief Inspector Hezbak of Thebes at your service."

When the two chariots pulled up to the dead archer's body lying face-down in the road, Nathan and Malik stayed in their chariot while Herihor and Hezbak examined him. There was no doubt that the bolt killed him instantly before he fell from his chariot. He still held his bow in a clenched fist.

Hezbak turned him over and exclaimed, "I know this man!"

"You know him?"

"He was a palace courier in Thebes. He came to my office once to take a confidential message to the palace. I thought he was Vizier Nakhte's private emissary, now I'm not so sure. He must work for the Black Falcon."

"If that's true, then the Black Falcon wants Malik and Nathan dead. You need to find the Black Falcon as soon as possible."

"I agree and I know just how to do it. I'll corner my prime suspect as soon as I set up the trap."

"Well, make it quick. Not only are these two in mortal danger but Sarina and her family are also. I'll double the guard on Jasmine House and at the Menkaure pyramid station."

After they buried the two bodies in the sand they returned to the Saqqara garrison at a slow trot. Hezbak rode with Nathan and Malik and explained his presence in the Memphis area as part of his investigation into the stolen gold from Queen Hatshepsut's tomb. He preferred to not reveal how he intended to expose the Black Falcon and extract a confession from him.

CHAPTER 31

Mennefer, Temple of *Sobek*

"Do I know you?" Royal Master Scribe Bakenmut asked the man who stood in the shadows of the temple dedicated to the reptile-god *Sobek*. "Step into the light so we can speak face-to-face like men."

Inspector Hezbak had summoned Pharaoh's royal scribe with a simple scribbled note on cheap parchment stating that he had information about the Black Falcon. This was sure to intrigue his prime suspect enough to come to the remote shrine on the Nile. The Temple of *Sobek* near the Mennefer Palace was modeled after the Temple of *Kom Ombo* in the *Ta-Seti* nome below Aswan. The *Sobek* Temple was dedicated to the reptile-god with a human body and the head of a crocodile which was said to possess magical, protective powers. The temple was surrounded on three sides by a crocodile-infested swamp and usually devoid of priests and worshippers since the large creatures often slithered through the complex unhindered. The inspector counted on Bakenmut feeling secure under the protection of *Sobek* in this out-of-the-way place. The Medjay official wanted a voluntary confession without resorting to violence; but if force became necessary, he was prepared.

The Chief Inspector stepped into the dim puddles of light cast by torches around the circular temple stone wall; he wore a pressed white linen Medjay tunic with his official gold credentials around his neck on a scarlet ribbon. He was no longer undercover in a soiled scullery apron. The kitchen odors of chopped onions, shallots, and garlic had been scrubbed from his pores. He was clean-shaven and smelled of expensive perfume. As many times as he had served meals to the master scribe in the palace banquet hall, he was certain that he wouldn't recognize him now.

The two adversaries stood ten feet apart and looked at one another with cautious, appraising eyes. Like two predators in a standoff, they waited to see who would make the first move. Hezbak took the initiative.

"I know who you are."

"Everyone knows who I am," the master scribe replied coyly. "The question is: Who are you?"

"I am Chief Inspector Hezbak of the Theban Medjay. I am here to arrest you for the theft of national treasures from the tomb of Queen Hatshepsut."

Bakenmut pretended to look mystified. "Arrest me? Why would you want to arrest me?"

"I know who you are," Hezbak repeated. He stepped forward. "You are the Black Falcon. I arrest you for high crimes against Pharaoh, the royal family, and the people of Egypt. You will come with me to stand trial before the Theban Court of Justice and face death by the Grand Inquisitor."

"The Black Falcon? Arrest, trial, execution? I am the Royal Master Scribe who is above the laws of The Two Lands! And you are what? Nothing but a policeman!"

"I am the Medjay Chief Inspector of Thebes." Hezbak advanced until he was a foot away from the arrogant master scribe. His face was grim with determination. "You *will* come with me. On the other hand, you might have a fatal accident along the way and never reach Thebes." He glimpsed a hint of fear in Bakenmut's face like a fleeting shadow. The royal official stiffened and drew himself to his full height.

"You listen to me," he demanded, "I cannot be prosecuted. If you touch me I'll have *you* arrested."

"What about Pharaoh and Vizier Nakhte? Are you above them also?"

"Those fools!" he mocked. "Our 'king' is so senile that he can barely feed himself. And Nakhte busies himself with so many royal ceremonies and religious rituals, that he knows nothing about what really goes on in The Two Lands. He leaves the nation's important business to me. I stole tons of gold from under their noses and they knew nothing—Those fools!" The master scribe's venomous words hissed from between clenched teeth.

"What of the Egyptian Army?" Hezbak asked. "Aren't you afraid of a military takeover if what you say is true?"

"The military does what the Big House tells them to do. The generals obey all royal orders like good soldiers. Besides, who do you think writes those orders? Me!"

"I've heard enough. Come with me." The inspector grabbed Bakenmut by his arm and spun him around. In seconds his wrists were tied with a woven linen cord and he pushed the Black Falcon toward the river.

"Not so fast, policeman," a voice behind him commanded. He felt the point of a spear press through his light tunic and into his back. He released his grip on the prisoner.

"It took you long enough, Imani. Untie my hands," Bakenmut snapped.

When he was released, he rubbed his wrists and turned on the Chief Inspector whose hands by then were tied behind him with the same cord.

Flanked by the Deputy Architect and Thethi, Bakenmut leaned into Hezbak's face and laughed. "So who's under arrest now? Now who's going to face the Theban Grand Inquisitor?"

"Theban Grand Inquisitor?" asked Imani. "I thought we agreed to feed his carcass to *Sobek*?"

"Of course we did, you fool! Don't argue with me!" The royal scribe rolled his eyes.

He beckoned for a heavily tattooed mercenary waiting in the shadows to come forward. "Feed him to the crocodiles. Make sure he's bleeding but still alive when you throw him into the water. I don't want a single piece of his body to be found."

"I know what to do," the hired muscle replied with no emotion.

Before Hezbak was led to the river and a gruesome death, the master scribe mocked him one last time.

"So now you know the identity of the Black Falcon, for all the good it will do you. You may take that knowledge to your death." He plucked Hezbak's gold Medjay identification card from the ribbon around his neck, admired its heft, and put it in his pocket. "I wonder what those two troublemakers and their sister will say when I show them this?"

Unshaken, the inspector gave Bakenmut no satisfaction, even facing death: "When you go to sleep tonight you'll wonder if one of my emissaries is waiting in the dark to slit your throat; or it might be something sweet slipped into your breakfast tomorrow morning; or it could be an adder swimming in your bath or a deadly insect in your bed. One day soon the Black Falcon will die a horrible death. Very soon!"

The hulking thug pushed Hezbak into the darkness toward the reptile-infested papyrus thickets along the river bank. Bakenmut hid the tremor of his hands in the folds of his royal robe. The inspector's threat unnerved him to the core. Even after he heard a splash and a blood-chilling scream in the distance, the Medjay's prediction still echoed through his mind: *"One day soon the Black Falcon will die a horrible death. Very soon!"*

CHAPTER 32

Giza Plateau, Jasmine House

Iset dismissed the kitchen and house servants for the night after the family's dinner was set on the table. Malik and Sarina felt that their parents had something important to say. Serious conversations at the dinner table, when they were both younger, were often stern lectures that ended in tears and shouting. A similar tension was in the air tonight.

Hatep picked at a chicken wing; his wife pushed food around her plate. Sarina couldn't stand the tension any longer.

"We know something's bothering you two. Tell us what it is, please."

Hatep set the chicken on his plate, dipped into the finger bowl of scented water, and wiped his hands and mouth with a napkin. He rehearsed this conversation with Iset last night, but he wasn't sure how it would sound now.

"This is difficult for me to speak about. It involves the balance of *ma'at* in our family. Your mother and I love you two very much. We have had many fine seasons of peace and stability in our family—in spite of small difficulties along the way. I don't want our family broken apart any further but it might be unavoidable."

"You and mother are getting divorced!" Malik exclaimed in disbelief.

"No!" Iset said quickly. "That's not it at all."

"Then what's all this talk of our family being broken apart?" Sarina asked.

Hatep searched for the right words. "Months ago the God of the Hebrews turned the river to blood and then a string of plagues came as one upheaval after another tore apart our nation. Of course, you know this. The plagues have taken their toll on our family too."

Hatep sipped from his cup before he continued. "I no longer believe in the gods of The Two Lands. This belief, or lack of it, cuts to the core of what it means to me to be Egyptian. This God of the Hebrews is so much more powerful than the gods of our forefathers. Those gods cannot protect us from harm. Now I see that the gods of Egypt were fabrications of ignorant priests and money-hungry men. Months ago, in a fit of rage and despair, I smashed the statue of *Osiris* at the entrance to Lotus House. Your mother threw her lucky locust amulet away and cursed *Khepera* and the pantheon of insect gods when the swarms attacked us. I never thought I'd admit this out loud: *there is no other God than Jehovah.*"

Sarina breathed a sigh of relief. "Father, I agree with you," she said softly.

"Me too," Malik added quickly. "I believed that before we moved here to Giza. Ben-Judah told me about the promises of Abraham. The land of Canaan is waiting for the Hebrews and anyone who will join them." Malik wasn't sure how his father would take his next statement. "I want to go with them when they leave Egypt for the Promised Land."

Hatep looked down at the table and then up at his son. "This is as I suspected, which is the reason for our talk tonight."

His wife had a further admission: "The reason our family is split is because I too want to follow Moses to that Promised Land."

"And Father does not?" Sarina asked. Her parents had had their differences on many issues, but this sounded ominous.

"I'm not sure…" her father admitted. "What I mean is, I haven't made up my mind yet whether to stay in Egypt or go with the Hebrews. The day will come soon when Pharaoh lets them leave. If I decide to go with them, then we will go together as a family; if I stay here, then your mother is willing to remain with me, for better or for worse. You, Malik, seem to have your mind made up to go."

"Yes, I want to go to Canaan with Ben-Judah, Nathan, and his family," Malik said firmly. "In one year I'll be old enough to leave without your blessing, but by then it would be too late. I hope you'll give me your blessing now so I can leave with them soon."

Malik looked at his sister. "I assume Sarina wants to leave too."

"No!" Sarina said with sudden conviction. "What I mean is: Yes, I want to go to the Promised Land also, but like Mother, I will stay with the one who will be my husband one day. He's Egyptian and I think that he will choose to stay here."

Her mother and father were stunned by her announcement.

"And who might this future husband of yours be and why have we not met him?" Hatep demanded.

"Oh, you've met him, Father. And you too, Mother."

"Well...? Speak young lady!" Hatep's impatience was building.

"I intend to marry General Herihor. Wherever he goes, I will be by his side."

Sarina's father slammed his fist on the table and the dishes clattered. "He's old enough to be your father—I forbid it! Why has he not followed our tradition and spoken to me first about this?"

Sarina faced her father calmly. "First, only a little more than ten years separates our ages, which is not that much these days. Second, he hasn't spoken to you because he doesn't know about my plans yet. I will discuss our engagement with him at the earliest opportunity."

Iset rose from her chair to calm her husband. He sputtered and his face turned bright red. "Calm yourself, dear," she soothed, "we don't want to call the physician at this late hour." She stood behind him and rubbed his shoulders.

"You see, Father, I have everything planned for us. The difference in our ages is immaterial. The general is clearly in love with me and I with him—the evidence is obvious. I'm convinced that it's only a matter of time before he asks me to marry him. I don't see anything wrong with moving our marriage date forward, especially since the final plague is imminent." Her confidence that the general was in love with her and would soon become her husband bewildered her parents. What Sarina described flew in the face of centuries of family tradition. Their daughter was being irrational! Apparently the general knew nothing of her wedding plans, but that didn't seem to diminish her certainty that they would be married.

"It seems to all depend on you then, Father," Malik bluntly summarized the evening's discussion. "Your decision will determine the future of our family. Here's the way I see it: whatever you decide, Mother will remain with you. According to Sarina's unfathomable estimation of the romantic situation, she'll marry General Herihor and move into a tent in the Saqqara military garrison. When the time is right, I'll head east with Ben-Judah, Nathan and his family to the Promised Land."

"I think I'll go to my room now," Sarina announced, having dropped a bombshell on her family.

Malik stood at the same time. "This enlightening family talk has worn me out too. I'm going to bed." He helped himself to a drumstick and headed to his room.

Hatep barely felt his wife rub his shoulders. He stared into the flickering flame of the oil lamp and was stunned by what had just happened. His family was finally shattered beyond repair. The God of the Hebrews was tearing his country, his family, and his soul to shreds.

Saqqara, Amun Corps Garrison – General Herihor's Quarters

An inner battle was also taking place in General Herihor's private quarters. After he dismissed Kahn, he sat in the shadows away from a small lamp on the wall. It was eight months since the first plague. The gods of The Two Lands had been humiliated by the Hebrews' God and this confounded the Egyptians. Even the disc-god, the source of all life in the heavens and on earth, had been blotted out in a show of supernatural power. *Amun-Ra's* incarnation on earth, *Men-kheper-ra* Thutmose III, was a straw in the wind compared to the God that the Hebrews called *I AM*. With the keen mind of a military tactician, Herihor made a logical assessment of the balance of forces and concluded that the mightiest army in the world would be crushed in an instant if the God of Israel chose to do so. Thus, it was futile to fight against Him; Herihor was an Egyptian soldier who had taken an oath to serve the Great One; he was the Commanding General of the Amun Corps; a battle-tested leader of 10,000 soldiers; he was trained to fight Egypt's enemies and his nation was under attack. So what would he do now?

If it was suicide for him and his men to attack Almighty God, what could he and his men do? Surrender? No, Pharaoh would never allow that. Most of his fellow soldiers would consider him a traitor if he ordered them to lay down their weapons before the omnipotent God worshiped by mere slaves. Surrender was out of the question. He could easily imagine what the Mennefer Palace would order if their wise men came to the same conclusion. The Amun Corps would be ordered to attack the Hebrew slaves instead of their God. Then what would he do?

Across the room, his golden *wesekh* with engraved bees awarded for his great victory reflected the lamp's shimmering flame. It symbolized the pinnacle of his military career. He had given up a life of wealth and physical comfort for the hard life of a soldier. Why? His loyalty to Pharaoh, to the gods of the ancient people of The Two Lands, and to his comrades in the Amun Corps and Leopard Charioteers; these motivated him to pursue excellence as a soldier. None of that seemed worth dying for now. So what was left?

His mind formed an image of Sarina on that day months ago when she visited him at the Karnak garrison in Thebes to tell him she had broken the royal cipher. She looked so serious when she spread her calculations on the table and tried to explain the mysterious jumble of letters to him. Her beauty, self-confidence, and youthful passion captured his heart that day. He smiled when he remembered how Sarina confounded the skeptical master scribe of the Amun Corps with her brilliant mathematical skills and then enchanted the old scribe with her easy smile and light laughter. Their afternoon lunch in the shady garrison courtyard was a cherished memory revisited hundreds of times on sleepless nights.

Herihor, brave warrior, decorated national hero, commander of the Leopards, and youngest general in the history of Egypt made his decision. He extinguished the lamp and crawled into bed under a cool linen sheet. He would speak with *Amkhu* Hatep soon about his daughter. She was definitely a woman he would die for!

CHAPTER 33

Goshen Nome, Heliographic Station

Two elder Hebrew brothers left the tower before the orange ball of the sun peeked over the flat horizon of the Nile delta. The grasslands and grain fields that never cooled at night were shrouded in a suffocating haze that gripped man and beast between the damp earth and scorching sun. Working on a tower above the mud, the two heliographers were fifty feet closer to the sun than everyone else in this flat delta.

"Do you want to start writing the message, or shall I?" Elias asked his Egyptian partner.

"Did you understand what our two visitors told us?" Hakamun replied, ignoring the question.

"I'm afraid so. Before the alert goes out to all stations though, it needs to be worded precisely as Moses and Aaron instructed us."

"Go ahead and do that, then. I need to stretch my legs and see if the well has any clean water left. I'm thirsty already."

While Hakamun descended in search of drinking water from a shallow well a quarter-mile away, Elias tried to clear his mind and organize his notes. He still couldn't believe it: Moses and Aaron wanted them to alert the nation about the final plague. He still didn't understand how they knew to come to them. The two leaders of the Hebrews had been expelled from the Mennefer Palace and the presence of Pharaoh. How did they know about the helio network? He supposed it was no longer much of a secret since it had been first used to warn of the hail and lightning plague almost two months ago.

Elias' pen scratched Moses' precise words on the papyrus while he referred to his notes. After this plague, his fellow slaves would be free! Of course, Pharaoh could always change his mind again, but this time the slaves would leave anyway with the consent of the Egyptian people and with gifts of gold. In fourteen days, at midnight, the God of the Israelites would Himself pass through the nation of Egypt and kill the firstborn of every family and every beast.

With this dire prediction came instructions about how to avoid death. As the Israelite blinker carefully documented the necessary preparations, he wondered at the simplicity of God's commandment. Elias and his young wife could save their little boy by simply obeying God: clean their one-room home, pack a bag with clothes, make loaves of unleavened bread, cook and eat a meal, and dab lamb's blood on the lintel and doorposts. He wondered how many people would bother to do those simple, uncomplicated tasks. Most Hebrews would do them. On the other hand, most Egyptians probably wouldn't.

Elias had finished writing the message when Hakamun returned with a pottery jug of water.

"This is cooler than water out of the canal, and a lot cleaner too, so drink up my friend." Hakamun handed him the jug and picked up the draft. Elias watched him read his handiwork as he quenched his thirst.

"This is good. It's long for an alert message, which is understandable since this will be our last one, but it explains everything thoroughly. I wonder how many people will do what Moses and Aaron said to avoid the plague."

"I was wondering the same thing. What about you?"

"What do you mean?"

"You're the firstborn in your family, right?"

"Yes, but..."

"So will you do what it says? It seems clear enough to me."

"I'm not sure. I've never been particularly religious. I figure we'll all die someday anyway."

"Then what?"

"Who knows? Besides, the god that's causing all these plagues is your god, not mine. Why would your god care about an Egyptian government flunky like me stuck on a tower in the middle of a swamp?"

"I can assure you that He isn't only God of the Israelites. Look, Hakamun, I'll make you a deal. Come home with me tonight, my wife will make us a nice meal, and we'll talk more about this warning. When the fourteenth day comes, you're welcome to share a lamb dinner with us in our room and then you can decide where you want to go after that."

"I don't have a family, so that sounds like a good enough plan. Besides, your wife *is* a good cook! We need to put this message onto the network now so it reaches Aswan by tonight."

"Egypt will be in an uproar by the time this makes its way to all the towns and villages." Elias climbed onto the heliograph seat while Hakamun adjusted the mirror for maximum intensity and correct bearing angle for the relay station in Iunu.

Ten minutes later, after confirming that the message had been received, the two helio operators discussed what they would say if a government official ever questioned them about who authorized the transmission.

Mennefer, Great House Palace

A palace helio operator burst into Scribe Gobe's reception area and handed him a large sheet of papyrus. The fact that this message wasn't entrusted to a regular palace courier meant that it was more urgent or sensitive than usual. He skimmed the text while the senior operator caught his breath and awaited further instructions. Gobe's heart raced when the paper's significance sunk in.

"Who sent this?" he demanded in his most authoritative voice.

"It originated from the Goshen station up north, sir. We received it on relay from Iunu."

"I can see that from the header! On whose authority was this material sent?" Gobe knew that the vizier would ask this very question.

"I don't know, sir."

"Well, find out!" Gobe barked. "Was this forwarded to anyone else?"

"Of course sir. The routing tag shows it was forwarded to all stations. That's standard practice for an alert message of this type."

"I don't know what you mean by 'standard practice' but recall this message immediately from the network!"

"We can't do that. It's been repeated to two or three stations down the line by now. A recall will never catch up to it with that much lead time. May I leave, sir? I have other work to do." He wanted to avoid interrogation by the vizier himself—an unnerving experience in the best of times. It would be even more unpleasant today.

"Get out of here!" Gobe's mind raced as he thought about what this meant for him and his position as the vizier's personal scribe. He had to somehow warn Bakenmut without compromising their arrangement; there wasn't time to make a copy of the full text for his secret sponsor.

He knocked on the vizier's office door and entered with a huff to give the impression that he'd just received the helio message. He stood before Nakhte and handed him the papyrus when he looked up from the work on his desk. Gobe watched his face as he read the text.

"Interesting, did you read this?"

"I just skimmed it, sir. It was obviously of high importance so I brought it straight to you," he lied. "I hope that was the correct thing to do."

"Of course, this will certainly stir things up." Nakhte gazed absently out the window at the Temple of *Ptah* in the distance.

"Would you like me to summon Royal Master Scribe Bakenmut, sir?"

"What? Oh, yes. That sounds like a good idea. He needs to read this and give me his advice before we take it to Pharaoh."

Gobe left the vizier's office to brief Bakenmut about the message and to tell him the vizier's reaction so he was prepared in advance. He knew his sponsor would appreciate his initiative.

Nakhte and Bakenmut discussed the matter a few minutes later. They agreed for now to set aside questions about who originated the message, which they had no doubt was an authentic statement from Moses, and to take it to Pharaoh with a recommendation that he grant the Israelite slaves freedom to leave Egypt within fourteen days. If he agreed, then it would buy them time to formulate a coordinated national strategy. The Great One could always amend his decree between now and then, or, as he had done many times before, reverse his decision when the impact of the plague became more clear.

No sooner had they read the message aloud to Pharaoh in his private quarters and given him their recommendation, than they had their answer. He would *not* give in to Moses' latest demand, no matter how severe the consequences. Vizier Nakhte delicately reminded his sovereign that every one of Moses' predicted plagues had come to pass. If this one were even remotely possible, it would mean the death of Pharaoh's own son, the next Ruler of The Two Lands. The second most powerful man in Egypt averted his eyes from the defiant stare of Thutmose III at this suggestion. Even Pharaoh's calloused advisors were stunned by his indifference. Pharaoh dismissed them.

"We must stop this madness!" Bakenmut hissed as they walked back to the vizier's office.

"Do not speak, Master Scribe. Not here." They walked in silence through the palace corridors while news spread about the plague and Pharaoh's refusal that would kill thousands of Egypt's firstborn sons.

Vizier Nakhte dismissed Gobe and locked the door to his office. He and the master scribe pulled their chairs close together in the middle of the room so they could converse in hushed tones away from prying eyes or ears.

"He's insane!" Bakenmut hissed.

"Keep your voice down! I agree that he is a calculating, hard-hearted ruler who believes that he is a god. He has convinced himself that this time he will beat the God of the Hebrews. You and I realize that he would rather destroy Egypt, even if it leads to the death of his own son, than give in to the demands of an Israelite slave."

"We can't let him wipe out the country. I'd kill him myself if I thought it would change things."

"Your loyalty to The Two Lands is admirable, Bakenmut, but you won't need to do that deed yourself. I anticipated this situation months ago and have a plan to take care of it. We'll discuss it in a few days when I can gather my associates and their resources. We'll decide on a date to end the destructive reign of the 'Great One.' Let's meet at the Temple of *Sobek* to finalize the plan."

"I look forward to that." Bakenmut smiled at the irony of meeting at the familiar location where human sacrifices were fed to the crocodile-god. The location suited him.

"Meanwhile, we have Pharaoh's last order, which I am in agreement with, by the way. A joint operation by the combined Amun Corps and Ammit Corps will be more than sufficient to exterminate any mass gathering of Hebrew slaves before they can leave the country. In fact, we should wait for them to gather in one place before attacking. It will be an easy operation for our military."

"Would you like me to draw up the official orders?"

"Yes, thank you. I'm glad you're fully on board with my plan to put our country back on its path to glory."

"With you as the next Pharaoh?"

"Of course. And you as my vizier." The two chuckled at their cleverness.

Royal Master Scribe Bakenmut left Nakhte's office suite with barely a nod to Scribe Gobe. He would write the military order and then focus on his own plan that meshed only partly with what the vizier had in mind. The difference was who would end up being the next Pharaoh of The Two Lands.

CHAPTER 34

South Giza, Menkaure Heliographic Research Station

Sarina normally did not transcribe entire helionet messages, but she could tell that this one was extraordinary. As soon as she saw the plague alert preamble, she called for Uriel to set up her portable desk and fetch fresh papyrus, ink, and quills. The transmitting blinker in the Mennefer Palace anticipated that his colleagues in Giza and Saqqara would want to copy the complete message in precise hieratic script so he waited several minutes before sending at a rate that allowed accurate transcription. There would be time later to make copies in *sekh shat* or in other languages for wider distribution.

Even at the slower sending rate, it required Sarina's full concentration to mentally convert the flashing helio code into flowing cursive. Even she struggled to accurately ink each character while keeping pace with the sender. Enough fragments of the alert's contents registered in another part of her consciousness to elevate her pulse and breathing. During a pause she called for more paper and another quill.

When she completed the message, she sent confirmation of receipt even though her Menkaure station was still unofficial. The blinker at the palace would understand her appreciation.

She devoted the rest of the morning to making copies for Akhenat to post in the Giza bazaar and Uriel to read aloud in the artisan and slave villages around the pyramid construction sites. She would not wait for the main Giza station nearby to distribute the announcement.

While she made copies in her careful handwriting, Sarina had time to think about arranging a meeting with General Herihor before the date of the plague—fourteen days from now. She couldn't remember if he knew any more about his birth. If he was the firstborn and didn't do what Moses instructed... No, she didn't want to think about that. She had put her faith in the God of Israel when the plagues began and trusted that she and Herihor would somehow be together forever. If only there was a way to go to the Saqqara garrison now and speak to him. She was certain that he would return her feelings.

After sending off Akhenat and Uriel with copies of the alert, she climbed down from the summit of the Menkaure pyramid and reclined on a cot in the dim storage room. More than four hours of intense mental concentration and meticulous copying had exhausted her. The granite blocks still retained some coolness of the night. She succumbed to the weariness of her morning's work and drifted to sleep.

"You have a dispatch, Miss."

The guard's voice sounded like it was miles away. How long had she been asleep? He stood in the doorway outlined by the glare of the afternoon sun.

"Are you awake, Miss?"

"Yes. Did you say a dispatch?"

"Yes, Miss." The soldier took one step into the room.

"Who is it from?" Sarina was still in a sleepy haze.

"It's from the general, Miss. General Herihor."

She leapt from the cot and snatched the dispatch from the soldier's outstretched hand. She was wide awake now. She broke Herihor's official seal and unfolded a single large sheet of papyrus folded many times into a thick package and covered with dense script. She caught a smaller piece of papyrus before it fell to the floor and gave a short gasp when she read it.

"Thank you," she said to dismiss the soldier when she realized that he was still standing in the doorway. Like all soldiers who deliver sealed messages from generals, he was curious about the contents. All he knew was that Sarina had reacted instantly to whatever the general said. He and his fellow bodyguard would speculate about that for the rest of the afternoon.

With hardly a glance at the large sheet which was an army scribe's transcript of the plague alert which she already had, she read Herihor's note again and again. After his official garrison duties were finished for the day, he would come to the Menkaure site to see her in private before she went home. The word "private" was underlined. That was the word that caused her to gasp.

General Herihor's chariot slid to a halt in a cloud of dust at the south base of Menkaure's pyramid. He nodded to his military driver and stepped off the platform onto the warm sand. Sarina's two bodyguards snapped to attention and greeted him with professional salutes. When his eyes landed on her waiting in the dwindling sunlight, he broke into a wide smile.

"You received my message," he said nervously when he stood before her.

"I did," she replied with a beaming smile.

The two guards and Herihor's driver watched the couple while pretending to busy themselves with the horses.

"Why don't we watch the sunset from the top of the pyramid?" he suggested.

"Yes, that would be nice," she agreed.

When he took her hand to help her climb the granite blocks, the general glanced back at his men with a scowl that sent them scurrying. The couple would still be in view of the guards but would not be overheard.

Their climb ended when they reached the limestone floor where the gold capstone, pillaged centuries ago, had once rested. The portable heliograph machine stood at the center of the open space. They sat on a pink granite block polished by the wind and a century of blowing sand. Herihor did not release Sarina's hand.

"Do you know why I wanted to speak with you in private?" he asked.

"Yes," she replied. He would have to get used to her habit of anticipating the obvious.

"You do?"

"I have been in love with you since we first met on the roof of Lotus House last year. You have decided that you are in love with me too. Now, we can speak of plans for our future together."

He was confounded that it had taken him so long to decide what had been so clear to her from their first meeting. "How did you know that?"

"Oh, my dear general, women just *know* these things. Still, I would like to hear it from your own lips." Sarina waited for Herihor to form the words. He might be the commander of ten thousand troops, but his heart was thrown into confusion by this beautiful woman under a colorful desert sunset framed by ancient, glowing pyramids.

"My feelings for you began when you visited me at the Karnak garrison and we had lunch in the courtyard with Nathan and your brother. Since then I thought of you every day."

The radiance of her face matched the golden sky around them.

"I often wondered if a beautiful woman like you could ever love a battle-scarred old soldier like me. The army is all I know and it's a hard life. I have very little to offer you, but I can't bear to be apart from you. If we survive this next plague, will you be my wife?"

"Herihor, I will go with you wherever you wish."

"Even if I wish to follow Moses to the Promised Land?"

"*Especially* to the Promised Land!"

They sat in the darkness atop the Menkaure pyramid and talked about what was in store for them in the next fourteen days. Those days would pass quickly before a plague from God wracked Egypt for the last time.

Sarina easily accepted that her general was probably from an Israelite bloodline. He had researched his family lineage and concluded that his Egyptian adoptive parents obscured the records to make his birthright unknowable. He was definitely not an Egyptian. She understood his deep desire to return to the land of his forefathers.

Herihor would speak with Sarina's father in a few days and obtain his blessing to marry his daughter. More importantly, the general had to find a way to leave the Amun Corps and join the slaves' migration to the land of Canaan without being executed as a traitor. He and Sarina were willing to risk all of this to begin a new life together in a land neither of them had ever seen.

Giza Complex, Jasmine House

After dinner that same evening, Sarina announced to her mother and father that General Herihor had asked her to marry him in the near future. She would tell them later that he intended to leave his command of the Amun Corps to journey to the Promised Land. Her parents' reactions were predictable.

"This is such great news!" Sarina's mother exclaimed. "General Herihor—a national military hero—will be my son-in-law!" She cried and embraced her daughter. "Then that settles it," she said to her husband. "Now, at least most of our family will stay together in Egypt. Only Malik will leave with the Israelites."

Hatep embraced his daughter and managed to give her a forced smile. "Will you live with the general in his quarters at the Saqqara garrison?"

Sarina hesitated—she realized that she had to tell them the full truth. "No, we won't."

"Then you can live here with us!" her mother exclaimed.

When Sarina didn't answer, she sensed her parents' confusion.

"We will not be staying in Egypt." Her eyes glistened when she looked up at her father. "We will be going with the Israelites to their— our—new homeland. Herihor intends to resign his command after the last plague and we will leave Egypt together."

"Can he do that?" her father asked.

"Can he do what?"

"He's commander of the national Amun Corps. Can he leave just like that without Pharaoh's permission? He's one of Egypt's top generals!"

"That is something he is trying to figure out. One way or another, he is convinced that he must join his people in their exodus."

"*His* people? What do you mean?" Sarina's mother put her hand to her mouth.

"He's an Egyptian general. He can't just leave like that," her father persisted.

"I think what Sarina is trying to say is that he is not… Egyptian." Her mother gathered her meaning.

"Herihor is a Hebrew by birth," Sarina announced. "He only recently discovered this. It changes everything, especially considering the significance of this last plague. If he is truly a Hebrew then he has a divine obligation to Abraham, his ancient blood-relative, and to his God to obey Him and return to the land of Canaan which is at the center of all God's promises. Nothing, and no one, will stand in his way from doing that, especially me. I will gladly go with him as his wife."

Hatep slumped in his chair. His family's *ma'at*, or whatever was left of it, had finally disintegrated. Malik would leave with Nathan and his family on what he thought would be an exciting adventure; his daughter would marry a military deserter—and a Hebrew at that—to depart on a perilous journey a few days later; and his wife only agreed to stay with him out of marital loyalty; her heart and soul were with the Israelites.

His world had crumbled and he didn't know what to do. That wasn't entirely correct; he did know what to do but he didn't want to admit it. He would brood about it for a few more days and see if anything changed. Postponing a decision was much easier than dealing with the inner conflict.

Hatep rose from his chair and walked to his daughter who was still apprehensive about her parents' reactions. He bent down and kissed his daughter on the forehead.

"I feel tired. I'm going to bed," he announced.

CHAPTER 35

Giza Complex, Jasmine House

Four days passed since Sarina's stunning announcement of her intended marriage to General Herihor and their planned departure to Canaan. Even her marriage ceremony would be different: Ben-Judah agreed to sanctify their union in a private Israelite ritual. Hatep had regained some control over his emotions and attempted to bring his household back to a more calm routine. He returned home early from work and spent his afternoons sitting with Iset in the courtyard that was devoid of flowers or shrubs. His outward appearance was as normal as he could manage, however it took all of his willpower to keep from erupting inside.

"I'm going for a walk, dear," he said. Hatep paused briefly to kiss his wife on his way past the table set for dinner. He didn't notice her questioning look. He turned his back to her and headed for the front door.

"But the duck is ready to eat—it's one of your favorites." The aroma of herbs and spices rose from the steaming platter.

"Go ahead and start without me. I need some fresh air."

Iset watched him walk away from her. "Are you feeling all right, dear?" she called out in concern. Maybe he was coming down with something. The stagnant canals could breed the fever during this time of year.

"I'm fine. Don't wait up for me." He turned the corner and a few seconds later she heard the front door close.

Ever since Sarina's news, her husband had been acting strangely. He spent more time than usual in the dark on the rooftop after dinner; his appetite had dropped and she was concerned for his health. Also, why had he not said anything about his visit to Ben-Judah last night? When Rachel mentioned this morning that the Master had been to her house, she feigned knowing about it. What did her husband and the Hebrew teacher have to talk about?

Iset's worry included more than her husband's visit with the crippled slave. The threat of the last plague loomed over them like an ominous cloud. Malik was at Nathan's house and missed dinner for the third time this week, which was unlike him. Sarina returned from the Menkaure helio site and went straight to bed. Now Hatep went for a walk without dinner—something he'd never done before—and told her not to wait up.

She called for the dinner slave and told her to clear the table.

"But Ma'am, nobody has touched a thing. What do I do with all this food?" The young servant was confused by her lady's order.

"Save a cold plate of duck and vegetables for the Master and another for my son. You and the servants take the rest. Bring a cup of fruit juice to my room when the table is cleared."

South Giza, Menkaure Heliographic Research Station

Hatep reached the worn peak of the Menkaure Pyramid in the fading dusk and paused to catch his breath and look out over the dim landscape. The looming pyramids of Khafre and Khufu were almost aligned in the last rays of a setting sun at his back. Menkaure's Temple sat at the end of a long causeway below him in the shadows of a depression in the red dirt. It was quiet except for a slight breeze that whispered around the sharp corners of broken stone. The day's heat would diminish within an hour.

He sat on the same smooth limestone bench where Herihor and Sarina spoke of their love for one another only a few days earlier. Now Hatep's pent-up fury against Egypt's gods—the consuming anger that washed over him that night months ago at Lotus House—had returned. When he smashed the black idol of *Anubis*, he thought he had released a lifetime of false illusions. The gods of Egypt were nothing compared to the God of the Hebrews. Plague after supernatural plague convinced him of God's superior power. Yes, he was convinced of this. However,

Almighty God now demanded more of him than rejection of his false gods. He had stolen the hearts of his wife and daughter and now threatened to take the very life of his only son.

According to Ben-Judah, he faced a stark choice similar to the Hebrew patriarch, Abraham. This time, it was his own self-will pitted against God's command: either do exactly what God instructed to avoid the next plague or God's Angel of Death would kill his son at midnight in ten days. The fact that Sarina was the eldest wasn't the issue. It was obvious that the *LORD* intended to strike deep into the core of what was most precious to Egyptian and Hebrew families. The eldest son embodied his father's life and pride, his mother's dearest joy, the family's future and prosperity. The terrifying predicament pitched Hatep's will against God's will. There must be some way to keep my dignity and self-respect, he thought, without losing my son. Hatep fell to his knees as starlight, whispering wind, and blowing dust enveloped him.

Hatep came to his feet much later to gaze out at the fires of the Mennefer Palace dying in the distance. He had no idea how long he'd been kneeling under the bright stars. He'd spoken to God—an unfamiliar act that Ben-Judah assured him was not only possible but natural—and he knew that God heard him! A lifetime of sin had been taken away. Not only did he talk to God, but God answered him! All around him, the gleaming white Tura limestone was illuminated by billions of stars in the Sky River that arched over him like a gleaming, milky wave. Even the twin peaks of Khafre and Khufu floated over the dark curtain of the Giza plateau. He looked straight up at the swath of stars and smiled to himself. He opened his heart to the God of the Universe and He answered him!

The steep descent took longer than expected. Being careful to not twist an ankle or worse, he felt his way past the crumbling layers of bright stone until he reached the stratum of black basalt on the bottom third of the ancient structure. His pace slowed as he lowered himself from pieces of stone larger than a house. If there were more light, he could have taken the easier route that he used to reach the summit hours earlier. When he finally stepped onto the sand at ground level he easily wove his path home through piles of construction debris and low brush.

When the pair of soldiers guarding his front door challenged him as he approached out of the darkness, he felt better knowing that at least they were alert and protecting his family.

"Did you men eat dinner?" he asked them cheerfully with his hand on the front door latch.

"Yes, sir...we did." His question, at any hour, was unusual for the taciturn master of Jasmine House. He usually either ignored them or uttered a rough grunt in passing.

"I hope you enjoyed the roast duck. It's one of my favorites. Well, good night!"

The guards thought it best not to return his merry salutation. They would quietly speculate about the man's strange behavior later.

Hatep entered his house and closed the gate behind him. He must wake Iset and tell her about tonight. Her husband was a different man with a new heart! He knew she would understand.

He must see Ben-Judah first thing in the morning.

CHAPTER 36

Mennefer, Great House Palace

It seemed inevitable to Vizier Nakhte that, without his intervention, Egypt would be decimated by the final plague and continue its decline because of Pharaoh's resolute stubbornness. He couldn't stop the plague that would come the next day, but he could position himself to lead the nation in a new direction when the naysayers saw that Pharaoh was insane to resist the Hebrew's *LORD* further. The nine plagues that had built up to the threatened death of the firstborn sons had not changed the unquestioning devotion of most Egyptians to their Pharaoh. For all their lives, Vizier Nakhte, Royal Master Scribe Bakenmut and Royal Priest Metjen had been complicit in perpetuating Pharaoh's charade of divinity and concern for his people. That had come to an end. It was now time to salvage as much as they could of the nation's *ma'at*.

Before Nakhte initiated his final plan to take over The Two Lands, the others had suggested that the Great One be given one last chance to agree on a new direction for this proud and powerful nation. When they gathered in Pharaoh's receiving room with their advice to stop the plague of death by releasing the slaves, they again ran into their sovereign's heart of stone.

"Absolutely not!" he replied to their suggestion. "I will *never* release the Hebrews—Never!"

"But Great One, what about your own son? What if he dies as Moses threatened?" the royal priest asked.

"My son was sent to Libya a week ago. The God of the Hebrews has no power over him if he is not in Egypt." Pharaoh smiled at his clever ploy to outmaneuver God. "The plague is only against the land of Egypt. The Hebrews' God has no influence elsewhere."

"I beg to differ." The vizier hazarded an outright contradiction. "The threat was against Egyptians everywhere. We received reports that some of the plagues such as the locusts and frogs extended well beyond our borders. You must see that the God of the Hebrews knows no boundaries."

"Do you dare speak against me?" Pharaoh screamed. "I am the supreme god of this nation! I tell you that no threat in the world will change my mind!"

It was finally clear that their leader was blind to all facts about the past plagues and his mind was closed to rational reasoning. His iron-willed obstinacy would prove fatal. Nakhte was convinced that Pharaoh's heir would die that night in Libya. He was also certain that Pharaoh himself would perish in a palace revolt the next day when the preventable nation-wide tragedy came to light. He nodded to the other visitors indicating that it was time for them to leave. He lowered his eyes and bowed to Pharaoh on his way out. After he led the entourage a safe distance away, he felt a sense of relief that the farce of Pharaoh's government would soon end. Their supreme leader barely noticed their departure.

Memphis, Temple of *Sobek*

The meeting at the Temple of *Sobek* later was auspicious according to the entrails read by Bakenmut's personal seer. The details of the morning sacrifice, the seer said, assured him that all his activities that day would be successful. Bakenmut was pleased with himself as he walked along the reed-lined stone causeway elevated a few feet above the marsh that led to the secluded shrine of the crocodile god. Since the gods guaranteed his success, he had no concern about being seen here in broad daylight. News of a final plague had thrown the city into such chaos that it was unlikely anyone would take special notice of top palace officials gathered to pay homage to *Sobek*.

Vizier Nakhte was waiting at the shrine with a dozen of his personal bodyguards when Bakenmut strolled up the path to the pavilion shaded by large awnings. Gobe, Nakhte's personal scribe, stood next to him. Bakenmut was accompanied by Imani and Thethi. What the vizier didn't know was that the master scribe had very dangerous men on his payroll—brutal, ruthless criminals—who knew how to kill a man in seconds and wouldn't hesitate to do so.

With a mild sense of irritation for having had to wait, Vizier Nakhte motioned for the visitors to join him and Gobe at the edge of the pavilion away from the guards.

"Now that you are here, I will go over the plan for the day after tomorrow. You heard the 'Great One'." His sarcasm seethed with frustration with the supreme leader. "He has brought his own death upon himself. In two days a new leader will guide The Two Lands to glory instead of to confusion and shame!"

"I'm certain of that, Your Excellency. Have you chosen a royal name for yourself?" Bakenmut asked. Having pondered a pharonic name for himself, he assumed that this was prominent in the other man's mind too.

"I was thinking that Serqet III would suit me."

"It does suit you," Bakenmut said smoothly. "That would make you the third of the powerful Scorpion kings in a revived Narmer Dynasty. Thutmose III will feel the sting of the scorpion—how appropriate."

"Enough of that," the vizier said. "It's time to explain the sequence of events between now and the start of a new dynasty." Nakhte paced before the men with a thrusting step that matched his excited face. "Less than two days from now, before dawn after the plague runs its course, when the palace guards are most likely to be the least alert, my men will overpower them and execute Pharaoh in his bed." The image of a spear through the feeble monarch's body thrilled him.

"Will you be there to see it?" Bakenmut asked, even though he knew the answer.

"No. I'll be at the Temple of *Ptah*. All the palace priests and officials, with you at the forefront, my friend, will gather there at dawn supposedly to pray for our nation. I will announce the untimely death of Pharaoh and, not incidentally, the death of his male heir in Libya from the plague. The government will be mine and I will proclaim a new Narmer Dynasty. You will step forward and urge the stunned crowd to recognize me as Serqet III. Then I will appoint you the Supreme Vizier. How does that sound?"

"Brilliant! I could not have thought of a better transition. Swift and decisive. The Temple of *Ptah* is the perfect site for such a momentous occasion."

"That is not all. We must deal with the departure of the Hebrew slaves and the paralysis of the country. We'll blame Pharaoh's death and Egypt's misfortunes on them. When the people see that the slaves are responsible, they will naturally seek revenge. The Hebrews will be slaughtered."

"How will you do that? I understand that they are already gathering near Ramses and Succoth by the hundreds of thousands in preparation for their journey to Canaan. One or two million people by then will be unstoppable." The master scribe was curious if Nakhte had thought through his actions beyond simply assassinating Pharaoh.

"My plan is still evolving. The Hebrews will head toward the land of the Canaanites, but we don't know their exact route. Will they go north through the Sea of Reeds marsh, or will they take a southern path? My plan is to pin them against either the reed marshes or the Red Sea and trap them where they will feel the full strength of the Egyptian Army. Our troops will pick them off like hunters shooting into thick flocks of quail. What a sight that will be!"

The master scribe wondered if this was just fantasy or if the orders had been issued. "Does the Army know of this? It may not be as easy as you imagine."

"I have not informed them yet. Your first order as the new vizier will be to the Amun and Ammit Corps. They will be the pincers of the new Scorpion King to annihilate the Hebrews!"

In Bakenmut's mind, all that mattered was getting rid of Vizier Nakhte and making himself the new Pharaoh. After that, the real Scorpion King could accomplish whatever his mind imagined.

When the vizier left the Temple of *Sobek* with Gobe and his platoon of guards, Bakenmut's spirits soared with thoughts of becoming the new Pharaoh by this time tomorrow. He and his two associates waited in the open pavilion of the temple until the vizier and his guards were out of sight across the causeway. Imani and Thethi searched the temple building and grounds and assured him they were alone.

"This is almost too easy!" he exclaimed with glee. "That fool will do most of the work for us."

"How's that?" Imani asked.

"He'll take care of Pharaoh for us. All we need to do is take care of *him*! We'll allow his plan to unfold just as he described. Then, on his way to the Temple of *Ptah,* he will meet his demise and I will announce the tragic deaths of both Pharaoh *and* the vizier. Then the court will crown me Pharaoh!"

Bakenmut explained how the Black Falcon's gang of thugs would ambush Nakhte at dawn on his way to the temple and clear the way for him to ascend to the throne. He would return to the palace now and draft orders for the two army corps to chase the Hebrew slaves eastward until they were trapped against the marshes or the sea. His orders would direct that their attack be without mercy.

"What do you want us to do?" Imani asked.

"I have loose ends to tie up that you will take care of before I become Pharaoh. First you, Thethi, will observe the assassination of the vizier on his way to the Temple of *Ptah.* Do not get close enough to be seen by the assassins or any passersby. Be sure that he is dead so that there is no chance of a wounded vizier showing up to spoil my plans. And Imani, I have a chore for you which I think you will enjoy. It will take care of a problem that has been irritating me for months. Tomorrow night, take some of my most skilled men—I suggest Antosh and two others—and murder Hatep and his family; especially his son and his Hebrew slave friend. Those two have been nothing but trouble for me since they found the secret tunnel to Queen Hatshepsut's tomb. Better yet, take the two alive after you kill their families so that I can watch them suffer in the last minutes of their life. If anyone else in the household dies when you take those two that's no concern of mine. Can you handle that, Imani?"

"It would be a pleasure to see those two slowly die," he replied licking his lips.

"One cannot be too sentimental about these things; you have the makings of a vizier yourself! Meet me at the Temple of *Ptah* at dawn after the plague when I will inaugurate a new age of power in The Two Lands. Yes, I believe I will use the 'Scorpion King' name myself to replace the 'Black Falcon'!"

CHAPTER 37

Goshen Nome, Heliographic Station

"We should have sent these messages yesterday," Hakamun said on the night before the final plague.

"Why's that?" Elias asked. He was busy drafting a note to Sarina with information on their plans to join the Israelites already clogging the highway heading south from Goshen to Memphis.

"It will still take us a couple of days to reach Ramses. We should have started yesterday."

"We already talked about this. My wife spent all week preparing tonight's meal. We'll stay at my house tonight and leave before dawn tomorrow. Don't worry, we won't be left behind." Elias hoped that his boss, and friend, wouldn't back out now and leave for Memphis on his own. He'd be better off staying with him and his wife and child in the house tonight.

"We're stuck out here at the far end of the helio net. There's probably nobody left at the Iunu station anyway."

"Why don't you send them a flash and see." They were both anxious to finish their last transmission and leave.

"Are you almost done?" Hakamun asked a minute later. "I received a short reply from the Iunu station. They said to hurry up because they're leaving in an hour."

"I want to get this last message just right." Elias jotted down that they would meet Sarina, Malik, and Nathan again somewhere, though he didn't know exactly where. It was a difficult way to say goodbye.

"Here it is," he said to his friend who had been anxiously pacing the helio tower platform. Hakamun took the paper and skimmed it quickly.

"That looks good, I'll send it now." He climbed into the transmitter's seat on the tall, copper machine. It was locked into position aimed at the Iunu station. Elias adjusted the mirror.

"All the blinkers know Sarina. They should know how to forward it to her at the Menkaure pyramid. Tell them to hurry," Elias reminded him.

"Oh, so now you're in a hurry too?"

"Ask them to let us know when they get an acknowledgement from her."

It took only a few minutes to send the message. It didn't matter who else read it since all the helio stations were being shut down. Even those sites manned by Egyptian loyalists realized that links in the national information network were collapsing.

Twenty minutes later they both saw the flash of acknowledgement from Sarina relayed through the Iunu station.

"That's it!" Hakamun announced. With a flick of his wrist on the worn blinker handle he sent their last transmission.

Goshen closed.

South Giza, Menkaure Heliographic Research Station

The short farewell message from Hakamun and Elias was a welcome relief for Sarina. It was hard for her to imagine what her life might have been like if she hadn't been curious about the flashing signals of light across the river in Thebes and Karnak. That was less than a year ago. She and Herihor would be married when he joined her soon and they would leave together for the Promised Land.

"Uriel, come here." Sarina called for the slave boy. He trotted to her from his mat in the shade where he kept papyrus sheets and writing instruments ready.

"Yes, Miss?" He was always eager to please this woman whom he nearly worshiped.

"Call Akenhut from the storeroom and tell the two guards to come here, please. We'll be closing the station for the last time."

Uriel gulped in disbelief. "For the last time, Miss?"

"I'll explain when everyone is here. Go now."

Her assistants and bodyguards gathered with glum faces under the awning out of the blinding sun.

"I thank you with all my heart for your loyalty to this station and especially to me. You are more than workers and servants. You are my friends." She looked into the sad eyes fixed on her every word and tried to keep her composure. "Our nation is torn apart by plagues from God and millions of Hebrew slaves gather in Ramses and Succoth. The helio network is shutting down and this station will be dismantled; there is no reason for us to remain here. I think it would be best for you to return to your homes or army units. I urge you to follow the instructions for protection from the death that will fall on our land tonight. There is nothing further that we can do here." The fatigue of the past months was catching up to her. She sat back in her chair with a sigh.

"Can I go with you?" Uriel asked as he handed her a cup of water.

"My advice to each of you is to return to your families and help them through this terrible test from God. Uriel, your parents will be worried if you don't go with them. And you, Akenhut, go home to your cousins. Whatever they choose to do tonight, they need you with them."

"What about us?" one of the guards asked.

"Shouldn't you report back to your unit?"

"Our direct orders from General Herihor were to protect you at all hours no matter what happened. That means we stay with you to the very end. With respect, Miss, we will not leave you."

"Well, I'm going home now." Sarina rose from her chair. "You can join the guards protecting Jasmine House and we'll see what happens tonight."

General Herihor and Sarina had agreed that she should bring the portable helio machine with her on their journey. It might prove useful when they crossed the desert of Sinai. Sarina oversaw the final disassembly of the instrument and made sure that the mirrors were carefully wrapped. Uriel packed the papyrus, pens, and ink in a bag.

The contingent from the Menkaure experimental helio station left the top of the ancient pyramid for the last time and went their separate ways. When Sarina said goodbye to Uriel and Akenhut they were in tears. Her stoic bodyguards walked behind her wondering what would happen that night and who would be alive by morning.

At that very moment, Royal Master Scribe Bakenmut issued military orders in the vizier's name directing the Amun and Ammit Corps to attack the departing Israelites at dawn.

Passover - Exodus

(c. 1446 B.C.)

'For I will pass through the land of Egypt on that night,
and will strike all the firstborn in the land of Egypt, both man and beast;
and against all the gods of Egypt I will execute judgment:
I am the LORD.
Now the blood shall be a sign for you on the houses where you are.
And when I see the blood, I will pass over you; and the plague shall
not be on you to destroy you when I strike the land of Egypt.
'So this day shall be to you a memorial;
and you shall keep it as a feast to the LORD throughout your generations.
You shall keep it as a feast by an everlasting ordinance.

Exodus 12:12-14 (NKJV)

But the children of Israel had walked on dry land in the midst of the sea,
and the waters were a wall to them on their right hand and on their left.
So the LORD saved Israel that day out of the hand of the Egyptians,
and Israel saw the Egyptians dead on the seashore.
Thus Israel saw the great work which the LORD had done in Egypt;
so the people feared the LORD, and believed
the LORD and His servant Moses.

Exodus 14:29-31 (NKJV)

CHAPTER 38

Saqqara, Amun Corps Garrison

General Herihor walked among the tents of his garrisoned command at dusk speaking to individual regiments. He spoke about the coming plague and of their need to be prepared for the worst. He appealed to all, but especially to those firstborn sons, to seek refuge under the blood of the lamb. The general refrained from giving a direct order to apply lamb's blood to all the regimental buildings. That act had to be an individual step of faith and not something they were compelled to do by a superior officer. Most of the soldiers, hardened combat veterans who had faced death many times, weren't interested in Egypt's gods and especially not the God of slaves. Threats from false deities of Egypt or the God of the Hebrews made no impression on them. They didn't care. That night, only a few soldiers sought divine protection in spite of their comrades' mockery.

When General Herihor sat down to his evening meal with a handful of men in his private quarters, darkness had already come to the Saqqara garrison. Khan, his private aide, valet, and cook, had prepared food for the general and three bodyguards. Following the strict instructions of his superior, Khan had meticulously cleaned the spartan living quarters, monitored the health of the young lamb for the past week, and packed unleavened bread for a deployment on short notice.

Before the meal, General Herihor sprinkled lamb's blood on the doorposts and locked the door of his quarters from the inside. He was uncertain about what to do next since he knew nothing about the customs of the Hebrews. He would improvise a solemn speech for the meal.

"I wanted all of you to join me because for some of you it may be our last meal together." He gestured for his aide and bodyguards to sit around the food before him. The puzzled soldiers set their weapons aside, removed their armor, and sat on the floor across from their general. They had shared many sparse meals together in the field of battle or on desert exercises, but never before had they eaten a meal with their commander in his private quarters.

"I've spoken with each of you about tonight. I don't know if you've chosen to stay here out of loyalty to me or because you believe that the blood on the doorposts will protect you. Either way, it has been your personal choice. You may still leave at any time, if you wish."

"I speak for the rest of the men," Khan stated. "We would gladly give our lives for you. We've seen the power of this God of the Israelites and we believe that He will exact a full price from Egypt tonight before the slaves depart in the morning. Nothing will stop His judgment. We will remain here and then go wherever you go." The others nodded in agreement.

"I'm humbled and honored by your trust. Tonight *is* different from all other nights. That will become clearer in the coming days. Meanwhile, we thank the One True God for His kindness to us as we eat this meal together."

To their continued astonishment, Herihor served his men first and poured each a cup of wine from his private supply. They devoured the meal of vegetables, unleavened bread, and roasted lamb as only hungry soldiers can. When they finished, there was nothing left except the bones and a large stack of bread to take with them in the morning.

The relaxed after-dinner atmosphere was the right time for General Herihor to take the men around him into his most intimate confidence. He told them of his Hebrew heritage and his intention to leave the corps, join the Israelite exodus, and travel to the Promised Land. Again, he gave them an opportunity to leave but they each swore to go with him. They then discussed how the small band of men could secretly leave the Amun Corps without being caught as deserters and traitors.

"Does this mean that we will not attack the Hebrews?" one of the men asked.

"I will not give the order nor will I lead an attack on God's people. My plan is to bring the Amun Corps into the desert where they will camp before we make our escape to the other side. My disappearance should slow an attack until another officer takes command. I do not believe that the God of the Hebrews has brought them or us this close to freedom to be slaughtered by the army. God will find a way to bring His people to the Promised Land, with or without us."

CHAPTER 39

Giza Complex, Jasmine House

The first Passover was a night like none other in history. The events would be memorialized for millennia by generations of Hebrews as the night that the *LORD* of Hosts brought them out of slavery by His great power and mighty hand. Egyptians and their gods would be crushed in a wave of death that spared no household that did not shelter under the blood of the lamb. The night spelled redemption for the oppressed and humiliation for the oppressors.

It was also a night like none other for Hatep and Iset. Egyptians and Israelites in their household had worked side by side with them preparing to join the bands of slaves in Ramses.

"Reuben, are you sure all the food and supplies have been loaded?" Hatep asked his horse slave.

"Yes sir. I personally secured the loads on the remaining three wagons and two chariots."

"Only the essentials, right?"

"As you instructed: no furniture, decorations, fancy clothing, or fine tableware. Just food, cooking utensils, heavy tunics, blankets; enough to carry us on our journey for several months."

"You're a good man, Reuben. I'm sorry I never appreciated you before. This journey would not be possible without you."

"It is the *LORD*'s doing, sir. I'm only a slave."

"We'll have to do something about that. First, let's go inside and see what the women have prepared for dinner. I understand that Ben-Judah is here with a special blessing."

The master and his horse slave made a final check of the animals. When they left in the dark before dawn he wanted the horses well-rested and watered.

Reuben watched his master dip parsley in a bowl of lamb's blood and splash it on the doorposts and lintel. He then locked the doors from the inside.

The largest room inside Jasmine House had been cleared of furniture with the heaviest items pushed against the walls. Rugs and pillows covered the pink granite floor. Bowls and plates of steaming vegetables were arranged in a cleared space in the middle of the room. Female voices accompanied by clanging utensils in the distant kitchen announced more food on the way. When two women entered the room with a gigantic platter of lamb it signaled that it was time to begin the meal.

Hatep, head of the house, called everyone together. Children ran from all directions to join the adults reclined around the feast. Iset joined her husband with Malik and Sarina on either side of them. Hatep gestured for Asher to lead the blind teacher forward to the seat of honor between him and Iset. Asher, Rachel, and Nathan joined the circle along with Reuben, his wife, and their children. Another horse slave and his family, a few farm workers and kitchen girls, and the four Army guards filled the room.

"As head of Jasmine House, I welcome you all to this special dinner. Some of you are uncomfortable eating with our family tonight, but I assure you that this is the first of many times that we will eat together. We are united by our desire to follow the God of Abraham to the Promised Land of Canaan. Tonight begins that great journey." Hatep sensed some of the uneasiness beginning to melt away. Even the soldiers had removed their armor but were still unsure what to expect. "Ben-Judah will explain more about tonight's observance."

The blind teacher waited for the room to quiet. "Tonight is a special night of celebration and anticipation. God brought Jacob and his family to Egypt more than four hundred years ago because of famine and drought in Canaan. He and our forefathers found protection in their brother, Vizier Joseph. We have been slaves under a long line of Pharaohs since Vizier Joseph died. This meal—called a *seder* in our language—will be cemented into the memories of the sons of Jacob as a special memorial of our freedom."

He asked Hatep and Reuben if the dinner preparations were completed in accordance with God's instructions.

"Yes. The lamb was carefully picked out of the flock ten days ago and Reuben watched to ensure that it remained without blemish," Hatep said. "We observed its preparation for the meal: its death was swift and not a bone was broken. Before we entered the house tonight, I used a bundle of parsley, dipped in the lamb's blood, to splash the lintel and doorposts as God instructed. The door is now shut and bolted."

"Very well," Ben-Judah said. "And your house has been cleaned of leaven?"

"Yes," Iset spoke up. "It was cleaned for seven days; Reuben's children and their friends inspected every corner of the house."

"The lamb was cooked properly?"

"Over an open fire as you instructed."

"My nose confirms that!" He said with relish. "However, I must ask you another question because I am blind. Is there enough bread for tonight's meal?"

Laughter across the room revealed the answer. Piles of unleavened bread over a foot high surrounded the platter of lamb.

"The girls have baked for days. We have enough bread for at least two weeks," Iset replied. "Much of it has already been loaded on the carts."

Ben-Judah held out his hand and asked for one loaf of bread.

"This loaf, "he began, "is the special bread of hope. We call it *matzah*. It is set aside for those who are not with us tonight but whose hearts are united with ours. Among them is Sarina's beloved general." Sarina blushed at the mention of her future husband. "Many others share this hope having chosen to follow the God of Abraham in spite of threats and difficulties. I pray that God will protect them as they prepare to leave Egypt. May we meet in the Promised Land, if not before.

"Is it dark yet?" the blind man then asked.

"Yes teacher. May I light the lamps now?" Nathan was eager to help and stood to fetch an ember from the kitchen.

"No my son, that is for the ladies of the house. Perhaps Iset and Sarina would do that for us."

Soon the large room was lit by oil lamps on pedestals around the room and along the walls.

The meal began with Ben-Judah offering the first cup of wine—the *kiddush*—as a cup of blessing. When the kitchen girls brought basins of water for everyone to wash their hands, the blind teacher asked someone to wash his hands ceremonially as his "servant" for the evening. Astonished silence fell over the room when Hatep reached for the old man's hands and placed them in the basin. He washed them and dried them on his own tunic. Iset and the others could not believe their eyes. Hatep was indeed a different man!

With a smile and a gesture from the evening's host, everyone was finally encouraged to eat. Adults and children stuffed bread with warm lamb and garnished it with parsley, figs, nuts, cinnamon, dried thyme and rosemary. They dipped more bread into the juices in the platter. Garlic and more herbs spiced heaping plates of leeks, cabbages, onions, kale, and spinach. Satisfied sounds of feasting soon gave way to singing.

During a lull in the celebration, Ben-Judah lifted a broken piece of *matzah*. Mothers hushed their children so everyone could hear him. "This is the bread of affliction which symbolizes our many years of slavery. It is an invitation to all who are hungry to join us on our journey. Let future generations celebrate with us. Tonight we are in Egypt; next year may we be in the Land of Israel. This year we are slaves; next year may we be free."

After a round of "Amens" Ben-Judah took a cloth napkin which he wrapped around the broken piece of bread and tucked under a plate. A few adults near him noticed this unusual move. Nathan asked the teacher to explain its meaning.

Speaking as a prophet for his people, Ben-Judah revealed something new to them: "This broken bread represents God's Anointed One who will one day be broken to deliver us *forever*. Tonight Moses, our redeemer, delivers from slavery in Egypt. One day God's Redeemer will come as the Holy Lamb of God to free us forever from the bondage of sin."

Reuben's young son asked a brief yet profound question. "Why is this night so different from others?" The child's clear, innocent voice grabbed everyone's attention. The adults smiled at his simplicity. Ben-Judah answered him and generations of children to come. Nathan, Malik and Sarina would remember his answer and teach it to their boys.

The old rabbi spoke directly to the child. "'Why is this night so different from others?' you ask. You are wondering why we are eating unleavened bread and so I will tell you. Pharaoh will finally let us leave Egypt so we must do so quickly before he changes his mind." The adults nodded their heads and murmured agreement. "There is no time to waste waiting for loaves of bread to rise into your favorite shapes like fish or birds. We must eat flat, unleavened *matzah* in our hurry to leave. We will eat it for many days on our journey, so I hope you like it!"

Amid laughter, he continued. "Why do we eat bitter herbs tonight, you ask? Why else but to remember our years of slavery that crushed us in servitude. Your grandfather and his grandfather and his grandfather before him only knew back-breaking work in the flooded grain fields, grinding mills, granite quarries, and brick pits. You are young and will never know what it means to be a slave; but when you eat herbs that set your teeth on edge, you will recall the starvation and hardships of your ancestors."

Egyptians in the room that night had a glimpse of the hardship of slavery that they willfully ignored all their lives. They realized that their culture of arrogance, privilege, and luxury were what held Israelites in perpetual bondage. That was about to change.

"Finally, we are reclined around the room on rugs and pillows as a sign of our freedom. We will no longer be forced to gulp our food standing in the grain field or stone quarry under the taskmaster's cruel whip while our owners relax on plush couches. We are free to recline, drink wine and eat bread in peace with our families. That is why tonight is so different from other nights."

Again, the room resounded with "Amens" and satisfied agreement from the slaves in the room. Hatep and Iset felt shamed by what Ben-Judah had said. Hatep's thoughts reached back to the years that he thought his treatment of slaves was benevolent and kind. It might have been comparatively so, but it was still humiliating bondage that tore husbands from wives and children from parents.

A distant scream broke their pensive interlude. It was midnight.

Soon, more shouts and screams drifted into the room out of the darkness. Almighty God filled the night with terror.

"This is the plague to end all plagues. We remember the plagues that began months ago when water turned to blood and will end tonight with the death of Egypt's firstborn sons throughout The Two Lands. In a few more hours we will be free." Ben-Judah offered the final cup of blessing to close the meal. The noise of death and anguish outside threatened to drown his soft voice. Later, Israelites and Egyptians rose together from their comfortable positions to prepare for the long journey ahead.

"Before you leave I want to say something on my last night as Master of Jasmine House." Hatep had everyone's attention and they sat down again.

"There is no need for you to wait for your freedom. I grant all my slaves full freedom from obligations of servitude to me and my family. That applies to everyone here and those servants and field workers who have already departed. Not only are you not bound to me or this house, but you are free to take whatever household articles or food that remains in the storehouses. Reuben and Asher have packed the carts and chariots to the maximum, so whatever we don't take will be left behind for others."

"Thank you, master!" Reuben said in genuine appreciation.

"I am no longer your master, Reuben. It was difficult at first for me to learn your name but I trust you will remember mine."

"I will try, sir," he laughed.

"I have a gift for Ben-Judah." Hatep walked to a carved wooden box against the wall behind him and lifted its gilded covering. "This is the gold *wesekh* given to me by Pharaoh himself. I have no further use for it." He placed the heavy necklace in the teacher's hands. The weight of so much gold caused the old man's arms to sag. "My debt to you and your adoptive family is worth more than the value of this gold," Hatep declared.

"May I give a gift also?" Iset asked her husband.

"Of course, do you have gold jewelry that I don't know about?" His wife's eyes sparkled at his humor; others in the room recalled her extravagant shopping expeditions to the Theban bazaar.

"Nothing that you don't know about, my dear." She opened another chest and lifted out a wooden box three or four times the size of the one that held Hatep's *wesekh*. "I wish to give my jewelry to Rachel. The emerald necklace and earrings will match your eyes, my dear. There are many gold chains, bracelets, and earrings too and some other trinkets that you might like. You were once my handmaiden but now I consider you my sister."

"I realize that my friend Nathan thinks he already owns Sapphire," Malik added, "but in case it isn't official enough, the black stallion is his." Nobody heard him amidst the joyous commotion at the meal's end, but Nathan acknowledged his friend's generosity by clapping his hands over his head. He and Malik would drive Sapphire and the heavily loaded chariot to Ramses in a few hours.

The room broke into loud applause at the wealthy Egyptian family's generosity. They were now part of the mixed multitude of tens of thousands of other families preparing to leave Egypt.

Malik and Nathan received approval from Hatep to open the front door of the house to check on the horses tied in the stable. Reuben followed them into the cool, pre-dawn darkness. Before they had walked but a dozen steps, Nathan's mother called him back.

"Nathan, there are some wool blankets at home that need to be packed into a wagon. We'll want them for the cold nights in the desert." Rachel told her son where to find them. He and Malik left together at a trot.

"We'll be back in ten minutes," Nathan shouted over his shoulder.

CHAPTER 40

Giza Complex, Jasmine House

Chaos surrounded the milling human and animal activity outside Jasmine House that was further pronounced in the darkness before dawn. News spread among Hatep's other released slaves that his estate storerooms were open for anyone who needed food or supplies. All the family's wagons and chariots had been loaded a day earlier and there was still food to spare. Scores of other slaves with their makeshift carts pulled by donkeys and oxen added their voices to the fray. The caravan from Jasmine House was ready to leave when Rachel asked Reuben if he had seen Nathan and Malik.

"Who knows in all this confusion?" he exclaimed in exasperation as he tried to control Sapphire. The high-strung horse, already unhappy about having to pull a heavily-loaded chariot, was crowded to the side by a goat cart whose young driver tugged at its reins.

When Rachel found Iset, the two mothers became more worried. "They should be back by now," Rachel insisted.

"Where else could they be?"

"They could be anywhere—who knows?"

Iset eventually found Hatep in the mayhem and asked him what they should do.

"We can't wait any longer," he insisted. The two mothers didn't want to hear those words. "When did you send them for the blankets?" he asked.

"Almost an hour ago," his wife replied.

"Well, we need to join the rest of the traffic that's already filling the highway from Giza to Ramses or we'll be left behind. I don't want to become separated from the main Giza group. It will only get worse when we merge with those coming from other directions."

"What will we do? We can't just leave them behind!" Iset was becoming more distraught by the minute.

"They could still be in the caravan but with another family. Obviously something has happened, but we have to trust our God to take care of them. They're probably in the crowd somewhere and we'll come across them by the time we reach Ramses tomorrow."

Hatep tried to calm the two women. "At least they're together so they'll look out for each other. Nathan is a sensible boy; he'll do his best to keep Malik from doing something too adventurous."

"I hope you're right," Iset said with little conviction. "Just in case, I'll leave them a note on the front door in case they come back after we leave. Where should they meet us?"

"Tell them to take the main road to Ramses and then follow the crowd to Succoth. If they find Sapphire then they'll find us. Now, we need to leave. You two walk beside the wagon carrying Reuben's children." Hatep spun around and shouted for the lead wagon to begin moving.

Iset returned to the house where she wrote a short note to Malik and Nathan containing Hatep's instructions. She pegged the papyrus to the front door and prayed that God would protect her son and Nathan.

Mennefer, Temple of *Ptah*

While he waited for news of the assassinations that would propel him into history as the next Pharaoh, Bakenmut paced around the cool central courtyard of the Temple of *Ptah* in the pre-dawn light. Scribe Gobe, now a reluctant accomplice to the assassinations, kept his distance from the mercurial master scribe. He was terrified of this man who could erase human life so casually.

Referred to by residents of Mennefer as the *Hut-ka-Ptah*, or the Enclosure of *Ptah*, the temple in the larger Sacred Precinct was a covered temple with a roof supported by dozens of closely spaced granite columns, each carved and painted with likenesses of the gods *Ptah*, *Sekhmet*, and *Nefertem* in various poses and embellished with depictions of their exploits. The thick columns and low roof gave the enclosure a coolness that drew tourists and worshippers. It was empty this morning because the midnight death had touched almost every family in Egypt.

Incense from an offering in the adjacent temple to the *Apis* bull wafted on a slight breeze from the direction of the river. Sweet, soft voices from a priestess chorus lifted Bakenmut's spirits until he realized that it was now well past dawn and he hadn't seen any palace priests or officials gathering for prayer as Nakhte assured him they would.

"Where is everyone?" he demanded out loud. "Everyone should be here by now."

"Maybe there has been some delay," Gobe observed. His boss was ready to explode.

"Obviously there has been a delay, you fool!"

The master scribe spun on his heel and headed for the front door of the temple. Gobe kept at a safe distance and waited in the shade. Bakenmut stepped into the sunlight and glanced at the colossal granite statues taller than the building that represented silent sentinels of *Ptah*. They stood guard in a row before the taller, brightly painted pylons. Apart from a few morning food vendors and six heavily painted priestesses, none more than twelve years old, giggling in a corner, nobody else was in sight. His irritation would give way to fear if he yielded his mind to further speculation. He decided to redirect his anxiety into anger.

Muttering curses to himself, he was about to buy a cup of persimmon tea from a vendor to calm his nerves when he noticed the dust cloud from an approaching chariot. The chariot's lone driver skidded to a stop before the broad flight of steps. It was Thethi.

"What news of the vizier?" the royal scribe called out before the diminutive draftsman reached him.

Thethi brushed the dust from his tunic and straightened his kilt. There was a smile on his face.

Bakenmut threw a silver piece to Gobe with a curt order to bring him a cup of tea. He didn't bother to offer one to Thethi or his scribe.

Thethi hurried to keep up with the master scribe who walked at a brisk pace into the temple courtyard where he stepped into an alcove behind a statue of Ramses II where they could speak in private.

"Tell me everything," Bakenmut said when the two were in the secluded space. Thethi wondered why they couldn't talk in the open if the man before him would soon be the next Pharaoh.

"Yes, Nakhte is dead. I saw his murder with my own eyes. He walked alone in the darkness on a path a mile from here. Your men cut him down without a sound."

"That's it? No cry of helplessness, no pleading for mercy, no scream to the gods?"

"Sir, you told your men to kill him. There were no instructions to prolong his departure to the afterlife."

"Yes, of course. I only hoped that he'd died with betrayal as his final thought."

"It was so fast that I doubt he had much of a final thought."

"So it's done." His earlier anger gave way to fiendish pleasure.

Gobe handed Bakenmut his tea when they stepped out from behind the statue into the courtyard.

"Where is the palace entourage to proclaim you the new Pharaoh?" Thethi asked.

"I don't know." His mind was elsewhere savoring the thought that the vizier was finally gone. He hated the man almost as much as he hated Pharaoh.

"Sir..." Gobe said.

"Don't bother me! Can't you see I'm thinking?!"

"Sir, there's a man at the entrance with a message for you."

"Well, send him in. What are you waiting for?"

"Sir, he's... well, the guards won't let him into the temple precinct. He's not properly dressed. He insists that he needs to give you the message personally."

Bakenmut downed his tepid tea, tossed the empty cup to Gobe, and hurried to the entrance. When he saw him he understood why his messenger was prevented from entering. Antosh was not only dressed in a tattered loincloth, but his muscular tattooed arms displayed almost one hundred kills and he stood a foot taller than any of the temple guards. The short sword in his belt shone with a fresh film of oil. A platoon of armed temple guards watched him from the temple door and hoped that there would be no trouble. They were surprised that the well-dressed official exiting the temple, evidently someone of high position and wealth, would have anything to do with the barbarian who waited on the steps. Bakenmut and Antosh walked several paces away from the guards and stood with the mercenary in the shade of a looming pylon.

"This better be important," Bakenmut growled. He had no fear of the menacing hulk before him. They had a long history of "beneficial mutual interests" that guaranteed the man's loyalty.

"One of my men does occasional contract work for the vizier and was part of his team hired to assassinate Pharaoh." Antosh began his terse report with no more emotion than he would have used to order breakfast. "They entered the palace in the dark and went straight to the Great One's bedroom. There were no guards or servants anywhere. They searched all levels of his residence and he was gone. The stable hands reported that he and a contingent of servants and soldiers on horseback left the palace just after midnight. Nobody knows where they went."

"So Pharaoh is not dead?" Bakenmut eyes widened with disbelief and his voice trembled.

"He was not murdered in his bed this morning according to the vizier's plan, which is all that I'm reporting."

The sight of another chariot speeding down the wide avenue toward the temple distracted Bakenmut from asking any further questions. He dismissed Antosh curtly and watched the vehicle stop behind Thethi's chariot at the curb. Deputy Architect Imani stepped down and told the drivers to move both chariots into the shade. He ran up the stairs where Bakenmut waited impatiently.

"I hope you have good news."

"It is mixed, I'm afraid."

"Tell me that Hatep and his family are dead."

"They are not. In fact, they are far from it. They departed with their freed slaves to join Moses."

"What? He's Pharaoh's Royal Master Architect and a national hero awarded the title of *Amkhu*. How could he be leaving his homeland with that rabble?"

"We tried to get close to the family at their home but there were four army guards protecting them and forty or fifty slaves and servants milling about. With just me and three of your men, we couldn't do a thing. Still, we managed to come away with something."

"What was that?"

"Those two teens. While we watched the house, they left their family compound and walked to the nearby slave village. We picked them up easily with only a minor scuffle."

"What did you do with them?"

"They're trussed up in Thutmose's pyramid as you instructed."

"But they're alive?"

"Yes. We drugged them, but they'll be awake in a few hours."

Bakenmut paced excitedly back and forth thinking about what he would do to those two pests. Imani broke his focus to ask about the large gathering of palace officials that was supposed to be at the temple that morning. When he gave Imani a quick update, he saw Antosh standing nearby with what appeared to be another report.

With a gesture for him to approach, the roughly-dressed mercenary gave a brief summary: "Pharaoh is encamped in Saqqara planning to combine the two Army corps into one force. He will personally lead an attack on the Israelites. I thought you would want to know this." Antosh walked away.

"I didn't think the Great One had it in him. For months he's been close to death from the plagues and diseases. He's tougher than he appeared."

"What will we do now?" Imani asked.

"We'll travel south to Saqqara tomorrow or the next day to join our Great One in his slaughter of the Israelites. I'll make some excuse about missing the summons of his royal court to accompany him for the revenge attack. My news of Vizier Nakhte's unfortunate death at the hands of robbers may open an opportunity for me to be the next vizier. Before we go to Saqqara, however, I want to remove Imhotep's giant golden cylinder from Pharaoh's pyramid and stash it away. My first priority before we leave this city is to settle a score with those two troublemakers!"

CHAPTER 41

Giza Complex, Unfinished Pyramid of Thutmose III

Nathan awoke with the vague sense that he'd felt this miserable nausea before. He couldn't remember when or why. When he finally recalled the *Per-Nefer* House of Mummification, he moaned, turned his head to his left and threw up. If it was the same drug, he remembered now, then his head would throb and his stomach would soon churn into full revolt. Sure enough, his stomach obliged with a repeat performance. He felt each blood vessel throbbing behind his eyeballs. Drugged *again*! He was sitting up this time and he felt another body next to his. Thankfully, this body felt alive.

"Malik!" he shouted—too loudly. A bit softer the next time, "Malik. Is that you?"

The person next to him began to wretch violently. Last night's Passover dinner shot away from him onto the floor.

Several rounds of low groans and vomiting brought Malik back to consciousness.

"Nathan?"

"I'm right here. How do you feel?"

"Gross. Rotten. Smelly…I just threw up on myself. On top of that, I'm blind."

"You're not blind. Wherever we are, it's totally dark. We're inside some sort of tomb judging from the dry, dusty smell. My eyes are wide open too and I can't see a pinpoint of light."

"Is it another plague?"

"No more plagues, remember?"

"Are we in a mortuary with dead bodies?"

"I don't think so. I don't smell chemicals or decaying flesh—just stone dust."

"That's a comfort. I think." He spit bile away from his friend.

Nathan tried to loosen the rope around his wrists but it was so tight that the struggling cut off circulation to his hands. He stopped moving and waited for feeling to return to his fingers. When he attempted to reach over and untie Malik's hands, he found that impossible. Whoever trussed them up knew what he was doing.

There was no sense of time in the absolute darkness. They alternated between dozing and waking for what could have been minutes or hours. Rolling on their sides helped the blood circulation somewhat, but hunger and thirst soon began to gnaw at them. Their retinas became so hypersensitive in the dark that they saw swarms of fireflies in rainbow colors flying before their eyes. Even their hearing played tricks on them.

"I hear voices," Malik exclaimed. He was wide awake, but he woke Nathan from a dream about flying above the Great Place Valley and Hatshepsut's tomb.

"I've been hearing voices and seeing things for hours," his friend retorted, still half-asleep.

"No! I mean I *really* hear people talking. They're coming this way."

Distant echoes preceded flickering torches that became brighter. Two men, dressed in neatly creased linen tunics worn by professional scribes and administrators, rounded a corner and stepped into the room where Nathan and Malik were bound.

"Hey!" Malik shouted. "Over here! Let us loose!"

A man who looked vaguely familiar held his torch above Malik's face and smiled. Both captives squinted and turned away from the blinding, sputtering flame. After checking the knots tying their hands and feet, the torch-bearer used his flame to light more torches on the walls. Soon the entire area was illuminated.

"Aren't you going to untie us?" Malik demanded.

"Oh, did we forget to untie you?" The men laughed.

"In case you missed it, you're prisoners!"

"What for? We didn't do anything." Nathan couldn't figure out why these two strangers would hold them hostage.

"You are so mistaken. You upset a perfect robbery scheme and nearly got all of us arrested." The older of the two stood before Malik.

"Imani!"

"That's right! The day you found that tunnel drawing in Thethi's desk was the day you sealed your deaths and the deaths of your family. We've been waiting for this day to even the score for all the trouble you've caused us."

Thethi joined him and sneered. "When the Black Falcon gets here you'll wish you were dead. You can't imagine how mad he's been since you spilled your guts to that Medjay Chief Inspector. He's looking forward to dragging out your payment for that."

As if cued by an invisible script, Imani and Thethi looked up to see Royal Master Scribe Bakenmut approach holding a flaming torch.

"Who are you?" Malik demanded when the man came into his field of view. Suddenly he felt energized by the thought that this might be the Black Falcon. He had to hear it from the man's own lips.

"I am who you think I am, Malik, son of Hatep. Your sister is the traitorous code breaker. My men know me as the Black Falcon, but soon I will be Vizier Bakenmut." He turned to Nathan. "And you are the slave Nathan, son of the Hebrew slaves Asher and Rachel. Yes, I know all about your two families. I've taken care of them and now I'll take care of you."

"What do you mean? What have you done to them?" Malik wrestled against his restraints and tried to stand. He fell and scraped his face on the stone floor.

To cause more anguish and dampen their spirits, Bakenmut toyed with them: "At my orders, both of your families and a handful of innocent servants were murdered outside your home this morning by a troop of my men. At the same time, you were captured and brought here. I'm surprised that you didn't hear their screams for mercy. I wish I'd been there to see them suffer, especially your father. I hear that he cried like a baby when my men took your sister."

"No! That's not possible!" Malik shouted in tears.

"You animal!" Nathan screamed.

"So you see, suffering later by my hand will not seem so bad now that all your hopes are gone. You'll welcome death."

While Bakenmut taunted his two prisoners, Imani and Thethi examined the large gold cylinder in the center of the high-vaulted chamber. They caressed the strange engraved symbols on its surface without understanding what they meant. They didn't want to interrupt their leader while he baited the prisoners in preparation for their torture.

"Just so you realize how hopeless things are for you, let me tell you what I did to the famous Chief Inspector Hezbak. He became too nosy around the palace and eventually discovered my identity. Unfortunately for him, he thought he could outsmart me. He accused me in private but my men captured him and threw him into the river at the Temple of *Sobek*. I heard his screams that night when the crocodiles tore his body to shreds—So much for your Medjay accomplice."

Malik and Nathan slumped against each other with their heads bowed in defeat. They quietly sobbed after hearing that the Black Falcon was responsible for their families' deaths.

"Boss, I think you should look at this." Imani called him over to the gold cylinder. "How are we going to move this thing?"

"It must weigh over two thousand pounds," Thethi added.

"I'll get some men to help us. We'll move it using rollers after we tip it on its side. We have plenty of time to do it right."

"What about them?" Imani pointed to the two prisoners.

"I'll come back to them later. Whatever fight was in them before is gone now."

The three men left the center of the large room and exited back through the pyramid's main entrance corridor, talking as they went about how they would move the cylinder from the pyramid out the back tunnel to the *mastaba*.

When they were gone, the two friends realized that the torches continued to burn along the walls of the chamber. In spite of what they had heard about the deaths of their families, Nathan grasped at a glimmer of hope. "Now that I know where we are, there should be a way out of here."

"I'm sorry, Nathan."

"I'm sorry about your family too, Malik."

"No, besides that I mean I'm sorry because all of this is my fault. If I hadn't found that tunnel drawing and taken you to explore Queen Hatshepsut's tomb, our families would still be alive. Now we're both going to be tortured and killed."

"Don't blame yourself. It wasn't like you forced me to tag along."

"What makes you think there might be a way out?"

"The last time we were here we came in through Prince Ankhaf's old abandoned *mastaba* to the tunnel. The room with the black flux box powering the *Breath of Osiris* must be on the other side of that door over there."

"So what? If we can't get untied we'll never make it out that way."

"I recall that Imhotep had some tools in that room. If we can crawl there, we might find something to cut or saw through these ropes. It's a long shot, but worth a try."

Hours later, they had only managed to wriggle halfway across the room. Drenched in sweat, ankles and wrists bloodied from the exertion, and dehydrated, they passed out on the cool floor in front of the gold cylinder.

CHAPTER 42

Saqqara, Amun Corps Garrison

Pharaoh's traveling carriage spewed a cloud of red dust behind it and sped into the Saqqara garrison at dawn accompanied by minimal royal fanfare. Generals Herihor and Intef had barely enough warning to line up a greeting line of available soldiers. A single trumpeter sounded the Great One's royal flourish across the encampment.

"He looks half-dead," General Intef, commander of the Ammit Corps, observed under his breath. The robust, barrel-chested general had little respect for a Pharaoh whom he considered a feeble-minded invalid. Better that the military should rule The Two Lands, he thought, than a tired old man on his last legs. He and General Herihor watched as servants gingerly lifted the emaciated monarch out of his travelling carriage and into a gilded, covered sedan chair borne by six black Nubian slaves in purple loincloths. Without a single glance at the line of troops standing at attention, Pharaoh's servants carried him straight to the two generals. The officers bowed to the ground before him.

"Stand!" the weak but sharp command left no doubt about Pharaoh's impatience.

When they stood in obedience and looked at the dark brown, shriveled form of Thutmose III he seemed lost in the pillows and blankets.

"Are you ready to attack the Hebrews?"

They had agreed that General Intef would speak for both of them. "Not as yet, Excellency." He gave a shallow bow to avoid eye contact.

"My orders were to attack them at dawn! This disobedience is treasonous!"

"If the Great One would allow me to explain, I can assure you that we are doing the best we can, under the circumstances." A thin veneer of professionalism barely veiled the general's outrage. Nobody, not even the Pharaoh, would accuse him of being a traitor.

"You have twenty thousand soldiers among your two corps. That is enough to decimate an unarmed rabble of slaves, no matter their number."

"As you are aware, O Great One, the God of those Hebrew slaves killed many in The Two Lands at midnight last night and all the firstborn among our soldiers have died. We are still counting the dead, but our numbers could be down by as much as half. It will take us at least one day, maybe two, to bury the dead, assess our remaining mix of forces, and reorganize ranks into a fighting force. Some horses of the Leopard Charioteers and the other mounted regiments have also been lost to the Angel of Death." General Intef finished his report without mentioning that it was only a partial estimate. Innumerable desertions also took place during last night's slaughter that further diminished their official ranks. If they ended up with half their original numbers he'd be surprised. He and Herihor hoped that the severity of the losses might change Pharaoh's mind about attacking.

"That is unacceptable!"

"But Great One..." Intef began his objection and regretted it immediately. It was pointless.

"Silence! Both of you are relieved of your commands. I will take control of the combined corps. The Army of Egypt will conquer those infuriating Hebrews once and for all. You have today and tomorrow to assemble a united corps of Egypt's finest warriors. If they are not ready to attack in two days you will pay with your lives. Dismissed!"

Generals Herihor and Intef bowed deeply and walked away.

"That fool will get us all killed!" Intef said as they walked away.

"At least we have two more days to live. He'll cut your life shorter if those words get back to him." Herihor wanted to return to his headquarters tent from which he could oversee what was left of his corps. Only it wasn't *his* Amun Corps any more. Pharaoh had relieved him of command but still expected him to reorganize his men and merge them with the other corps. The deranged old man wanted to lead a diminished army against two million slaves!

Still, Herihor could feign loyalty to Pharaoh as long as he didn't have to kill Hebrews. He had to think of a way to disappear from the army and join his future wife and her family among the refugees following Moses across the desert. He looked east at a white cloud rising into the sky and backlit by the glow of a sunrise. That must be dust raised by Moses and the marching Israelites. His future was somewhere under that cloud.

Between Ramses and Succoth

Two million slaves, interspersed with some believing Egyptians and a mixed multitude of non-Israelites, made their way to Succoth. When word reached stragglers in Ramses that the Egyptian army was preparing to attack them, they relayed that information ahead to Moses and hurried forward for relative safety among the main group. News of an imminent attack served to energize the idle and undecided stragglers, but fear and anxiety added to the strain of tribes and families who had abandoned their homes to follow a prophet most of them had never seen.

Fear gave way to anger when they realized that Moses was leading them into the Eastern Egyptian Desert where they were sure to die of thirst and hunger. On top of that, he had chosen the more difficult route that would pin their backs against the Red Sea!

"I think we should turn back and return to our homes," one of Hatep's ex-slaves said as they sat in a circle and ate bread and leeks for breakfast. The former field hand felt that his new-found freedom gave him the right to speak as an equal among the others.

"You're talking nonsense," Hatep said.

"The army will cut us to shreds. The only weapons we have are hoes and sticks. They have archers on chariots that can put out your eye at two hundred yards. We should turn back."

"Enough of that talk!" Hatep spoke as the unofficial leader of the caravan. He looked to Asher and Reuben for support.

"Listen to Hatep," Reuben insisted. "How will you return to Giza against the tide of people going east? If anyone had a reason to go back it would be Hatep and his family. Yet, there's no one among us more determined than him to trust God."

"I'm just saying that Moses seems bent on getting us killed by taking us to a dead end. It's sure suicide," the grumbler persisted.

Hatep had enough of the man's complaints. "Look, you can go back if you want. My family and I are risking our lives to follow the God of Abraham, Isaac, and Jacob to a land we've never seen. When we decided to join God's chosen people by the faith of Abraham we knew there'd be no turning back. If you want to go back, then go, but don't discourage the rest of us with your complaining!" He stared at his former servant while he chewed his meager breakfast.

The former slaves squatting around the campfire pondered what this wealthy Egyptian *Amkhu* said about giving up everything to follow the God of Abraham. How could Hebrew slaves do any less? Reuben admired his former master all the more.

CHAPTER 43

Giza Complex, Unfinished Pyramid of Thutmose III

Malik was the first to wake up. Nathan awoke a few minutes later from a delirious dream. Two or three torches around the room sputtered with their last flames.

"We should pray," Malik said through cracked lips. "We should pray for a quick, painless death."

"No my friend, we should ask God to somehow deliver us from that evil monster." Nathan tried to sit up but he didn't have the strength. "If God can send a deliverer to free an entire nation of Israelites, then He can free two miserable creatures like us." He prayed for both of them before he drifted into a mercifully calm sleep.

The noise of men returning to the main chamber brought the two back to consciousness.

"What have we here?" Imani said when he found the bent shapes in the middle of the room. Gobe, who had joined the group along with four stocky workmen, dragged the two back to where they had been leaning against a column and dropped them to the floor like sacks of grain.

Bakenmut pointed the four workmen who carried wooden rollers and coils of ropes to the golden cylinder. He ignored the prisoners for the moment and looked around the dim chamber.

"When I was here last, Imhotep energized those glass globes in the ceiling with some sort of light. I think the source was in that room." He pointed to a door in the distance. "Imani and Thethi, go figure out how to make them work."

Within minutes, the objects in the ceiling gave off a soft hum and a golden glow. They gradually became brighter until they illuminated the entire pyramid vault. A mellow hum from the back room was accompanied by a similar, though higher pitched, yet pleasant purr from the golden cylinder.

The cylinder's intricate and elegant engraving still captivated their attention when they gathered around the center of the room. The amount of gold in this one object was staggering.

"This treasure will be my ultimate prize," Bakenmut announced. His accomplices lusted after even a small piece of the golden cylinder.

First, he gave instructions to the workmen: "Before we tip this over and move it on rollers into the abandoned *mastaba*, I want you men to go into the tunnel through that far room and make sure the floor is clear and level. Once we get this moving on the rollers it should take less than an hour to push it out of here."

After the workmen departed, he turned to admire Imhotep's mysterious handiwork. "Imani, how are we going to tip this thing over without damaging it? I don't want to mar the carvings or chip it."

The architect stepped to within an arm's length of the gold and peered at the tubes that exited from its top and disappeared into the high ceiling above. The instant he touched the golden surface he jerked his hand back in surprise.

"That thing's alive! I felt it buzz up my arm!"

"It's making the sound of a thousand bees," Thethi observed. "And it's becoming louder. The sound is coming from *inside* the gold!"

The humming of the gold so fascinated him that Imani moved closer to touch it again. A blue glow that highlighted the deeply etched characters on the surface looked inviting. He timidly reached out again and the blue glow enveloped his fingers. A sharp "Crack!" reverberated against the stone walls and he flew back onto the floor. Imani climbed to his feet on shaky legs. His fingers and hand were numb. It was not a pleasant sensation.

"Never mind that for now," Bakenmut said indifferently. "When the workmen come back, I'll have them use wooden poles to tip it over onto the rollers and then that noise should stop. I'm not concerned if it sparks and kills them. They're expendable."

He turned to his accomplices. "There's more gold in the queen's side-chamber. I want you three to collect as much of it as you can and stash that in the abandoned *mastaba*."

"I saw the entrance to the side-tomb off the main corridor when we came in," Gobe volunteered.

"Good. Retrieve as many articles as you can carry and forget anything that isn't gold or precious jewels. I saw a small chariot in the tomb that you can use to haul it in."

After the three left on their errand, the Black Falcon stood alone to admire his treasure from a respectful distance. The buzzing sound grew more annoying. He would have Imani find a way to stop the racket without extinguishing the lights in the ceiling.

Malik and Nathan watched their tormentor warily. He was focusing more on his gold than on them which suited them fine. Nathan stifled a cry when he felt something furry brush his bare arms bound behind him. He strained to look but his stiff neck wouldn't cooperate. He felt it again. A soft squeaking sound made no sense until he realized that whoever, or whatever, it was was trying to untie his wrists.

Tiny hands worked on the knots for several minutes before giving up. He then felt something moist against his wrist accompanied by a gnawing sound. His hands were loose! Nathan flexed his fingers and wrists behind him without giving his freedom away in case Bakenmut looked in his direction. The bewildered look on Malik's face matched his own.

"Don't say anything," Nathan whispered through clenched teeth.

He then saw that Malik's hands were free too. A small, chocolate face peaked over Malik's shoulder.

It was Tik-tik! The appearance of the trained monkey meant that Imhotep must be nearby.

To their bewilderment, the monkey swung up onto a statue of an oversized armored figure and let out a blood-chilling screech to get their captor's attention. Bakenmut jumped at the inhuman scream. His wide eyes followed the agile monkey as it ran across the room where he screeched again before hopping into the room with the black energy box.

"Stupid monkey!" he muttered. He turned his attention back to examining the inscription on the gold cylinder.

Malik and Nathan exchanged satisfied grins. A few minutes later they heard a deep rumble. Bakenmut's head swung around to find the source of the roar. He ran into the room that led to the *mastaba* tunnel at the same moment that a cloud of dust blew out the door, blinding him.

"Quick, untie your feet." Malik and Nathan groped at their knots with aching fingers urged on by a rush of adrenaline. When the ropes came loose, they tried to stand but had no strength in their legs.

"I think Tik-tik triggered a cave-in. Remember Imhotep said to be careful of booby traps?" Nathan said. The deep roar of the *mastaba* tunnel collapse still reverberated around the room and they no longer needed to whisper.

Malik crawled on his knees toward the cylinder. Blue light filtered through the dusty haze and enveloped the object. It was past its initial humming and buzzing; it now filled the room with a high-pitched, piercing howl. About five feet away from the cylinder, Malik's hair stood straight out from his head and he felt a fascinating, tingling sensation.

"Get back here! The Black Falcon could return any moment." Nathan couldn't believe what his friend was doing. If that thing gave off another spark it would make Imhotep's muscle stunner seem like a toy.

Another thunderous roar came from the opposite side of the room that led to the main tunnel entrance and the side corridors to the queen's vault. Someone, probably Imhotep, must have triggered another cave-in, but that was the only other way out! At least they would only have to deal with Bakenmut and not his henchmen or workers, Nathan thought.

Imhotep's monkey emerged from the settling dust with a yelp. Proud of triggering the *mastaba* booby-trap, he spent a full minute carefully brushing dust from his face and body with his tiny hands. His grooming done, he raced across the room and jumped onto another large statue. He beckoned them with waving arms and a sharp whistle. Malik couldn't take his eyes from the glowing cylinder.

Fed up with his friend's ill-timed fascination with the pulsing blue light, Nathan grabbed Malik's arm and pulled him away. Snapped out of his trance, he joined Nathan and crawled on hands and knees toward Tik-tik. The strange monkey hopped up and down and whistled louder. He wanted them to hurry!

The two felt stiff after being tightly bound and immobilized for almost three days. In spite of wanting to stand up and walk, all they could do was hobble forward on hands and knees in a painful waddle. When they finally reached him, Tik-tik slipped behind the blocky pedestal of the giant statue. They stared at a waist-high door that led into blackness.

"Are we supposed to crawl in there?" Nathan asked.

"Not if you have a better idea." Malik squeezed ahead of him into the small opening.

Tik-tik gave a loud scream and pointed behind them. Bakenmut had emerged from the energy room covered in thick dust. He had to rub his eyes before he could locate the monkey. When he peered through the cloud he noticed Nathan crouched at the base of the statue and ready to enter the crawl space. Their eyes met for a split-second before Nathan squirmed into the dark hole followed by their scampering rescuer. Tik-tik pulled on a lever, a hidden mechanism immediately slammed a heavy wooden door behind them, and they were plunged into total darkness.

Knowing that their nemesis was a few feet behind on the other side of the door gave them the impetus to press ahead in the cramped confines of the passageway. It led down, which didn't make sense as a way of escape, but they were in no position to argue. Crawling down a black tunnel with a monkey didn't make much sense either.

Royal Master Scribe Bakenmut, the infamous Black Falcon, was in a blind rage. Outsmarted again by two teenagers! He cursed and banged and pulled on the small fortified door until blood covered his hands. All avenues of escape for him were sealed. Chunks of limestone that weighed tons blocked the *mastaba* tunnel. Granite slabs had fallen into slots to secure the main passageway that exited to the surface. His only hope was to break down the wooden door between him and the two escapees. If they could escape that way then so could he.

The ear-splitting, warbling wail from the gold cylinder drowned out the sound of another granite slab when it slid into place behind the wooden door. He put his hands over his ears to block out the sound but it made no difference. The high-pitched, penetrating whine was driving him insane. Little did he realize that it would grow louder and louder until his eardrums ruptured. Pent-up energy of the *Breath of Osiris* inside the cylinder would eventually be released through the golden conduit in the ceiling and into the sky in a monumental blaze of beautiful blue-white electrical plasma.

The two crawling figures followed Tik-tik's incessant chatter in the dark which encouraged them in a strange way. If they hadn't followed his noise, they would have become lost in the maze of side tunnels and dead ends. Their path down finally turned upward. Hope replaced despair for a few minutes longer. Their lives would never be the same since their families were dead.

Warm air with a fresh smell of palms announced freedom ahead. Even though it was night when they emerged from a simple opening at the base of Thutmose's pyramid, light from the stars overhead breathed new life into their exhausted bodies.

They forced themselves to stand in the sand on wobbly limbs and walk toward a clump of palm trees.

"I wish I had something to lean on," Malik said.

"Will this do?" They never heard Imhotep approach out of the shadows. The brilliant inventor, never one for elaborate greetings, handed the startled young man his walking stick.

"You sent Tik-tik for us!" Nathan exclaimed.

"Of course I did. I instructed him to wait until you were out of harm's way before he released the *mastaba* booby-traps. I'm glad everything worked out for you. When monkeys are given complicated instructions, one never knows what will happen."

"We need to get to Jasmine House. I want to see my parents one last time." Malik could not hold back his tears.

"They are gone." Imhotep replied.

"We know that. The Black Falcon murdered all of them when he captured us. He actually enjoyed watching our reaction when he described how his men murdered our families and many slaves too."

"Obviously I did not make myself clear." Imhotep searched for the right words. "Your parents are *not* dead. Your tormenter lied to cause you more anguish. Of course, you had no way of knowing the truth. You have been that monster's prisoners for almost three days and your parents left soon after you disappeared. They and many others joined the Israelites in Ramses. By now they must be in Succoth and well on their way east toward Canaan."

Elation replaced misery when they understood that the Black Falcon had lied to them; tears of joy replaced heartache. All their pain and suffering would be forgotten when they reunited with their families.

"We need to get to Succoth right away then," Malik said.

"That will be difficult." Imhotep handed him the paper that his mother left on the front door of Jasmine House. He read it quickly and handed it to Nathan.

"So what, we'll find them somehow."

"What Master Imhotep means is that there's a lot of desert between us and them by now. We need time to regain our strength and by then they'll be a hundred miles away. We can't catch up with them by foot in time."

"You are correct," Imhotep agreed. "Besides that, Pharaoh has combined his two Army corps and they are maneuvering from their Saqqara garrison to Succoth as we speak. You would have to go through lines of soldiers ready to kill any Israelite they come across. Thus, you cannot reach them by walking across the desert."

"So, our parents are alive, but you're saying that we'll never see them again?"

"No, that is not what I am saying."

"Master Imhotep, with all respect, you are talking in circles. Could you be more clear?"

"I apologize. In my reluctance to state the obvious through minimal use of words, my explanation was too short." His mind sifted through words and phrases to express his meaning with both economy and precision. Nathan and Malik grew more impatient.

"Tik-tik will take you to the *Eye of Horus* which is fueled and ready to fly. You will soar in it over the desert and the army. If you leave in the next few minutes you may catch a favorable wind in the desired direction. Is that more clear?"

"Yes!" the two friends shouted in unison. Tik-tik jumped onto Imhotep's shoulder and clapped his hands while baring his teeth in a wide grin.

"Come with me. We must launch the *Eye of Horus* immediately to reach the proper altitude before the sun rises." He turned without another word. Nathan and Malik hobbled after him across the sand as fast as they could.

CHAPTER 44

Giza Complex, Imhotep's Aerodrome

When they reached the makeshift aerodrome where Imhotep kept the *Horus Eye*, blood circulation and some feeling had returned to the two young men's legs. It was still dark, so they sensed rather than saw the tall wooden frame that supported the lighter-than-air machine. A segment of the night sky was devoid of stars where the limp silk bag drooped like laundry hung on a clothesline to dry.

Imhotep retrieved a burning wick from a nearby censer and used it to light fuel in the metal bowl suspended above the passenger's basket. A red glow became fire that illuminated the inside of the balloon. Looking up into the billowing envelope above him, it seemed bigger than Nathan remembered it. In twenty or thirty minutes it should take on its full shape and be ready to launch.

"Have you flown it recently?" Malik asked while they watched warm air ripple up inside the bag.

"Alas no, the pieces were in storage after it was shipped down the river from Thebes. My assistants readied it for flight only a few days ago after they modified it to my specifications."

"So this is a maiden test flight?"

"Yes, but you are an adventurous one, Malik. Are you disappointed to be testing this new *Horus Eye*?"

"Not at all! I can't wait to see what Giza and Mennefer look like from above."

Nathan was more cautious. "What exactly does 'modified' mean? And what will happen when the *Horus Eye* flies without a tether?"

The twinkle in the old inventor's eye worried Nathan even further. "Ah, I wondered if you would think of that. Cut loose from its tether, the balloon will drift wherever the winds take it. You were thinking, 'What if I want to go in a different direction from that of the wind?' Is that what concerns you?"

"Among other things, yes," Nathan admitted. "So what should we know about this new air machine?"

"First, you have already noticed that the balloon is larger than the one you flew above the Great Place. This one is almost twice the volume, so it can carry more weight and fly higher." Imhotep lit a torch and lifted it above his head taking care to hold it away from the suspended basket and balloon. The woven basket hanging below the balloon was in the shape of a reed boat, but larger and with unusual mechanisms at either end of the passenger compartment.

"Those look like fans!" Malik exclaimed.

"They are fans, but when these fans spin they push the basket and balloon forward in the direction you choose. You change directions using that large rudder above your heads just as you would the rudder of a ship."

"But what makes the fans turn?" Nathan asked. "Is there something under the floor of the basket?"

"Yes! I already explained to you how flux was stored in that black chest in the pyramid to feed energy into the golden cylinder. There is a flux box under your feet."

"I hope it doesn't spark like the muscle stunner you made for General Herihor. I wouldn't want that thing going off under me while we're up in the air." Malik laughed at the absurdity of his suggestion. He looked to Imhotep for confirmation that the black chest wasn't dangerous.

"No, of course not. I built a small machine that uses the flux to spin the fans. As long as there is energy left in the box, they will push you forward. Here, I'll show you how to turn them on so you only use the fans to change direction. There's no sense using them if the wind is taking you where you want to go."

After Imhotep showed them how to use the rudder control and turn the fans on and off, the inventor stepped out of the basket and admired his craft. "Take good care of her. My prayers are with you on what will be the first and last flight of this *Horus Eye*."

"You're not coming with us?" Malik asked.

Imhotep shook his head and a surprisingly cheerful smile crossed his face. "I loaded the craft with as much fuel as possible. My presence would only limit your range and duration of flight. You will have to fly her by yourselves. Tik-tik will go with you to untangle the control ropes and straighten any folds in the silk bag."

The thought of leaving Imhotep behind was unsettling but they could understand his reasoning. He had logically balanced his options and concluded that their best chance of rejoining their parents was if he sent them on their own.

"Master, please tell us what to expect in the flight," Malik figured that their inventor friend didn't want to dwell on his decision to stay behind.

"Yes, so this is how I foresee things developing for your voyage: The wind, light as it is now, will strengthen as the day progresses due to the sun's thermal effects. It should carry you toward Succoth and the cities where the largest numbers of Israelites are likely to be. You will be able to tell if you are heading in the right direction when you are at a high altitude. Steer the *Horus Eye* toward the main gathering of the exodus."

"What else do we need to know?"

"If we meet again I wish to know all the details of what it is like to fly as high as the *Horus Eye* can take you and steer against the direction of the wind. Returning to earth is more unpredictable. It is the most dangerous part of the journey."

"By 'returning to earth' do you mean like *crashing*?" Nathan knew there had to be a drawback to their aerial escape.

"Not necessarily. You will eventually either run out of fuel for the hot air or you will no longer fly toward your objective. I suggest releasing some of the hot air gradually when you see that your fuel is almost gone so that you have some altitude control. If, however, the winds shift you *away* from the departing Israelites, you must begin a rapid descent or you will lose the distance gained in your flight. In that case, the longer you delay landing, the farther you will have to walk."

"I remember how to release the hot air vent, so that's not a problem." Malik said.

"Be careful though, because releasing it too fast will cause you to fall quickly and hit the ground with great force."

"Great. So that's the *crash* part." At least Nathan knew what he had to look forward to.

By now the *Horus Eye* strained against its ropes. Tik-tik was in the support webbing and waited for his master's command to launch. The inventor looked at his two friends for what might be the last time. "You have grown from boys to men in the past months. Our times flying over the Great Place Valley were special for me. I wish you safety of flight," his eyes twinkled when he looked at Nathan, "and a soft landing." He waved his hand in a warm farewell.

Tik-tik scampered to the top of the balloon and released the ropes that tied the balloon to the support arms. Imhotep cranked the mechanism that retracted the four arms of the thin restraining structure. The *Horus Eye* lifted into the night sky without a sound.

With hardly any sensation of movement, the *Horus Eye* flew in a gentle arc over the dark pyramid complex of Giza. A dot of light from a single campfire passing below was the only perspective of their speed or altitude. For a long time they said nothing. Tik-tik fell asleep curled up in a tight ball on the floor of the reed basket. They would engage the fans when it got light enough to see, so they sat on woven reed benches and stared into the night.

Imhotep walked away from the aerodrome until he was almost a mile away from the pyramid where he had an unobstructed view of the structure built to honor the Pharaoh. According to his calculations, the *Breath of Osiris* could erupt at any time. He sat on the warm desert sand and waited.

Inside the pyramid's central vault, the royal master scribe lay unconscious on the floor. His eardrums had burst not long after the two teens escaped and the pain had become so unbearable that he passed out. Blue exoflux engulfed every object in the vaulted room, including his body on the floor, which vibrated with energy. The purpose of the golden cylinder was to accumulate flux energy from chemical reactions inside the black box. When the time was right, a tiny switch inside the cylinder released all the pent-up energy in a split-second into the tubes through the ceiling to the golden capstone at the apex and up into the night sky. It should repeat the process as long as the chemicals in the black box lasted.

When Imhotep felt the sandy ground shake beneath him he knew it was time. As soon as he squinted his eyes, a blinding blue-white flash illuminated the sky like a bolt of inverted lightning from the ground. Energy rose from the sharp apex of Thutmose's pyramid and branched up and out in all directions in the largest manmade electrical display ever created. The *Breath of Osiris* looked exactly as Imhotep had envisioned it; he clapped his hands in excitement like a child enjoying a magic show and then covered his ears when the thunderclap swept over him.

The bright flash of exoflux spread across the black sky in a beautiful white and blue web of sparks that blinded Nathan and Malik for a moment. Spots danced before their eyes. Tik-tik jumped onto Malik's shoulder and screeched in his ear. The passengers in the *Horus Eye* watched thin strands of ionized air branch up so high into the sky that they thought it might touch the stars. Peals of distant rolling thunder reached them seconds later.

Bakenmut's inert body on the floor of the pyramid's vault was reduced to a pile of ash by the split-second flash. One thing that Master Inventor Imhotep miscalculated was the amount of energy that would leak from the cylinder into the room when it discharged its exoflux. Blue sparks incinerated everything but metal and stone before exiting through the ceiling. Then the flux energy reversed its leakage back to the chemical black box which exploded in a shower of sparks. The *Breath of Osiris* would never illuminate the Giza sky again.

A deep purple hue on the eastern horizon announced dawn high above Egypt before any rays of sunlight reached the ground below them. When tinges of red and orange overtook the floating balloon, they made out the glowing tops of pyramids behind them and the dark Nile in shadows ahead. Their slow movement was finally perceptible by watching the ground. Farms, buildings, and canals crawled past as if in a lazy dream.

"What did you make of Imhotep's celestial display?" Nathan asked.

"Leave it to him to come up with something so spectacular. I don't know what else to say."

"I hope he's all right."

"If I know him, he'll turn up again someday."

By the time a sliver of golden sunlight peeked over the sharp horizon and reached the city of Memphis, the giant pylons of temples, symmetrical rows of tombs, and Pharaoh's ornate Mennefer Palace stood in stark relief against the long shadows. The Nile was a winding blue ribbon outlined by an emerald green fringe extending out for a mile from both banks and feathering into the tan desert.

"Are we heading in the right direction?" Nathan broke the reverential silence.

"I think so. If my geography is right, Ramses is slightly to our left and Succoth should be straight ahead. So far so good."

Nathan added a few more lumps to the fire. "We still have plenty of fuel to keep us at this altitude. As the day warms up though, we'll have to use more."

They lapsed into silence again, enthralled by the panoramic view of Lower Egypt that no human had ever seen this way before.

Malik broke the silence a few hours later. "I don't suppose Imhotep packed any food."

As if Tik-tik understood his words, the diminutive monkey awoke and blinked in the sunlight.

"Food, Tik-tik, where's the food?"

He hopped to a bench and lifted the seat, revealing loaves of unleavened bread wrapped in a rough cloth and a jug of water. Imhotep thought of everything!

"I wish I'd asked sooner!" Malik laughed.

They ate and drank while they watched the landscape roll by below them. Exhausted from their ordeal with the Black Falcon and claustrophobic escape from the pyramid, they fought the urge to sleep lest they lose altitude or miss a shift in the wind. In spite of their attempts to stay awake, they nodded off to sleep until Tik-tik's screech jolted them awake.

Judging from the location of the balloon's shadow that traced a path on the ground below, it was past noon; they were moving faster than before they fell asleep. Had Tik-tik alerted them to a wind shift? When the agitated monkey climbed onto the rope mesh above their heads and pointed to the horizon, they discovered why he had woken them.

Off to their right, far away on the horizon, a crisp white cloud stood out against the bright blue sky.

"That must be dust from all the people marching across the desert." Malik wanted to sound confident, but a trace of uncertainty betrayed him. They turned on the fans which caused the floor under them to vibrate and the whirling blades in front created a warm breeze. Using the rudder like Imhotep showed them, the *Horus Eye* gradually turned toward the dust cloud. Soon they sat back and steered straight toward the cloud.

"That means that we're getting closer to our families by the minute, right?"

"I suppose so. At least we're moving in the right direction."

"What else could that cloud be?"

"It could be a desert dust storm."

Nathan hadn't thought of that. "Can the *Horus Eye* fly through a dust storm?"

"Do you want to find out?"

"No! I insist that we *not* find out. Can we steer this thing around it?"

"Maybe, but for now we'll keep going in this direction. If it's a dust storm, we'll land and find shelter before it reaches us or we reach it. I want to watch for a while before we change our course."

"Alright, I'll keep my eyes on that dust cloud too." Nathan was glad that his reckless friend was thinking of their safety, for once. He also thought it wise to say nothing more and let Malik examine the cloud. He stoked the fire for the second time in fifteen minutes.

Shadows lengthened on the ground as Malik continued to concentrate on the cloud.

"It's not a dust cloud," he concluded. "It's located about where the Israelites should be but it's not moving. A dust cloud would be the color of the desert and should move. This keeps its tall shape, doesn't move, and it's gray and white."

"Like a rain cloud?"

"Something like that. It's as if we're being drawn straight to it."

"That's good, right?" Nathan was growing more nervous by the minute.

"How much fuel is left?"

"Less than an hour's worth at this rate. The sun will set about then too. I think we should start our descent now so we don't, you know, hit the ground really hard…in the dark. Imhotep thought that might not be a good idea."

"I want to keep going as long as we're moving in the right direction. I can feel the fans turning slower so there may not be much flux energy left to spin them. I'm certain now that the cloud marks where the Israelites are. We'll keep burning fuel for as long as we can."

"My next question is 'Then what?' but since you won't give me the answer I'd like, I'll give it more fuel…" Nathan added fuel and looked at the small amount left in the bin.

While Malik concentrated on their movement toward the cloud, Nathan watched the ground below them. Lengthening shadows caught his eye. In a few minutes he saw campfires and realized what he saw.

"Malik, I think we're flying over the Egyptian Army. They're camping for the night and there are thousands of them. I saw horses and chariots too."

"Maybe we'll outrun them if they've stopped for the night."

No sooner had he said that, than the wind shifted noticeably. The cloud directly before them appeared to swing to their right. Instead of flying east, they were flying north. If they continued to turn like this they would reverse course and fly back over the encamped army.

"We need to descend *now*," Malik announced.

"What a coincidence!" Nathan threw his hands up at the irony. "The fans stopped spinning and we're out of fuel."

Malik sorted through the maze of small ropes that hung over their heads. He searched for the control line to vent hot air from the top of the balloon so they would descend. All the ropes looked alike in the dim light.

"I think it's this one." Malik pulled on the rope but nothing happened. He expected to hear a hiss from above and feel them drop as the air escaped. He pulled it again but still felt no change.

"I was thinking," Nathan began. "If the sun has set and the outside air cools faster than the warm air inside the bag, shouldn't we *gain* altitude even though we're not adding more heat to the air inside the bag?"

"I suppose so. Then we'd need to release even more hot air to descend." Malik wrapped both hands around the rope and gave it a hard jerk. A rush of air above them meant that the balloon was finally venting. Their stomachs told them that the *Horus Eye* was dropping fast.

Nathan groaned, closed his eyes, and clenched the railing with both hands.

CHAPTER 45

Eastern Egyptian Desert

By the time the *Horus Eye* descended close to the desert floor, shadows obscured features on the ground that might have warned them to brace for impact. They felt the craft plummeting in the dark but had no perception of their true altitude. They hit the ground with a resounding crash and bounced back into the air. Imhotep designed the basket with woven layers of dried papyrus and bulrush reeds to crush and absorb the energy of just such a disaster; the result was that the humans and primate tumbled out of the basket unharmed. They landed in an area of soft sand. The empty, twisted shell of the basket rebounded a second time and shattered in pieces against a rock outcropping. The silk bag snagged on a boulder and ripped apart.

Dazed, but glad to be alive, the two survivors wobbled to their feet and looked around. Tik-tik jumped into Malik's arms.

"Did you see where we landed? We have to keep away from the Egyptian soldiers." Nathan hated the thought of being taken prisoner a second time. After what they'd been through with the Black Falcon, he couldn't bear having his hands tied again.

"We're in the middle of their encampment. If they saw the *Horus Eye* come down then my guess is they'll be here in a few minutes."

No sooner had he spoken than he heard gruff voices nearby.

"I found their flying reed ship! Keep looking!"

Torch in hand, an Egyptian soldier confronted them. Two other soldiers pointed spears at their chests.

"Sit down!" the torch bearer commanded. Malik and Nathan obeyed.

Tik-tik scampered into the brush before the soldiers noticed him.

"Over here!" they called to the other soldiers. "It's two lads!"

Soon a squad of soldiers surrounded them and tied their hands with leather straps. Their raw wrists protested but they gritted their teeth and listened to their captors discuss their fate.

"One looks Egyptian and the other looks like a Hebrew slave. We have to do something with them." Their leader appeared to be a sergeant. He was uncertain what to do next.

"Let's kill them and bury them in the sand," one said. "I don't want to babysit two boys. Besides, we need to get ready for tomorrow's attack." Several other soldiers muttered in agreement.

"I don't have a problem with executing the slave but the Egyptian might be a commander's son trying to reach his father. We'd be sorry if we harmed him."

His statement gave Malik an idea.

"What corps are you with?" he demanded.

The sergeant was surprised at his question. "We are Amun Corps, the Leopard Charioteers! Why?"

"General Herihor is your superior. Take us to him."

"I will do no such thing until you explain yourself."

"Were you in the battle of the Great Place Valley of the Kings last year when the Nubian and Libyan invaders were defeated? Did you fight in the South Canyon under Commander Herihor?"

"Why, yes. It was a great victory for the Leopards. Everybody knows that."

"Then you saw the *Horus Eye* fly in the sky that day over the Great Place Valley and guide your charioteers into the heart of the enemy attack. I and my slave sent you that information. We landed here in the same *Horus Eye*."

Malik figured he'd continue to lay it on thick. "I am Malik, son of *Amkhu* Hatep, Royal Master Architect and honored friend of the Great One." That seemed to get the soldier's attention.

"I remember now," the sergeant smiled for the first time since their capture. "Pharaoh gave you that black stallion and fancy chariot. I marched in the palace courtyard that day."

Malik perked up. "And Commander Herihor was rewarded with the *wesekh* of golden bees and promoted to General of the Amun Corps." He prayed they'd not ask him why he crashed in the middle of the army's bivouac. The tables would be turned if they knew he and Nathan had flown in from Giza and descended by mistake in their midst trying to join the Israelites.

The sergeant was finally convinced. To their relief, he ordered them untied. "I'll take you to General Herihor." They left the crashed airship behind and walked, or rather marched at double-time, flanked by their armed escort, through row upon row of tents and campfires to the Amun Corps' field headquarters.

Malik was startled when Tik-tik landed on his shoulder from a nearby tree but he said nothing. The little imp might come in handy again later.

Eastern Egyptian Desert, Amun Corps Field Headquarters

Primitive, smoking oil lamps lit the inside of the large army tent. A dozen senior officers huddled around a table covered with large maps drawn on durable parchment. General Herihor used a pointer to trace lines depicting their areas of responsibility.

"The main Israelite camp is here in the ten miles between the large hill of Migdol and the sea. Our scouts estimate that they number almost two million people. Another hundred thousand clog the road back to Baal Zephon. To their north is the village of Pi Hahiroth."

The sergeant stepped into the headquarters tent with Malik and Nathan at his side. He had instructed them to wait in silence next to the tent entrance until the general acknowledged their presence.

General Herihor continued to outline the disposition of troops from the two corps and Pharaoh's instructions to attack the next day. General Intef and his Ammit Corps would come down from the north through Pi Hahiroth and the Amun Corps would press forward due east through the stragglers in Baal Zephon, over Migdol, and into the heart of the Israelites camp pinned against the Red Sea.

"What about that pillar of cloud and fire between us and them?" one of his commanders asked. "I've lost some of my best scouts probing it."

Before he could answer, Herihor glanced up and saw Malik and Nathan standing by the tent flap. His eyes bulged in surprise and he was about to say something before he clamped his mouth shut. He looked down at the map to regain his composure and took a deep breath. His men were concentrating on the map and didn't notice his reaction.

"That...that's something we'll deal with at our morning staff meeting. Everyone meet here before dawn and we'll go over our attack plan. Dismissed."

The general turned to a scribe as his commanders filed out of the tent. He gave him instructions to prepare copies of attack orders for the morning meeting and dismissed him.

The tent was quiet while he stood with his back to the entrance. After a minute of silence, he whirled around to face the sergeant.

"What do you mean by interrupting my commanders' meeting? And who are these young men?" his face was contorted in rage.

The sergeant had never seen his commander act like this. "Sir, the Egyptian boy said he knows you. I thought it best to bring him here where you could verify his story."

"I've never seen him in my life! How dare you bring civilians into my command center! They could be spies or assassins. Tie them up now!"

"But..." Malik tried to speak but Herihor cut him off.

"Silence! Sergeant, tie them up *now*!" he shouted.

The puzzled soldier called for the guards stationed outside the tent to bind the two prisoners again. He also gagged them so they could not protest. What had gotten into the general?

Malik saw Tik-tik slip quietly into the shadows.

When the guards left, the general approached the sergeant who snapped to attention and stared straight ahead. He was about to be reprimanded by his general and was sure that he wouldn't like it.

"Listen to me, Sergeant," Herihor's low growl was edged with restrained fury as he paced before his subordinate. "I will interrogate these two spies myself. I cannot believe that two dirty, bedraggled *children* who appeared in my camp out of nowhere and claimed to know me, deceived you, of all people. I will extract the truth from them myself. It disgusts me that I must do your job for you."

"Yes sir!" The confused sergeant dared not flinch a muscle.

"Leave my presence and tell the guards outside that I will not be disturbed. Ignore any cries for mercy that you hear from these whelps." Herihor removed a gleaming dagger from his belt and flashed it in the lamplight an inch from Malik's face.

The soldier could not believe what he saw out of the corner of his eye.

"Sergeant, you are dismissed!" he barked over his shoulder.

"Yes sir!" He saluted and hurried out without glancing back.

"Now I'll watch you squirm," he heard his commander snarl at the Egyptian young man.

CHAPTER 46

Eastern Egyptian Desert, Amun Corps Field Headquarters

General Herihor stood over the two figures bound and gagged on the floor with the dagger's tip pointed at Malik's face. The young Egyptian instinctively flinched. He tried to move away but the general grabbed him, turned him over, and pushed his face into the dirt. He cut the rope with one flick of the razor-sharp knife. In seconds, he had cut Nathan's wrists free too. After returning his dagger to its sheath he stepped back to watch them remove their cloth gags. Tik-tik ambled into the lamplight from under a pillow with a downcast, shamed look and a low whistle before he climbed onto Malik's shoulder.

"I apologize for the charade in front of my sergeant. I hope you understand that I could not jeopardize our escape."

"You sure had me convinced," Nathan said.

"Escape?" Malik rubbed his wrists and flexed his hands.

"I plan to leave tonight. Your appearance here presents a slight departure from my plans. By the way, where is your sister? Why aren't you with your families? I couldn't believe my eyes when I saw you standing in my tent!"

Malik and Nathan took turns telling him of their capture and imprisonment in the pyramid, the revelation of the Black Falcon's identity, the booby trapped tunnels and their eventual escape with Tik-tik through a dark tunnel. When they mentioned their flight all day in the *Horus Eye* and crash into the army camp less than an hour ago, he exclaimed: "Incredible!"

They drank juice, ate cold meat and bread, and prepared to leave.

"I'll summon Kahn to join us," the general said. "Stay seated there with your hands hidden behind you in case someone looks in."

He left the tent and they heard him speaking with the guards outside in a loud, gruff voice. When he returned, an old Egyptian soldier whose rugged face bore the scars of many battle campaigns followed him. His missing left arm and decided limp meant that his fighting days were behind him. His quick eyes took in the two dirty young men sitting on the floor.

"This is my personal servant, Kahn. He will accompany us to the Israelite lines. For the life of me I cannot figure out why he is still with me, but his loyalty is unquestioned.

"Kahn, this is Malik whose sister I am about to marry, and this is his friend and Israelite slave, Nathan."

"Ex-slave," chimed Malik. "My father released all his slaves on the night of Passover. He's always been my best friend too. I also cannot understand why he sticks with me, after all the trouble I've gotten us into."

"Never a dull moment," Nathan grinned. Kahn stared at both of them without blinking.

"When I change out of my officer's uniform into a soldier's tunic and Kahn and I step through the back of my tent, we'll become traitors to Pharaoh. This is not because I hate Egypt but because the so-called Great One no longer deserves my loyalty. He is no deity. His arrogance has brought The Two Lands so such destruction that it may take centuries to recover, if at all. My heart now belongs with the God of Abraham. If we are separated I want you to continue on to rejoin your family and give my undying love to Sarina."

Herihor explained how they would leave through the rear flap of his tent and make their way through the camp toward the Israelite lines. When officers arrived for the morning meeting, they would discover his absence, but by then he hoped it would be too late. No doubt it would cause some disruption or delay the attack for several hours until his men received further instructions from Pharaoh and another officer took command. When he changed out of his officer's uniform into the simple tunic of a foot soldier, Malik and Nathan followed him out the back of the tent into the dark with Kahn close behind them.

The four walked unchallenged through rows of army tents, small campfires, and soldiers sleeping in circles around dying embers. There were no guards monitoring the middle of the encampment since thousands of troops encircled them. Alert sentries were spaced at intervals around the outside edge of the camp between them and the Israelites.

"Let me do the talking when we meet any guards." Herihor covered his face with a head scarf. The tents and campfires thinned in numbers and they could see the glow from the pillar of fire in the distance. They continued for about a hundred more yards until an armed soldier stepped out of the bushes into their path.

"Who is it?" Only their vague shapes were distinguishable.

"There are two of us with two prisoners. We're returning them to the enemy lines."

"Returning them? Why?"

"These two teenagers wandered into the camp during the night and they want to go back home to their mothers. They present no danger to us. Let us pass."

"On whose authority?" The guard found the story suspicious.

"General Herihor himself. I have a pass with his seal on it." He extended a slip of paper in the guard's direction. He took it for a moment and returned it.

"I can't read it in the dark. Do you give me your word?"

"Yes. On my word, we were sent by General Herihor to return these boys to their parents."

He remained standing in their way. "What is the password?"

"Password?"

"Nobody comes or goes without giving the day's challenge password. You could still be traitors. I'll call my commanding sergeant if you answer incorrectly. What is the word?"

Herihor felt Khan tense next to him. Both were prepared to overcome the sentry, if needed. The general tried to remember the word for the day. He'd issued it through his scribe less than twenty-four hours ago and now his mind was blank. He braced for a fight with the sentry.

"The password is...*Montu*" Khan spoke clearly.

Everyone held their breaths. The guard hesitated.

"That's right," Herihor repeated, "*Montu*."

"Correct. You may pass." He stepped aside so the two soldiers and their prisoners could continue down the path.

"Don't forget the password," the sentry reminded them. "You'll need it when you return."

"I'll remember it," Herihor promised. They could breathe once again.

After several minutes walking away from the sentry along a dark, indistinct path in the desert scrub brush and toward the fire in the sky, they felt free to speak.

"That was too close," Nathan admitted.

"You can thank Khan for knowing the password. I think I'll remember it—*Montu* is Egypt's god of war—for the rest of my life!"

"Where are we going now?" Malik asked.

"We'll continue in this direction for a while and then skirt around the pillar of fire until we run into an Israelite sentry or patrol."

"What do you think it is? The fire, I mean." Malik could see individual flames from less than a mile away. "We watched the pillar of cloud all day from the *Horus Eye*. It transformed itself into fire when the sun set."

"It's some sort of protective presence standing between the army and the Israelites. I heard some say it was the Angel of the LORD guarding His people. Egyptians die when they come too close to it. We'll be sure to keep our distance."

They walked single file for another twenty minutes before they saw evidence of a flickering campfire ahead. Not sure what to expect, they slowed their pace when they saw crude tents through the dried brush one hundred feet ahead of them.

"Stop there!" Even though they'd expected it, the challenge startled them. The sound of running feet from opposite directions meant that they were surrounded.

They didn't resist when strong hands shoved them toward the campfire. A struggle would be pointless; after all, they wanted the Israelites to capture them. Somehow, Herihor had to convince their captors that they were not spies and wanted to join them.

After roughly searching the four, they relieved the Egyptian soldiers of their knives and made them sit in the dirt under watchful eyes. The guards, farmers dressed in dirty field clothes and armed with pitchforks, hoes, and pruning hooks, stepped aside when their leader came into the firelight rubbing sleep from his eyes.

"So who are you and what are you doing here?" He resented the interruption in the middle of the night.

Herihor thought it best to tell their captors the full truth. It was obvious from their tunics and crude insignia that they were Egyptian soldiers. When he said he was an Egyptian army general in disguise and a Hebrew by birth asking for asylum, the farmers jumped to their feet.

"It's a trick!" one of them exclaimed. "There must be others out there ready to attack us!"

"He can't be Hebrew!"

"He must be a spy!"

"Settle down, men. The Shekinah Presence between us and our pursuers has protected us from attack so far and these men, aside from a couple of knives, don't seem like formidable attackers. Just to be safe, tie them up for now. We'll take them to Naphtali's camp in the morning and see what the council of elders says."

"How do I tie up a one-armed man?" one of the farmers asked.

"Do I have to do all the thinking around here? Tie it behind him to his belt. How much trouble can a one-armed man be, anyway?" Kahn struggled to keep a straight face.

Their interrogator turned to Malik and Nathan. He looked them over with a wary eye.

"You two look pitiful. What's your story?"

Nathan spoke for him and Malik. "My name is Nathan, of the tribe of Judah. I want to reunite with my family but I don't know where they are."

"Moses is still trying to organize this hodgepodge of slaves and freeloaders by tribes, or at least that was his plan when we gathered at Ramses. Much of Judah is gathered next to him at the Red Sea fifteen miles or so from here. You won't be seeing them today, though. What about him?"

"This is Malik, my friend. He's Egyptian but he and his family have professed faith in the *LORD* of Abraham. His family joined mine to go to the Promised Land."

"Them and a million other people…, so what's your connection with these two?" He pointed to Herihor and Khan.

"The general is engaged to marry Malik's sister. That's why we need to stick together."

"Well, well. Isn't that a romantic little story—if it's true. There are some Egyptians among us who say they trust in the Holy One of Israel too. I don't believe most of them—they have their own reasons for coming with us or they could be Pharaoh's spies. Time will tell. Here's what we'll do: the two soldiers stay tied up and under guard as possible spies. You two are free to go. If you make your way to Migdol over that hill east of us by daybreak, you'll see camps along the shore. Judah is to the north and Benjamin is to the south. Moses, Aaron, and Miriam are camped between the two. It might take you two or three days to cover the ten miles to Judah's camp, given how tight everyone is packed between here and the shore."

"We'll stay with our friends, if that's all right," Nathan said and Malik nodded.

"Suit yourselves," he shrugged. "I'm going back to sleep for another hour before our relief arrives at dawn. Then we'll take you to Naphtali's camp."

Satisfied with their leader's decision, the farmer-guards set down their makeshift weapons and sat around a fire which they stoked with dry branches. More than a few distrusting eyes remained on their captives.

Like farmers everywhere, their captors were up before sunrise. They shared some bread, gathered blankets and a few supplies and began their march in the cool desert air. Their leader estimated that they would reach Naphtali's camp in a couple of hours.

Nathan and Malik followed in a single file and kept Herihor and Khan, hands still bound behind them, in view ahead of them. They walked through tightly spaced camps of families with screaming babies, braying donkeys, and wagons overloaded with possessions. Chaos raged around them and their pace slowed to a standstill every few minutes.

"Somebody is following them up ahead," Malik said to Nathan in a low voice.

"Following who?"

"That tall man up ahead in the black turban has been walking about five paces behind the general for the past fifteen minutes. He came out of nowhere and hasn't taken his eyes off of him."

"How can you tell in all this pandemonium? He doesn't look suspicious."

"I'm going to ask him what he's doing." Malik took off at a trot to catch up with the tall man whose black turban towered over the throng around him.

"Wait! I don't think we want any trouble." Nathan hurried to catch up but he was too late.

Malik reached the stalker and tugged at his sleeve. The man ignored him as he continued to watch Herihor intently.

Malik pulled on his tunic again. "Why are you following him?" he demanded.

In one swift motion, the tall pursuer spun around, grabbed Malik by his tunic, and thrust his gaunt face into his.

"Go...away!" He pushed him aside and resumed his steady stride behind the general and his aide who walked ahead through the crowds watched by a single guard.

Before Malik or Nathan could object, someone grabbed their arms from behind and pulled them aside. Another man dressed in a similar black headdress held them in a tight grip. He was much shorter than the other man but not as thin. A black scarf covered his face.

"Malik...leave him alone!" he hissed.

The mention of Malik's name instantly got both of their attentions.

"Who are you? What do you want?"

"We'll wait here until Hevel figures out a way to release your two friends. I must say, I never expected to see you two here. It wasn't part of the plan."

"What plan? What's going on?"

Their interceptor relaxed his grip on them and searched for Hevel's black turban bobbing above the crowd. Not seeing it, he motioned for them to come with him.

"We need to catch up with them. He'll make his move soon."

Malik and Nathan stayed where they were. "Not until you tell us who you are and how you know my name," Malik insisted.

"Medjay Chief Inspector Hezbak...again." The turbaned man removed his scarf and performed an exaggerated, theatrical bow.

"But the crocodiles ate you at the Temple of *Sobek*!" Nathan blurted out.

"Obviously not, my friend. Did the Black Falcon tell you that?"

"Well, yes... among other things."

"And you believed that thief and liar."

The two were stunned to see the chief inspector alive and shamed by their gullibility. Hezbak pulled them at a trot to catch up with Hevel.

The black turban came into view again and they walked in the line of people struggling to push their way through the crowd about ten paces behind him. A loud commotion erupted as people behind them turned and pointed into the sky. A hushed murmur overcame them.

It was daybreak and the pillar of fire had transformed itself into a tall, billowing white cloud. It was moving high in the sky over them. Everyone watched as the wind picked up and their protecting cloud raced east toward the Red Sea!

Hevel and Hezbak used the distraction as their cover to pull Herihor and Khan behind a wagon stacked with furniture. The lone guard walking behind the prisoners stared into the sky and never noticed their escape. Within seconds, they were untied and Hevel grabbed some ragged farmer's tunics from a nearby wagon. After changing out of their army uniforms, the two soldiers blended in with the other ragged refugees.

Nathan and Malik were bewildered and hurried to keep up. Their friends were free, but where were they going?

"I was beginning to wonder about you, my friend," Herihor said to the inspector.

"I didn't get your reply to my message until yesterday afternoon. The Israelite checkpoints were loose and unprofessional but there were so many of them. Hevel didn't spot you until about an hour ago. The protecting cloud came along at just the right time."

It took them most of the day to reach the promontory of Mount Migdol. It wasn't really a mountain, but an escarpment fault line dividing the desert plateau on the west from the seaside plain that descended in a gentle slope for ten miles to the shore of the Red Sea. The top of the steep cliff offered an unobstructed view of a dense camp more than two miles wide that filled every inch of land between them and the dark blue sea.

"I'm familiar with this terrain," Herihor said recalling yesterday's map and battle plans. "Something must have happened to prevent the army's attack this morning. They'll probably come from the north along the seashore tomorrow morning and slaughter everyone." He gazed to either side of him at the rivers of humanity on foot and in carts plodding north and south from the height of Mount Migdol onto the already crowded plain. He wondered what would happen when all the Israelites reached the sea.

"Maybe not," Nathan sounded optimistic—almost cheerful.

"What do you mean?" Hezbak asked.

"Do you think that God brought His people here to die? Don't you think he would also be able to stop the Egyptians and deliver His people? This is Almighty God who controlled all the plagues. If our captor last night was right, then what they called the Shekinah Presence is hovering above Moses' camp there." They pointed to the cluster of tents under the cloud. "It wouldn't surprise me if Moses was receiving instructions from God at this very moment. Our families are somewhere there in Judah's camp." He pointed to the lines of tents that paralleled the shoreline to the north of the cloud.

"General," Khan spoke up, "we should camp here for the night and not try to descend the steep slope in the dark with that rabble."

Herihor agreed. "Maybe you can find us some rations? Anything will do." His servant slipped away to see if a few copper pieces could buy enough food and wine to satisfy the general and his friends.

Each had to settle for a small loaf of unleavened bread and an ear of corn roasted over a meager fire. Soldiers preparing for battle often ate less than that. They found shelter in a hollow space in the hillside and huddled together for warmth. A fierce wind picked up during the night.

CHAPTER 47

Eastern Egyptian Desert, Mount Migdol

General Herihor and Kahn took in the landscape before them from their high vantage point on Mount Migdol. Experienced eyes surveyed the coastal plain between them and the Red Sea.

"What's your military assessment, Kahn? Are they preparing defensive positions to repel an attack?"

"No sir. It looks to me like they're getting ready to move again. I see more order than I expected; somebody's giving them mobilization orders. For the life of me, I can't figure out where they think they can go pressed up against the shoreline like that. They'll be slaughtered when the army comes upon them from the north."

"You're right about their organization, though. It's an hour past dawn and already everyone is packed and ready to move. Not quite military precision but an impressive mobilization for that many civilians. They seem to be waiting for something."

Nathan and Malik stood beside the general at the edge of the Migdol cliff and looked in awe on the panorama with deep blue water in the background.

"The cloud moved during the night after the wind picked up," Nathan observed. "It's behind us again."

"Between us and the army," Herihor observed. "I'm not sure how long it'll stay there. Whoever is in charge of the combined corps—probably Pharaoh by now—is executing his attack strategy. If I were directing them, I'd press for a fast sweep around the cloud and attack while the slaves have their backs against the sea."

Eastern Egyptian Desert, Combined Army Corps

General Intef objected to Pharaoh's order for a direct frontal attack on the Israelites. The mysterious cloud stood between the Egyptian Army and the renegade slaves. His adamant resistance and insubordinate language put him in mortal danger.

"Great One, this is a useless maneuver. That cloud swallowed hundreds of my men. The enemy must be using some kind of chemical smoke screen to kill anyone who approaches. Thousands more will die."

"I don't care!" Pharaoh shook his bony finger at the defiant general. "Send more soldiers! There must be a way to overwhelm it. Do whatever it takes!" Blind fury energized the ruler of Egypt who could barely stand on his own. How dare anyone or anything stand in his way!

"Thirty of my best archers perished this morning. I will *not* send more!" No one argued with Pharaoh like this and lived. Grim defiance sealed the general's fate.

"Take him away!" shouted the thin monarch from his elevated chaise. Two muscular palace bodyguards grabbed the rebellious general in iron-like grips and carried him away flanked by two more guards. The King of Egypt trembled with uncontrolled rage. Regimental officers stood paralyzed in a semicircle around him. First General Herihor had disappeared during the night and now General Intef was gone too.

"You're a fool!" the corps commander screamed in the distance. "You'll kill all my men for nothing!"

Thutmose III gathered his satin robes and with help from two servants descended from his upholstered platform. For a few moments he managed to stand unaided before all that remained of the leadership of the Egyptian Army.

"I am in command of this army! Anyone who dares to disobey me will be cut down for treason." Nobody dared move a muscle.

"Who is in charge of the Leopard Charioteers?" Pharaoh demanded.

A soldier dressed in leather armor with the orange plume of the regiment in his helmet stepped forward. "I am, Great One."

"How many chariots can you muster from both corps?"

"My elite charioteers number approximately eighty. I might gather a total of five hundred or so from all the other regiments. Some chariots are barely serviceable and I lack archers to man them all."

"You will organize as many chariots as possible into one fighting force. If you cannot do this then I will find someone who can." His meaning was clear.

"I will do it, Great One. What do you wish me to do with them?"

"I will lead them to the north around the cloud. We will then attack the main contingent of Hebrews and kill as many as possible. The rest will be brought back into slavery more oppressive than they ever knew." By force of will he stood erect before his commanders. "All ground troops will move east in a direct frontal attack to distract the cloud away from the attacking chariots. That poisonous smoke cannot stop ten thousand soldiers!" Pharaoh's foolhardy claim meant that he would send the entire Egyptian ground army to its death for the sake of one final, desperate maneuver.

No senior advisors remained in his royal court. No experienced generals remained to lead his army. He was gambling everything in a single desperate act against the escaping Hebrew slaves. The stone-hearted supreme leader of Egypt—Ruler of The Two Lands between the First Cataract and the Great Sea—would defy the God of Israel to the very end.

Eastern Egyptian Desert, Red Sea

Horses stamped in the sand while the tribe of Judah and a mix of Egyptians and other nationalities looked at the distant shore in the east with longing. Behind them and to each side, refugees, packed and ready to march, stretched for ten miles. The question was where would they all go? The wind had blown all night and now the air was still and damp.

Some former slave women in Hatep's now-enlarged family caravan sensed that there was no way of escape. They begged him, as their leader, to return to Giza and Memphis. Iset urged them to stay and trust God. Even Ben-Judah reminded them that the Angel of *Jehovah*, in the form of the pillar of cloud and fire, would protect them from attack and provide a way of escape if they trusted in Him. Two million anxious Israelites pressed at their backs.

Moses ordered the twelve tribes to wait on the shoreline until God opened a way of escape. Judah's leaders in turn passed the order to elders who relayed it to heads of families. Hatep called the men in his caravan together. He thought it ironic that he, a former slave owner, was now following orders from an elder in a Hebrew tribe.

"Asher, I want you and Reuben to select a few capable men to help you and move down the shoreline to keep carts and wagons away from the water's edge. I don't want any vehicles stuck in the wet sand."

No sooner had the men dispersed along the beach to keep people and heavy-laden vehicles away from the wet sand, than a hot blast of air whistled down from the sky above and raced perpendicular to the shore in both directions. Everyone looked up. The strong wind had suddenly burst out of the clear blue sky.

The Red Sea water gradually receded from the sandy shore. Men, women, and children gaped at the shells, rocks, and white sand exposed in the morning sun. The water quickly moved away from them. Where was it going?

"Look!" A child pointed up the beach to the north. "Mountains of water!"

The hot wind in the sky reached hurricane strength. Silent observers, scarfs covering their faces and crouching together for shelter, watched as blue water piled up on either side of the gathered multitudes and receded—tall, aquamarine cliffs on either side lay bare a valley on the seafloor. The unnatural watery heights spread apart as millions of onlookers gawked in disbelief.

"There will be time to cross over to the other side. Wait on the *LORD*!" Hatep urged those around him who wanted to rush onto the newly exposed seafloor and escape from the approaching Egyptian army. He knew that their wheeled vehicles would become stuck in the wet sand. The hot wind and sun must dry and harden the sand first. Some stepped onto the soft sand and discovered that he was right. Hands pulled them back onto the dry beach.

"God is faithful," Hatep uttered in a calm voice. Iset stood next to her husband and admired the tremendous power of God.

"Did you ever think that God's way of escape would be *through* the Red Sea?" she asked him.

"He's opening a path of safety for His people. I can see the opposite shore through the hazy spray. From here it looks like the mountains of water are higher than the gray mountains of Shur in the Wilderness of Sin. If we keep order, and wait, we should reach the other side by sunset. All the Israelites will be on the other side by tomorrow at this time." He looked behind at the pillar of cloud that stood between them and the Egyptian army. Yes, God was very faithful.

An hour later, Hatep noticed that some men were venturing onto the white sandy bottom of the Red Sea to test its ability to support traffic. He sent Reuben with a staff to probe the way before them. He came back with a broad smile.

"It's good enough to support carts as long as they take their time. I suggest as many people as possible walk and not ride to lighten the weight of the carts and wagons."

Apparently that was the conclusion for miles up and down the shore because a cheer went up around them. Like a wave moving from the beach to the dry seafloor, the historic exodus from Egypt began. By nightfall the first slaves would taste freedom from Egypt.

Caravan leaders urged care when crossing the uneven rises and dips that still held puddles of seawater and slippery seaweed. People picked up stranded fish and other sea creatures for a meal on the other side.

Those who walked near the mounds of water stopped to stare up at them. Children screamed in delight when large sharks and flashing schools of small fish swam above their heads and peered down at them. Cautious parents did their best to keep them away from the vertical water suspended in the air, not sure what would happen if they touched it. Those who pressed hands to the stretched surface found it cool and elastic. Torn between fascination with God's miraculous handiwork and an urge to get to higher ground, they pressed forward.

Far from the watery edges, Hatep and Iset walked side by side in the hot sun leading Sapphire through the unfamiliar smells of dead fish, drying coral and dank seaweed. Ahead of them Reuben led a pair of horses pulling a wagon piled with supplies. Ben-Judah steadied himself on the wagon atop a mound of bagged millet.

Halfway across the Red Sea, the wagon dipped into a rocky hole that Reuben didn't see. The load shook violently and almost knocked Ben-Judah from his seat. A wooden wheel was stuck in a deep rut. Reuben crawled under the tilting wagon, examined the partially submerged wheel and assured Hatep that he could get the wagon moving in a few hours. The supplies first had to be unloaded so they could lift the wagon out of the hole. The rest of their caravan continued walking while Hatep and Reuben stopped to discuss what to do. Other families and their belongings shuffled past in a steady flow.

"I'll stay here with two of the farm hands and work on the wagon. I think you should continue with the others while there is still light." Reuben was insistent.

"And the supplies of food?"

"We'll guard them. When you extricate the wagon, we'll reload the bags of millet and meet you on the other side by morning. Don't worry. I'll look for Sapphire and then find you!"

Agreeing that this was the best course, Hatep lifted Ben-Judah out of the wagon and carried him to the chariot where Iset cleared a place for him on a rug and wedged him between two wooden chests.

"You are very kind, Hatep." The old teacher's voice was weak after days of jostling across the desert and now over the dry bottom of the Red Sea. He couldn't see it, but he believed that God could do anything.

"Carrying you is the least I could do after all you've done for us, Rabbi. You led me to faith in the God of Abraham, Isaac, and Jacob. In a few hours you will be a free man on your way to the Promised Land. Did you ever think that this day would come?"

"In my lifetime? I hoped it would be so, as did my father and his fathers before him. God has been faithful all these centuries since they came to Egypt under the protection of Vizier Joseph. Who could have imagined this miracle? I'm being carried by an Egyptian through the Red Sea to my homeland!"

When the tired old man settled in the overloaded chariot, Hatep and Iset led Sapphire steadily toward the distant shore where they expected celebrations to erupt when the Israelites experienced real freedom for the first time.

CHAPTER 48

Eastern Egyptian Desert, Mount Migdol

"They look like ants crawling across the sand." Nathan's observation echoed the thoughts of the other men around him. Earlier that day, they had watched the distant waters of the Red Sea pull away from the shore of Egypt to open a pathway to the distant shore. From ten miles away on Mount Migdol, which was no more than a large hill, the mounds of blue water bordered a broad sandy highway through which the multitudes on the shore funneled in a constant, dark stream of humanity.

"It's time to join them," Herihor said. "The slowest caravans on the mountain have descended to the plain below us. If they can all reach the far shore without mishap by tomorrow morning, it will be a miracle."

"Miracles seem to be normal today," Nathan observed.

Their descent from the height of Mount Migdol by sunset was easier than they expected. The ten-mile walk to the dry seashore proved more difficult. Although the six men could move more quickly than most because they had no baggage, they walked among thousands of families struggling with unruly livestock, rickety hand carts, over-loaded wagons, and hungry, crying children. Not only were the exhausted travelers at the tail of the convoy making slow progress, but abandoned broken vehicles and discarded supplies from those at the forefront of the crossing impeded them. The men halted their progress every few minutes to help push aside stuck vehicles, attend to the injured, or reunite lost children with their parents in the noisy crowd. They urged people to abandon nonessentials and press forward.

"So that's what the bottom of the sea looks like," Malik said when he stood on the beach and peered at the sand and rock that had been churned by thousands of human and animal feet. "It looks like a muddy dirt road."

"Don't sound so disappointed, Malik. I've never seen the *top* of the sea." Nathan was in a hurry to reach the other side. "There aren't many more people behind us, so let's keep moving. We should all make it by morning."

Nobody dared mention it, but they feared that the water might not stay suspended in the air much longer. After walking along the towering north wall of water for half the night, their small band stopped to look at the surreal moonlight shining through the translucent water. A giant black shape swam back and forth eyeing them from above and silhouetted in the blue-gray luminescence.

"So is your God really doing this?" Khan asked the general.

"He is *Almighty* God!" Herihor assured him. "You didn't think that the gods of Egypt could do this, did you?"

"If I wasn't seeing it with my own eyes, standing before a mountain of water held up by invisible hands, I would never believe it. This is a God worth trusting."

"Then let's follow Him to the Promised Land!"

After another hour of steady walking along the wall of water, Herihor made an observation: "I think the water is slowly moving in toward us."

Everyone nearby halted to stare at the bottom of the wall where it met the seafloor. It was definitely moving!

"We should turn away from the wall toward the center of the opening but continue going east to the shore as quickly as we can. We'll make it in another hour or two."

Every few minutes their eyes glanced over at the wall; sea water seeped from under the bottom of the wall and flowed onto the sand. If God removed His divine restraint, they would all die instantly.

"We're almost there!" Herihor urged them onward. How would he find Sarina and the others among millions of people?

Eastern Egyptian Desert

Both maneuvering arms of the Egyptian Army were unaware that two million Israelite slaves and thousands from dozens of other nationalities were crossing the Red Sea at that very moment. Continuing with their plan from that morning, six hundred chariots and other wheeled military transports swept north around the cloud of protection and then back south through the low hills. At dusk they camped several miles away from the broad path that cut across the Red Sea seafloor carrying a stream of escapees to the Wilderness of Sin. The other force composed of Egypt's infantry, under inexperienced leaders, hesitated in their frontal attack on the billowing cloud that consumed anyone who approached it. Junior infantry lieutenants withdrew to recover their losses and wait. On the other side of the cloud the Israelites walked across the Red Sea.

During the night, a squad of drivers and archers at a Leopard Charioteers encampment in the north talked about the massacre that they would unleash in a few hours.

"We've seen worse than this," their sergeant said philosophically as he leaned back on his blanket and gazed into the campfire.

"Not under Pharaoh's command though," someone said. The circle of soldiers murmured in agreement.

"True," an older battle-hardened veteran admitted. "I'd charge into a Hittite brigade for General Herihor. The 'Great One' might have fought with troops in his day, but he's no tactical genius. I predict that he won't go into battle with us tomorrow."

"So what's his plan?"

"He'll order us to kill as many Hebrews slaves as we can." It sounded obscene the way he said it so casually.

"But why? Just for his personal vengeance?"

"Mostly, I think. There's no way to make it seem otherwise."

"What will it be like?" a rookie driver asked. "I mean, attacking civilians bunched up against the sea like that? Is that something the Leopard Charioteers should do?" He had misgivings about slaughtering helpless men, women, and children.

Some of the others, old-timers with combat experience against Hittites, Canaanites, and other savage nations in the eastern desert or in the jungles of southern Kush, expressed their distaste by spitting into the sand. Did they find the rookie's doubt offensive? Or was it Pharaoh's plan to have his army slaughter defenseless Hebrews?

"General Herihor would never stand for it," one of them finally said and spat into the fire.

"But the general's a traitor," another responded. "He ran away. Now we have Pharaoh as our commander."

"Listen, orders are orders," their sergeant broke in. "We do what we're told."

Some of his men still grumbled. "Mark my word," one of them said, "we'll take many casualties. If I were a farmer defending my wife and kids, I'd fight to the death with anything I could get my hands on. Six hundred chariots attacking hundreds of thousands of slaves with pitchforks and shovels might not be as easy as you think."

"Sounds like a stupid cause to die for, if you ask me." That bold observation by the rookie driver echoed in the minds of the others as they tried to snatch an hour or two of sleep before dawn.

CHAPTER 49

Eastern Egyptian Desert

The flaming pillar floated down from Mount Migdol and hovered above the beach where the shoreline had been the day before. Its light illuminated the few remaining Israelite stragglers who trudged over dry ground to the opposite side of the Red Sea. Finally, those who crossed during the night were close enough to hear cheers of encouragement from the shore.

The Egyptian Army approached the shore from two directions. The archers' chariots, led by Pharaoh in a wagon outfitted to carry him on an elevated reclining throne, proceeded at a measured pace toward the pillar of fire that was transformed into a cloud after dawn. The marching infantry battalions crested the top of Mount Migdol, stopped in bewilderment when they saw the Red Sea parted before them, and marched down to join up with the chariot regiments.

While the charioteers waited for the ground troops to line up in orderly formations, the squad sergeant from the night before gathered his men. He had to shout above the chatter about the dry seafloor that extended into the distance. They would have to cross the exposed seafloor to reach the escaping Hebrews, even if it meant attacking them on the other side in the Wilderness of Sin.

Just as the sergeant thought he would, Thutmose III stopped his luxurious carriage on a rise and motioned for the archer regiments to go around him and continue forward. As soldiers marched past their Pharaoh, they looked away with barely concealed disgust. This was as far as he would go to "lead" his army into battle. It was obvious that he considered them expendable.

"Listen up!" the archer squad leader shouted. "We have orders to drive onto the sand and see if it will support our chariots. Four chariots will go out and probe the surface while the other chariots stay in formations with their assigned regiments. If the surface is passable, we'll return to what was the shore and march to the opposite side ahead of the infantry and finish our mission."

"What about Pharaoh?" a voice called out from the line of chariots. "Why isn't he leading us?"

"Silence!" the squad leader shouted, even though the same question was on his mind.

As horses walked onto the sand of the seafloor, archers used the shafts of their spears to test the ground. It was dry and packed from a day and night of Hebrew traffic. The solid sand and crushed seashells were more than sturdy enough to support their chariots.

When they turned around, the novice chariot driver commented to his archer companion about the wall of water nearby. He didn't know what to make of the claim by their regimental commander that the sea-goddess *Anuket* would give them victory over the Israelites.

"If *Anuket* opened the path for us, then who opened the path for the Israelites? It doesn't make sense to me."

"You think too much," his archer, older and supposedly wiser, growled.

"By the way, I can't swim. If that water starts falling while we're crossing, I won't be able to swim to shore."

The archer smacked him on the head. "If that wall of water comes down, it won't matter. We'll all be dead. Now drive so we can get this mission over with and go home!"

More than an hour later the assembled military might of Egypt had formed into long columns with the orange-plumed Leopard Charioteers in the lead, followed by five more regiments of mismatched chariots. Ten thousand disheartened foot soldiers marched behind the chariots in ragged columns identified by their colorful ensigns, banners, and streamers.

Pharaoh's royal wagon, distinguished by its bright purple awning with gold fringe, remained on the shore atop a small rise. Thutmose

III would wait for certain victory before joining his troops. He wasn't taking any chances now. In his heart he knew that the *LORD* of the Hebrews had won. All he cared about was how his name would be remembered in Egypt's archives.

Bottom of the Red Sea

General Herihor and his five exhausted companions had worked through the night and into the morning helping the last of the Israelites reach safety. They fixed broken wagons that had been overloaded with useless furniture and possessions donated by Egyptian masters in the hasty departure. Herihor anticipated an army attack on the stragglers at dawn and urged the others to empty wagons of possessions, load them with women, children, and injured and hurry eastward as fast as possible.

When they saw the land of the opposite shore rising ahead of them they knew that they had done all they could.

"We're almost there!" Malik shouted. He drove a wagon pulled by two horses who were exhausted almost to death. Nathan was beside him in another wagon with tired, crying children and their mothers. Bedraggled fathers nearly crawled behind them to reach the shore.

The crowd on the beach parted to let the last of the refugees through. The cloudy pillar was now high in the air above a spot further down the shoreline where he assumed Moses was camped. All eyes were on the approaching Egyptian Army.

The Leopard Charioteers had orders from their new general to move at a walking pace so that the foot soldiers could keep up with the chariots. The elite horsemen and archers chafed at this order; they were used to racing at high speed toward an enemy to achieve surprise and strike them unprepared. However, speed would have been impossible in this case since abandoned possessions, shattered vehicles, and subsea rocks littered their path. A voice behind the Leopards' commander gave a frightened shout: "The water is moving!"

He held up his hand to stop the column's forward movement. "Scouts!" the leader shouted. Further instructions were unnecessary. Two mounted scouts raced toward the walls of water to investigate and returned within minutes with confirmation.

"Sir, they're moving toward us at the speed of a slow march. They'll reach us in twenty or thirty minutes."

The commander looked around for safer ground but saw none. He would continue to obey orders and proceed ahead. The farthest wall of water was still more than a mile away. Maybe they had enough time to reach the opposite shore.

"Move more to the south, pick up the pace, and follow me in a close column!" He angled his men away from the approaching blue wall. Even if they continued at a full gallop he knew they'd never make it.

A mile away on the other side of the opening, the wall of water was not only moving forward but beginning to fall apart. Water flowed in a steady stream onto the seafloor from under the wall and wind-driven waves splashed water over the top. It moved steadily toward the army.

At the rear of the marching infantry, the commander of the last battalion stopped when he heard shouting behind him.

"We're trapped!" a soldier screamed in panic. He ran past the lead officer throwing his weapons aside and ripping off his armor.

"Sergeant, stop that man for leaving his post!"

From atop his horse, the battalion commander turned to see that the two walls of water had come together behind him and were racing in his direction. His entire battalion, officers, sergeants and footmen, rushed ahead to escape. He prodded his horse to a trot and stepped on fellow soldiers who had tripped and fallen in the sand. They were trapped!

"We'll never make it," the rookie chariot driver observed in a shaking voice when it was obvious that in a few minutes five hundred feet of water would crash down over him and his comrades.

He looked at the glorious Leopard Charioteers decked in their orange plumes for the last time. In an instant, Almighty God released mountains of water that crushed the Egyptian army in full view of its arrogant Pharaoh. Waves of thunder rolled over the shore as the Israelites watched in awe from the opposite shore.

The combined Amun and Ammit Corps of the mighty Egyptian Army disappeared in the Red Sea in an instant. Those who did not die at the hand of the Angel of Death on the night of Passover perished at the bottom of the Red Sea.

Thutmose III, Great One of The Two Lands, Pharaoh of Egypt, closed his eyes to block out the nightmare of men and horses thrashing in the churning water. His mighty army was gone!

"Take me back to my palace," he said to his servants. The royal carriage attendants stared in horror at the carnage.

"Now!" he screamed.

He drew the curtain of his coach and buried his face in a pillow. Finally, the mortal ruler of Egypt admitted—the *LORD* is God!

CHAPTER 50

Wilderness of Sin

The people of Israel broke into a song of praise to their Mighty God when the Egyptian Army disappeared before their eyes. The song rang for millennia:

> *The LORD is my strength and song,*
> *And He has become my salvation;*
> *He is my God, and I will praise Him;*
> *My father's God, and I will exalt Him.*
> *The LORD is a man of war;*
> *The LORD is His name.*

Then they turned their backs on the last remains of life in Egypt to recover their strength for the long journey ahead. While some went about the chores of setting up camps, others stood on the shore still in shock from what God had done that morning.

"How will we find our families?" Malik was tired of running and wanted the comfort of a hot meal. Jasmine House, with its bubbling fountain and flower garden, was gone forever. He wanted to see his parents.

"They'll be with the tribe of Judah," Herihor speculated. "It shouldn't be difficult to find them."

When they came across members of Judah's tribe it turned out to be impossible to find specific individuals among them. A census performed a year later would put the number of men, women, and children in the tribe of Judah at 186,000. The chaos of that first day in the wilderness was something the adults would never forget. Nobody knew any of their neighbors and members of other tribes had yet to find their leaders. There was no way to find a lost relative or friend in the swirling turmoil.

"We'll be looking for days. There must be a way to find them without asking person-to-person." Malik's frustration had reached its limit.

"I have an idea," Nathan said. He saw a cart piled with bales of hay and climbed to the top.

"Hey! Get down from there!" its owner protested. "That's hay for my horses!"

"I'll just be a minute." Tik-tik jumped from Malik's arms onto the bales and scampered up Nathan's back to get a better view.

Nathan put two fingers in his mouth and let loose a loud whistle. He waited. Then he whistled again.

"What are you doing?" Herihor called. By now their party had gathered around the stack of hay while the wagon's owner fumed.

"I'm calling for Sapphire. Listen for his answer."

"I don't hear anything," Malik muttered.

Nathan whistled again and again.

Then Tik-tik gave a screech and pointed.

"He hears Sapphire!" Nathan scooped up the monkey, jumped from the hay wagon, and took off at a run in the direction his tiny friend showed. The others were doubtful that a monkey could pick out the sound of a specific horse among all the other animal noises, but they followed for lack of a better plan.

Within twenty minutes, Nathan saw Reuben and a few other men tending horses that they had unhitched from the family's chariots and wagons. Sapphire was one of them. The men had staked out a patch of scrub grass for their stable.

"Reuben!" At Nathan's call, the horseman turned in surprise.

"Nathan! I feared I'd never see you again!" He threw his arms around the young man in a tight hug. "And Master Malik!" He embraced the two as if they were his own sons. They returned his hugs.

Sapphire snorted for his attention and Nathan rubbed the stallion's nose and hugged his neck too.

"You heard me! What a smart horse you are!"

"Where are my parents?" Malik asked.

"Look for the campfires over there and you'll find them." He stiffened when he noticed four men dressed in dirty clothes. "And who are they?" he demanded.

"You know General Herihor. The other soldier is Khan, his personal aide. And you know Chief Inspector Hezbak too and his assistant Hevel."

After giving the inspector a scowl of recognition, Reuben turned his attention to the general. "Sir, I know a young lady who will be very happy to see you! Come, I'll take you to her right away." He gave brief instructions to the two men helping him with the horses before he waved the others to follow him.

Sarina burst into tears of joy the moment she saw Herihor running toward her. She held him in her arms.

"I thought I'd lost you," she said between sobs.

"Not a chance. Our God brought us together; I knew I would see you again."

"Maybe you were confident of that, but I wasn't so sure. Promise me that you'll never leave me again?"

"I can't imagine what could separate us."

After Nathan and Malik were reunited with their parents, Reuben took Hezbak aside. He needed to set matters straight between him and the inspector who had disrespected him back at Lotus House.

"I never thought I'd see the Medjay out here in the desert, let alone see you again."

"Nor I you, horse slaves must be in high demand in this crazy bunch. Correction…*horse masters* must be in demand. I respect a man who knows how to get things done."

They eyed each other and then broke into laughter. "I'll show you around the camp if you promise not to tell anyone you're a policeman."

"*Ex*-policeman." They laughed again and after they found Khan and Hevel they went back to the corral where Reuben kept the horses.

"Might you be a man who knows his way around horses, in spite of missing an arm?" Reuben asked Kahn.

"Forty years with the Leopard Charioteers. I know a few things about horses."

Reuben broke into contagious laughter. "As I suspected! Then you can teach *me*!"

After dinner, Herihor and Sarina spoke with Ben-Judah about performing a wedding the next day. They arranged for him and her father to preside over the first marriage, as far as they knew, in what people were calling the *Nation of Israel*. Iset rushed about finding suitable food and decorations for the celebration amid the clutter and confusion of their meager belongings.

"Can I pry your husband-to-be away from you for a short while?" Hatep asked his daughter when they returned in the early evening from speaking with Ben-Judah.

"That depends on how long 'a short while' is," she joked.

"It could be longer than you wish," he replied cryptically. "Someone important wants to speak with him."

On that vague note, he took Herihor by the arm and led him out of the family camp.

"Why all the secrecy? Where are we going?"

"I'll tell you before we get there, but now I need to pay attention to directions so we don't get lost."

It took a half-hour to wend their way through the closely spaced camp sites.

"We're almost there, so I'll stop here and tell you what's up." Hatep looked around to be sure they couldn't be overheard.

"We've been summoned to Moses' tent for a meeting. All I know is that two very important men wish to speak with a certain general of the Egyptian Army. I doubt you are in any kind of trouble, though."

"That's reassuring. So what's it about?"

"I'm told that these men have a bold vision for Israel that somehow includes you. Let's find out what they want."

The two men approached a roughly fenced campsite that seemed no different from all the others except for alert guards who stopped them at the single entrance. Hatep explained the purpose of their visit and, after casting doubtful looks at Herihor in his dirty worker's tunic, they pointed them to a nearby tent.

Another guard at the tent was expecting them and showed them in where two tired Hebrews reclined on rugs. They stood to greet their visitors.

"I'm Joshua, son of Nun," the younger of the two announced. The thin, unassuming figure that stepped forward with his hand outstretched in greeting had a smile that immediately wrapped them in its warmth. His friendly appearance was combined with a steely determination of purpose. "This is Caleb, son of Jephunneh. You must be Hatep and Herihor." The statement, not a question, still made them feel welcome.

They sat on rugs and someone set cups of tea on the rug before them. Joshua began what soon sounded like an interrogation.

"Both of you are Egyptians of great reputation. Pharaoh himself decorated you both for heroism, or so someone told me. Titles and honors aside, you both have years of experience in your areas of specialty. You both now claim to be followers of the God of Abraham. Please explain how you came to be here with us."

For the next thirty minutes both Egyptians gave their testimonies of faith in the One True God. Joshua and Caleb were surprised when Herihor told them that he was actually Hebrew by birth and adopted by Egyptian parents.

Satisfied with their explanations, Joshua continued: "Are both of you willing to do whatever is asked of you to help us claim our place in the Promised Land?"

"I don't see what I can do," Hatep responded. "I'm a tomb architect and I don't see much need for my skills in the foreseeable future."

"Same here," Herihor laughed. "My army's gone and it looks like my future is in farming or livestock."

"Do you believe that God is faithful to the promises He made to Abraham? That He will make Israel a great nation in the Promised Land?"

"Of course!" the two visitors replied. Ben-Judah had explained this truth and they believed it with their whole hearts.

"God promised that *all* the land of Canaan will be ours." Joshua's firm and confident tone made it sound as if he had spoken these words many times before. "I believe that He will give us all the land that He said is flowing with milk and honey. It is currently occupied by Canaanites, to say nothing of a long list of other nations—Amorites, Hittites, Perizzites, Hivites, Jebusites—who won't take kindly to our moving in. We *will* take it as our God-given land!"

"I've fought Canaanites and Hittites before," Herihor stated. "The Egyptian Army defeated some of them but we had to retreat before we could claim full victory. They'll not be easy to conquer, especially by a nation of farmers. You'll need a huge army to clear them out of that land."

Joshua and Caleb waited for Herihor to draw his own conclusion. The general's thin smile turned into a wide grin. "An *Israelite Army*." Joshua and Caleb nodded in encouragement.

"A *very large* Israelite Army."

"Yes!" Joshua's excitement was contagious. "We think that an army of three hundred thousand or more troops will be needed to clear the heathen nations from the land of Canaan; thirty times larger than your single Amun Corps, but you know better what it would take." He looked at the general for any hesitation. Seeing none, he continued.

"Are you willing to train an Israelite Army to take over the land of Canaan?"

"Yes, I will train it, but who will lead it?"

"I will." Joshua said with a simple, clear-eyed confidence that Herihor had never seen in a military leader. Absent was the brash, presumptuous self-confidence of an ambitious officer.

"Yes," Joshua explained, "I know that I'm young and inexperienced, but you'll teach me and our young men what we need to know to be soldiers and generals. More important than that is the fact that Almighty God is on our side. We cannot clear the land of idolaters ourselves, but He can. He promised to be with us every step of the way. If you and I build the army then God will lead us into the Promised Land and give us victory. I am certain!"

The charismatic man before him was barely twenty years old but showed not a bit of arrogance. The general had been around self-driven, self-important military men all his life. Generals and commanders did not rise through the ranks without large egos driving them. An unshakable faith in *Jehovah* energized Joshua; he betrayed not a hint of pride. Herihor would learn much from Joshua in the future about an unwavering faith in God.

"What about me?" Hatep asked. "I don't have anything to offer the army."

Caleb spoke for the first time. "You may be a tomb architect, but people tell me that you have mobilized thousands of workers to build great projects for Pharaoh. I want you to help me organize the twelve tribes so we can function as a single nation under the leadership of Moses and Aaron. We need to teach our tribal leaders self-discipline and organization if two million of us are to survive as one nation in the wilderness and in Canaan. I believe you can do this, with God's help."

It seemed that Caleb had more faith in God than Hatep had.

"I will do whatever is necessary," Hatep promised.

General Herihor thought he should seal his promise with Joshua and Caleb as well.

"Even if I never live to see the Promised Land myself, I will gladly do my part to train your people—*my people*—to claim the land that God promised to Abraham."

"Then there's no time to waste! Come with Caleb and me to speak with Moses about starting our training tomorrow."

"But I'm to be married tomorrow…" Herihor protested.

"Very well, then. You may start our training the day *after* tomorrow. Now, we must speak with Moses before you change your mind!"

"Change my mind about Sarina? Never!" Herihor replied with a serious face.

"That's not what I meant, General." Joshua's easy chuckle reassured Herihor that he understood fully. "You'll need a sense of humor after Moses explains what God has planned for you."

EPILOG

The Israelites became a great nation and theocracy at Mount Sinai with the *LORD* God as their King. Sadly, because of national unbelief and disobedience, they spent forty years wandering in the wilderness. The books of Exodus, Leviticus, Numbers, and Deuteronomy contain the divinely inspired account of the new Nation of Israel, led and protected by Almighty God,

None of our principle fictional characters lived to see the Promised Land. What happened to them? Their lives in the desert set the stage for exciting adventures under Joshua and Caleb in the Canaanite invasion and its various military campaigns. The Israelite army mostly cleared the land of idolatrous Canaanite peoples after almost a generation of war.

Malik and Nathan

Both of our main characters married and became part of the tribe of Judah. They fathered many sons and daughters and rose through the ranks to military prominence in Judah. Malik's love for high-risk adventure never diminished throughout his lifetime. He eventually became a general and commanded the entire Judean Army. His bravery was unmatched in battles against the desert enemies of Israel and his sons were no less valiant in the invasion of Canaan. Nathan's cautious and analytical temperament distinguished him in a much different way. He became an anonymous spymaster who learned the dialects of the Midianites, Amalakites, Amorites, and other peoples of the desert. Few knew of or appreciated his silent contributions to Israel's victories.

The sons of Malik and Nathan fought beside Joshua and Caleb to conquer Canaan in the name of the God of Israel.

Herihor and Sarina

Herihor, the Hebrew and former Egyptian Amun Corps general, was a key figure in the new Israelite Army. He spent the rest of his life transforming former slaves and their sons into skilled soldiers with a love for the *LORD* of Hosts and for Israel's freedom. The army's first combat action against the Amalekites convinced him, as if he needed convincing, that the *LORD* of Hosts would fight Israel's battles and guide His army to victory. The power of God similarly defeated Sihon, king of the Amorites. Herihor, like others of his generation, died without ever seeing the Promised Land.

Besides raising a family of boys destined to follow in their father's footsteps, Sarina persuaded her husband and Joshua that the Israelite Army needed a mobile solar signaling network to coordinate the movements of what amounted to twelve large, independent armies. Bezaleel and Aholiab, skilled craftsmen in metals and clever designs who later crafted the Ark of the Covenant and other articles in the tabernacle, built brass replicas of Imhotep's small portable heliograph that Sarina carried from the Menkaure pyramid station. Word spread about the signaling devices that moved with the army and a few old blinkers, Hakamun and Elias among them, stepped forward to train others. The Israelite Helio Network was instrumental in coordinating the large-scale movement of Israel's people, supplies, and troops across the desert and into Canaan.

Hatep and Iset; Asher and Rachel

When Moses tasked Caleb and Hatep with organizing the twelve tribes so that millions of people could assemble and move as a unified nation across the desert, the problem seemed insurmountable. It couldn't be done without God. The heads of each tribe—good, well-meaning men overseeing tens of thousands of clamoring families—needed to learn that the God who brought them out of Egypt and across the Red Sea would also meet their physical needs in the desert if they would only trust Him. With Asher's help, Hatep came to appreciate the fact that creating order out of chaos ultimately was a spiritual challenge and not solely an administrative or operational task. It took more than two years of training, but the result was a diverse people who looked to God for their daily provision while they observed Hatep's rules for the efficient distribution of food and water and the fair allocation of land for grazing their herds.

Iset and Rachel settled into tent life as desert nomads. They excelled as mothers and grandmothers by raising children to serve the *LORD* as well as organizing scores of women skilled in the arts to sew tapestries and coverings for the tabernacle of God's Presence.

Chariot Regiments

Each tribe formed its own regiment of elite charioteers patterned after the Egyptian Leopards. Reuben joined his namesake tribe and commanded the Reubenite Bulls Regiment. Hezbak and Hevel remained in Judah where they learned archery and horsemanship. The Judean Lions regiment eclipsed all others in inter-tribal marksmanship and racing competitions. The Lion Charioteers were at the forefront when Joshua led the Israelite Army into their first battle in the land of Canaan.

Rabbi Ben-Judah

This kind, faithful teacher spent his last year as a free man in the loving care of his adoptive family. He died after hearing the sound of God's voice and his family buried him on the slope of Mount Sinai. He witnessed the blessings of more miracles by God than he could ever have imagined.

Imhotep

The Royal Master Inventor of Egypt remains an enigma to this day. Legends and myths about him have circulated through the centuries in many cultures giving him an aura of mystery and intrigue. Some say he flew in a replica of the *Horus Eye* and landed in the middle of the camp of Israel a month after they passed through the Red Sea. Others claim to have seen him conversing with Joshua and Caleb. There are no official records of these reported sightings.

There are references to his name and depictions of his fantastic inventions such as the glowing light globes and the *Horus Eye* on the walls of ancient Egyptian tombs and pyramids. Although the drawings appear to be abstract, the reality behind them is plausible. A faded sketch of the *Breath of Osiris* is all that is left of his spectacular monument to Thutmose III.

Whether he lived later among the Israelite nation or his children carried his ideas and inventions with them to the Promised Land, it is possible that we have not heard the last of his genius.

Ark of the Covenant

In a twist of history that nobody could have foreseen, Bezaleel melted the ornamental gold *wesekh* of bees awarded to General Herihor, the heavy gold collar presented to *Amkhu* Hatep, and Iset's serpentine gold *meket* armlets and *masektu* bracelets along with other gold treasures from Egypt. That gold became the mercy seat between the cherubim of the Ark of the Covenant—God's place of presence and worship in the new nation of Israel.

All fictional characters in *Flight from Egypt* contributed to the Nation of Israel that God created in the desert of Sinai from a mixed multitude of former slaves, Egyptian refugees, and strangers from other lands. God alone receives the glory for defeating the greatest army in the world; the *LORD*'s sovereign hand through history continues to this day as He fulfills His eternal promise to Abraham, Isaac, and Jacob that they will be a great people, live in a rich land, and be a blessing to all mankind.

AFTERWORD

The Egyptian, Hatep, and other characters in this book, found peace with the LORD God the same way countless others have through the ages: by faith in the God of Abraham. The Bible tells us that Abram (later named Abraham) . . . *believed in the LORD; and He* [God] *accounted it to him* [Abram] *for righteousness.* (Genesis 15:6) God accepted Abram because he believed (trusted) in what God said about Himself and not because he performed a ceremony, did good deeds, or lived a righteous life. He simply believed what God told him.

Faith or trust in God's revealed truth about Himself has always been the basis for individual salvation—coming into a right relationship with God. This was the case for Noah and his children before the Flood, for those who lived in the time of Babel, for Abram in Chaldea, for Israelites enslaved in Egypt, for Christians in the first century, and for us today. However, the scope and content of God's revelation has progressed from early, observable creation, to the accumulated, preserved writings of the apostles and prophets in the Bible about the Lord Jesus Christ. (Hebrews 1:2; Ephesians 2:20, 3:5; II Peter 1:20-21)

Our completed Bible has more revelation about who God is than at any other time in history. This divinely inspired book—the Word of God—also shows us who we are and how we can be right with Him. (II Peter 1:3) It shows us how infinitely offensive our sin is to God (Romans 3:10-12, 23); He cannot allow anything sinful into His holy presence. (Isaiah 59:2; I John 1:5) As painful as it is to admit, the Bible brings us face-to-face with the reality of our sin. We cannot "buy off" God to earn His favor, do something good, or promise to stop sinning, because all that is impossible. (Isaiah 64:6-7; Hebrews 11:6) Instead, God has a solution to our most pressing sin problem. We must believe Him and approach Him *by faith* on His terms.

The infinite offense of our sin against a holy God requires infinite compensation by a perfect person. God sent His Perfect Son, Jesus Christ, to earth to die as a human being in our place. (Romans 5:8) The idea that God's own divine Son, the second person of the Trinity, would shed His blood on the cross of Calvary as an infinite substitute for our sin should awe us like a bolt of lightening. Jesus' death is not some distant, dry, abstract fact. The historical, divine Jesus of the Bible died for *me personally* so all my sins would be forgiven; so I would be right with God and so I would be born into God's family! (John 3:3, 7; I John 2:2)

How does someone benefit from this wonderful truth? The simple answer comes straight from the Bible: *believe on the Lord Jesus Christ and you will be saved.* (Acts 16:31) Faced with the impossibility of paying for your sin or earning your way into heaven, you must come to God His way if you want to be right with Him. (John 1:12-13; 14:6) You have a wonderful opportunity that is freely offered: believe on God's Son as your sin substitute and receive Him as your Savior. As humbling as that might be for you to do, it is what God says is your simple part in His plan. This offer of a free, perfect salvation is given to anyone who will believe God and accept the person and work of His Son *by faith.* (Acts 2:21; Romans 10:13) Will you believe God, receive Jesus Christ as your Savior, and be born into God's family?

More information about how to have a relationship with Jesus Christ can be found at www.michaelvetter.net